THE SUN'S BRIDE

Spring, 266 BC

When Isokrates, helmsman of the Rhodian warship Atalanta, encounters a pirate vessel off the Lycian coast, he finds himself caught up in affairs of state more deadly than the naval battles he's accustomed to. Among the pirates' victims is a beautiful woman, the mistress of a king, who is fleeing to her lover's enemy with news that will start a war to engulf the whole of the east . . .

THE SUN'S BRIDE

Gillian Bradshaw

Severn House Large Print
London & New York

This first large print edition published 2009
in Great Britain and the USA by
SEVERN HOUSE PUBLISHERS LTD of
9-15 High Street, Sutton, Surrey, SM1 1DF.
First world regular print edition published 2008 by
Severn House Publishers Ltd., London and New York.

British Library Cataloguing in Publication Data

Bradshaw, Gillian, 1956-
   The sun's bride
   1. Naval history, Ancient--Fiction. 2. Pirates--
   Mediterranean Sea--Fiction. 3. Mediterranean Region--
   History--To 476--Fiction. 4. Mediterranean Region--History,
   Naval--Fiction. 5. Historical fiction. 6. Large type books.
   I. Title
   813.5'4-dc22

   ISBN-13: 978-0-7278-7783-3

Printed and bound in Great Britain by
MPG Books Ltd, Bodmin, Cornwall.

Cui dono lepidum novum libellum
Arida modo pumice expolitum?
Janice, tibi, namque tu solebas
Meas esse aliquid putare nugas.

One

It was too early in the year for pirates. *Atalanta* certainly hadn't expected to meet any. She was a brand new galley, just out of the naval shipyard of the island republic of Rhodes, her sides gleaming with fresh paint and her hundred and twenty oars sanded smooth and white. Her helmsman was taking advantage of the un-seasonally calm April weather to shake down a new crew while her trierarch stayed behind arguing with the ship chandlers. Her maiden voyage had been southeast along the Lycian coast, with two overnight stops in friendly ports. Now she was on her way home.

The yell from the bow-officer penetrated the decking and resounded along the dim sweaty oardeck where the helmsman was consulting with the bo'sun: 'Longship there! Ai! It's a hemiolia, a *hemiolia*! It's got a merchantman under tow!'

Several of the less experienced oarsmen miss-ed their stroke. There was a clatter of oars strik-ing one another, an indignant yell of pain, and an eruption of oaths. *Atalanta* lurched, then tilted noticeably to port.

Damophon, the ship's bo'sun, rolled his eyes in disgust. He strode along the benches, rapping

7

the handles of the offending oars with his timebeater's mallet and yelling, *'One* an' two an' three! *One* an' two an' three! *I–don't*–care–what's–going–on–above-deck! *You–boys*–keep–the–beat!'

The oars steadied again, though the younger oarsmen were craning their necks, trying to get a glimpse of the hemiolia out the oarports – stupidly, because it was impossible to see anything from the rowing benches. The leather oarsleeves that stopped water from running down the blades blocked the view almost entirely.

Isokrates, the helmsman, had already scrambled up on deck, blinking in the bright sunlight. *Atalanta* had been proceeding at an easy pace, with only half her oars manned; the rest of her oarcrew were above-decks, enjoying a mid-morning meal in the fresh air. Most of them had now crowded against the port rail, making the ship list. The weather was chilly enough that some had pulled on a light cloak, but most followed the usual shipboard custom of going naked. Isokrates was confronted with an un-appealing row of salt-scurffed backs – short and tall, stocky and scrawny, hairy and smooth – their buttocks all chafed red from rowing and shiny with grease from the bench cushions. He grabbed the nearest shoulder and thrust its owner angrily toward the companionway. 'To your stations!' he yelled. 'Stop gawking, you stupid farmboys, you're unbalancing the ship!'

That brought a massed turning of sheepish faces. They began to obey, and the shuffling

8

crowd blocked his way forward to the look-out. The mast was unstepped – no point setting sail when the light breeze was contrary – so he jumped up on to it, ran along it with his arms out-stretched for balance, and jumped off again.

Nikagoras, the eighteen-year-old bow-officer, was perched on the ship's forefoot, leaning out above the figurehead and pointing excitedly. Beyond him the Mediterranean gleamed brilliantly blue under a cloudless spring sky; they had just rounded a headland, and to starboard the Lycian coast rose steep and green. The ships revealed by the turn were perhaps six stadia distant on the port bow – and yes, one was indeed the long, low shape of a hemiolia, with a round-bellied merchant vessel towed behind her, like a fat man behind a fierce thin dog. Even at this distance Isokrates could see that the hemiolia was decked, her benches roofed over and the outrigger that held her upper tier of oars enclosed in an oarbox: she was a fighting ship, not a courier.

'It's a pirate, sir!' Nikagoras exclaimed excitedly – then, less confidently, 'It is, isn't it?'

'Maybe,' Isokrates said warily. Many pirate ships were hemioliai, but not all hemioliai were pirates: some were perfectly respectable naval vessels. They were small galleys, armed with a ram and propelled by an oarcrew of fifty; they had one bank of oars stem and stern, but two banks amidships – the extra 'hemi-' or 'half', file of oarsmen that gave them their name. The fact that this one was painted a pale blue that made it harder to pick out against the water was suspicious, as was the fact that it was towing a merchantman – pirates, like all galleys, had large crews and very limited storage space, and so tended to seize merchant vessels to carry off their loot. It was possible, however, that the roundship contained military supplies.

The hemiolia, however, promptly made her status clear by a flurry around her stern: she was preparing to cast off the merchantman and run. Even at this distance her crew would have noticed the gleam of *Atalanta*'s standard, recognized the gold sun-disk of Rhodes, and realized that they were in the worst possible trouble. Rhodes was an implacable enemy of piracy, and *Atalanta* was a far more powerful ship. She was a *tri*hemiolia, a 'half-three', with two and a half banks of oars and a hundred and twenty oarsmen.

'All oars!' Isokrates roared at once, and ran aft.

Now there was pandemonium as every oarsman on the ship tried to get to his place at once. From below, Damophon's voice resounded in outrage as the newcomers pushed their way on to the benches and the men who'd been there before fouled their neighbours. All rowing came to a halt, and *Atalanta* coasted forward in a succession of bumps, jolts and curses.

Heart pounding, Isokrates went to his own station: the command chair in the stern, directly behind the helm. Kleitos, the tiller-holder, gave him a nod as he passed; he returned it, his head swimming with a flurry of considerations. *Atalanta* was much faster than the hemiolia – that is, she *should* be much faster, but would she

10

prove so, with this half-trained crew? Oh, he should've ordered all crew to the oars the moment he first heard the hail – it was just that he hadn't trusted Nikagoras to get the identification right; the youth didn't have any shipboard experience to speak of, he'd been given his commission because he was the trierarch's nephew, but his education had been in rhetoric and *philosophy*, Fortune protect the navy!

Atalanta was getting under way again, though. The ship's piper had been roused from his break and was playing something steady and not too fast, with Damophon striking out the beat on the big drum amidships. First the thalamian oars, the lowest tier, began the stroke – *one* and two and three, *one* and two and three. The middle, zygian tier, joined in, if a bit raggedly, at least without any more fouling. Finally, the uppermost, thranite, oars completed the set, their smooth entry betraying the fact that all of the ship's professional oarsmen were in this, the most difficult position. The oarcrew was a promising one: a lot of youngsters doing their naval service; a good number of professional oarsmen, citizen and foreign, recruited by the trierarch's willingness to top up the state wage; the bare minimum of hard cases scraped up from the docks. They'd been shaping up well; Damophon knew his job.

Were they doing well enough to catch that pirate, though? There was a yelp forward as one of the oarsmen caught a crab. From the sound of it, he'd ended up with his head banged against a beam by the neighbouring oar. Mistakes slowed a ship. What if they slowed *Atalanta* so much that the chase failed? What if they had to go back to Rhodes and admit that a pirate had appeared right in their path, and he, Isokrates of Kameiros, had let it get away – on his very first sole command?

Isokrates glanced unhappily up at the standard just above his head. His view of it was half-obscured by *Atalanta*'s stern post, but the gold-leaf shone so brightly that even so it blazed at him: the all-seeing Sun, the lover and protector of Rhodes. He remembered the story of the Sun's son Phaethon, who'd borrowed his father's blazing chariot and disastrously failed to manage it.

Not a good parallel, he told himself firmly. If the pirate got away because *Atalanta* had a raw, half-trained crew, well, that was life at sea – but they *ought* to be able to catch the bastard. He knew this bit of coast well, and he'd refreshed his memory on the journey out. It might be his first command, but he was no Phaethon, no novice unaccustomed to handling the reins. Warships had been his life for over a decade: he'd spent every summer since he was sixteen at sea, and every winter working in the shipyards. His record was as good as that of any man in the navy, and better than most.

There was certainly no point in longing for the absent trierarch. The main qualification for the trierarchy was enough money to outfit a ship: the position was assigned to wealthy citizens as a form of tax. *Atalanta*'s trierarch knew merchant ships very well, but, by his own admission, hadn't set foot on a warship since he completed his naval service at the age of eighteen. Even if he *had* been on board, he would have expected Isokrates to make the naval judgements: he'd hired him for just that purpose.

'Helm to starboard,' Isokrates ordered, indicating the bearing to the tiller-holder with angled hands. Kleitos nodded and shifted the tiller-bar so that the two great steering oars tilted just a shade. Isokrates stood and walked forward to get a better view, taking care to move with calm deliberation. A helmsman was supposed to remain unflappable in all circumstances. The oarcrew were all below-deck, but the deck-soldiers and sail crew might find his act encouraging – and even if it impressed nobody else, acting calm made *him* feel better.

The pirate had been heading west when he first saw her, but now she was bearing north, all her oars beating frantically. The abandoned merchantman was already well behind her, and *Atalanta* was closing with the roundship fast. The merchant was of average size, perhaps a hundred and thirty tons, finely made, her hull clean and her two masts straight and sound; she had a figurehead at her prow and a standard at her stern, but Isokrates couldn't make out what either was supposed to represent. There was a ragged line of armed men along her side: they raised their shields and hefted their spears as *Atalanta* approached, then jeered loudly as they realized that the trihemiolia was going after their comrades on the galley. Another small group huddled on the foredeck waved vigorously as the trihemiolia swept past: captives, presumably, since they were all fully dressed and mostly women. From the bow Nikagoras waved back, and gave a whoop of glee.

Isokrates walked back to his place again, grinning. The coast to the north was steep and rocky, full of inlets and small islands: the hemiolia was hoping to duck out of sight. She'd find, though, that her pursuer was too close to lose, and already positioned to cut her off from that concealing shore – and only a little further to the northwest lay the long, long sweep of Phoinikos beach, where there would be no hiding place.

Simmias, the second officer, came over as Isokrates took his seat again. 'You want me to tell Damophon to speed up the stroke, sir?' he asked eagerly.

Isokrates shook his head: a faster stroke would increase the risk of fouling. Simmias looked disappointed, and glanced anxiously toward the fleeing hemiolia, further away than when they first spotted her.

'Don't worry!' Isokrates told him. 'She can't keep up that pace for long.' *Atalanta* could: her greater concentration of oar power meant she could equal the hemiolia's speed with a slower stroke – provided, of course, she didn't foul too many of her oars too often.

Simmias, still unhappy, looked pointedly over Isokrates' shoulder at the merchantman. That fine ship and her cargo would, if rescued from pirates, become salvage, and, by long custom, *Atalanta*'s crew would share the bounty. To rescue her, though, they'd have to find her again, and the roundship was certainly going to flee: the pirates sailing her would be as eager to get away from *Atalanta* as their fellows on the hemiolia.

'She won't get far,' Isokrates assured his second. 'There's not much wind.'

'Yes, sir,' said Simmias. He was still unhappy. If their pursuit of the hemiolia lasted into the afternoon, the merchantman would have a very good chance of getting away, even in a light wind. The night would hide her, and by morning she could be anywhere. There was no help for it, though: a Rhodian naval vessel couldn't possibly break off the pursuit of a pirate in order to make sure of a salvage claim.

'Go talk to Nikagoras and Polydoros,' Isokrates ordered, to get rid of Simmias. 'Come back with recommendations for where to put the deck-soldiers when we catch our quarry. I want three options.'

'Yes, sir.'

Isokrates leaned back in his seat. The piper was playing a line dance now, the notes high and clear; the ship, surging with each stroke of the oars, moved to the tune like an accomplished dancer. He closed his eyes, feeling the cool rush of air against his face. For a moment he was filled with a stark joy. *Atalanta* was his: this spear fifty paces long, this bronze-tipped thunderbolt driven by a hundred and twenty gleaming wings, this weapon fit for a god – was *his* to direct!

He had loved warships since he first set eyes on them. He had been about four then, and he had sat on his father's shoulders to watch the fleet procession during the Festival of the Sun in Rhodes town. He could remember nothing else about that festival, but the ships were still clear in his mind's eye: a long line of them, gliding one after another through the harbour entrance, the wings of their oars beating, the painted eyes on their prows bright as the eyes of eagles, their bronze beaks garlanded with flowers. As he grew up, his schoolwork was always full of their scribbled images.

He was not alone in his enthusiasm. Every Rhodian knew that the navy was the defender of the republic's freedom and the protector of its wealth. Most boys looked forward to their obligatory two summers of naval service and took pride in it. Isokrates, though, had had reasons to make a career of it. When he'd completed his time he'd enlisted again, as a professional oarsman, despite his father's furious demands that he come back to the family farm. Over the next eight years he'd been promoted to oarbinder, to tiller-holder, to bow-officer. He had no expectations of ever becoming wealthy enough to be a trierarch, but as *helmsman* he was executive officer of the ship, subordinate only to the trierarch. The rank he held – *this* new, just-gifted glory – was the summit of his hopes.

Then he thought of Phaethon again, and opened his eyes, suddenly afraid that his pride would ruin them all. He glanced over at the coast: had he forgotten some secluded cove? Were there hiding places to the west after all?

There was a wide patch of duller water just to

16

starboard. He stared at it for a moment, then jumped to his feet and stepped out on top of the oarbox to look.

Yes: it was the hemiolia's wake. *Atalanta* was catching up. Those frantic oarbeats were weakening. Probably the oarcrew had been tired even to start with – it couldn't have been easy, towing that merchant. Now their muscles wearied and their breath grew short. Desperate as they were to escape, they could not maintain the pace.

A steep, green headland jutted out ahead; some distance from its tip was an islet, rough and stony, with a few scraggy pines on its peak. The hemiolia moved to starboard, as though she meant to round the islet on the landward side. Isokrates watched her, frowning. Her commander must know that if he didn't lose his pursuer soon, he'd lose his ship instead. It was very likely that he would try something as soon as he was out of sight behind that islet. What, though?

Simmias reappeared, with Nikagoras and Polydoros, the chief of *Atalanta*'s small contingent of deck-soldiers. 'We've got the suggestions for the dispositions, sir,' the second officer said respectfully.

The three options were to position the two archers in the bow, amidships, or the stern, with the nine spearmen protecting them. It wasn't very imaginative, but it was hard to improve upon. Isokrates glanced again at the fleeing hemiolia and made up his mind.

'Station the archers amidships,' he ordered. 'And tell Damophon to prepare to ease the zygian and thranite oars on my command.'

17

'Ease them?' asked Simmias, alarmed. 'Sir...'

'Ease them!' Isokrates decreed, cutting off the protest. He hesitated, then admitted to himself that he had done nothing to earn Simmias' unquestioning obedience, and that the second was entitled to an explanation – even if he was a greedy, sour-faced whiner. 'I think she's going to try to use that little islet to double back and dodge us. As soon as she's out of sight we'll slow down and move to port, so we catch her when she rounds it.'

Simmias scowled. 'What if she keeps on going? Or, ai! ducks behind that headland while we're hanging about waiting for her to come round the rock?'

'Then we'll catch her up again. We're tracking her wake: how's she going to shake us off?'

Simmias looked sullen, no doubt thinking of the merchant ship. Nikagoras, however, beamed. 'So if we're wrong,' he said delightedly, 'we still catch her, but if we're right she rows right under our ram!'

She almost rowed *into* the ram, rather than under it. The pirate reappeared around the western tip of the islet just as *Atalanta* cruised up to it. The two ships were close enough that Isokrates could make out the expression of horror on the face of the hemiolia's bow-officer, close enough that he was afraid of a ram-to-ram collision. 'Port helm!' he shouted urgently, and 'Archers fire at will!' *Atalanta* curved away to glide slowly past the hemiolia. The archers had a point blank range and plenty of time to pick their targets.

Unfortunately, there were not many targets to be picked. The pirate's oarcrew were protected by the decking, and there were no deck fighters or sail crew to be seen. Presumably they were on the roundship – or pulling an oar. The pirate bow-officer, however, went down with an arrow in his shoulder. The archer who'd hit him yelled excitedly and snatched another arrow to the string. The prize target would be the tiller-holder.

No more arrows flew, however, and as the hemiolia's stern came into view Isokrates saw why: one of the pirates was standing before the helm, holding a woman in front of himself as a shield, a knife at her throat. The pirate's eyes sought the commander's seat, found Isokrates, and held. He was a man in his prime, tall and strong, with a thick black beard; his dark eyes burned into Isokrates' with furious challenge. The woman was dressed only in a sleeveless linen chiton, her long brown hair loose and tangled over her pale shoulders. Her face was bruised and blood-streaked; her expression was one of misery and shame.

'Rhodian!' yelled the pirate. 'Let's bargain!' Then the ships had passed.

'Port, full turn about!' Isokrates shouted furiously.

Kleitos leaned into the tiller bar; from below Damophon's voice could be heard calling for the port crew to ease oars, for the starboard crew to pull hard. Ordinarily he would have sped up the stroke as well, but, wisely, he kept to the same steady rhythm. A minute later *Atalanta* had

19

turned about and was heading back the way she had come. Her course wobbled as the port oars resumed the stroke unevenly.

Isokrates was waiting in the prow by then, furious and sickened. The woman was probably the wife or daughter of somebody important; the pirate commander must have taken her off the merchantman to keep her more securely. Now he was trying to use her to buy his freedom. How, though, could Isokrates justify such an exchange? Releasing a pirate might save one woman, but it would condemn scores of others to abduction and slavery.

How could he stand by, though, and watch as a beautiful young woman was murdered before his eyes? He hated to see women abused – hated it with a stomach-wrenching passion born out of dark memories. Perhaps he could offer the pirate a different bargain: hand over the woman and live; injure her and die.

The hemiolia had eased oars: to try to run now would be futile. As *Atalanta* approached, Isokrates saw that the pirate leader had dragged the woman out on top of the oarbox next to the sternpost. She knelt passively, gazing down at the dark blue water under the hemiolia's stern, while he stood over her, holding her by the hair, his knife held out so that they could all see it.

'Easy oars!' Isokrates ordered. *Atalanta* coasted forward; below-decks, the oarcrew began asking one another what was going on, and Isokrates added another order: 'Silence!'

The two ships coasted forward with no sound but the whisper of water along their sides,

Atalanta's momentum steadily diminishing the blue space between them. As they came within hailing distance, Isokrates studied the pirate intently. There was a jagged scar on the man's right arm and shoulder – good. That would help in tracking him down.

'Rhodian!' the pirate yelled again, as the trihemiolia's tall prow loomed over him. 'You know who this bitch is?' He jerked her head back, exposing her throat. 'King Antiochos's favourite, that's who! You want to restore her to her grateful lover – or explain to him how she died?'

He seemed about to say more, but at that moment the woman twisted and bit his arm. The pirate yelled, and she tore out of his grasp and hurled herself into the blue water, leaving him with a fistful of hair.

Isokrates gaped in amazed delight. His first instinct was to throw himself into the water after her, but he was *commander*, and couldn't possibly abandon ship. He had no idea, though, what sort of commands a commander was supposed to give in such a situation. The pirate looked up furiously into Isokrates' face – then dived after the woman.

Isokrates' paralysis broke. 'Anyone who can swim!' he yelled. 'Save the woman! Kill that murdering bastard! And helm to starboard, to starboard!'

Atalanta swerved to starboard as no fewer than four of her deck-soldiers and three of her sail crew leapt into the water.

'To starboard!' Isokrates shouted again,

21

hurrying back to his station. Filled with an exhilarating hatred he yelled out the deadly order: 'All oars, rush speed!'

The rhythm of Damophon's mallet on the drumhead picked up. *Atalanta* swung round in a great curve to starboard, her speed steadily increasing. The sea foamed at her bow and paled where her great bronze ram moved beneath the surface.

The hemiolia was slow to react. Her oarcrew, below-deck, hadn't seen what had happened, and her bow-officer was wounded. *Atalanta* had almost completed her circle before the first few oars began to beat. They weren't enough to provide much steerage way. The ship began to turn her prow toward her opponent, but moved as sluggishly as an old donkey. The trihemiolia, now at full speed, approached her at the perfect oblique angle from behind.

Isokrates stood behind the tiller-holder, the emotion of a minute before now lost in an over-whelming concentration. Too fast and he risked damage to *Atalanta*; too slow, and their opponent might survive the blow. 'Wait for it, wait...' Back oars!' he yelled. There was a lurch as the oarcrew obeyed. He braced himself and added the final command, 'Ship oars!' And then came the prolonged, tearing crash as the ram struck, ripping open a bloody gash along the hemiolia's side.

The impact threw Isokrates forward and he caught the arm of the command chair to prevent himself from stumbling into Kleitos. He let it go again, yelling for the men to back oars –

unnecessarily, because they were already doing so, as hard as they could, though with a great deal of excited fouling. *Atalanta* twisted, askew in the water as her ram shuddered in the guts of its victim. There was a horrible groaning of wrenched timbers. Above it sounded the screaming of men: the pirate's oarcrew, trapped beneath the deck of their shattered ship as the sea rushed in. *Atalanta*'s own deck tilted as the hemiolia began to go down, still impaled on her enemy's ram. The trihemiolia's oars laboured. Then, with a great cracking of timber, she backed away. The hulk finally slid from her ram and began to settle in the water.

'Easy oars!' Isokrates ordered, and *Atalanta* coasted slowly back from her victim. He could picture the scene on the pirate oardeck: the water flooding in, the shafts of the suddenly useless oars, with their heavy counterweighted ends, waving about in the growing dark, the desperate men, many of them injured, clawing at one another as they tried to force their way to one of the narrow hatches. Even as he watched, a few drenched oarsmen scrambled on to the deck. Most of their comrades wouldn't make it.

He drew a deep breath, blinking at shameful tears, all his savage joy quite lost. He told himself that he did not pity the pirates – they did not deserve to be pitied! – that it was the ruin of a ship that tore at his heart. Instants before the hemiolia had been whole and beautiful: now it was a wreck full of dying men.

Simmias and Nikagoras came up to report *Atalanta* undamaged and her crew unharmed, apart from a few scrapes and bruises. The second officer was sullen: he undoubtedly would've preferred to take the hemiolia intact and sell it as a prize. Isokrates wondered how he thought he could've done that and still gone after the merchantman. *Atalanta* did not have the crew to move both warships at any speed, and only a fool would try to employ the pirates.

As for Nikagoras, his eyes were wide and his face pale. When he finished his report he gestured at the wretches on the deck of the swamped ship and asked, 'Do we help them?'

Isokrates drew another deep breath. A truthful answer was 'Yes – if you call it *help*.' The men would suffer the fate they'd inflicted on others: they would be sold as slaves. Ex-pirates, however, did not make trustworthy domestic servants or goatherds: ordinary citizens wouldn't want them. They would probably end up working in the mines and quarries of neighbouring kings. Some might be ransomed by friends or family, but most would die within a few years. Letting them drown might be kinder.

'We'll take them off the wreck in another minute,' he said. 'When it's finished settling.'

'Get the *akrostolion,* too,' said Simmias, with a grin of triumph. That was the ornamental finial at the high curving peak of a ship's stern, traditionally collected as a trophy by a victorious galley. 'How many galleys come home from a training cruise with an *akrostolion*, eh?'

One of the survivors lost his footing and slid into the sea; he floundered back on board with the help of his friends, and the handful of men splashed over the deck to the tabernacle of the mast, the only part of their vessel still above water. Isokrates suddenly remembered the woman and the men who'd jumped in to rescue her.

'Where are our people?' he asked, terrified that he'd run them down.

In fact, they were comfortably astern, a little knot of heads moving slowly toward the islet. The hemiolia had still been drifting forward, and had been well clear by the time she was rammed. It was precisely the situation he'd envisaged when he gave the order to circle round – but he hadn't even looked for his crew members as the ships closed, and the thought that he might have killed them with their own ship gave him cold shudders.

The swimmers turned back from the islet when they noticed *Atalanta* moving toward them. The trihemiolia slowed, turned her side, and let down the boarding ladder at her stern; Isokrates anxiously counted the bobbing heads as they approached. Eight: all seven of the men, and it seemed that they had the woman safe! It was better fortune than his carelessness deserved. He owed the gods an offering.

The seamen scrambled aboard, the first man taking the woman's hand to pull her up, while the others showed her where to put her feet. The men were shivering – the sea was cold, this early in the year – but elated; the woman was pale and silent. The drenched linen of her chiton clung to her slim body, showing with disturbing clarity just how beautiful she was. Isokrates was not

25

sure whether he believed that she was a favourite of King Antiochos – what would a royal mistress be doing to get herself abducted by pirates? – but she was certainly beautiful enough. He felt an embarrassing stirring in the groin, and wished fervently that he had some clothes on. Officers were supposed to wear a tunic – knee-length, bleached linen, pinned on the right shoulder with a Rhodian sunburst. Nikagoras and Simmias were both correctly dressed, but Isokrates had taken his off; he'd been working with the oarcrew, and he'd wanted to keep it clean. He quickly turned his eyes away from her, thinking of the cold sea to make his embarrassment subside.

'Well done!' he told the swimmers, shaking the hand of the nearest and trying to remember his name – Kleophon, that was it, one of the spearmen. 'Well done, Kleophon, and ... Heliodoros...' He made sure he got all their names. 'You all did very well, and I'll report your courage to the trierarch.'

'Well done the ship!' replied Kleophon, grinning. 'Sir, we didn't do as well as we might've done. Their chief got away.'

'What?'

'When he saw all of us coming, he swum off. He was heading for that little island, like us, but he was going a lot faster, since we were all trying to support the lady.' The spearman shook his head. 'To tell the truth, sir, I'm glad we don't have to try to climb that buggered rock with the bastard throwing things at us.'

Isokrates had almost forgotten the pirate

26

leader, and he looked over at the islet in irritation. It was too steep and rocky to approach closely with the trihemiolia – a gust of wind or an unforeseen current might thrust the ship against it. He could send swimmers over, of course – but there was a danger that they might injure themselves against the rocks, or lose their weapons in the sea. Besides, the roundship still needed to be rescued. No, he could not spare the time to hunt down one stray pirate.

'Well, may the gods destroy him!' he said. 'Let him starve there, or let him try to swim to the mainland, and drown. You men should dry off and go warm up; get yourselves a ration of wine.'

He took a breath and turned to the woman. It was easier to control himself now: she stood with her shoulders hunched and her arms wrapped around herself, shivering, her hair in wet rattails. The sea had washed the blood from her face, but left a bruised cheek and swollen lip plain to see. Her dark eyes were huge. Was she really the mistress of a king? He had no idea how you were supposed to address a royal mistress. Would she be a respectable woman or a whore?

Again he saw her turning to bite the pirate chief, then flinging herself into the sea. He supposed that such ferocity wasn't respectable – but it had been honourable and brave, and his heart leapt at the memory. She had not given in; she'd preferred death to becoming the coin her enemy paid for his freedom.

'Welcome aboard *Atalanta*, Lady,' he said,

giving her the respect she'd earned. 'You're safe now. This is a Rhodian ship, and no one aboard will harm you. We'll take you home.'

She burst into tears.

He always hated it when women cried: it tied knots in his stomach – though the lady's tears were understandable, after what she'd just been through. He noticed Nikagoras watching her with admiration, and, with relief, handed the problem over to him. 'Nikagoras, look after her – find her a towel and blanket, get her some food.' Nikagoras moved eagerly to obey, and Isokrates gave a sigh of relief and went down to the oardeck to speak to the rest of the men. The oarcrew never saw anything of a battle, and he knew from his own experience how much they appreciated an early report from the man in charge.

The oardeck was warm, after the breeze out-side, and dark, after the bright sunlight. What light there was filtered through the louvres on the underside of the oarboxes, or fell through the three hatches which led to the deck, or trickled through chinks between the oarports and the leather oarsleeves. The benches sat in tiers either side of the central gangway: a step down for the thalamians; a step up for the zygians; two steps up and one out for the thranites. The hull nar-rowed, though, stem and stern, squeezing out the thalamian benches at each end. The whole long space was divided by cross-beams, floored with sand-and-gravel ballast, and crowded with naked oarsmen. Its new-ship smell, of pitch and pine, was already giving way to the familiar stink of flesh, sweat, oil, and mutton-fat cushion-grease.

The men were leaning on their oars, talking animatedly about what it had been like to ram another vessel – a new experience for most of them. They fell silent, though, when Isokrates came down the ladder. The expectant faces stared at him, half of them – since he'd come down the central hatch – twisted about to look at him over their shoulder. The faces, like the benches, were in tiers: bearded men's faces, spotty youths, scarred faces and smooth ones. Isokrates knew many of them. He'd worked with most of the professional oarsmen on one ship or another; he'd worked with some of the dockyard toughs during winters in the shipyard – and fought with a couple of them, too. He had no illusions about them, but now he was suddenly flooded with affectionate pride: this motley collection of farmboys and city poor, of tough professionals and dock scum, had, even half trained, done all that their city asked of them.

'Well done!' he told them warmly. 'We've sunk our first pirate. The bastard was headed west, towing a roundship full of loot – and you can bet on it that most of that loot was men, women and children, *freeborn* men, women and children, snatched off their farms or fishing boats and with nothing to look forward to but slavery. We put a stop to that. Some of you never set hand to an oar before this spring, but there's not a ship in the fleet that could have done more.

'Now, we had to leave that roundship to go after the pirate, but we're going to go back for her. We'll have to hurry to catch her before nightfall. I know you're tired, and I know you have blisters, but those people on the roundship are praying to the gods that we'll come rescue them, so we can't rest yet. We'll be going south, so we'll have the wind with us. I'm going to get the mast stepped, so we won't need all of you pulling at once, but those of you who are pulling need to pull hard.'

One of the thranites – a professional oarsman, and an Athenian, not a Rhodian – yelled, 'What about the hemiolia?'

'She's swamped,' Isokrates told him, and bluntly answered the real question. 'We're taking what's left of her crew off, and we'll look for the hulk on our way home. If we find it we'll tow it back for what we can get for the timbers and the bronze – but the roundship's worth more. She's a fine vessel, worth eight or nine thousand unladen, and probably still carrying some cargo. If we find her, we'll be entitled to claim salvage at something like two thirds her value.'

The Athenian grinned and gave him a thumbs up.

All the other men were grinning too, and one of the portside zygians punched the air and let out a cheer, *'Io!'* The rest took it up, *'Io, euge!'*

Isokrates grinned back at them, and punched the air in reply. *'Euge, Atalanta!'*

Two

The survivors of the swamped hemiolia proved to be Cretans.

This was no surprise: half the pirates in the Aegean were from Crete. Cretans seemed to consider it a brave and manly thing to enrich themselves by stealing other people's property or freedom. Even the deaths of most of their company did not seem to have convinced them of the merit of abiding by the law. They submitted to captivity with noisy bravado, some of them insisting that they would be ransomed, others threatening the vengeance of their chief, whose name, it appeared, was Andronikos of Phalassarna.

'You didn't catch *him*, did you?' jeered one of the survivors. 'You watch: he'll get us out – and make you pay for this!'

'Really,' said Isokrates drily. 'If he has a ship that can take ours, why was he slumming it in a hemiolia?'

The pirate was reduced to glowering. Isokrates assigned Simmias to question the men, but he had little hope of getting truthful answers.

It was past noon by the time *Atalanta* started back to where she'd encountered the roundship; as expected, the ship was nowhere in sight, but

31

the prospects for finding her again were good. The breeze continued light and unsteady from the north, and they were immediately west of the rocky headland of Lycian Olympos. To disappear the merchantman would have to beat around that headland, and there hadn't been enough time for her to do anything of the sort. Isokrates posted men on the yardarm to scan the shore and check the breeze, but he was satisfied that the roundship had fled south – or southeast, or southwest, but the closer she sailed to the wind, the slower she would be. The trihemiolia raced southward over the blue water, her mainsail and boatsail drawing and her oars beating in shifts, half the men rowing, half resting. Isokrates took the helm, telling Kleitos to rest. The tug of the tiller bar under his hand gave him a thrill of delight. *Atalanta* moved like a falcon – the same short, strong beats of the wing, the same deadly grace.

Nikagoras interrupted his contemplation of his ship's excellence by coming aft, escorting the woman. She had a blanket draped round her like a cloak, and only the edge of her chiton showed. Her loose hair was a mass of wind-blown tangles.

'She wants to talk to you,' Nikagoras explained. 'Well, she asked to talk "to the trierarch", but I told her Uncle Aristomachos was in Rhodes.'

The woman looked at Isokrates uncertainly, then turned a questioning gaze back to Nikagoras. It was only too clear that she found it hard to believe that this naked seaman, gaunt, dirty and unshaven, was the trierarch's stand-in. Isokrates cursed himself: here he could've impressed a beautiful woman – a woman who was undoubtedly full of gratitude and admiration! – and he'd failed because he hadn't put a tunic on. It was just that it was hard to get cushion-grease out of bleached linen, and what use were you to a half-trained oarcrew if you stayed away from the oars?

'Excuse me that I'm not dressed,' he told the woman, curt with embarrassment. 'I've been working on the oardeck. I am Isokrates of Kameiros, helmsman of *Atalanta*.'

'If you are in command, then it is you I must speak to,' said the woman, though she modestly turned her eyes toward the decking. She spoke Greek with the long vowels of the Ionians and a cultured accent, and her voice was soft and melodious. 'Isokrates – of Kameiros? You're not Rhodian?'

He forced a smile: properly he should have introduced himself as 'Isokrates son of Kritagoras', rather than by his hometown – but he preferred not to mention his father. 'Kameiros *is* Rhodian, Lady, one of the three cities which joined together to found Rhodes-town.'

'Oh. Oh, yes, of course: Lindos, Kameiros, Ialysos, the sons of the lovely nymph Rhodos. I did know, I just ... Sir, you said earlier you would send me home, but when my ship was taken, I was on my way to Alexandria. I need to get there as soon as possible. Will it be possible for me to continue my voyage?'

Isokrates shrugged. 'That depends on the captain of your ship – and on his backers, and on

33

how you booked your passage.'

She frowned. 'His backers?'

'The owners of the ship and the cargo. Or was it a private venture?'

'Oh! I ... I don't know. I booked with the captain at the harbour. I paid in advance.' Her eyes darted up to him uneasily, then away again.

He stood a moment, looking at her downward-turned profile in its tangle of hair: a long nose, bruised mouth, beautiful dark eyes. She was perhaps twenty, too old to be respectable and unmarried – and yet she had booked the voyage herself? She had paid the captain at the harbour-side, rather than going through a male relative and some wealthy shipowner friend? With an ordinary woman, he would've suspected that she was running away from a cruel husband – but why would a royal concubine run away? More pertinently, why would a concubine of *King Antiochos* run to *Alexandria* – the home of Antiochos's greatest rival?

He could think of one rather unsettling answer to that question – but maybe she wasn't a spy. Maybe she *was* just a runaway wife, and the pirate had lied about her status to increase his bargaining power, or she'd lied about it to the pirates, to keep them from raping her.

'Are you what the pirate said?' he asked bluntly.

A swift, indignant glance of those dark eyes. 'I am a *free woman*, sir, the daughter of Kleisthenes of Miletos, a member of the Guild of Dionysiac Artists. It's hardly proper for you to question a freeborn citizen about such things!'

34

This was not the grateful tone he'd expected! It was also much more aristocratic than he'd expect from a concubine, so maybe she was a wife. He tried to tell himself that if she *was* an Egyptian spy, the republic of Rhodes wouldn't want to know about it. The island tried to stay on good terms with all of its neighbours – which frequently meant remaining officially ignorant of their differences with one another. You couldn't be expected to take sides in a quarrel you knew nothing about.

He sighed: that argument was rubbish. *Unofficially* the island always wanted as much information as it could get. Kings, as everyone knew, were dangerous neighbours, always hungry for dominion, and Rhodes had kings to the north, south and east. The republic was a power in the Aegean, controlling not just the island of Rhodes itself but several smaller islands and a chunk of mainland Caria – but it was a *minor* power, totally outmatched by the kings around it. If it was to retain its independence, it needed to know what they were up to. He hoped he could hand this over to somebody else quickly: he knew nothing about diplomacy.

'May I at least know your name, Lady?' he asked politely.

She frowned and didn't answer. He wondered whether her silence reflected a spy's need for secrecy, or whether it was simply the ordinary reluctance of a respectable woman to give her name to a strange man.

'Someone may ask after you,' he coaxed. 'I need to be able to reassure them that you're

35

safe.'

The frown deepened, but she answered. 'My name is Dionysia. Daughter of Kleisthenes of Miletos, as I said.'

He nodded. 'Daughter of Kleisthenes, the first thing we need to do is to *find* this ship of yours. If we do, and if we manage to save her, we'll escort her to port and get a salvage agreement signed and sworn. Then...'

'How long will that take?' she interrupted. 'What's involved? All your men are talking about this *salvage* business. Does the captain have to *pay* you for saving his ship?'

The scornful tone stung. 'Lady, as everyone knows, we Rhodians attack pirates wherever we find them! However, under Rhodian sea-law, anyone who rescues a ship, from wreck or from piracy, is entitled to a share of the value of the vessel and its lading.'

She stared in alarm. 'What? A share of the ship and everything on it?'

'Lady, that ship was *lost*, along with everything on her – including you. Anyone who wanted to get her back had to fight the pirates for her. How many men are willing to fight without any hope of reward? The Rhodian law on salvage has been accepted by seafarers all over the Middle Sea, for the very good reason that part of a ship's value is better than nothing-at-all-less-ransoms!'

'But what am I supposed to *do*?' she demanded, her voice wobbling alarmingly. 'Alone in a strange port with no money?'

He realized that she was *frightened*. They had

36

rescued her from the pirates, but she was still trying to escape whatever-it-was – angry husband or vengeful king – that lay behind her. He was ashamed of his indignation: after what she'd been through, it was astonishing that she even had the composure to speak to him. She had been struggling to keep that composure, but his impatience had fractured it. 'Forgive me,' he said, in a much gentler tone. 'You don't need to worry. Salvage only applies to ships and their ladings – that is, cargo carried in the hold. Persons and personal property are exempt.'

Gentleness, or perhaps relief, made her eyes suddenly wet. 'Oh! I'm sorry, I ... I ... I was just ... I know you saved my life. When your ship came round that headland and everyone started screaming that it was *Rhodian*, it was like ... like a *god* appearing at the end of a play to set everything right! I shouldn't have...'

'Please don't worry!' he said urgently, afraid of another bout of tears, and, to distract her, hurried on with the answer to her question: 'If we find the ship, the salvage claim should be agreed within a few days. Phaselis, where we'll go tonight if we can, is a friendly port, and accepts the Rhodian sea-law.'

The distraction seemed to have worked. 'Phaselis? Does that not belongs to King Ptolemy? You're not going straight to Rhodes?'

'Not tonight. Rhodes is two full days' pull. We can get back to Phaselis in a few hours, if your roundship doesn't lead us too much of a chase. We have a standing arrangement there; they let our ships use the northern harbour. Can you tell us anything about the roundship that might help? How she's crewed, what she's carrying? And the pirates aboard – how many of them are there? How are they armed?'

The woman drew a deep breath. 'The ship is called the *Artemis,* after the goddess. She's Ephesian, and I think she's fairly new. That's what I was told, anyway: that she's new and fast. The captain's name is Philotimos, and there were a dozen men in the crew.'

Even a 'fast' roundship was slow compared to a galley – but applied to an unoared merchant, the term often meant that the ship could sail close to the wind, which sped up most journeys. Isokrates at once began to worry that their quarry had gone so far west or east that they would miss her. No, he told himself nervously: she *couldn't* have gone west, because *Atalanta* would have seen her, and as for east, there was the headland in the way. There hadn't been *time* for her to disappear, not with the wind so light and so unsteady. *Atalanta* should carry on southward: they would raise her soon.

'They were going to Alexandria with a cargo of wool and wine,' Dionysia was continuing, 'but the pirates drank some of the wine and threw the woollens overboard. You see, they had all these poor people they'd kidnapped...' She broke off, her jaw clenching.

Kidnapped and abused: it was what pirates did. The more decent sort of pirate would offer their victims for ransom first; the more brutal would sate themselves, then offer the remains to the highest bidder. He suspected they were dealing with brutes here. 'They threw the woollens overboard to make room for the captives,' he prompted.

She nodded. 'We were three days south from Ephesus when we were attacked. They came out of the north, from the Lycian coast, like an arrow from a bow. It felt as though we were tangled in a snare, or wading in mud, we moved so slowly. There was nothing we could do to get away. They threatened to ram us, so the captain had to surrender. They ... they put a lot of men aboard...'

'How many?'

'I ... I'm not sure. The captain had sent all of us passengers down to the hold when the pirates came up, and the pirates kept us there. They had seventy or eighty men in all, though – I saw that later, when we put in. They had some more men waiting on the coast with the captives and some goods they'd stolen. You asked how they're armed – I saw, oh, twenty or thirty spearmen, and some men with bows as well, and a couple of others with slings and bags of lead shot. The rest had knives and cudgels. They were all bloody, brutal men. They'd killed people in Lycia – they were *laughing* about it, how they'd killed men when they tried to defend their wives and children! The captives were nearly all women, children and boys. We spent the night at this inlet on the Lycian coast, and the men all got drunk and...'

'Sail!' yelled the lookout up on the yardarm. 'Sail to the west! It's a roundship! I think it's *our* roundship!'

Isokrates' heart leapt with relief. 'Bearing?' he yelled back eagerly.

'Southwest! She's maybe thirty stadia away!' The lookout indicated the bearing with an out-flung arm

Isokrates closed his eyes a moment, trying to visualize the roundship's course and estimate her speed, trying to choose the most direct line he could take to intercept her. He pulled the tiller gently, and felt the force of the water as the steering oars tilted. The trihemiolia's prow turn-ed southwest; her sails flapped, and the sail crew hurried to trim them. 'Bearing?' he called again, and got another arm gesture.

He let out his breath slowly and returned his attention to the woman. 'We have a little longer before we catch her up. Did you have more questions?'

She looked down, tugging at the edge of her blanket cloak. 'I had only the one question, sir: whether I'll be able to continue my voyage to Alexandria.'

'Oh. Yes. Well, as I said, it depends on the captain of the *Artemis* and on his backers – and, I suppose, on whether he's got enough cargo left to make it worth his while sailing to Alexandria. He'll have to settle the salvage claim before he does anything else. If the ship belongs to a reputable syndicate, it's easy: he just pledges the money on their behalf. Even if it doesn't, I suppose he could borrow the money to settle the claim, then continue to Alexandria, and pay off the loan once he gets home with the proceeds of the voyage. On the other hand, he may decide to sail straight home, or sell the ship and what's left of the lading in Phaselis. I don't know what he'll do, I'm afraid.'

She bit her lip. 'What about the money I gave him for my passage?'

Money was obviously a worry. He wondered if she could *afford* to buy passage on another ship. 'I'm sorry. I don't think you'll get it back. If he does decide to continue the voyage, though, he'll probably honour your agreement.'

She looked unhappy, but said only, 'Thank you, trierarch.'

'Helmsman,' he corrected her. He hesitated, then offered, 'Lady, if you can't continue your voyage to Alexandria, we would be happy to offer you passage to Rhodes.'

That brought a look both hopeful and wary, which he met openly. 'It would be much easier for you to find another ship in Rhodes,' he pointed out. 'It's a bigger port than Phaselis, and there's a lot of Alexandria trade heading out this time of year. And we owe you something for taking yourself out of the hands of that pirate and scuppering his bargain.'

At this, she looked down again quickly. 'Thank you. If ... if I can't continue on the *Artemis*, I may accept your kind offer.'

He wondered guiltily if he ought to do something to *ensure* that she couldn't continue on the *Artemis*. If she was a spy, and if she had information about King Antiochos so important that she needed to carry it to Alexandria in person, then the Council of Rhodes definitely wanted to talk to her.

41

No, he thought with relief, there was no need to choose between duty and pity. *Artemis* had lost much of her cargo and was closer to home than to her destination: it was very unlikely that she'd continue her voyage. He could help the lady and serve Rhodes at the same time.

He glanced forward, and found the sail the look-out had spotted earlier, on the starboard bow: *Atalanta*'s oars were carrying her toward it as though the roundship were standing still. 'If there's nothing more, you should go below,' he advised Dionysia. 'I hope there won't be any fighting, but there may be, and if you stay below you can be certain of not being shot. The spot next to the water supply is coolest.'

She opened her mouth – then closed it again and took herself off to the hatch. Nikagoras tried to accompany her, and Isokrates had to order him to his station forward.

Tangled in a snare, he thought appreciatively, or wading in mud: the merchant ship was no faster now than when the pirates took her. As *Atalanta* sped toward her, it quickly became certain that this was indeed 'their' roundship, with her two masts and clean hull. The sails, which before had been brailed up to the yards, shone white, the foresail full, the main yard pulled round forward of the mast, like a folded wing pushing the vessel westward. The figure-head and standard which had baffled him before he could now identify as the goddess Artemis and the bee emblem of Ephesus – though, to be honest, the bee still looked like something squashed on the floor.

The pirates had seen them coming, of course, and as they drew closer it became possible to make out a crowd on deck. It glinted here and there as the sun caught on spear-points and shield-rims, and Isokrates frowned unhappily. Dionysia had said there'd been seventy or eighty men in total: that was a lot of men for one hemiolia to carry all the way from Crete, but pirates did tend to pack as many fighting men aboard as they could. If one assumed that the hemiolia's oars had been fully manned, that still left more than twenty pirates on the roundship. That number undoubtedly included most of the fighting men, stationed there to keep the captives under control. *Atalanta*'s deck-soldiers would be outnumbered.

He could supplement them with the oarcrew, of course; most of the rowers had some military training. Weapons were scarce, though. Oarcrews didn't have the money to equip themselves with expensive swords and spears: they had a knife and a sling with a handful of shot, at best. *Atalanta* herself was supposed to be their weapon, but they couldn't use the ram, not against a merchant ship stuffed with captive women and children. The thought of throwing raw young recruits, most of them not even armed, against veteran pirates was nauseating. He imagined taking the trihemiolia back into port, imagined the friends and families of the new recruits waiting to welcome them home after their first cruise – imagined the wails when he handed over the bodies of the dead. No: he would not try to board the roundship.

If need be, *Atalanta* could row rings round *Artemis*, showering her with arrows and sling-stones – but it would be a long and weary business, laying *siege* to a ship at sea! He wondered, too, if these pirates would, like their chief, try to bargain with the lives of their captives. He needed them to surrender.

The pirates must know that they couldn't prevail against a trihemiolia of the Rhodian navy – but they might hope that if they held out, they could shake off their pursuer under cover of darkness, and hope for rescue from their friends. They hadn't witnessed the hemiolia's destruction: they'd be hoping that it had managed to escape.

Atalanta's figurehead – the legendary huntress she'd been named for, smirking in a short tunic – now had the hemiolia's *akrostolion* tucked under one arm like a bouquet: would that be enough to convince the pirates that their ship was lost? Maybe not: it wasn't a very distinctive stern ornament. He needed to show the pirates that there was no hope of rescue; more, he needed to convince them that if they shed Rhodian blood, they should be afraid of Rhodian vengeance. He glanced round, then beckoned Polydoros, the commander of the deck-soldiers.

He came, spear draped over his shoulders, and gave Isokrates a look of inquiry. He was a heavy, ugly man of about thirty, much scarred and with bad teeth; Isokrates had already pegged him as one of the brightest and most competent men on the ship.

'Take one of our prisoners,' Isokrates ordered,

44

'put a rope round his waist, and when we catch up with that roundship, push him off the fore-foot. I don't want him damaged, but if he yells a lot, so much the better.'

Polydoros grinned. 'Give the bastards a show, is it? Good idea!'

When *Atalanta* caught up with her quarry, Isokrates gave the order to ease oars, then took them starboard of the merchant at about half a stadion's distance. Polydoros had picked out the youngest and most nervous of the prisoners; now he frogmarched the protesting youth forward, arms lashed behind his back and rope about his waist. Isokrates couldn't see the forefoot of the ram from his seat in the stern, but when the shrieks of 'No! No!' rose in pitch, he turned the trihemiolia's prow toward the merchant, making sure that the pirates all had a good view of their comrade.

There was a burst of angry yells from the pirates, accompanied by Rhodian jeers. Isokrates handed the tiller over to Kleitos and went forward. Two of the deck-soldiers joined him as he did so, holding their heavy wood-and-oxhide shields high to each side to protect him and themselves.

The young pirate was dangling just above the water, his head level with the figurehead's knees, his feet kicking madly. The rope was cutting into his ribcage and he was struggling to breathe. Polydoros gave him an occasional poke with the boat hook to make him swing. The *Artemis* was close enough now that Isokrates could make out the faces of the men on deck, glaring from behind their own shields: he had no doubt that they'd recognized one of their own. There were a couple dozen of them, and most were armed. Others crouched behind the shield wall, only their feet and the tops of their heads visible: the archers, probably. The small group of passengers on the foredeck had disappeared. He hoped they had simply been imprisoned in the hold.

'Cretans!' Isokrates shouted, leaning out past Polydoros's shield.

'Rhodian queers!' somebody shouted back – but there were no arrows. He took that as a good sign.

'Your chief Andronikos didn't surrender!' he yelled. 'Because of that, your ship's swamped, and most of your friends are dead! You can see what sort of treatment you're going to get if you fight! Heave to, turn that ship over to her own crew, and you can keep your lives. Resist, and I swear by the Sun who sees all I'll have the lot of you hanging along our oarbox like so many gaffed fish!'

There was a silence broken only by the sound of wind and water, and the gasping of the pirate dangling from the forefoot. One of the pirates struck his spear against his shield in a warlike fashion – but the others didn't follow suit.

'Surrender and you can live!' Isokrates called. 'Surrender, and you can hope! I swear it by the Sun!'

One of the pirates threw down his spear and shield, and then another did, and another, until only the warlike one was left. He swore angrily,

46

but made no resistance as the helmsman turned *Artemis* ponderously into the wind and his fellows went to open the hatches and let the merchantman's own crew free.

Philotimos, captain of the *Artemis*, was a tall, barrel-chested man with a disconcertingly high-pitched voice. When he found himself master of his own ship again, he took his ship's boat over to *Atalanta,* and vaulted up the ladder to shake the hand and slap the back of everyone in reach.

'May the gods bless Rhodes!' he shrilled. 'May the great goddess favour you! Ah, I thought I was going to spend the rest of my life quarrying stone in some black mine! Good fortune and victory to Rhodes forever! Which of you is the trierarch?'

'Isokrates is helmsman,' Nikagoras supplied. 'Our trierarch is in Rhodes.'

Isokrates had managed to fetch his official tunic and pull it on; he came forward, and was slapped on the back so hard he stumbled.

'May Artemis the Great bless you!' piped the captain. He looked round, beaming, then exclaimed. 'Ah, and you even rescued my passenger!'

Isokrates glanced in the direction of his stare and saw that Dionysia had come back up on deck.

'She's a favourite of King Antiochos!' the captain informed them proudly. 'She admitted it when we were seized, and produced a packet of letters to prove it. You'll have a royal reward from him, I'm sure!'

47

Dionysia gave him a look of dismay: obviously this was something she'd have preferred the Rhodians not to know.

'Captain,' Isokrates said hastily, 'I hope you have made your prisoners secure, but it's best if you get them ashore as soon as possible. We can escort you as far as Phaselis.'

'Phaselis, eh?' grinned the captain. 'A good friend of Rhodes, isn't it? And willing to draw up a salvage contract, I've no doubt.' He glanced round them and grinned wider. 'As far as I'm concerned, you're entitled to every last obol!'

It was a long way back to Phaselis, around the Olympos headland and then almost due north, which meant that the wind was contrary, and the *Artemis* had to be towed. It was night by the time they arrived – a moonless night, with a faint haze over the stars which worried Isokrates as a sign of a change in the weather.

Phaselis had three harbours: north, central and south. The central one was for the galleys of King Ptolemy, who reckoned the city as his; merchant shipping used the large southern harbour; and visiting warships usually ran up on to the sandy beach of the north cove. *Atalanta* and *Artemis* parted company.

There was a watchman on the northern cove, but he knew *Atalanta* and made no difficulties about their arrival: they'd spent the previous night on the same beach. The trihemiolia's exhausted crew ran their ship stern-first up into the spot they'd used before, and secured the prow with anchor-stones. It was about the fifth

48

hour of the night, and they'd been rowing on and off for sixteen hours: they were too tired even to eat. Isokrates left the men to make camp; he needed to report the action and get someone to take charge of the captive pirates.

It took a while, even with the help of captain Philotimos, who'd come ashore on the same errand. At last, though, they found the house of the right official, woke him up, and got him to rouse the garrison. Isokrates returned to his ship with a small contingent of spearmen, two of them bearing torches.

Atalanta by this stage looked more like a tent than a ship: her mast, unshipped, had been propped against her stern, and her mainsail, pegged down with belaying pins, formed a sheltered area on the dry sand where most of the men had bedded down side by side, wrapped in their cloaks. More were asleep under an awning made from the boat sail on the foredeck.

Isokrates checked that the two deck-soldiers posted guard were awake, then collected the pirates and turned them over to the troops from the Phaselitan garrison.

When the city's men had marched off with the prisoners, the beach was left dark and utterly still. The haze over the stars had thickened; the sea, gleaming like black silk, barely lapped at the shore. Isokrates wearily climbed the boarding ladder, his hands and feet finding the rope rungs his eyes could barely see. He made his way over to the commander's seat: the area behind it, which was sheltered by the overarching curve of the stern, was traditionally reserved for

49

the ship's ranking officer. He stepped into the shadow – on to something soft.

A woman screamed, and he stumbled back. The stern watchman came running up, a darker outline in the dark night. 'Oh!' he told Isokrates. 'I forgot to tell you: Nikagoras told the Milesian lady she could sleep there.'

'Yes,' came a woman's shaky voice from the darkness.

Isokrates had managed to forget about her. 'That's where *I'm* supposed to sleep!' he said aggrievedly, too tired to care how it sounded.

'Oh,' she replied unhappily. 'I didn't know.'

He wished Nikagoras awake, so he could curse him – then instantly saw that he was being unreasonable: the bow-officer had given their passenger the only semi-private space on the ship. The one really at fault was Isokrates himself: he should have sent her back to the *Artemis*. He hadn't wanted to transfer her when the ships were at sea, though – what if she fell in? – and then when they arrived in Phaselis he'd been *tired,* worried about the prisoners, and eager to get *Atalanta* run up on shore so that everyone could rest. He should, though, have remembered her, and found her a room in town.

It was too late now to send her anywhere. 'Well, stay where you are,' he told her grudgingly. 'I'll find somewhere else.'

'Thank you.'

'Sorry I woke you,' he muttered, and stamped off.

Three

Isokrates woke early, still tired, to the sound of rain.

He lay still for a few minutes, curled up on the gangway of the oardeck, listening to the drumming on the decking above and the splash of waves on the beach. Then he groaned, uncurled, and got up. The oardeck was full of sleeping bodies – more of them than when he'd gone to sleep, which must mean that some of the men under the awnings had got wet and come inside. He picked his way over and around them and climbed through the stern hatch.

The waters of the north harbour were dull with rain. Rivulets streamed off *Atalanta*'s canted deck and cascaded from the ends of her oar-boxes. The wind was gusting from the northeast. Inside the harbour the waves were small, but he could see flecks of white on the water beyond the bar. It was cold, too. He had taken off his tunic again, though he was still wrapped in the cloak he'd used as a blanket, and he immediately wished for the warmth of another layer.

He splashed disconsolately over to the wet command chair – then recoiled: Dionysia was still in the space behind it, huddled in the angle of the upcurving hull timbers on a pile of bench-

51

cushions with her blanket wrapped tightly around her. With her bruised face and loose, tangled hair she looked like the survivor of a shipwreck, and he felt a stab of pity.

She started to get up when she saw him, and he gestured her to stay where she was. 'Never mind. I only got up to look at the weather.'

She settled in a sitting position, pulling the blanket up to her chin. 'I would've thought you could see – and feel – it anywhere.'

He snorted ruefully. 'I need a view out to sea.' He pulled his cloak about himself more closely. He was once again uncomfortably aware of his body, this time not because it was exposed but because it was so plain – tall, gaunt and big-boned, with the bad skin of years of poor food. He knew, too, that his face was too long, with a big nose and heavy eyebrows; his speech was plain uncultured Doric. Dionysia was beautiful as a goddess, even in her shipwrecked state. 'I'm sorry I didn't think to take you into the city last night,' he told her. 'I should've seen to it that you had a room somewhere you could wash and change clothes and sleep in a bed. This...' he waved a hand at the damp length of his ship, 'this is no place for a lady.'

She awarded the apology a weak smile. 'I was much too tired to go anywhere last night, and I couldn't have faced another set of strangers – though I'm sorry I took your sleeping place.'

He shrugged. 'I've slept on the oardeck before. No, I'm sorry I didn't do better for you – and that I woke you up.'

'In truth,' she said slowly, 'I didn't sleep until

52

you had.' She met his eyes. 'It was only after you stepped on me and went off apologizing that I really believed I was safe among decent people, and that no one would come at me during the night.'

He'd suspected that the pirate chief had raped her. It had all along seemed probable: that she was the mistress of a king would have made the man want to prove himself a king's equal, and any self-controlled intention about returning the royal property intact would've gone overboard once the Cretans were drunk on *Artemis*'s wine. He had not wanted to probe, though: most women who were abused by pirates were desperate to conceal the fact, afraid that husbands or fathers would blame them for it.

He'd been assaulted himself, back when he was a raw sixteen-year-old farmboy struggling to survive in the shipyard barracks. He could still remember the hot shame, the impotent anger.

'You made a great fool of that pirate,' he told her, wanting to say something to ease the pain of that unacknowledged injury.

Her eyebrows curved upward.

'When you jumped in the sea,' he elaborated. 'One minute he had a treasure in his hand; the next, a fistful of hair. You should've seen his face!' He mimicked the pirate's expression of furious disbelief and waved an imaginary clump of hair.

She looked bewildered for a moment – then smiled. It was a hesitant smile, almost shy, and when he saw it he knew that it was real, and that

53

until that moment she'd faced him from behind a mask.

'He thought he could use you,' he told her. 'He was wrong. You defeated him.'

She drew a deep breath, then released it, shivering a little. 'I was desperate.'

'You were very brave.'

Her eyes searched his a moment, looking for flattery and not finding it. The smile reappeared, tentative and uncertain. 'Would you really have bargained with him, if I hadn't jumped?'

He hesitated. 'Yes. I wouldn't have let him go, but I would've agreed to let him surrender on conditions. He might've kept all his men alive and together, and arranged for friends back in Crete to ransom them.'

'I'm glad you sank his ship.' She raked her fingers through her tangled hair, pausing at the crown of the head, where that fistful had been wrenched out. 'They were evil men. Now they can't harm any more innocents. Do you think that ... that foul Andronikos is still alive?'

'Perhaps,' Isokrates admitted reluctantly. 'If he's a good swimmer, he could've made it to the mainland. I gave his description to the garrison commander here, but ... he didn't seem very interested.'

He scowled at the memory of the commander's off-hand manner: *'Cretan pirates, eh? You Rhodians keep yourselves busy, don't you?'* A dangerous attitude: Lycia itself, with its deeply indented coastline, was ideal pirate territory. If the authorities relaxed their vigilance, there would soon be more Lycian pirates than

Cretan ones.

'I doubt that he'll spare anyone to make inquiries in the countryside,' he told Dionysia. 'I'm sorry. I just didn't think I had the time to go after him, not with the *Artemis* sailing off in the opposite direction.'

'No,' she agreed. 'Those people on the *Artemis* needed rescue just as much as I did.' She drew another deep breath. 'We all of us owe you a great debt.'

'Lady, we Rhodians set ourselves against piracy because we live by trade. What we did yesterday was what this ship was built for. When we go home every man on *Atalanta* will be boasting of how we sunk the famous pirate Andronikos on our very first cruise, and all our friends will be envious. We'll get our share of the salvage, too, and our share of the money from selling those pirates. We're blessing the gods for what happened yesterday! You don't owe us anything.'

'Was Andronikos famous?'

Isokrates hesitated. 'I think I might have heard of him. I'm not sure. But by the time the men have been back in Rhodes ten days, he will have become a monstrously famous pirate and the captain of a whole flotilla, which we skewered on our ram like so many partridges on a spit.'

That won him another of the shy smiles, and he grinned at her. 'I should check the weather and see if I can work out how soon we can go back,' he told her. He stepped out on to the top of the oarbox and stared at the sea to the north, holding a hand up into the rain to feel the wind. The sky was an unrelieved gray, and the chill air had the heaviness that promised more wet weather to come. The choppy sea was already on the edge of what a galley would tolerate – warships needed calm water – and it looked like it was going to get worse. 'It's not going to let up today,' he concluded, shaking his head and stepping back on to the deck.

'Well, at least you weren't planning to go anywhere.'

He looked at her in surprise. 'I was planning to set off back for Rhodes!'

She blinked. 'What about your salvage agreement?'

'I was going to leave Nikagoras to settle that.'

Her straight brows drew down. 'I thought ... that is, you'd offered me passage if...'

'Yes, certainly! But I don't need the contract settled to do that. I spoke to Philotimos last night, and he's already said he's not going on to Alexandria.'

They had discussed the *Artemis* and her cargo while waiting for the garrison commander to produce men to take charge of the prisoners. Philotimos had also revealed why he could be so cheerful about the Rhodian salvage claim: *Artemis* and her cargo didn't belong to him. The ship had been built and outfitted by a newly formed syndicate in Ephesus, and the captain had merely been hired to sail her to Alexandria.

'He said there's no point going on with the hold half empty,' Isokrates continued. 'He's going to go back to Ephesus, and offer to complete the voyage for his backers once the ship's

56

fully laden again.'

Dionysia looked troubled. 'I thought...' She stopped abruptly, giving him a distrustful look he didn't understand.

'It'll be a while now before we can set out,' he told her.

She regarded him a moment in silence. He had thought her eyes beautiful the day before, when she was shaken and afraid; now that she was calmer, he was struck by the cool intelligence in that dark gaze. 'You didn't ask about what Philotimos said,' she observed suddenly, 'that I have a packet of letters from King Antiochos. Why not?'

'You named yourself a free woman and told me that it was no business of mine.'

Her lips curled in distaste. 'And you no doubt drew your own conclusions from that.'

He hesitated, trying to puzzle out the reason for the change in tone. 'Rhodes is not subject to King Antiochos,' he told her. 'It's not our business to keep track of his friends for him.'

Her eyebrows rose. 'Rhodes supported Antiochos in the last war. In fact, I distinctly remember the king saying that he owed his victory to Agathostratos and the Rhodians.'

'Ptolemy was using pirates to harass his enemy's shipping,' Isokrates replied at once. 'It hurt our trading ships and our livelihoods: we had to fight. When the war ended, though, we were very relieved to be friends with Egypt again: if we lost the Egyptian trade we'd all go bankrupt. Lady, if I tell you that the kings are stronger than us, I won't be saying anything you don't know. We try to stay friends with them because we don't want them as enemies – but that doesn't make us their subjects.'

'So you have no interest in the *royal reward* Philotimos was promising you yesterday?' she asked bitterly.

He finally understood what the trouble was: she thought he was eager to get back to Rhodes so that he could hand her over to the king. He hesitated again – then, with a sense of relief, decided to be honest: the truth was less discreditable than her suspicions. 'Lady, I don't serve the King of Syria – or the King of Egypt, or any other monarch. I serve the Council and People of the Rhodians! Yes, I was interested by what Philotimos said about a packet of letters. I've suspected from the first that you have some information you mean to give King Ptolemy, and I was hoping that if I took you to Rhodes you might be willing to give it to us as well. But I don't have any plans to return you to King Antiochos against your will. I swear it by the Sun! As far as I'm concerned, you're welcome to continue your journey – and I didn't lie when I told you that it would be much easier to do from Rhodes.'

She looked at him intently, biting her lip.

'I'm guessing that you badly need to make this voyage,' he told her. 'And that the pirates have left you short of funds to continue it. I'm sorry for it – but it isn't the fault of Rhodes. I think we've earned the right to be treated as your friends – or, at least, the right not to be treated as enemies.'

'Say I do have some information,' she said slowly. 'Would the Council of Rhodes be willing to pay for it? And what would they do with me once they had it?'

'I ... I think they'd be happy to pay for copies of your letters. And afterwards they'd send you on your way and pretend they knew nothing about you.'

'The letters are nothing. I just brought them along to prove who I am – that I really was a friend of the king.' She bit her lip again, the tips of her teeth white. 'How do I know that you're telling the truth?'

'Lady, *I* don't speak for the Council! But I'm giving you my best guess – and I do know something about what the Council is like. We Rhodians have a *democracy*. We elect our councillors, and we know who they are and what weighs with them. If Antiochos suddenly sent letters all over the Aegean demanding that anyone who found you should return you forthwith, the Council probably *would* send you back – but I haven't heard that he's done that, and I'm assuming that King Ptolemy is in this game, too. When two kings are involved, Rhodes won't want to offend either of them. If we admitted we knew what you were doing, we'd be expected to support one side or the other. If anyone asks, it would be safer and easier to say something like, "Oh, yes, we did save her from pirates – but she told us she was on her way to visit her brother in Alexandria, so we sped her on her way. How could we possibly have known she had information King Antiochos wanted to keep secret?" '

'Antiochos won't send out any letters,' she said dismissively. 'He's probably relieved that I've disappeared – though he probably thinks I've gone home to Miletos.' She regarded him earnestly. 'Would your Council grant me passage on the next ship to Alexandria?'

He spread his hands helplessly. 'I would've *thought* so. I would've thought they'd put you on a courier ship straight there, if that's what you want. But, as I said, I'm not a member of the Council.'

She gazed at him a minute longer, her eyes full of hope. 'Your guess sounds reasonable to me. When can we set out for Rhodes?'

It was not for another two days: the weather got worse before it got better. The rain drove in from the east, then turned to hail and thunder; the sea beyond the bar was stormy. *Atalanta*'s crewmen had brought along at most light cloaks, and there were only five pairs of sandals on the whole ship. The men crowded into the taverns of Phaselis to stay dry, and the tavernkeepers complained to Isokrates that there was no space for better-paying customers – or, alternatively, that Rhodians had damaged the furnishings brawling with the locals. As for the men themselves, they complained of greedy tradesmen, of cold and damp and bad food. Phaselis had a standing arrangement with Rhodes for the provision of basic supplies for the crews of visiting galleys, but this amounted to little more than barley cakes and olives – and the olives they were given were starting to go off.

Isokrates was continuously busy: trying to get credit enough to buy cheese and onions and wine; pacifying the tavernkeepers with apologies and promises; cadging straw from a livery stable and borrowing sails from *Artemis* to wall in their awning so the men could sleep dry.

Apart from the sails, *Artemis* was a source only of headaches. *Atalanta*'s crew looked at the ship sitting in the harbour – ten thousand drachmai at anchor! – and loudly wondered why they couldn't have their share *now*, when they needed it. Everyone in Phaselis, too, seemed to know that the Rhodians were due salvage, and expected Rhodian payment in cash. It was no use Isokrates explaining that the salvage hadn't been agreed yet, and that even when it had been, Philotimos didn't have the cash in hand, and could only pledge it on behalf of the syndicate that employed him. Agreement on the salvage proved harder to reach than expected, too, even though Philotimos remained cooperative. There was confusion about how the value of the ship and its cargo should be assessed, about whether the salvage should be half or two thirds of that value, about what port dues and fees should go to Phaselis. Nikagoras, whom Isokrates had hoped would take charge of the matter – after all, the boy belonged to a family of merchants! – turned out to have no idea how to go about it; in the end Isokrates had to draw up the agreement himself, with advice from the Phaselitan councillor who represented Rhodian interests.

There were questions, too, about the captive

61

pirates, who numbered thirty-one in total. The commander of the city garrison – a smooth, fast-talking man whom Isokrates instinctively distrusted – offered to buy them all for eighty drachmai a man. Isokrates didn't want them on his ship, but he was unwilling to turn them over to the soldiers of King Ptolemy. In the end, he had to pledge Rhodian credit for their guards and their upkeep until another ship came to collect them.

After two wet and weary days, however, the sum of six thousand drachmai – a whole talent of silver! – was agreed in salvage, a document was drawn up, and Philotimos pledged the money on behalf of his syndicate. That same evening the rain stopped.

The next morning, their third in Phaselis, dawned calm and clear. Deeply relieved, Isokrates ordered the men to strike camp and sent the borrowed sails back to *Artemis* with a message of thanks. The messenger also spoke to Dionysia, inviting her to come on board.

The ex-concubine had returned to the *Artemis* on their first day in Phaselis: it seemed she had a cabin there, which saved her paying for an inn. Isokrates had been surprised when he learned this – only the very rich travelled in cabins. Ordinary people just rigged themselves shelters on decks, and Dionysia hadn't seemed wealthy. When she turned up, though, quickly on the heels of Isokrates' messenger, he had to revise his estimate.

She was much changed from the bedraggled survivor they'd hauled out of the sea. A long chiton of pale gold peeked out from under a dark gold wrap; her smooth brown hair was piled high on her head and secured with a gold chain, and there were pearls in her ears. She was followed by an attendant – a sour-faced woman of middle age – and by two sailors carrying a heavy chest of luggage. Only the bruise on her face, now turning green at the edges, showed that this was indeed the same woman. Isokrates gaped at her. An elegant woman like this was as out of place on a galley as an emerald in a begging bowl. If she'd looked like this before, he would never have suggested that she travel with them.

He would never have spoken to her so freely, either, nor have looked forward – as he had – to seeing her again. He had hoped to gain another of those sweet smiles, perhaps even make her laugh. The strength of his disappointment revealed to him just how much he'd been hoping, and he cursed himself: he should've known that a king's mistress was far out of his reach. He was puzzled, too. Why had she been worried about paying for a passage to Alexandria, when she was wearing pearls which would buy her way there and back again?

'Good health!' she exclaimed, smiling at him. 'Where can I put my luggage?'

They couldn't fit the chest on to the oardeck without repacking all the supplies of food and water, so Isokrates ceded the space behind the command chair. The two sailors who'd carried the chest went back to *Artemis*, but it seemed that the woman who'd trailed Dionysia was her

63

own maid; she had been on the *Artemis* and had been rescued along with the other victims of the pirates. She was a thin, dark creature, fortyish, with eyes that watched the crew with the flat unblinking gaze of a snake. Her name was Dyseris, and it was evident from her demeanour that she strongly disapproved of her mistress's notion of travelling on a warship. She and her mistress were found a place amidships, on the tabernacle of the unstepped mast; Dionysia perched there with a smile, but Dyseris glowered.

The men stripped off, and, with extravagant howls at the chill of the water, dragged the ship back down into the sea. They scrambled aboard, laughing and shouting, and piled below to take their places on the rowing benches. The wind was from the east; the sail crew shook out the boat sail at the prow, and Isokrates took the tiller. *Atalanta* glided slowly out into the south harbour of Phaselis, propelled by the wind alone. By the time she reached the open sea, the men were all in place; the piper struck up a tune, and Damophon began to beat time. Suddenly a hundred voices were roaring out a shanty:

> *The pig has an acorn, and that he likes to eat,*
> *Me, I've got a girlfriend, who is much more sweet!*

The maid Dyseris stalked over to Isokrates. 'Sir!'

He was glad that he was properly dressed and officer-like. He almost protested that the impropriety of the situation was not his fault – and anyway, wasn't he owed some gratitude, for rescuing the lady? – and the maid herself!

'My mistress has delicate skin,' said the maid. 'Can we have an awning to protect us from the sun?'

It was the first of many requests: Dyseris also wanted a pitcher of water, with a cup for her lady to drink from ('you can't expect her to gulp from a jug like a sailor!'); a screen to protect her from the breeze; and a screened-off area at the stern so that the women could relieve themselves in private ('since it seems this ship doesn't contain such an elementary convenience as a chamber-pot!'). The sailors who had to rig these for her were not at all put out; in fact, they competed with one another for the honour. They hadn't really believed before that they had rescued a king's mistress; this fussiness convinced them that they had, and they regarded her and themselves with great satisfaction.

A few hours into the voyage, Isokrates steered past the islet where they'd rammed the hemiolia; as he'd expected, the hulk had broken up in the stormy weather. A few timbers were visible on the rocks, but that was all.

The crew were relieved: the few drachmai they would've earned from the timber and bronze weren't worth the hard work of towing a waterlogged hulk. As they continued on, they left off the sea-shanties and instead launched on a more formal hymn, though one that was a perpetual favourite of Rhodian oarsmen:

For the Sun bears toil in every day,
without ceasing in any way
his horses run when rosy Dawn...

Suddenly the deep voices were joined by a clear soprano which floated above them:

... rises from Ocean to heaven each morn
where the furrowed wave bears his hollow
bed
that Hephaistos' hands have laboured
to fit with gold...

Dionysia's voice was so strong, and so pure, that the rowers fell silent to listen. She sang on for a few bars alone, then stopped, shaking her head and laughing. She went over to the central hatch and called down, 'You have to sing too!'

'I have a kithara,' she told Isokrates a little later, when she came aft to fetch a scarf from her luggage. 'Would it be safe to take it out here at sea? Or would the damp air damage it?'

Isokrates could only shake his head uncertainly. He had had a basic education, which had included just enough music for him to recognize a professional musician when he heard one. 'People don't usually play kitharas on galleys,' he managed. 'Not good kitharas, anyway. Sometimes somebody will accompany the piper on an old pot that doesn't mind the odd splash of salt water.'

She smiled. 'It's a *very* good one. It was my father's. He won the kitharist's crown once at Delphi.'

Isokrates was impressed: the music festival held during the Pythian Games at Delphi was the most prestigious in the Greek world. 'Then you *definitely* need to keep it safe.'

She nodded, as though this was the answer she'd expected. 'A pity. I haven't played for days.' She stretched out her hands with their slim strong fingers, then looked up at him again. 'Does the Guild of Dionysiac Artists have a house on Rhodes?'

'Oh, yes!' he agreed. 'A good big one, near the theatre.' The Guild had branches in most Greek cities and was very active in protecting the interests of its members; professional musicians and actors joined it as a matter of course. 'You said your father was a member, didn't you? Would they let you stay there?'

'I don't know,' she admitted. 'I could ask.' She was silent a moment. 'My father used to talk about taking me on tour with him. I used to day-dream about it – foreign cities, cheering audiences, excitement and adventure. Instead...' she shrugged. 'There was King Antiochos. Papa still hoped that one day he and I could go on tour together, but it never happened, and now he's dead.'

'I'm sorry.'

She gave him that sweet smile. 'Maybe I'll be able to join the Guild in my own name now. It's what I want to do. I hope ... do you like music?'

'Everybody likes music! I'm not a – an educated man, but I like to listen, when I can. I would've thought you could join the Guild. Your voice is beautiful.' Even as he said it, he knew that the words were the ignorant reassurance of an admirer, and clenched his teeth on them, too late. Dionysia's look became wary, and she excused herself.

As the sun was going down they reached the island of Megiste. This island – like several others close to Rhodes – was legally part of the Rhodian republic, its citizens able to vote in the Rhodian Assembly. The Rhodian navy had shipsheds and barracks there, and supplies for visiting galleys. The men were cheerful: they would sleep under a roof that night.

Dionysia's maid declared that her lady would stay in an inn. The two women were escorted into the town by Nikagoras, who eventually returned with the news that Dyseris had been unimpressed by any of the Megistean inns, but had settled for the best one. Isokrates began to feel embarrassed at his assumption that Dionysia was short of money.

The good weather held; the following morning dawned clear and calm. Dionysia and her maid returned to *Atalanta* in good time, and the trihemiolia set out on the final leg of her voyage.

Rhodes lay east-northeast of Megiste, a day's sail away. The breeze, though light, was still easterly, and *Atalanta* was able to step her mast and use both her mainsail and boatsail. Isokrates nonetheless insisted that the men row, in shifts: after all, the voyage had been intended to shake down the oarcrew. They made good time, and the island came into view in the afternoon.

Isokrates recognized the shape when it was still only a blue shadow, and corrected their course just slightly: the harbours of Rhodes were best approached from the southwest: strong northerly winds and a fierce current often made the northeastern approach impossible.

The seas around Lycia had been uncrowded so early in the season, but here in Rhodian coastal waters they met more traffic: a roundship bearing the standard of Egypt, rolling along to the south; then another, with the Rhodian sun, bearing north. Then a quadrireme appeared from the direction of the mainland – a larger galley than *Atalanta,* with four files of oarsmen arranged two men to an oar in two oarbanks. She had only half her oars beating, though, and those moved slowly: another oarcrew in training. *Atalanta* stayed ahead of her without difficulty.

The city of Rhodes appeared: a mass of red-tiled roofs enclosed by massive walls of grey stone. Isokrates turned the tiller over to Kleitos the tiller-holder, and went forward to the prow, where Dionysia was standing with her maid. She gave him a smile as he came up, then turned her eyes back to the city before her. Nikagoras was already beside her and it seemed he was pointing out the landmarks. Isokrates felt a stab of resentment, and struggled to suppress it: the bow, after all, was where Nikagoras was *supposed* to be – and Isokrates would have to be very foolish indeed to think either of them had any hope with a woman like this one.

'The big temple's to Athena of the City and to Zeus,' Nikagoras was explaining, waving at the white blur atop the hill of the acropolis. 'The smaller one, there, is to Pythian Apollo.'

'I thought you Rhodians honoured the Sun above all the other gods,' Dionysia said, frowning slightly. 'Or do you think Apollo and the Sun are really the same divinity?'

'Some people say that,' Nikagoras replied, then proceeded to show off his education. 'Others say no, the Sun is one of the Titans, the son of Hyperion, while Apollo is the son of Zeus. My philosophy teacher doesn't believe any of the myths; he says that the only god is reason! Me, I don't think mortals can say anything for sure about the gods. The temple of Athena is very fine, though; you'll have to see it! But it's true we Rhodians honour the Sun most of all. You know the myth?'

'The Sun was driving his bright chariot across the heavens,' Dionysia recited, 'when, looking down, he saw a beautiful nymph, a daughter of Ocean, rising from the sea. Her name was Rhodos, and he fell in love with her and made her his bride.'

'That's the story,' agreed Nikagoras, grinning. He flung out his arm in a gesture Isokrates suspected he'd learned in his rhetoric class. 'And there she is, the Sun's bride, as beautiful as ever! Almost as...'

Isokrates knew he was going to say 'beautiful as you!' Dionysia obviously thought so, too, because she interrupted with a quick, 'But a *rhodos* is also a flower, isn't it? I've always wondered – is it or isn't it a kind of rose? The word is almost the same, but the image you put on your coins doesn't look like one.'

Nikagoras was only slightly put out. 'It's a

70

rose hibiscus. It grows all over the island. There's a park there, near the temple, where a lot of it grows – see that green patch? And that, just to the north – that's the roof of the covered concert hall, just there – see? It's new, seats nearly a thousand people; the ceiling is painted with the nine Muses. And that golden spire, that's the Tower of the Winds, in the marketplace. My family's house is just south of that.'

'Oh!' exclaimed Dionysia, but not at the interesting location of Nikagoras's house: the angle of their approach had suddenly given them a view of the northern harbour – and the statue there. Taller than *Atalanta* was long, the bronze image of the sun-god stood beside the harbour entrance, one great arm raised to protect the island he loved. His halo was gilded, and seemed to glow as brightly as the late afternoon sun that shone upon it.

'The Colossus of Rhodes,' Nikagoras said proudly. 'Chares of Lindos built it. They used the money from selling the siege engines left behind by Demetrios the Besieger. He never took Rhodes, you know, though he tried for a whole year, and it was the greatest siege in the history of the world. The siege engines fetched three hundred talents!'

'The sun of Rhodes shines bright,' Dionysia murmured, gazing at the statue with awe.

Atalanta rowed past the sheltering hand of the Colossus and into the military harbour, and Isokrates went aft again. He might as well devote himself to his job: their return would give him plenty to do, and whatever had he hoped to gain,

71

anyway, going forward?

In her home port, there was no running *Atalanta* up on to a beach: she had a shipshed of her own. There were a few formalities to be completed before the doors of that shed were opened, though. The delay was apparently long enough that news of their arrival spread: Isokrates was discharging the crew when there was an angry shout from the shed entrance. He looked up, and found Aristomachos the trierarch bearing down like a galley preparing to ram. He jumped down from the ship, ignoring the boarding ladder in his haste, and hurried to meet his commanding officer.

'You're three days late!' roared the trierarch. Aristomachos was a burly, sharp-eyed man in his early thirties; he was dressed in a fine linen tunic and a very fine red cloak, but the cloak was askew, disarranged by its owner's vigorous temper.

'Yes, sir,' admitted Isokrates. 'The weather...'

'The bugger-arsed weather can only explain two fucking days!' exclaimed Aristomachos. 'It was a filthy *training exercise*, by Apollo; how can you come in three days late from a *training exercise*?' He caught sight of Dionysia, who was peering down at him over the railing, and his jaw dropped. 'By Apollo! What is your girlfriend doing on *my ship*?'

'Sir, she's not...'

'Where's my nephew?'

Nikagoras descended from the trihemiolia. 'Here, Uncle.'

'Well, I thank the gods for *that*, anyway! Your

72

mother's been on at me for two days now: where's my boy, is he drowned, is he stranded penniless in some horrible foreign port, why didn't you go along yourself to keep an eye on him?'

Nikagoras looked disgusted. 'Sir,' began Iso-krates.

'So what's the story? And who, by the Lady of the Crossroads, is that woman?'

'She's the mistress of King Antiochos!' announced Nikagoras proudly. 'We rescued her!'

Aristomachos's sharp eyes darted swiftly to his nephew. 'From what?'

'From the pirates,' explained Nikagoras.

There was a moment of silence. 'Indeed?' Aristomachos asked, in a much milder tone. 'What pirates were these?'

Nikagoras beamed. 'Their chief was called Andronikos. They were cruising along west of Phaselis, on their way back to Crete, Uncle, but when they saw us they ran! We chased them, and then we *rammed* them! Only eight of them on the hemiolia survived!' He seemed to have forgotten all the horror and pity he'd felt when he actually witnessed the events he recounted. 'And then we went and rescued the ship they'd seized to carry away their booty. It's a very fine ship, Uncle – the *Artemis,* a hundred and thirty tons, just built by the syndicate of Stephanos and Miltiades in Ephesus. It had a hundred and twelve amphorae of wine from the Cayster valley still aboard. The salvage comes to a talent of silver!'

Aristomachos's eyes flew back to Isokrates,

then checked the grinning faces of the men and officers, who had all stopped to watch the show. Finally his gaze went to the ship's prow, where *Atalanta*'s figurehead still clutched her wooden stern-ornament bouquet.

'Well,' said the trierarch at last. 'Well, well done! Pirates, eh? I would've thought it was too early in the year.'

'Yes, sir,' Isokrates said tactfully. 'I was surprised when I saw them. I suppose *they* thought it was too early in the year for *us*.' He beckoned Dionysia. 'Sir, this lady is Dionysia, the daughter of Kleisthenes of Miletos and, as Nikagoras said, a companion of King Antiochos. She was on her way to visit her brother in Alexandria when the pirates seized her ship.'

Dionysia, just down from the boarding ladder, straightened her cloak.

'Lady, this is Aristomachos son of Anaxippos, trierarch of *Atalanta*.'

Dionysia gracefully inclined her head. 'Sir. I must thank you and Rhodes for my preservation. I believed I was lost forever until your trihemiolia found us. She is well-named: the Calydonian huntress of legend was no swifter, nor more deadly.'

Aristomachos began to smile 'Well,' he said again.

'I hope you are not offended that I accepted your helmsman's kind offer of passage from Phaselis. The *Artemis* was returning to Ephesus and I was at a loss how to continue my voyage.'

'No, not at all! Isokrates did very well to offer.' Aristomachos glanced at Isokrates again, then reached up to slap him on the shoulder. 'Very well indeed! I look forward to hearing the whole story. Isokrates, you will join me for dinner this evening. Ah, Lady...' Aristomachos drew himself up, tugging at his dishevelled cloak. 'I hope you will accept the hospitality of my house while you are in Rhodes.'

Dionysia gave him an enquiring look. 'You are very kind sir, to offer it. May I ask, though, whether it would be proper? For all that I've arrived so suddenly and shamefully on a war-ship, I am, I assure you, not a lewd woman.'

'I never believed otherwise, Lady,' Aristo-machos declared gallantly. It was probably true that he had never believed that a king's mistress would sleep with him. 'You are right, now I think of it: it would not be proper. Allow me to offer you hospitality on behalf of my married sister. Nikagoras!'

The young bow-officer looked brightly at his uncle.

'Go put your mother out of her misery, and take this lady with you – no, wait! I'll come along with you, and introduce her. Isokrates, I'll expect you at my house in about an hour.'

'You are very kind, sir,' murmured Dionysia, while Nikagoras beamed. She'd be staying in *his* house now! Isokrates' heart burned, and he cursed himself for a fool.

Four

Coming back to Rhodes usually left Isokrates feeling flat and low. On a ship there was order and purpose, and he was an important man; on Rhodes he was just another poor sailor ashore. Returning to his lodgings that evening with his small sack of luggage, the change seemed more depressing than ever before.

He had a rented room in the house of an oarsman's widow. It was a small, shabby place, and it stank of drains and the neighbouring fish market. He had taken it when he first moved out of barracks. He was only an oarbinder then, and it was cheap; he could afford better, now that he was a helmsman, but it was close to the ship-yards and to the porticos and taverns frequented by navy men – and besides, he knew that his landlady couldn't afford to lose the rent-money. When he knocked on the door, he could hear one of her children crying.

The landlady, an ugly bad-tempered woman by the name of Atta, opened the door with a cooking spoon in one hand. 'Oh!' she exclaimed, regarding him resentfully. 'I didn't expect you back. I haven't cooked for you.' His rent was supposed to include the evening meal, but Atta had two children to support on a meagre income:

food was always short. Even when she did cook for him, she never cooked enough.

'That's all right,' he assured her. 'The trierarch invited me to dinner.'

The crying child, a five-year-old girl, stopped wailing and came over to embrace Isokrates' knees. She gazed up at him hopefully, her slobbered face breaking into a smile. He had a soft spot for little girls, and often slipped her crusts of bread or pieces of fruit. On this occasion, however, he'd brought nothing, so he merely rumpled her dirty hair. 'Good health to you, Leuke!'

Atta impatiently seized her daughter's shoulder and jerked the child off. 'Stop that, Leuke! He doesn't want your nasty snot all over him!' Isokrates wasn't sure whether she suspected his motives for befriending the girl, or whether it was simply that there wasn't much affection in her life, and she was determined that her children should not go wasting any on the lodger.

Leuke began to cry again; her mother ignored it, except to raise her voice as she said, 'You're late back, Isokrates, sir. Was there trouble?'

'We ran into a pirate.' For a moment he was tempted to go on, to tell her, 'We sank him; we rescued a shipful of captives and the beautiful mistress of a king' – but somehow the events seemed exaggerated and unreal, here in a small house in one of the poorer quarters of Rhodes.

Atta wasn't really interested anyway. 'And chased him over the horizon, and were caught by the weather,' she concluded, returning to the hearth to stir her cooking pot – 'Leuke, stop that

77

wailing! I've had enough of it!'

'Harpalos *hit* me!' wailed Leuke. Harpalos was her brother, a seven-year-old bully.

'And if you don't stop, *I'll* hit you, too! – Isokrates, sir, those things you're wearing could use a wash. If you leave them, I'll clean them tomorrow.'

Atta charged for that service – but it did need doing. 'Thank you.' He went into his room, stripped off his officer's tunic and changed into his best woollen one. He tossed his summer cloak on over it, despite the fact that it was musty and that the moths had got into it over the winter: the only other cloak he had was the heavy sea-cloak he'd worn on *Atalanta,* and it was covered in cushion-grease and sand. There was no time to wash and visit a barber: Aristomachos would just have to take him as he came. He told himself – as he always did before a meeting with a trierarch – that all citizens were equal in law, and he should not allow himself to be intimidated by money and noble ancestors. As usual, he was not entirely convinced. A bad report from Aristomachos could ruin him.

'A letter for you came a couple of days ago,' Atta told him as he came back through the house. 'I put it in your room: did you see it?'

He hadn't, and went back to check. It was from his father. He stared at it a moment, then went out again without picking it up. He did not particularly want to hear anything his father had to say to him: it could wait until he'd finished his business with Aristomachos.

The trierarch's house was near the marketplace, on the eastern side: a good location and a very fine house. Aristomachos lived there alone, apart from his young son and his slaves. His wife was dead and he'd married off his fourteen-year-old daughter the previous year: it was that absence of respectable women from the house which made it 'improper' for him to play host to Dionysia. A slave admitted Isokrates to the stone-paved entrance hall and brought him a basin of water to wash his hands and feet before escorting him to the dining room.

Aristomachos was already reclining at the table, eating olives from a Corinthianware dish; he waved for Isokrates to join him. There were no other guests, which was a relief: Isokrates was unsure how much secrecy would be required, so at this stage, the fewer listeners the better. He took his place on the couch next to his captain.

'My sister was a study,' Aristomachos commented, taking another olive. 'She didn't know whether to hug me for bringing her darling boy home intact, or hit me for foisting a royal whore on to her as a guest.'

'Lady Dionysia isn't a whore,' Isokrates said flatly.

Aristomachos tossed his olive pit on to the floor. 'No? What was she doing travelling to Alexandria, then, alone except for a maid?'

'Running away,' Isokrates replied at once. 'She has some important information, sir. She's hoping to sell it to Ptolemy, but I persuaded her to offer it to the Council as well, in exchange for a swift passage to Alexandria. I promised her that if it affects two kings, we'll want to pretend we don't know.'

Aristomachos regarded him a moment; lying side by side on the couch, their faces were only inches apart, and Isokrates could smell the olives on the other man's breath. The trierarch grinned. 'They told me you were sharp as a new knife! Tell me everything.'

Isokrates told him, quickly and plainly, everything that had happened since they first sighted the pirate. Aristomachos's slaves brought in the meal as he did so, and he snatched bites of grilled fish punctuated by a salad of parsley and onions, while the trierarch ate in appreciative silence.

At the end of the narrative, Aristomachos beamed and slapped him on the shoulder. 'A pirate sunk, a nice fat salvage claim, and my ship and everyone aboard safe home again: well done! You were cheated over the salvage, but not badly. Refusing to sell your captives to that shark – that was good! Eighty per man is much too low. I'll send a ship to fetch them tomorrow, if the weather holds.' Aristomachos was the sole owner of one trading ship, and a shareholder in another five: it was the source of his wealth. 'But let's get back to the matter of the royal spy...'

'I don't think she's that, either.'

Aristomachos raised his eyebrows. 'You said she was running to Ptolemy!'

'Yes.' Isokrates paused, trying to sort out his impressions. 'I think something happened at Antiochos's court, something that frightened her badly. She's running to Ptolemy because she thinks he'll pay for news of it, but she wasn't one of his spies. She said she was bringing the packet of Antiochos's letters to prove who she was.'

Aristomachos grunted thoughtfully. 'I see your reasoning: a proper spy would have a contact and a password. Where did you say she was from?'

'Miletos.'

The trierarch considered that a moment. Miletos, like most of the cities of the Asian coast, had been under the control of King Ptolemy until the war a decade before; however, unlike most, it had genuinely welcomed its transfer to King Antiochos. The Milesians had suffered greatly under their Ptolemaic governor, and had been so grateful to Antiochos for ridding them of the 'tyrant' that they'd given their new monarch the title of 'the God'. A Milesian concubine was an unlikely candidate for a Ptolemaic spy.

'Any idea what her news is about?' Aristomachos asked.

Isokrates shook his head. 'I didn't even ask. Sir, she's hoping to *sell* information: asking her to give it away for free would only have made her suspicious. What I do know, though, is that she's afraid – and that she's in a hurry. She booked passage unseasonably early, on a ship she was told was fast, and she was eager to continue the voyage as soon as she could, despite an experience which would leave most women refusing ever to set foot on a ship again. I think it means something, too, that she didn't ask help from Ptolemy's garrison in Phaselis. Maybe she would have, if we hadn't been there, but, even so, the fact is she preferred us to them. She's hoping for a reward for her information. I've convinced her that *we're* not going to steal that reward by delivering the news ourselves – but Ptolemy's servants are another matter.'

The trierarch shook his head unhappily. 'I don't like this business at all. It's a chancy spring. The world's been holding its breath since the new year.'

There was no need to ask what had happened in the new year: everybody knew. In January King Ptolemy the Loving Brother, who'd ruled Egypt for nearly forty years and made his kingdom the greatest power in the Aegean, had died. It was a natural death, and the succession had passed smoothly to his son; the new king, Ptolemy the Benefactor, was a mature man and reputed to be intelligent and energetic – but still, the death of a king unsettled the world.

'How many others know about this?' Aristo-machos asked, after a moment of silence.

'I don't think *anyone* else is aware, sir. As far as I know, I'm the only one the lady told about it. I suppose others could have noticed what I did – that there's something very strange about a woman like that travelling by herself – but the first day we were busy with the pirate, and after that everyone seemed to believe the lie about a brother in Alexandria. I suppose most of the others aren't aware of the detail which made me suspicious – that she booked the passage herself at the harbourside. Your nephew is the one who's had most to do with the lady, though, and it's possible he...'

'No,' Aristomachos said confidently. 'Nikagoras is a fool. Oh, he's showing some signs of interest in business, I admit; he may amount to something in a few years. But now? He doesn't see a problem unless you point it out, and then he'll accept the first explanation he's offered. Besides, he thinks that Milesian courtesan is a goddess sprung from the foam of the wine-dark sea, and all his thinking about her is done with his prick. So you not only found out about this; you managed to keep it secret!' He slapped Isokrates on the shoulder. 'I did well, picking you to run the ship for me.'

He'd had friends who'd recommended their protégés for the place; he'd told Isokrates that when he offered him the position. 'But I want someone keen and sharp and hungry,' he'd said. 'Someone who'll make my trierarchy a success. Your name came up.'

Aristomachos had less naval experience than most men of his class: he'd concentrated on his merchant ships since finishing his military service. His family's wealth had suffered badly from some poor investments by his father, and he'd been obliged to build it up again before he could qualify for a trierarchy. Now he was trying to make up for lost time. Without naval experience, he had little chance of being elected to any position of real influence.

'I hope never to give you cause to regret your choice, sir,' Isokrates said sincerely. Aristomachos's approval, and the reputation of a man who could make a trierarchy a success, meant he would have his choice of ships next year.

Aristomachos smiled, but the smile faded quickly. 'I don't want to take this to the full Council,' he said at last. 'No group that large can ever keep a secret. My friend Xenophantes is a president this season: I'll get him to bring a couple of his colleagues here to the house.' The Council had five presidents, who took turns chairing its meetings. 'They can listen to what your girlfriend has to say and decide what to do about it.'

'She's not my girlfriend.'

Aristomachos grinned. 'Then the more fool you! She was singing your praises loudly all the way to my sister's.'

Isokrates' heart gave a lurch, and he looked down at his plate. He thought of Dionysia in cream and gold, and of his shabby little room at Atta's: there was a gap there which couldn't be bridged. 'You're my commander,' he told the trierarch levelly, looking up again. 'Praising me to you is doing me a favour. I saved her, and she's not ungrateful – and one of the things she's grateful for is that I left her alone.'

Aristomachos pursed his lips. 'The pirate...?' he made a graphic gesture.

'I didn't ask. It isn't something most women want to talk about.'

Aristomachos studied him a moment, then nodded. 'And you were out to win her trust. Well, since she trusts you, you can escort her to meet the presidents tomorrow. The fewer people who are involved, the better. Besides, the presidents may want to ask you some questions about how she got here. I'll send you a messenger tomorrow morning to let you know the time.'

Isokrates duly found himself knocking on the door of the house belonging to Nikagoras's family next morning.

It was approaching the fourth hour. He was still unshaven: he had slept late, and Aristomachos's messenger had arrived just as he was getting up, giving him time only for a hurried wash with a basin and a sponge. The slave who answered the door of the mansion looked down his nose at such a scruffy visitor and told him to wait outside.

He had been waiting barely a minute when Nikagoras hurried out, very elegantly dressed in a sleeved tunic and short cloak, but still unshaven and with his long hair still wet from the bath. He eyed Isokrates with open hostility. 'Why are you here?'

Isokrates straightened – taking full advantage of his height – and answered the hot look with a cold one. 'Your uncle sent me to escort the Milesian lady to his house to meet his friend Xenophantes. He's a president now and he wants to ask her the news of the court of King Antiochos.'

'Well, you can just go home!' said Nikagoras. *'I'll* escort her over to my uncle's.'

Isokrates raised his eyebrows. 'You expect me to take your orders over those of my trierarch, do you, *bow-officer*?'

Nikagoras had enough sense to hesitate. It was true that his family had people like Isokrates as tenant farmers; it was also true that Isokrates was currently his superior officer. 'We're not on a ship!' he protested resentfully.

'So you stop being a naval officer when you set foot on dry land, do you? Fancy. I never knew that.'

Nikagoras glared. 'You think you're so wonderful – standing there in that moth-eaten cloak, without a house of your own to go home to! I don't know why my uncle picked you as helmsman. There were plenty of *gentlemen* available for the place.'

The gibe about the cloak stung, and Isokrates replied with some force. 'What Aristomachos told me was that he wanted his trierarchy to be a success, and apparently he wasn't sure that the available *gentlemen* could deliver that. A man who's been appointed because of his friends and relations doesn't need very much in the way of ability – *does he*?'

Nikagoras flushed angrily. 'You ... you *goatherd*!'

'That's "you goatherd *sir*" to you. But the farm's vineyards, mostly, not goats.'

Nikagoras went a darker red, started to mumble an apology, then remembered his pride and swallowed it. 'Why did my uncle ask *you* to escort Dionysia, anyway?' he at last demanded resentfully. 'It's *my* house she's staying in!'

'Why do you think?' Isokrates replied. He was already regretting his words. It was never good to quarrel with a shipmate, and it was particularly pointless to quarrel about a woman who was going to disappear within a few days. She

86

wouldn't be Nikagoras's any more than she would ever be his, so why should he lose his temper? – even if the bow-officer *was* a dolt.

Nikagoras bit his lip. 'Did my mother ask him to keep me away from her?'

'I wouldn't know about that.'

Dionysia came out of the house, looking as fresh as the spring in a long cloak of pale green bordered with woven flowers. She smiled warmly at Isokrates and wished him good health; she greeted Nikagoras second. The youth started to glower, then recollected himself and put on his most charming smile. The maid Dyseris trailed after her mistress, sour as ever.

'They said you'd come to escort me somewhere?' Dionysia asked.

'To my uncle's house,' Nikagoras replied, before Isokrates could speak. 'His friend Xenophantes, who's one of the Council presidents, wants to hear the news of Antiochos's court.'

'Ah.' Dionysia shot a look of nervous question at Isokrates. He nodded, wishing he could say something to reassure her, but unwilling to speak in front of Nikagoras.

'My uncle's house is only a couple of blocks away,' the young man continued. 'I was just about to go out; why don't I come along as well?' He shot a challenging look at Isokrates, who set his teeth and said nothing. He could not forbid it.

They set off together. Nikagoras pointed out landmarks along the way and promised Dionysia a proper tour of the city later. She answered distractedly: it was quite plain that she was nervous about the meeting, and would have preferred it if she could question Isokrates about what he'd told the trierarch.

When they arrived at the house, Aristomachos came into the hall to greet them. He stared at his nephew in momentary surprise – then smiled. 'Ah, Nikagoras, good!' he exclaimed. 'Go over to Ephialtes' house, will you? Last night I sent him a message asking him to take *Thalia* to Phaselis to collect those pirates of yours, and I need to know when he can sail.'

Nikagoras almost protested this demotion to errand-boy, but discipline held: he sighed, shot a wistful look at Dionysia and a dirty one at Isokrates, and departed. Aristomachos showed his guests into the dining room.

There were two couches there now, and a single chair. The couches were occupied by three of the five presidents of the Council of Rhodes, all looking stern. Isokrates was familiar with their faces from hearing them speak in the Assembly, but had never dealt with any of them in person.

'This is Dionysia, daughter of Kleisthenes of Miletos,' Aristomachos told his guests. He did not sit down, but remained standing, leaning against the door. 'And this, my helmsman, Isokrates, who was in command of my ship when it rescued her from pirates. Lady, these gentlemen are Xenophantes, Thrasykrates, and Hagemon, presidents of the Council of the Rhodians.'

'We were told you had information about King Antiochos,' said Xenophantes. He was the middle of the three, a plump, red-faced man a little older than Aristomachos.

Dionysia seated herself in the chair and carefully arranged her cloak; Isokrates was impressed by her composure. 'Sirs,' she began, in her soft, cultured voice. 'I am grateful to Rhodes for my rescue, and – believe me – very well-disposed to the Rhodians, but I must beg you to understand that I can't simply tell you my news for nothing.' Her hands sought and clutched one another, giving the lie to that composure. 'I had property in Miletos, but I think I must now reckon that as lost: all my possessions are in one chest of luggage. My hope is that when I give my news to King Ptolemy he will grant me some patronage, but I can't count on it. I am not a courtesan, sirs, and I don't wish to become one. My training is in music, and all my life my greatest hope has been to become a musician like my father – but, as I'm sure you are aware, among female musicians, all but the most distinguished are disreputable. If I am not to be seen as a common harlot I need to keep my property intact.'

Hagemon, at thirty the youngest of the three presidents, leaned forward slightly. 'Was your father Kleisthenes the famous kitharist?'

She smiled at this, and nodded eagerly.

Hagemon smiled back. 'I heard him play, once at the Pythian Games and once here in Rhodes. The Muses favoured him with a great gift.'

'Thank you, sir,' said Dionysia, smiling more warmly. 'He taught me music himself, sir, and I hope to follow in his footsteps. But I need ... I need to arrive in Alexandria looking like a woman of quality, and I would prefer to arrive there *soon.*'

'I am certain that we can arrange your passage to Alexandria,' said Hagemon. 'It seems to me a very modest request.'

Thrasykrates, the eldest of the presidents, snorted. 'In exchange for what? We're buying a pig in a poke: we don't know what this "information" is. We don't even know whether this woman actually ever met Antiochos, let alone that she was in a position to have *secret knowledge* of his plans!'

Dionysia reached under her cloak and drew out a scroll. 'Letters from the king,' she said evenly. 'Signed and sealed by him. Can you recognize the royal seal?'

Aristomachos took the scroll, and unrolled it enough to reveal that it was composed of letters stacked one on top of another. He cleared his throat and read out the top one:

King Antiochos the God to Kleisthenes son of Chaireas, greetings. At the welcoming ceremony today we were much pleased by your daughter's singing and wish to hear her again; accordingly we invite you to visit us this evening and to bring her, so that we may delight ourselves with listening to your superb playing and her beautiful voice. Farewell.

'I was sixteen,' Dionysia supplied quietly. 'The king came to visit Miletos, and I sang at the civic ceremony to welcome him. My father accompanied me on the kithara. It was all very proper: us, two children's choirs, and actors and a chorus performing a specially commissioned play. My father had hoped the king might notice him – not *me*.'

Aristomachos read out the second letter.

King Antiochos the God to Kleisthenes son of Chaireas, greetings. The beauty and charm of your daughter have captivated us entirely, and we make bold to claim her from you. We grant to you the property described below, to compensate you for her loss and to be her dowry if she should marry. Farewell.

'That came the next day,' said Dionysia, smiling a little. 'My father wasn't sure whether to be outraged or delighted. He found it very high-handed – but on the other hand, the man *was* a king, and the property was substantial.'

Aristomachos turned over to the next page. 'This is the description of an estate in the Maeander valley ... hm. It makes the whole over to Kleisthenes son of Chaireas of Miletos, and it has what I take to be the royal seal.'

'Let me see,' said Xenophantes. He took the document and inspected the seal, then passed it to his colleagues.

'It sounds a good-sized place,' commented Hagemon.

'Yes,' agreed Dionysia. 'A manor house and an estate with six families as tenants. My father wasn't poor, sir, but we hadn't been rich, either, until then. My father was still unhappy at the arrogance of the king – but you don't say no to a king.' She sighed, and added bleakly, 'When he died last year Father was still making plans for what we'd do when the king tired of me.'

'But he hasn't tired of you?' asked Hagemon, with a charming smile. 'That doesn't surprise me.'

Dionysia looked away and shook her head. Aristomachos read out the next letter.

Antiochos to his beloved Dionysia, greetings. I cannot sleep tonight; the Egyptian cat has been yowling at me all day. How I wish you were here to sing to me and make me forget all my grief! Come quickly to Seleukeia to meet me, darling Dionysia; we will stay in the summer palace and eat peaches. I am sending a carriage. Come quickly! Farewell.

She looked down, then up again, her face determined. Aristomachos handed her the letters back. 'I don't think we need to read any more. It's clear enough that you were a favourite of King Antiochos – and plain, too, that something must have happened, for you to abandon him and your property and flee to King Ptolemy.'

'Yes,' agreed Xenophantes. He glanced round his colleagues, got two nods, and went on. 'In exchange for your news we will arrange for you to travel to Alexandria in a fashion befitting a lady, on the first ship available. Is my word on this sufficient, or do you wish us to swear to it?'

Dionysia inclined her head. 'I am sure your word is sufficient, sir. As I said, my debt to Rhodes is such that I am ashamed to ask anything in exchange for my news; it is only my necessity that compels me.' She drew a deep breath, closing her eyes for a moment, then opened them wide and said, 'My news is this: King Antiochos intends to divorce his second wife and return to his first.'

There was a silence, bewildered at first – then stunned. This was a diplomatic catastrophe. Antiochos's second wife, Berenike the Dowry-bringer, was the daughter of Ptolemy, and her wedding had been the keystone of the peace settlement between Egypt and Syria. The dowry she had famously brought to her husband consisted of Asian cities which had been at issue in the war.

'That's *lunacy*!' sputtered old Thrasykrates at last. 'He'll start another war!'

'I agree,' Dionysia replied at once. 'I tried to tell him that. He said that the old Ptolemy's dead, and his son needs to secure his position in Egypt before he can think about fighting a war with Syria – and even if he does decide to fight, Syria beat the father last time, and can beat the son now.'

'Lunacy!' repeated Thrasykrates, in horror. 'Syria only won the last war because it had help from *us*!'

'And from Macedon,' put in Aristomachos sourly. 'I love Rhodes as much as any of you, but let's not exaggerate our importance.'

'It wasn't Macedon that won the Battle of

93

Ephesus!' Thrasykrates protested. 'It was *us*. I was there!'

'Very well!' Xenophantes said impatiently. 'The fact remains, Antiochos won the last war at the head of an alliance, and he can't possibly count on that alliance backing him again – not if he's going to plunge men and ships and cities into bloody war just because he's tired of his wife! This idiocy could cost him his kingdom! *Why* would he do such a thing?'

'First, because he never liked Berenike,' said Dionysia. 'She's the "yowling Egyptian cat", if you didn't catch the reference. She's a proud woman, and she was always telling him how much better things were at her father's court in Egypt. Secondly, because of Laodike.' She glanced round the uncomprehending faces. 'Have you forgotten who she is, or did you think that once he set her aside, she was nothing? Believe me, if you'd ever met her you wouldn't make that mistake!'

'We know who she is,' replied Xenophantes testily. Laodike was Antiochos's first wife. She was his cousin, the daughter of his uncle Achaios; she had been queen for fifteen years and borne Antiochos four children before she was set aside in favour of peace with Egypt. Her divorce settlement had left her with an income as great as that of all Rhodes.

'She is a terrifying woman,' Dionysia said in a low voice. 'Ever since she was set aside she's been looking for a way to get back into power, and when she heard that King Ptolemy was dead she sent her younger son to invite Antiochos to

94

come visit her in Ephesus. Antiochos didn't need to go. All his friends told him so! He could've sent an envoy to learn what she wanted, or he could have asked their son to explain it to him. But no: he went himself. He said it was "to show respect", but I think really he must have been toying with the notion of getting rid of Berenike even then. He left Queen Berenike in Antioch and took half the court to Ephesus – overland, because it was too early in the year to sail.

'We arrived in the city ... oh, it was only twelve days ago! Laodike invited Antiochos to dinner at her mansion; he stayed the night. When he came back to his own household next morning he was saying that he had wronged her, that he should never have given in to the demands of Egypt and sent away the bride his father had chosen for him, or disinherited his sons. He cursed Berenike, and began to talk about sending her home. All his friends said what you did: that it was lunacy, that he would certainly provoke another war, and, what was more, he'd be condemned as an oath-breaker and a fool. He eventually agreed, but then he said he must explain it to Laodike. He ended up staying the night again, and in the morning he had made up his mind to divorce Berenike and refused to hear any arguments.

'That same afternoon, Laodike summoned me to her house – to sing for her, she said. I was afraid to go, but I didn't dare disobey. When I came into her hall, I found her already dressed in a purple cloak and wearing the diadem of a queen. She looked me up and down and said, "So you are the little warbler who's been keeping my husband's bed warm! It wasn't my bed then, so I give you leave to go home. But understand this: the king is mine now. If I come across you fouling my sheets, I will cut out that tongue that sings so sweetly, and give you to a friend of mine who will see to it that you are never seen again."'

Dionysia drew in a deep breath. 'I have absolutely no doubt she would do it. I thought of going home and living quietly on my estate. Then I thought, "What if Antiochos sends for me?" Because he would, you see. He wants Laodike back, but he would see no reason to restrict himself to her. She is a scorching fire, and he would want warm balm as well, women who flatter him and try to please him – and I pleased him. Right now he's happy with their reunion, but at the first quarrel, or even if he just needed soothing, he'd summon me. But he wouldn't protect me from her.' She shook her head. 'When I was arguing with him, I said that if he really couldn't do without Laodike, he should offer to keep her as his mistress, or even as a second wife – after all, his grandfather Demetrios had several wives at once! He replied that she was a free woman of rank and he would not disgrace her – he said that to *me*! And he couldn't even understand why I should be offended by it! To Antiochos, Laodike is a free woman, and all his other loves are slaves. You asked how he could plunge the world into war just because he's tired of his wife: it's part of the same thing. The men who would die, the ships sunk and cities sacked – they would all be

96

slaves. He would be sorry at their loss, but he would not be *ashamed,* because they are *his* men and ships and cities, and he has the right to dispose of them as he pleases. If Laodike killed me, he would be angry with her, but no more than if she'd killed a favourite horse: it wouldn't last more than a day or two.'

'Once a city has a king, everyone else in it becomes a slave,' murmured Hagemon. The other two presidents shot him a look of irritation: the saying was trite.

'So I decided I had to leave the kingdom,' Dionysia concluded. 'Once I'd decided that, I began to hope I might do more than save my own life. Antiochos has made his mind up to divorce Berenike – but he hasn't made any public announcement about it yet. If I know him, it will be a long time before he does: he *is* aware that he'll be criticized for it, and he doesn't like that. He likes to have Laodike wooing him, too, and he knows she'll be a lot less sweet and charming once she has what she wants. Until there's been a public announcement, Antiochos can still change his mind without too much embarrassment – and if he gets this news quickly, King Ptolemy might write a letter which would make him back down. That's a worthy cause, isn't it? To persuade a king to wisdom, and avoid a war that would kill thousands? So I booked a ship for Alexandria. I took my maid, my clothes, my jewels and my kithara. Everything else I abandoned. But three days into the voyage my ship was seized by Cretan pirates – and so, sirs, here I am.'

Five

Dionysia left Rhodes next morning, travelling in a cabin on Aristomachos's ship, the *Thalia*. *Atalanta,* however, accompanied her.

The Council presidents had been so outraged by Antiochos's conduct that they did not, after all, want to pretend to be ignorant of it. They took the point, however, that it would be easier for Antiochos to back down before his intentions became public knowledge, so they were being discreet. That discretion, and a lack of time, meant that there could be no meeting of the Council and Assembly – and without such a meeting, there could be no official embassy, since the presidents did not have the power to send one.

Aristomachos had suggested a way round this: *Atalanta* had rescued Dionysia, and could justifiably escort her the rest of the way to Alexandria. When she'd finished telling her story to King Ptolemy, Aristomachos would step forward to assure the king that, as the trierarch of the ship which had rescued her, he strongly disapproved of Antiochos's behaviour. It wouldn't bind the island, but Ptolemy would certainly read between the lines and understand that if it came to war Rhodes would not be supporting his enemy.

Aristomachos was delighted with his position as semi-official envoy. It was no secret that he intended to seek election to the Council once he'd finished his season as trierarch: that was the reason he was so eager for his trierarchy to be an outstanding success. To represent Rhodes before a king, however, was an even more impressive accomplishment, and the two things combined could put him in line for a presidency in a year or two. He threw himself into the mission energetically.

Isokrates was not sure what Dionysia thought of all this. He hoped she was pleased – to arrive in Alexandria escorted by a Rhodian warship would add weight and dignity to her own mission – but he feared she would believe he'd misled her. He could not ask her: he had no opportunity to talk with her privately, and anyway, he was frantically busy preparing his ship to set out again. The crew were not happy about it: they'd expected an advance on the salvage money and time in port to spend it. Isokrates promised them the delights of Alexandria instead. He hoped that Aristomachos *would* come through with a bonus or advance of some sort. It was customary, and the men knew they deserved it: meanness here would damage morale and the trierarch's reputation.

There was the letter from his father, too, to distract him. He'd known there would be nothing good in it, and he had not been mistaken:

Kritagoras to his son Isokrates, greetings. Our neighbour Theophrastos has a daughter, sixteen years old, whom I have asked from him as a bride. Since the son I have is rebellious and disobedient, I will get myself another. Farewell.

Isokrates' first reaction was an outraged *poor girl*! On reflection, though, he decided that the marriage was unlikely to take place: Theophrastos could do better for his daughter than a fifty-year-old widower who'd buried two wives already. The letter had been written to goad. The conclusion didn't help: the goad hurt. Rage at his father kept him awake that night, composing explanations of exactly where the proud, stubborn old man had gone wrong – words he could never say to his father; words which his father would never endure.

What was worse, his midnight meditations on his father ended up in a miserable contemplation of Dionysia and his own poverty. He thought he understood her worry about money better now: what she possessed seemed so small compared to what she'd lost that she was terrified it would all soon be gone. She had very little experience of buying and selling: she had gone straight from her father's house to the king's. The thought of how much courage it must have taken her to march down to the harbour and book herself passage touched him and filled him with admiration. He wanted to help her – and he knew he could do no such thing. His father might contemplate marriage, but he could not. He was much better off than he'd been as an oarsman, but still, he owned neither house nor land. He couldn't approach any respectable woman, let alone one accustomed to wealth. His funds stretched only to the occasional visit to a brothel, and he always left feeling depressed, pitying the poor slaves who worked there.

Marriage! he thought in disgust. Was he really so far gone?

Dangerous question: he was. When he thought of Dionysia's sweet shy smile, or her composure before the presidents, or her desperate leap into the sea – it *hurt*, with a kind of deep ache of wanting. It felt, more than anything else, like the homesickness he'd suffered his first years in the navy. He could remember lying awake in the barracks that first winter, picturing every detail of the farm where he'd grown up, from the blackened stones of the hearth to the scent of the pines on the mountains, the silence broken only by the distant tinkle of goat-bells. He had ached then with the same wanting, and the same certainty that he could not have.

That had passed, in the end, he told himself. Memory still caught him now and then with the odd pang, but the dark hours were over. He'd get over this, too, in time.

He was relieved when the night finally began to pale. Life ashore might be grim, but at sea he had a beautiful mistress in *Atalanta*. He got up, and went to check the ship and the preparations for the voyage to Alexandria.

It was a clear spring morning when they left the harbour. *Atalanta* rendezvoused with *Thalia* just beyond the Colossus, and the crews waved to one another. *Thalia* was a much bigger ship:

four hundred tons unladen, with two tall masts and a vast mainsail. She had been named for the comic Muse, whose laughing image formed her figurehead. She towered above the long, low shape of the trihemiolia. Isokrates craned his neck looking for Dionysia on the roundship's deck, but didn't see her: either she was in her cabin or on the other side of the ship.

Nikagoras was looking, too. As Isokrates turned away, the bow-officer's gaze crossed his, full of resentment. Isokrates sighed: couldn't the young fool see how stupid it was, to be jealous of a girl who was already on her way to another country?

The sail-crew hurried about *Atalanta*; the great mainsheet was made fast, swelling with the northerly breeze as the trihemiolia turned her prow to the southeast.

Thalia, with her wide beam and strong hull, might have struck out directly for Egypt, but *Atalanta,* like all galleys, tried to put in to shore at night if she possibly could: sleeping under an awning on a beach was a great deal better than trying to sleep curled precariously on a rowing bench. Accordingly the two ships retraced the route taken by the trihemiolia, stopping the first night at Megiste and then going on to Phaselis. The second destination was a detour, but only a slight one, and its purpose was to collect the roundship's cargo: Aristomachos had decided to sell the captive pirates in Alexandria. 'It gives us a good excuse to escort *Thalia,*' he told Isokrates. 'Nobody's going to wonder about why

102

a warship has to accompany a merchant ship, when the merchant has a cargo of pirates. And we should get a good price for the buggers in Alexandria: kings always need slave labour.'

Phaselis, however, lay north of the Olympos headland, and there was no chance that *Thalia* could get there from Megiste in a day, since she would need to tack against the wind. *Atalanta* went on ahead, to pay off the Phaselitans and make the arrangements.

It was a long pull, and they didn't arrive until nightfall; Isokrates and Aristomachos went to see the shifty-eyed garrison commander the following morning. Isokrates had expected an extortionate charge for the prisoners' upkeep before the commander handed them over. He had not expected to find the prisoners gone.

'Yesterday,' said the garrison commander happily. 'Sold for two hundred drachmai a man.' He grinned.

Aristomachos cast a frowning look at Isokrates, as though he doubted his subordinate's account of the arrangements. Isokrates, stung, objected, 'You were supposed to keep them until we came to collect them!'

The commander just shrugged. 'Yes – but you *know* you couldn't have done better than that! How many people want to buy pirates? I kept the money for you ... less the guards' wages, of course, and the cost of the captives' food, like we agreed. It came to two hundred.'

It did not – but that was a lesser matter. 'It was *agreed* that you would keep them for *us*,' Isokrates said angrily.

'We-ell, but...' Another shrug.

Isokrates guessed that the commander had taken a cut on the deal. 'Who bought them?' he demanded.

'Slave-dealer from Cos. Lysandros, he said his name was.'

The name instantly aroused Isokrates' suspicions: *Lysandros* meant 'Man-looser'. A moment's thought brought another suspicion: Cos, like Rhodes, spoke the Dorian dialect, different from that of the mainly Ionian cities roundabout – but similar to Cretan. 'This Lysandros,' he said sharply. 'He wouldn't have been a tall man, black-haired, with a scar like *this*?' he traced a jagged line on his right arm and shoulder.

The commander blinked in surprise. 'Yes. That was him. You know him?'

Isokrates glared in furious despair. 'I gave you his description! When I told you about the pirate chief escaping, I gave you his description!'

'Yes, but you said his name was...'

'Obviously he didn't use his real name! You criminal fool, you've just given the pirate chief his crew back!'

The commander was unimpressed. 'He said he was from Cos! He had a ship and men – and you *sank* his, or so you claim! Anybody can have a scar!'

'What sort of ship? How many men?'

'Nice little *akatos*.' That was a fast merchant ship, equipped with oars. 'A dozen men, I suppose. He came up here nice as you please, said he'd heard I had some pirates and he had a buyer for them.'

104

Aristomachos intervened. 'Who do you report to?'

The commander stared. For the first time he looked worried.

'Come, it's a simple question! If you don't want to answer, your men will tell me.'

'I answer to Aischines of Corinth,' the commander admitted reluctantly 'The commander of the garrison at Pydnai.'

'I am going to write to him with a full account of your bugger-arsed stupidity!' said Aristomachos savagely. 'Give us our talent of silver, and don't waste any more of our time!'

On the way back to the ship, Aristomachos asked quietly, 'You're confident that it was this pirate Andronikos?'

'Yes,' Isokrates said tightly. It was true that anybody could have a scar, but to assume that somebody with just such a scar, a Dorian accent, and the name of Lysandros would turn up in Phaselis to offer an improbably good price for those particular pirates stretched credibility to the breaking point.

'Where did he get the money?' wondered Aristomachos.

Isokrates had been wondering the same thing. Andronikos had leapt into the sea with nothing but a knife: where did he find a talent of silver to ransom his men, only eight days later?

'He must have had a second ship,' Isokrates said shamefacedly. 'This akatos he turned up with. His men *told* me he would ransom them. I should've taken it seriously.'

They walked on several paces in silence; then

Aristomachos shook his head. 'Even if he had another ship, do you really think it would've been carrying a talent of silver?'

The answer to that was, no. If he'd had a talent of silver, Andronikos would've kept it on his own ship, where he could keep an eye on it – just as he'd kept Dionysia, that other item of exceptional value. He couldn't have fetched the money from Crete, either. While it was true that an akatos with a determined crew could've sailed in the weather that had kept *Atalanta* port bound – it was more stable than a warship – still, no ship could have gone to Crete, raised a large sum of money, and come back against contrary winds, all in only eight days. And it was vanishingly unlikely that the akatos had managed to collect a whole talent of silver by raiding. The raid had been on the country areas of Lycia, and country people rarely had much coin.

'The coins were all from the same mint,' the trierarch continued quietly. 'Did you notice that?'

They had been given the silver in four leather satchels, each holding fifteen pounds. Aristomachos had made the garrison commander unpack them so he could inspect the coins and make sure they weren't being short-changed. Isokrates had indeed noticed that the coins were remarkably uniform – silver staters and tetradrachms, minted on the Rhodian standard that was used throughout the Aegean, but stamped with the head of King Antiochos the God. He hadn't really marked that as unusual – he'd only ever seen large sums of money when a ship's crew was paid off at the end of a season – but, now that Aristomachos had drawn his attention to the fact, it was obvious.

'He's a mercenary,' Isokrates concluded, disturbed by it. 'Either he was one all along, or, more likely, he's just sold his services, and those of his crew, in exchange for the ransom money.'

Aristomachos nodded. 'Only way he could've raised it. And we may not know who gave it to him, but we do know what kingdom they live in. An akatos could've taken the filthy bugger to Ephesus and back in eight days. I wonder how much of your girlfriend's story he knows?'

'She's not...'

'Yes, yes, I know!' Aristomachos sighed. 'Well, I'll write to that bugger-arsed garrison commander's superior, much good it'll do. And we'll set off at once. We've wasted our time; we can still save *Thalia* wasting hers. I'll use the silver to buy a cargo in Alexandria.'

Isokrates hesitated, then decided that he had to speak. 'The men are expecting some money in Alexandria, sir. They're due some. They captured those pirates. Sir, it's *important* that you give them some kind of bonus. They'll think badly of you if you don't.'

Aristomachos gave a bark of laughter. 'I'm going to buy *grain,* man, not slave girls and frankincense! Half a talent will be plenty. The other half can go to the crew, and they can have the rest of their money back in Rhodes. No need for them to spend *all* of it on Egyptian flutegirls. Satisfied?'

* * *

They met *Thalia* in the Gulf of Phoinikos at about noon. Her crew had been preparing to tack round the Olympos headland to get to Phaselis, and were pleased to be spared the labour. The two ships set sail for the south. The breeze continued from the north, and there was no need to row. *Atalanta*'s men sat about on deck or lounged on the benches, talking and playing dice. Isokrates was aware of tension with his bow-officer, and sullenness from his second, who was particularly eager to get his hands on the money – but it was nothing he could complain about.

When it began to grow dark, they steered the trihemiolia closer to the roundship. If a galley had to spend the night at sea, it generally tried to do so in the company of a more stable and capacious vessel – one that could carry more than a couple of days' supply of food and water. Isokrates had made sure that *Thalia* was provisioned with that in mind. *Atalanta* had brought her ship's boat along this time, towed behind, and Aristomachos ordered it made ready. When he had climbed carefully down into it, he gestured for Isokrates to follow him.

They rowed over to the roundship and climbed cautiously up *Thalia*'s boarding ladder. Ephialtes, *Thalia*'s captain, was waiting attentively at the top to learn what his employer wanted.

'Get some bread and sausage and wine over to the men on *Atalanta*,' Aristomachos ordered. 'Isokrates and I are going to talk to the Milesian girl.'

Dionysia had been coming forward, and heard

this. She raised her eyebrows, but said only, 'If this is official business, trierarch, we can speak in my cabin.'

She had been promised a cabin befitting a lady, and the Council had certainly delivered one. The room was small, but beautifully decorated with panels of carved and painted wood, and the couch was upholstered with tapestry fishes. A brass lantern hung from the ceiling, its flame shielded by panels of shaved horn.

Aristomachos looked around approvingly. 'Simonides did a good job on this. Should have, of course, for what I paid him.'

Dionysia seated herself on the couch. 'Your ship is indeed very fine, sir. Even Dyseris is impressed, and she's not easily pleased. Am I right, though, to think that I owe this visit to the absence of the cargo we were to have collected in Phaselis?'

The trierarch grinned. 'Sharp lady. Yes. Isokrates, tell her what happened.'

Isokrates wished himself elsewhere. Shamefacedly, he explained that the man who'd abused her was not only alive and free, but had a ship and a crew again. Dionysia listened in increasing dismay, and when he finished she turned her head away and stared at one of the wall panels.

'What we need to know,' said Aristomachos, 'is how much you told that pirate.'

She began to speak, then had to clear her throat and try again. 'Very little.'

'What did he know, then?'

'That I was a favourite of the king ... and, I suppose, that my travel arrangements were

109

suspicious.'

'He ever say anything about having another ship?'

'No.' Her hands clutched one another and, still staring at the wall panel, she added bitterly, 'It's not as though he was interested in *conversation*.'

'I'm sorry,' said Isokrates helplessly.

At that she looked at him. She shook her head fractionally. 'You had to worry about catching *Artemis* – I don't think he did have another ship.'

'No?' asked Aristomachos, interested.

'If he did, I should have heard *something*, shouldn't I? From one of the other men, if not from Andronikos; *somebody* should have said *something* about meeting up with it, or wondered what it was doing and how the men on it had fared – wouldn't you think?'

The trierarch grunted, then shot an assessing look at Isokrates. 'Your second questioned the men, didn't he? And he didn't hear anything about a second ship, either. So, Lady, you think Andronikos got the akatos from the same place he got the money?'

She nodded. 'He was ... he was the sort of man who takes risks. They call it daring and boldness, I suppose, when it goes well, and reckless folly when it doesn't. I can just imagine him deciding to go to Ephesus to see if there wasn't something there he could turn to his advantage. Oh, Apollo! I can imagine him cutting some poor fisherman's throat and taking his boat north to Ephesus. If he asked about me ... if it got to Laodike, she would have given him a ship and money and asked him to hunt me down before I

110

could get to Ptolemy.'

'You think that's what happened?' asked Aristomachos, watching her intently.

'I don't know. It could have. Laodike knows Antiochos at least as well as I do; she knows that he can still change his mind. She won't want any letters from Ptolemy to arrive until she's had a chance to secure her position.'

The trierarch grimaced. 'Should've asked more about it while we were in Phaselis. If he'd been asking about you, people would remember. Well, too late now! Don't worry! If the bitch-faced queen did ask him to hunt you down, he's not going to manage it. You're under Rhodian protection, and he can't touch you.'

Dionysia gave him a tired smile. 'I thank you, sir.'

'We will hunt *him* down,' Isokrates offered impulsively.

Aristomachos looked at him sideways. 'We will, will we?'

Isokrates found he had an answer ready. 'Do you want to leave him free to sail up and down the coast of Asia, sir, assured of a bolthole in Ephesus whenever he needs one?'

Aristomachos snorted appreciatively: the Aegean coast of Asia was a rich market, and Rhodian ships were to be found in every port of call. 'Put like that, no. Very well: soon as we get back from Alexandria, we'll go after the bastard.' He nodded to Dionysia.

She looked anxious. 'I hope, sirs, that you don't end up cursing the day I crossed your path. It will be awkward, won't it, for you to arrive in

111

Alexandria escorting an empty ship? How will you explain it?'

Aristomachos waved that aside. 'Won't be the first time I've sent a ship empty to Alexandria: plenty of grainships arrive like that. As for *Atalanta* – well, I'm a corrupt trierarch, obviously! I'm using the city's warship to guard my own silver, which I'm taking to pay for the wheat I'm going to ship to ... eh, Ephesus! If your king and half his court turned up unexpectedly at the end of winter, they'll be wanting grain and able to pay a good price for it. I'll make a profit on this voyage yet.'

Thalia and *Atalanta* sailed on southward for another three days of calm seas and light breezes. Aristomachos was horrified by the discomforts of a trihemiolia on the open sea, and after the first evening, made a point of stopping on *Thalia* instead, where he could sleep in the captain's cabin. Isokrates was uneasy about this: while it was reasonable enough, it didn't do the trierarch much good with the men.

On the third night the second watch saw a faint point of light on the southern horizon and steered toward it. The morning revealed Alexandria, a red and white blur against the flat green of the Nile Delta. Smoke hung above the great lighthouse which had guided them during the night, a streak of white in the pale blue sky, and the mirrors at the tower's height shone in the first light like stars come to earth.

Isokrates had visited Alexandria before: pirates and pirate-hunters both followed the merchant

112

shipping, and the sea-lanes between Alexandria and Rhodes were the busiest in the world. The route was so well-established that the Alexandrians had jokingly named an islet in the middle of their Great Harbour 'Antirrhodos', as though it and Rhodes faced one another across a narrow strait. Antirrhodos, however, was not used by merchant ships: it held a summer palace and private moorings for the king. Other palaces and gardens covered the whole of the eastern side of the Great Harbour. To Isokrates it had always seemed scandalous, that nearly a third of the city should belong to one man.

He liked Alexandria, though. It was spacious, magnificent, and above all, *alive*. The streets were wide, well-laid-out, and continually full of people from all over the world. You could buy anything in Alexandria – Egyptian linen, Chian wine, African ivory; the perfumes of Arabia and the pearls of India. You could hear the finest musicians and see the most spectacular stage plays and goggle at the most beautiful courtesans. In Alexandria, too, there was always something new – a musical statue, a giraffe, or, most stupendously, a double-hulled galley two hundred and eighty cubits long, rowed by four thousand oarsmen. This last was endlessly ridiculed in Rhodes – the monstrosity had barely been able to get itself across the harbour! – but everyone who'd seen it was able to drink out on the story ever afterward.

The ships docked separately, *Thalia* at the merchant quays, *Atalanta* in an area reserved for visiting galleys. This was a compound provided not only with shipsheds and landing slips, but also with a barracks and a small garden with a fountain of fresh water: Ptolemy reckoned Rhodes as a friend, appreciated the island's efforts against piracy, and made its navy welcome. The Egyptians weren't careless, however: the compound was guarded by Ptolemaic soldiers, and the Rhodians were questioned about their errand before they were allowed to put in.

Aristomachos informed the guardship that he was on a diplomatic mission to the king, and asked to speak to a superior officer. *Atalanta* was allowed to put in, and the men were given leave to enter the city. Aristomachos gave them fifteen drachmai each – with a bonus of another ten drachmai for the petty officers – and promised them more when they returned to Rhodes. The crew weren't overwhelmed by his generosity, but they were satisfied, and headed off into the city eagerly discussing how they'd spend it.

Isokrates began the task of checking over the ship's gear. Aristomachos interrupted him.

'You're due some of that silver, too,' said the trierarch. 'The officers' share comes to two hundred each – that's a hundred now.'

A hundred drachmai was a very respectable sum of money, more than three months' wages for an oarsman. The thought of spending such an amount during the few days they were likely to be in Alexandria was obscene. 'I'll take ten now, sir,' Isokrates said respectfully. 'I'd prefer it if the rest was kept secure until we get home.'

Aristomachos grinned and held out a handful

of coin. 'Take it. Buy yourself some new clothes.' Isokrates frowned, and he laughed. 'Oh Zeus! No, I *know* it's your own hard-earned money and you can spend it any way you like. But you'll find that clothes are cheaper here than in Rhodes. Linens, particularly, but even woollens, if you know where to look.'

Isokrates remembered the moth-holes in his summer cloak and took the money.

'As for the other hundred,' Aristomachos continued, 'if you like, I'll invest it for you. Give you a share in *Thalia*'s cargo, how about that? I expect to make between ten and fifty per cent profit selling in Ephesus. If you like, I'll invest your share of the salvage money, too.'

Isokrates didn't know how to respond. Part of him was suspicious; another part recognized that this was an opportunity not to be missed. Aristomachos was known to be a shrewd businessman, and the offer was one many merchants would envy. 'Thank you, sir,' he said at last.

Aristomachos grinned again. 'Wondering what I'm up to, are you? I'll tell you. You've quarrelled with your father and he's cut you off without a copper – don't look so offended, man! It's common knowledge. Now, most of the time, if I have to rely on a poor man, I make sure I give him money, so he won't be tempted to get some from somebody else. I won't do that with you; you'd just take it as an insult. I don't see, though, why you should suffer for being honest. So, my friend, I intend to help you use your *own* money to get rich!'

Again Isokrates was at a loss. 'Thank you,' he

managed at last. Aristomachos slapped him on the shoulder and marched off to harass the guards about when he could see someone in authority.

The trierarch's request for an interview with someone of a higher rank was eventually granted; his further request for an audience with the king was sufficiently urgent and mysterious that an appointment was made for the following afternoon. He promptly sent to *Thalia* to arrange for Dionysia to join him in good time for it. Isokrates found that he had somehow expected that he would attend the audience as well, and cursed his own stupidity. He was not a wealthy merchant, an envoy of the Council of Rhodes, nor was he a friend of kings: why in the world would he attend a royal audience? He went out drinking that evening, with Damophon the bo'sun and Polydoros the spearman, and finished in a brothel, dead drunk and depressed.

He went out into the city next day as well, shopping for a new summer cloak and eventually buying one of good quality linen, yellow with a border patterned in black. He returned to the ship wearing it, then sat about in the garden of the compound for several hours anxiously waiting for Aristomachos to come back. No one else was about: most of the men were off sampling the delights of the city, and the rest were recovering from them.

The trierarch didn't appear until dusk. When he did show up, Dionysia and her maid were with him. The Milesian girl was elegantly

116

dressed in a cloak patterned in rose and green, but she had a fold drawn well over her head, and when Isokrates hurried up he saw that she'd been crying. He looked at Aristomachos in alarm.

'The king already knew,' said the trierarch. 'Zeus! I could do with a drink.'

Isokrates had bought some rough wine as part of the basic supplies for the men; he opened the amphora and fetched some in a jug. Aristomachos drank several swallows of it neat, then topped the jug up with water from the fountain. He offered it to Dionysia; when she shook her head, he took several swallows more.

'I suppose it wasn't really a disaster,' he conceded, wiping his mouth. 'He wasn't upset with *Rhodes*. But, well, it seems that his sister had written to him complaining about the Milesian lady, and she didn't get the reception she hoped for.'

'I was a fool!' said Dionysia thickly, twisting the edge of her cloak between her hands. The composure she'd struggled to keep so long, through so much, had finally shattered: she sounded young and scared and utterly miserable. 'I just thought he might be *grateful*, to get the news quickly from somebody who was *there*; I thought it would make a *difference* that I disagreed with Antiochos and argued with him about it! I hoped...' She stopped, choking, and pressed the fabric against her face.

'He already knew?' asked Isokrates.

'Mmm. I don't think for long, though.' Aristomachos took another swallow of wine. 'Couple of days at most: he was still in a temper over it. Well, he has spies, no doubt, and between the pirates and the detour to Rhodes, the lady took longer getting to Alexandria than she'd hoped.'

'I should've expected it!' choked Dionysia.

Aristomachos grunted. 'Anyway, there was Ptolemy the Benefactor, in a temper about the insult to his sister, and who should turn up but a woman his sister's complained about? Not really surprising, I suppose, that he bore down to ram – but it wasn't a pretty sight. He called her a whore and said she might've been kicked out of Syria's bed, but she wasn't going to crawl into Egypt's. She tried to defend herself, and he jeered at her until she broke down in tears. This was all before I had a chance to say a word, mind you, and after he'd kept us waiting for two hours. So I stepped forward, and said my piece about how my ship saved the girl from pirates and she told us this news, and how I was dismayed, and that we'd brought her here as quick as we could in the hope that the king could sort matters out with his brother-in-law. I said we were keeping quiet about it, in the hope that Antiochos could be brought to his senses.

'At that the king swallowed his temper a bit, and said he appreciated Rhodes' *loyalty* – ha! – in coming to inform him, and that he valued our friendship. He said he would give me a letter to take home, and that he'd be writing another one to Antiochos. And that was that: his men showed us out.' Aristomachos took another swig of wine and swilled it round his mouth before swallowing.

'I was so *stupid*!' cried Dionysia, and pinched her nose, fighting to stop the tears. 'All I could think of was that I'd be *safe* in Egypt. I'd argued Berenike's cause, I'd tried to *help*! I wanted to stop a war! I should've *known* that nobody would care!'

Aristomachos made a noncommittal noise and offered her the wine again. Dionysia hesitated – then took the jug and choked some down.

'I'm sorry,' said Isokrates unhappily.

'It's my own stupid fault!' replied Dionysia, wiping her eyes. 'Oh, Apollo! I was hoping for *patronage*: how stupid is that? I was lucky they didn't clap me in irons and ship me off to Antioch for Berenike to punish as she saw fit! I think they *would* have done that, if I'd come here on my own. I was so *stupid*!'

'Well, we didn't think of it, either,' remarked Aristomachos. 'Cheer up, girl! Alexandria's not the only city in the world.'

She glared at him through her tears. 'Next you'll be telling me that I'll have no trouble setting up as a courtesan in Rhodes!'

The trierarch shrugged. 'Well, you wouldn't. If you're set against it, though, there's no reason you couldn't try your luck as a musician.' He waved a dismissive hand. 'Oh, I know, Alexandria's the Garden of the Muses and the House of Aphrodite: everybody from philosophers to fluteboys comes here in the hope of getting rich. Doesn't mean you can't get rich elsewhere. I did, for one.' He retrieved the wine, sloshed it meditatively, and had another swallow.

'It's true,' Isokrates said tentatively. 'Everyone

119

likes music. The Council spends thousands on festivals in Rhodes-town, and that's not counting all the concerts in the other cities of Rhodes. And our republic trades with everybody on the Middle Sea, so if you make a name in Rhodes, you've made it everywhere.'

She pressed her hands against her eyes. 'It's *harder* for a woman – unless you want to sell yourself, and I *don't*! How am I going to get started, without patronage and without any family to help me? My father's dead; my property is lost; Antiochos undoubtedly thinks I've betrayed him. All I have is one chest full of clothes and a few jewels – and if I sell them, Ihave *nothing*. I don't, I don't...' She stopped, and tried again, 'I don't *want* to be a whore! I *know* that everyone thinks I'm one already, but I'm *not*! I'm a *musician*!'

Aristomachos belched. 'You want my advice? Come back to Rhodes. You don't need a king to give you patronage: you've got three Council presidents! They were all impressed with you, you know, and Hagemon knows all the people in charge of festivals and the like. Oh, he'll try and see if you'll sleep with him, but if you're really good at music he won't insist on it. He's a lover of the Muses, he is. You go to him and ask about renting our concert hall, and I promise you, if you're good he'll pull some strings, book it for you himself, cheap, and tell all his friends to go listen. Then you give a big free concert during some festival when there are a lot of visitors in town – maybe with a couple of other acts, for a bit of variety, good amateurs who'll do it for

nothing if they don't have to pay for the hall –
and, well, you'll have got started, won't you?'

Dionysia stared at him, stupefied.

Her maid Dyseris spoke hastily. 'Sir? Are you
offering my mistress passage back to Rhodes?'

Aristomachos spread his hands expansively.
'Why not? Nobody else has booked that cabin.'

'Oh!' whispered Dionysia, smiling through
tears. 'Thank you!'

Six

There was a drawback for Dionysia in the offer of passage to Rhodes on *Thalia: Thalia* was, in fact, bound first for Ephesus – the last place she wanted to go. Aristomachos, however, was astonished at the very suggestion that the round-ship might divert: his profit would be reduced if somebody else's grain got to the overcrowded city first. Dionysia, he said, could either stay quietly in her cabin while the ship was in Ephesus – in which case there was no reason for anyone in the city to know that she was there – or she could pay to go straight to Rhodes on someone else's ship. She chose to stay on *Thalia.*

Aristomachos was summoned to another audience with King Ptolemy next morning, and returned to *Atalanta* carrying a letter from the king to the Rhodian presidents.

'He was very, very gracious this time,' he said, with satisfaction. 'Full of assurances about how dearly he cherishes the friendship of the Rhodians. Felt embarrassed, I think, about the way he laid into the Milesian girl in front of me. If the letter's as civil as he was in person, she will've done me a favour: the presidents will think I must be the best diplomat since Odysseus. Start rounding up the crew, will you? We leave tomorrow, weather and the gods permitting.'

Thalia's captain Ephialtes had spent the previous two days inquiring about grain supplies; now Aristomachos approved his choice, paid for it, and arranged for the ship's lading. The following morning *Thalia* and *Atalanta* set out northward.

The breeze was still northerly, as it would be for most of the summer: the direct route to Rhodes or Ephesus was impossible for any ship that relied on the wind. *Atalanta* accompanied *Thalia* northeast to Cyprus, then left the round-ship to sail northwest again, and rowed along the coast of Pamphylia, pausing at night to sleep and buy provisions. Aristomachos didn't like camping on a beach much better than he'd liked sleeping on a warship at sea. 'Zeus!' he complained, stretching the stiffness out one morning. 'To think I did this when I was sixteen and thought it was *fun*!'

They made a point of stopping in Phaselis to make inquiries about the ship which had collected the captive pirates. The harbour authorities there had a record of her: the *Nea*, out of Cos, shipmaster Lysandros. One of the dockworkers remembered her: 'Nice ship. Slimmer than most akatoi, with a prow sharp as a warship's. New paint ... oh, blue! to match the sea. One mast and ten oars; about thirty tonnes laden, I suppose. I was surprised when her master marched all those slaves aboard, though: would not have thought she was the right craft to carry troublemakers, and he had to pack them in so tight his crew scarcely had space to swing the oars.'

One of the harbourmaster's clerks confirmed, too, that 'Lysandros' had been asking about a woman whom the Rhodians had rescued from pirates. 'He said he was a friend of her uncle's. Oh, so you know about her? I suppose it was your lot rescued her! I didn't know anything, but a friend of mine told him she'd been on the *Artemis*.'

They arrived back in Rhodes fifteen days after they left it, and seven after their departure from Alexandria. It was May now, and the sailing season proper had begun. The harbour was crowded with merchant ships, and the naval shipsheds were almost empty: the trihemioliai and quadriremes of the Rhodian navy were out protecting Rhodian trade.

Atalanta had three days in port. Most of the crew considered the time much too short: several of them approached Isokrates to point out that they'd been rowing up and down the Middle Sea while most of the navy was sitting in port waiting for summer, and that they ought to be given a chance to spend their money – Aristomachos had given them the rest of what they were owed for the pirates. The second officer Simmias, however, complained that he was still waiting for his share of the salvage money from the *Artemis*.

'We all are,' Isokrates told him shortly. 'It hasn't been *paid* yet, Simmias.'

'The trierarch could give it to us on credit,' Simmias objected. 'Aristomachos has plenty of money.' He regarded Isokrates a moment with narrowed eyes and added, 'Has he given credit to *you*?'

'No,' replied Isokrates – then wondered if it were true. Aristomachos had said he would invest his first officer's share of the salvage money in *Thalia*'s cargo: was that the same as giving credit?

Simmias seemed to sense the doubt. 'We all worked hard to take that ship!'

'Simmias, if the syndicate dissolves or goes bankrupt, *nobody* will get that money. We're headed for Ephesus next: we can ask about the salvage money while we're there.'

Simmias accepted this, but he was puzzled, too. 'Why Ephesus?' The city was by no means a pirates' lair.

Isokrates told as much of the truth as he could without mentioning King Antiochos. 'You know we think that the garrison commander in Phaselis sold our pirates back to their chief? We want to talk to *Artemis*'s captain, to see if he can give us any information which would help us track them down.'

Two evenings later, when they arrived at Ephesus, Aristomachos gave much the same answer to the captain of a guardship who stopped them at the entrance to the harbour and asked their business.

'You want to talk to *Philotimos*?' said the captain of the guardship, with a hard look. 'He's dead.'

Isokrates remembered Philotimos's bone-jolting slap on the shoulder and piping enthusiasm, and was staggered. *'Dead?'* he exclaimed, improperly breaking into the conversation.

'Found drowned in the harbour ten days ago,' replied the captain of the guardship. 'He won't be answering your questions.'

There was a silence. Then Aristomachos sighed and said, 'May we come into port anyway? It's too late to find somewhere else to stop the night.'

The captain of the guardship grudgingly allowed this. It seemed, though, that with the king in residence Rhodian longships were less welcome here than usual: *Atalanta* was directed to a muddy beach on the north side of the harbour, outside the city wall and well away from the docks.

The harbour authorities knew, however, that longships needed to buy supplies, and when Aristomachos and Isokrates trudged across the mud that evening, with a couple of the oarcrew along to carry things, they were admitted to the city. *Thalia* was sitting tied up at the main docks.

Aristomachos went aboard at once. 'Don't expect me back this evening,' he declared. 'I swear by Poseidon and by Zeus the Guest, I've had enough of roughing it! I'm going to eat in the finest tavern in Ephesus tonight, and sleep in the master's cabin on my own sweet ship. I'll see you tomorrow.'

'Sir,' said Isokrates unhappily, 'do you really think it's wise to separate yourself from the ship?'

Aristomachos snorted. 'Why? What do you think is going to happen?'

Isokrates couldn't say – but he did know that he felt acutely uneasy. King Antiochos was somewhere in this huge city, and Aristomachos had just returned from a mission to the king's rival; Queen Laodike was here, too, and Aristomachos had on board *Thalia* a woman the queen wanted to get rid of. *Atalanta* was beached outside the city walls, and a man they'd hoped to speak to had been found floating in the harbour. It didn't seem to Isokrates a good time for the trierarch to cut himself off from all communication with his ship.

'I'll be fine!' Aristomachos said breezily, slapping his helmsman on the shoulder. 'You go do the shopping.' He scrambled eagerly up *Thalia*'s ladder.

Isokrates couldn't help wondering if what the trierarch really wanted was to try his luck in the passenger cabin. He tried to shove the unpleasant possibility from his mind, but it kept coming back. Aristomachos was a widower: there was nothing to stop him chasing freeborn women. He'd done a lot to help Dionysia, and she'd been grateful. He liked her, and he was not only wealthy, but clever and clear-sighted as well. If she disregarded that, she was a fool.

The image of them laughing together in that small panelled cabin gave him a hot, sick sensation in his stomach, and he felt a spasm of hatred for his trierarch. He tried to banish it. Aristomachos had done nothing to deserve hatred: in fact, Isokrates was beginning to like him. The only things he could really fault the man on were that he was overly careful with his money and reluctant to suffer discomfort. It wasn't his fault that Isokrates was poor.

He took the men on to the marketplace, bought wine and cheese for *Atalanta*, then trudged the weary way back to the ship, his imagination now showing him Aristomachos and Dionysia entwined in happy nakedness on that couch upholstered with tapestry fish.

He spent a restless night in the commander's spot under the sternpost, falling asleep towards dawn. He was woken by voices even before one of the oarsmen shook his shoulder and whispered, 'Sir! Sir!' in a tone of some urgency.

Isokrates staggered up and descended the boarding ladder, bleary-eyed and dishevelled, wrapped in his old sea cloak. The ship had visitors: an official and a file of spearmen. The official was a plump, pale young man in a long cloak gorgeously patterned in crimson and purple; he held a herald's staff of ivory entwined with gold serpents, and his pudgy hands were adorned with numerous rings. The sixteen spearmen accompanying him wore bronze breastplates and greaves, and helmets with purple-dyed crests; their shields were painted purple and decorated with gold stars, and the hafts of their long spears were banded with gold. *Atalanta*'s barefoot, half-naked crew stared at them with a mixture of awe and contempt, while her spearmen were torn between embarrassment and envy.

'Are you trierarch of this vessel?' the herald demanded, in a plummy Ionian tone.

'I am the helmsman, Isokrates of Kameiros.

Our trierarch's gone into the city.'

The herald was put out. 'Well, I am not going to chase about after him! You'll have to do instead.'

'Do what?'

The official drew himself up to his full height. 'I am Hyperides, son of Lysimachos, a royal kinsman! *Queen Laodike* sends me to the Rhodian ship, to invite the trierarch to her house! She is curious to know the errand which brings you here.'

Isokrates stared in confusion and misgiving. 'Oh!' he exclaimed stupidly. After a moment, he managed, 'We're honoured by the queen's invitation, of course, but it's – that is, she doesn't need to go to the trouble. We stated our errand to the guardship yesterday when we arrived. We were hoping for information about pirates from a man named Philotimos, who had a brush with some, but we've been told that he's dead. We were planning to leave again this morning.'

Hyperides sneered. 'You'll have to postpone your departure then, Rhodian. My instructions are to bring one of you to the queen, and since your trierarch isn't here, it'll have to be you.'

'I could go!' offered Nikagoras eagerly. Isokrates looked at him in astonishment, then realized that the youth had no idea that there was anything alarming about the invitation: he just wanted to meet a queen.

'I think not,' replied the herald. His tone and expression added, 'Who do you think you are, puppy?' with the superiority conferred by perhaps a whole year in age. 'You, helmsman – if you have anything better to wear than that cloak, put it on.'

'Certainly,' said Isokrates, feeling a bit sick. He didn't know why Queen Laodike wanted to speak to Aristomachos, but it seemed horribly possible that she knew about the meeting with King Ptolemy, and he was glad, now, that the trierarch wasn't on the ship. Was the title 'queen' an indication that her position was now public and official? He hadn't heard of any announcement. If she'd been wearing the diadem since the day after her reconciliation with the king, though, then Ephesus at least must regard her title as an established fact, whether it was official or not. Probably it was already too late for Antiochos to set her aside again without embarrassment.

His instincts were screaming at him to get the ship away *at once*, while he still could. It was entirely possible that war was about to break out – and the Syrians might already regard Rhodes as an ally of Egypt. To run away before they'd been threatened, though ... at best it would look ridiculous; at worst, it would cause a diplomatic incident. Laodike's title was still revokable. This invitation might well be motivated by a desire for information she could use to secure herself. Besides, Aristomachos was in the city ... probably on *Thalia*. If the authorities searched *that,* they'd find Dionysia, which might mean worse trouble. No, he would have to go meet the queen.

He'd brought his new cloak, carefully folded and stowed in his sack. He went back on to the ship to put it on, and was relieved when Nikagoras followed him, looking sullen. 'Get Simmias and Polydoros,' he told the young man, and delayed over the cloak until his subordinates returned.

'This may be trouble,' he told the three bluntly, in a whisper. 'Get the ship ready to go, and send to Aristomachos at once. Tell him not to wait for me beyond noon. And if you can't find him, or if the messenger you send doesn't come back – leave. You'll be more help to him coming back with a protest from Rhodes than sitting here.'

Nikagoras and Simmias just looked bewildered, but Polydoros swore. 'This is because of something he told the king in Alexandria?' he asked in a grating whisper.

Isokrates was grateful that at least one of his subordinates was intelligent. 'Possibly. I hope not, but it's better to be prepared.' He fastened his sandals, tossed the end of his new cloak over his shoulder, and descended the boarding ladder. He forced himself to walk away from the ship confidently, as though he had no doubt he'd be coming back.

His escorts set out toward the city, but turned aside before reaching the North Gate, taking a road which led inland to the left. Isokrates was surprised. 'Aren't we going to the queen's house?'

'Yes,' replied the herald Hyperides. He looked down his nose at such ignorance and added, 'She doesn't live in the city. There wasn't space there for a house fit for a great queen. Her mansion is about ten stadia away, over that hill.'

They walked on, silently apart from the muffl-
ed *clunks* of the soldiers' armour and the beat of
their footsteps. The road climbed the side of a
hill, Ephesus at their backs, the Cayster valley
hazed with blue before them. The sun shone on
a landscape of rich fields, green with spring and
studded with wildflowers; cows grazed the deep
pastures. Isokrates wondered if he'd panicked. If
the queen was merely idle and curious, his
desperate instructions were going to look very
stupid.

They crested the hill, and there below them lay
what could only be Laodike's mansion – a splendid confection of marble porticoes, cypress trees
and pools, with a cluster of stables and outbuild-
ings trailing behind it. Isokrates' escort marched
up to the columned front of the building. There
they were met by more soldiers and a doorkeeper. After a brief discussion, the soldiers of
the escort marched off along the side of the
house. Isokrates wondered whether they were
permanently attached to the queen, or if they
actually served the king. Then he wondered if
the king was staying in his wife's house. It was
possible – though also possible that Antiochos
was staying in the Ephesian citadel.

The doorkeeper raked Isokrates with suspicious eyes. 'Is he armed?' he asked Isokrates'
guide.

'They weren't *any* of them properly armed,
from what I saw!' replied Hyperides contemptuously.

'Did you check?' asked the doorkeeper.

'I'm unarmed!' Isokrates said sharply. He

shook out his cloak and spread his arms, letting the doorkeeper see for himself. 'Sir, I'm not fool enough to carry weapons to a meeting with royalty!'

The doorkeeper sniffed, but allowed Isokrates and his guide into the house.

They went through an entranceway paved with polished marble, into a courtyard where a fountain played, along a colonnade and into another courtyard. This one held a rectangular pool of dark water, flanked by rosemary and lavender bushes in stone urns. There was a vine trellis, now in full leaf, with a marble bench beneath it. A woman in a purple cloak was lounging on the bench, her arms wrapped about one bent knee. The royal diadem – a narrow ribbon of rich sea-purple – was woven into the intricate knot of her auburn hair. A couple of other women flanked her, one spinning, the other playing a lyre.

The queen looked up, then snapped her fingers. The lyre-player stopped midnote. Isokrates' guide continued forward a few steps, then prostrated himself face down on the paving stones. 'Good health, o Queen!' he exclaimed, sitting up again. 'I went to the Rhodians, as you asked, but the trierarch wasn't there. This is the helmsman.' He didn't give Isokrates' name. Probably he hadn't bothered to take note of it.

Laodike looked at Isokrates. She was younger than he'd expected, and prettier, with a pale oval face and green eyes. He wondered if she expected him to make the prostration, and hoped not. It seemed demeaning – and anyway, he didn't know how.

'Helmsman,' repeated the queen, raising her eyebrows. 'Where's your trierarch?'

'He went into the city this morning, Lady. I would be pleased to assist you in his place.'

'Would you?' Laodike stretched and lowered her raised foot to the ground; Isokrates noted, incredulously, that her sandals were worked with gold and studded with amethysts. 'What business does your ship have in Ephesus, then, helmsman? – and, by the way, I am a *queen*, not a mere *lady*.'

'Excuse me, o Queen,' Isokrates said carefully. 'I don't know the usages; I've never met a queen before. If I offend, it's through ignorance, not by intent. We came here hoping for information about some pirates from a man who was captured by them about a month ago. We were told, though, that he's dead. We were intending to leave again.'

'Pirates! How fascinating! Why do you want information about pirates?'

'La– that is, Queen, our trihemiolia's chief task is to hunt pirates. These particular pirates are ones we had an encounter with last month. We sank their ship and took the survivors prisoner. But we had to leave them with the garrison in Phaselis, and when we came back to collect them, we found that the garrison commander had sold them to someone who sounded very like the pirate chief. We were hoping we could catch them again before they do more harm.'

Laodike gave a small, self-satisfied smile and snapped her fingers; the lyre-player hurried up, listened to some whispered command, and ran out. 'Perhaps I can help you. But tell me more about this desperate sea-battle where you sank a pirate ship!'

Isokrates was puzzled. 'It wasn't a sea-battle, o Queen. All they had was a hemiolia!'

'And that's not a worthy opponent? Well, it hardly seems very brave of you, then, to sink them!'

'Sinking pirates isn't *brave*, it's ... it's like killing wolves when they prey on your flocks, or rats when they eat your grain. It's something you have to do, or lose your livelihood.'

Laodike smiled at someone who'd just entered the courtyard on Isokrates' left. 'Did you hear that, Andronikos? He thinks you're vermin.'

Isokrates whirled, and found the pirate chief staring at him. He recognized the man instantly, despite only having seen him once before, and despite the fact that the thick black beard was now neatly trimmed and the muscular nakedness covered in a scarlet tunic that partially concealed the distinctive scar.

Andronikos clearly recognized Isokrates, as well; his face was full of astonishment and rage.'What's this Rhodian queer doing here?' he demanded.

Laodike sniggered and held up an admonishing finger. Andronikos grimaced, bowed his head – then knelt and made the prostration. 'Excuse me, o Queen!' he exclaimed. 'I was taken by surprise. This is the man who sank my ship!'

'Oh, no!' exclaimed the queen girlishly. 'What, all by himself? In that case, your ship wasn't even sunk by a trierarch, because this fellow is just the helmsman. His ship's come all the way to Ephesus to ask about *you*: isn't that sweet?'

Isokrates had been clenching his teeth to hold back the angry exclamations; now he turned to the queen and said fiercely, 'This man is a pirate, o Queen! He raided in Lycia, murdering and robbing and carrying off freeborn persons to sell as slaves! You should not employ him!'

'Oh, be quiet!' snapped Laodike. 'He *was* a pirate; now he's a mercenary in my service. Rhodian, if it weren't for your ignorance of court manners, I would have you beaten for presuming to tell *me* what I should or shouldn't do. There was a girl you took off the pirate ship, a Milesian slut by the name of Dionysia. What became of her?'

So *that* was what it was about! The queen didn't know about the trip to Alexandria: she was still trying to hunt down Dionysia. Isokrates stood still a moment, trying to think. The pirate was back on his feet again, watching with the intensity of a dog watching a man eat. Isokrates knew now what had killed Philotimos. Andronikos had been told that Dionysia was on the *Artemis*, and so *Artemis*'s captain had been taken for questioning – but his answers hadn't been satisfactory, and his body had ended up in the harbour.

'She took ship to Alexandria,' Isokrates said at last.

'Ah.' Laodike leaned forward, elbows on knees. 'Well, this is progress! You helped her, did you? You took her to Rhodes! I'll have you know, Rhodian, that the woman is a thief; she

136

stole jewels from me and ran off!'

Isokrates gave her a look of disbelief. 'I know nothing about that.'

'I say she was a dirty *thief*, Rhodian – and you helped her!'

'You expect me to sympathize, when you employ a *pirate*?'

This created a stir: the woman who'd been stolidly spinning all this while stopped her spindle and stared; Hyperides exclaimed in indignation; Andronikos grinned. Laodike narrowed her eyes. 'Rhodian, if you are wise, you will be more respectful! Ignorance doesn't excuse all. I say you have helped a woman who stole from the house of Seleukos the Conqueror!'

'And I told you, I know nothing about that! You can't expect me to delve into the history of every woman who turns up in the hands of pirates! Zeus, there were twenty of them on the *Artemis* alone! I remember the girl you're talking about: that ought to be enough. She said she'd been a friend of King Antiochos, and she had letters from him to prove it; she said she was trying to go to Alexandria, where her brother lives. She was unlikely to find another ship in Phaselis any time soon, so I offered her passage to Rhodes. When we got there, we helped her book a cabin on the next ship bound for Alexandria.' He met the queen's eyes. 'If the king is angry because we helped someone who claimed to be his friend – well, does he want us to promise we won't?'

There was a silence. Then the queen asked,

'And you had no suspicions about the girl?'

'It wasn't my business, to ask about a king's love-life, or why he'd sent her away.'

Laodike sniffed, but Isokrates could sense her satisfaction. 'So she's in Alexandria?'

Isokrates nodded. 'The winds have been favourable. She must have arrived in the city last month.'

The queen made a face. 'Treacherous little whore! Well, at least she's not coming back!'

There was another silence. Isokrates was aware of Andronikos standing, thumbs hooked in his belt, hoping that this scrap would fall from the queen's table. He took note of the fact that the pirate, too, was unarmed. He might be in the queen's service, but she evidently didn't trust him with a weapon in her presence. Whatever happened next, it wouldn't happen *here*.

Andronikos, of course, had access to weapons nearby – weapons, and men to help him. All of Isokrates' hopes were back on *Atalanta*. He fought the desire to beg the queen for his life. The fear that tightened his gullet might be unnecessary – and if it was justified, begging was unlikely to gain him anything except the knowledge that he had shamed Rhodes.

'Was that all, o Queen?' he asked at last.

Laodike frowned and pulled her amethyst-studded sandals back up on to the bench. 'You displease me, Rhodian.'

'I am sorry to displease you. Rhodes has always tried to be a friend to the house of Seleukos.'

Her lip curled. 'And that in itself is *presump-*

138

tion! One little island, reckoning that somehow it's entitled to be *friends* with a kingdom that rules the whole East from Persia to the Gates of Arabia! My husband is a *god,* Rhodian!'

'So was Demetrios the Besieger, in his day. We sold his siege engines for three hundred talents, as you may have heard.'

Hyperides gave another indignant exclamation and took a step forward, raising his ivory herald's staff like a club. He looked to Laodike for permission, though, and she ignored him. Instead she stared at Isokrates a moment longer with those narrowed eyes – then gave a small, malicious smile.

'There's no need for my men to escort you back to your ship, is there?' she asked sweetly. 'I'm sure you can find your own way.'

Isokrates did not turn his head to see the pirate's reaction: he could guess it. He bowed to the queen and started back toward the entrance of the house.

'I haven't given you leave to go!' exclaimed the queen. He stopped and turned back to her, his heart beating hard with anger and desperation. From the corner of his eye he saw Andronikos make a hasty prostration and leave.

Laodike settled herself more comfortably on the bench, smirking. 'Tell me – what did you think of the little whore Dionysia?'

'I admired her courage and her dignity,' Isokrates replied honestly, 'and I pitied her. She was torn from her family by a king's whim – treated as though she were a slave and not a free woman – and when another whim struck the royal mind, out she went. I was glad we have no kings on Rhodes.'

The smirk was transformed into a look of outrage.

He pushed harder. 'The more I see of monarchy, the more I love our democracy.'

Laodike exclaimed wordlessly, pulled one of her sandals off, and threw it at his head; he managed to get his hand up in time to deflect it. The queen glanced along the colonnade, as though she was thinking of summoning her guards – then apparently thought better of it. 'Get out!' she ordered furiously.

He bowed quickly and got out. Now, if he could get away fast enough...

Isokrates' guide Hyperides caught up with him before he reached the next courtyard. The young fop ran up, flushed and puffing, seized Isokrates by the arm, and dug his heels in, halting them. 'You!' he shouted angrily. 'You're not allowed to wander about the queen's house on your own!'

Isokrates pried the clutching fingers off his arm. 'Then show me out. Your mistress just ordered me to leave.'

The young man scowled. 'That way,' he said, gesturing to the right along the colonnade.

'That's not the way we came in.'

'It's the way you go out!' Hyperides once more caught Isokrates' arm; Isokrates jerked away, and they stood a moment, glaring at one another. The plump youth was several inches shorter and obviously no fighter: Isokrates was tempted to knock him down and walk out.

140

Impossible. Hyperides was obviously someone of importance – and besides, he'd been acting as a herald, whose person should be sacrosanct. Isokrates grimaced and turned to the right.

Hyperides at once pushed in front of him.

They traced a zigzag route through the house – slowly. They wandered about courtyards and through splendid halls covered in priceless carpets; in and out of workrooms where startled serving women were weaving; through the kitchen and round about the garden. Isokrates was not aware of feeling fear, but the young man's mincing steps burned his nerves and set the blood pounding in his ears.

They reached the marble entrance hall at long last. Hyperides halted again. 'The doorkeeper will want a record,' he said loftily. 'Your name and city and so on. Wait here a moment: I'll fetch the record book.'

Isokrates nodded. As soon as the young man turned away, however, he walked directly to the heavy oak door, lifted the bolt, flung open the panel, and started running.

The herald and the doorkeeper both shouted indignantly; the soldiers on guard outside yelled, and one brought his spear up – but they were surprised and uncertain: they were supposed to stop people going *in*. Isokrates dashed past them and on to the road to Ephesus. His long cloak slowed him, so he pulled it off and, with a pang, dropped it: better the cloak than his life. More yells rose behind him – *Stop!* and *Wait!* Nobody, however, shouted, *Kill him!* so he kept running and did not look back.

141

He was pounding up the hill when something *cracked* off a stone in the road just beyond him. He glanced down when he ran past, but saw nothing: a missile from a sling, then, not an arrow. Still he did not feel frightened, even when there was another *crack* almost under his feet: he had no attention to spare for anything but running. His throat hurt and his legs ached already; it had been years since he ran far – but he had stamina from rowing. He wasn't going to stop.

Just as he reached the crest of the hill, something slammed into his back with a brute, numbing impact. He staggered, but managed to stay on his feet and keep going. Safe for a minute or two! They could not aim over the hill, and going downhill he'd be faster than they were coming up; he might be able to get out of range. If he got to the city, would they give up? He hoped, he *hoped* that they wouldn't kill him in front of witnesses. He hurtled desperately down the slope, each step a gamble against a twisted ankle and a headlong sprawl. The pain from whatever-it-was that had hit him had caught up now; it seemed to strike him again with each step, and he couldn't get enough air. Sweat was running into his eyes, and he could barely see the road in front of him; he stumbled over a rock, tripped, and cried out at the red-hot jolt along his back as he fell. He forced himself to his feet again, visualized himself at an oar, pulling hard to drive his ship away from a more powerful enemy: rush speed, *one* and two, *one* and two...

There was shouting all around him, and then an impact against his face. He felt for his oar, but his hands were numb. The ship had been rammed! He was filled with an immense, overwhelming horror: beautiful *Atalanta*! Ripped open, broken, wallowing in the bitter sea, all the crowded lives aboard her swallowed by the waves! His father's voice shouted at him – 'Worthless! You've thrown away everything to go running after worthless timber!' He turned his head away – and saw Agido.

Her face was calm and happy, beautiful again. His eyes filled with tears. She smiled at him tenderly and brushed his forehead with a gentle hand.

'Hush, Isokratidion!' she murmured. 'It will be all right.'

He tried to say her name, but his lips wouldn't move. She shook her head and, still smiling, backed away.

'Give him some water,' somebody suggested. A cup was put against his lips; he tried to drink, but it was hard to swallow. He felt dizzy and sick, and closed his eyes. There was a jolt of pain in his back, and he opened his eyes again and cried out.

'Gently!' said somebody. There were more voices after that, but he didn't listen to them.

Seven

Isokrates woke thirsty, sick to his stomach, and with a horrible pain in his back. He shifted, trying to find a more comfortable position, and somebody came over, helped him turn on to his right side, and offered him a cup. He drank, realizing only as he finished that he wasn't sure what he'd just swallowed or who'd given it to him.

'He's woken up!' the man who'd given him the drink called. It was Polydoros, captain of the spearmen; he grinned encouragingly and asked, 'How're you feeling?'

Isokrates groaned. Aristomachos appeared in his field of vision, face full of concern. 'You gave him the mixture?' he asked Polydoros.

'He took it all,' the spearman replied. 'You want some water now, sir? I'll go fetch it.'

He disappeared. 'How're you feeling?' asked Aristomachos.

Isokrates wasn't sure how to reply. The planking beneath him was familiar, as was the scent – seawater, pine, sweat and grease. He knew where he was – but he had a clear memory of losing it to the greedy sea. 'Didn't we sink?' he asked in a hoarse whisper.

The trierarch snorted and slapped his shoulder

– very gently. *'You* almost did. Are you up to telling us what happened?'

Polydoros reappeared, with the cup of water. 'Drink it up! You lost a lot of blood.'

Isokrates stared at him in confusion. 'Blood?'

'You ran up to the North Gate of Ephesus and collapsed in a bloody heap,' Aristomachos informed him. 'The city guards were going to take you to the citadel, but we realized what was going on and got you away from them.'

That made no sense. 'Slingstone!' he protested feebly.

'Slingstone? You had a filthy *arrow* in your back! You can have a look at it if you like: we kept it. Who shot you?'

He'd always thought an arrow would feel *sharp*. That blow against his back might've come from a club. He wondered queasily what it had done to him. He twisted his neck, trying to see over his shoulder, but it hurt, so he put his head down and lay flat on his stomach again.

'Just a couple of questions, if you can,' coaxed Aristomachos. 'Who shot you?'

'Andronikos. Or maybe one of his men. I didn't see.'

'Ah.' Aristomachos sat back on his heels, his expression grim. 'Was he at the queen's house, or did you meet him on the road?'

'He was at her house. He's a mercenary in her service.' There was something else, something important ... oh! *'Thalia*! *Thalia* has to get away! Sir, what the queen wanted was to find Dionysia.'

'Thalia left Ephesus this morning,' Aristoma-

chos told him. 'She'd finished her business the day we arrived. Rest easy, we're all safe.' He patted Isokrates' shoulder again. 'Did the queen order your death?'

Isokrates closed his eyes, trying to make sense of things. He remembered running down the hill, then remembered rowing desperately to get away, and the impact as the ship was rammed ... but no, she couldn't've been, she was here beneath him, alive with the movement of the oars. He was lying in the quiet, comfortable spot behind the command chair, and all his people were safe. He would sacrifice a lamb to the gods, to thank them for their great kindness.

Aristomachos was still waiting to hear whether the queen had ordered his death. 'No,' he managed, forcing his eyes open again. 'She knew Andronikos wanted to kill me. She wanted him to. She tried to arrange it so he could. But she didn't ... didn't give any order about it. When I ran the soldiers didn't try to stop me. I don't ... don't think they're *her* soldiers.'

'Most likely not,' Aristomachos said softly. 'Most likely they're her husband's soldiers, and if he asked them, "Did she order you to kill a Rhodian naval officer?" they'd give him a truthful answer. A mercenary now, killing a man because of a personal grudge – she can't be held accountable for that, can she? Useful that way, mercenaries.' The trierarch sat back, pursing his lips. 'I'm not sure we were right to leave Ephesus. If she wanted you dead, it was probably so that you couldn't tell the king what she'd questioned you about. What we should've done is gone straight to Antiochos and said, "Look what your bitch-faced wife is up to!"'

'When they came I thought maybe they knew about Alexandria,' Isokrates told him.

'That was what I thought, too, when Nikagoras told me what had happened. But they didn't?'

'No. I told her Dionysia had gone there. Nobody said anything about us going too. And I pretended to think the king sent Dionysia away because he was tired of her. She believed me.'

Aristomachos grunted. 'You know, I think the best thing we could do is tell the king. It's too late to go back to Ephesus today, though. We'll stop in Cos tonight. I'll leave you with some friends, see to it that you're properly looked after.'

Isokrates had been drifting off to sleep, but at this his eyes flew open again. Stay in Cos while his miraculously preserved ship went off without him? What if he woke, and found that this was nothing but a happy dream, and the reality was death in the salt water? 'No!'

'You rest,' Aristomachos ordered him. 'We'll talk about it later.'

They did not. Isokrates was deposited in the house of Aristomachos's Coan friends that evening, heavily drugged. When he woke up again next morning, *Atalanta* had already left.

It was like a bereavement. That moment when he had known that the ship had been rammed haunted him; he could not shake a conviction that now it would come true. His only comfort was that Agido had told him that it would be all right – but that was a shaky support for hope: she had not, after all, said anything about the ship.

Aristomachos's friends were wealthy, and Isokrates was well looked after. One or another of the household slaves came into his sickroom regularly during the day to check if there was anything he wanted. Cos was famous for its doctors, and a knowledgeable-seeming medic visited twice a day to clean the wound and mix remedies. On the second day he irritably told Isokrates that the wound itself wasn't that bad.

'The arrow was descending, and hit you at an angle,' he explained, laying splayed fingers next to the throbbing knot of pain, under the shoulder blade on the left side of his patient's back. 'It grazed the outer edge of *this* rib, then lodged in the inner edge of *this* one, instead of going straight into your lungs. It hasn't penetrated your vitals. If you'd sat quietly after being hit, you'd be back on your feet by now. But you kept moving, and that tore the wound and made it bleed heavily. It's the blood loss that nearly killed you, and that's what's reducing your spirits now.'

Isokrates thought of telling the doctor that if he'd sat quietly after being hit, he would be dead – but there seemed no point in arguing.

'You need to build your strength up again,' the doctor told him. 'You're underweight and ill-nourished as it is, and if you don't follow a proper diet now, you won't recover. When they give you broth, you must drink it up. None of this taking a sip and telling the attendants you'll finish it later.'

* * *

After the doctor left, Isokrates lay mulling over Agido's promise. It was only then that he realized that his memory of rowing to escape didn't make sense: he couldn't possibly have rowed after collapsing with an arrow in his back. It had been a kind of dream. How had he ever been stupid enough to believe otherwise?

Had Agido been a dream, too? He remembered her calm happy face – so different from that of the thing they'd cut down from the roof-beam! – and hoped desperately that she, at least, had been a true vision. *'Hush, Isokratidion! It will be all right.'* He prayed to the gods that it would be.

In the middle of his third day at the house there was a commotion in the corridor outside, and then Aristomachos came in, flushed and sweating. Isokrates exclaimed wordlessly in relief and struggled to sit up. The trierarch came forward and helped him! 'Well.' he exclaimed, beaming. 'You are looking better than you did, at any rate. They tell me, though, that you've been doing none too well.'

'You shouldn't have left me behind!'

Aristomachos snorted. 'You sound like my little son: *"Why* did you leave me behind, *I* wanted to come, *toooo!"* Don't be stupid. You were much too ill to travel.'

'You should have brought me anyway,' Isokrates said vehemently. 'All you could tell the king was what I said had happened. He must've wanted to question me himself.'

'We didn't see him.' The trierarch grimaced at Isokrates' look of surprise. 'We didn't see him, and yesterday we left in some haste.' Aristomachos lowered his voice and went on, 'When we arrived in the harbour at Ephesus, I told the guardship that I'd come to speak to the king about what had happened to my helmsman at the house of Queen Laodike. A friend of the king turned up that same evening to ask me about it, and I told him most of what I was going to say to the king. He went off looking worried.

'Yesterday morning the king's friend came back and told us that Antiochos would see us that afternoon. In the afternoon, though, he turned up again, and this time he said that the king was ill. "You should go home," he told me, and there was something about the way he said it that made me think he wasn't just trying to get rid of me. So I said, "Who's in charge of things while the king's ill?" and he gave me a look like he was relieved I was asking, and said, "The king's eldest son, Seleukos, the child of Queen Laodike." Then he said, "Antiochos met with the queen this morning, just before he fell ill" – which I took to be as plain a statement of suspicion as a courtier was likely to make. So I thanked him and gave orders to put out to sea at once, even though it was late in the day by then. Zeus! We hadn't even managed to top up our water supplies, and last night we ended up on some bugger-arsed little beach in the middle of nowhere without anything to drink.' Aristomachos sighed and stretched. 'Got another rough night ahead, too, if we're to get this news to Rhodes quickly.'

Isokrates was appalled and stunned. 'The
150

king's been *poisoned*? Because of *us*?'

'Oh, I doubt it was because of us. Most likely he got Ptolemy's letter within the last few days. That must've been the big thing: probably he was sitting there wondering, "Do I really want to go to war?" But us turning up when we did could've tipped the scales: the wife he was about to hazard his kingdom for has been trying to get rid of his favourite concubine; what's more, she's hired pirates who've gone about trying to murder the king's allies. Seems to me that if he wasn't thinking she's not worth it, there'd be something wrong with him.' Aristomachos rubbed the back of his neck. 'My reckoning is that he was stupid enough to tell his wife, "Dear, I'm sorry, but I'm going to have to set you aside again." I'd like to ask Dionysia what she thinks, though: she knows the people. Well, I had us stop in Cos to get food and water, and to check on you, but I intend to head straight on to Rhodes to let the Council know what's up. I was hoping you'd be well enough to come with us, but...'

'I'm well enough.'

'That's not what I heard from my friends.'

'I'm well enough. I couldn't settle before. I was afraid for the rest of you.'

Aristomachos snorted. 'What, afraid we'd get killed if you weren't there to keep us safe?'

Isokrates was embarrassed – and angry: he did not think he had deserved ridicule.

Aristomachos laid a hand on his shoulder and looked at him with a mixture of exasperation and affection. 'My friend, you and I both know what happens to wounds when they're left untended in rough conditions. I was never going to let that happen to you. The queen's people asked for the *trierarch*. If I'd been with my ship the way I should've been, it would've been me they took to meet her, and I don't think *I* could've outrun them. That's my life I owe you. I wasn't going to repay that debt with your death.'

'It wasn't...' Isokrates began – but Aristomachos interrupted him.

'Very well! You've had a few days' proper care and it's only a day's pull to Rhodes. I'll see about getting a litter to take you down to the ship.'

Riding down to the Coan harbour in a litter was simple enough. Getting up the boarding ladder on to the ship was much more complicated, but the crew all cheered him when he made it. He lay down in the hollow of the stern and listened to the sound of the ship getting under way. He had to struggle not to cry.

It was not as rough a night as Aristomachos had feared. When night fell, the wind continued light from the north, and the trihemiolia was able to cruise slowly and cautiously along the coast under sail while the oarcrew dozed. It was, however, quite rough enough for Isokrates. Aristomachos insisted on yielding the prime position behind the command chair, but Isokrates still found it impossible to sleep. The decking was hard, and it was impossible to find a position on it that spared his back; there was also a constant procession of men climbing out on to the oarbox to relieve themselves over the stern. Every time

152

he was about to doze off, the tiller-holder would alter course slightly to stay away from some headland or island, or to compensate for a shift in the wind, and then the sail crew would rush about adjusting the sails with a great thudding of feet and yelling of instructions. When morning came he felt feverish and wretched.

It was only a couple of hours after sunrise, however, that they arrived in Rhodes. Aristomachos shot off to speak to the Council presidents, but not before arranging for Isokrates to be carried to his own house. 'You'll stay with me until you're recovered,' he said, as though it were a matter of course.

Isokrates was very relieved: he did not feel nearly well enough to look after himself, and the thought of having to depend on Atta was frightening. At the same time, though, he was uncomfortable about relying on Aristomachos. For a poor man to accept the charity of a rich one was a good way to lose his independence. He liked the trierarch, but had no wish to become a servant. Still, what choice did he have?

Four of the oarcrew carried him up to Aristomachos's house on the eastern side of the marketplace and installed him in a guestroom. It was a large, airy room which opened on to a courtyard garden planted with jasmine and the Rhodian pink hibiscus; the couch was soft, spread with clean linen that smelled of lavender. Aristomachos's slaves brought him broth, put a soothing poultice on his wound, then left him to rest.

He was just going to sleep when Aristomachos

came in. 'I'm sorry!' exclaimed the trierarch. 'The presidents want exactly what you said the king would. They're here in the house, though. Can you manage to walk as far as the dining room, or shall I get someone to carry you?'

Isokrates sat up groggily and too fast, and almost fainted. Aristomachos tut-tutted and helped him on with a tunic. He managed to walk as far as the dining room, clutching the trierarch's arm for support.

The dining room was full: three couches had been arranged around the walls, and a chair by the door, and all were occupied. Isokrates had been expecting the three men who'd been there before, and was staggered to see that the matter now rated all five presidents, plus three very distinguished former presidents, presumably invited because of their experience in affairs of state. One of these last was the admiral Agathostratos, who'd commanded the Rhodian fleet in the last war, and won the Battle of Ephesus. Isokrates hung on Aristomachos's arm, gulping.

Xenophantes jumped up from the central couch. 'Here, lie down!' he ordered. 'We understand that you're injured.'

Isokrates was embarrassed, but took the vacant place. His head was swimming and he feared that if he had to stand he would faint.

He told the presidents everything he could remember about his meeting with Laodike. They listened intently and asked questions: Was he sure the queen knew nothing about the mission to Alexandria? Was it possible that she was ignorant of Andronikos' career as a pirate? Was he certain that she knew Andronikos intended to kill him? He answered honestly: yes, no, yes.

'Why was she so determined to find the Milesian girl?' Xenophantes asked with a frown. 'She can't *still* have expected to stop the news of her reinstatement from reaching Egypt! It's been a month, and the sailing season's started: she must know that somebody would've told Ptolemy by now!'

'I don't know,' Isokrates said wearily. 'It wasn't something I could ask about.'

'We'll have to ask the Milesian girl,' said Aristomachos. 'She should be here soon.'

Isokrates looked at him in surprise – then realized that yes, of course Dionysia would be in Rhodes by now, and of course the presidents would have sent for her.

Hagemon began tapping the arm of his couch; it took Isokrates a moment to recognize the ominous throbbing rhythm of a chorus from a tragic play. '"Just like a lioness,"' he murmured, '"hid in mountain wilderness, striking in savageness, she accomplished it." This Laodike seems the most infamous queen since Clytemnestra!'

Admiral Agathostratos frowned at him. 'We don't know she poisoned King Antiochos. He could genuinely have fallen ill, from anxiety over the matter and sleepless nights. Alternatively, some friend of the queen who hoped for advantages from her reinstatement could have poisoned him – or it could be that he isn't ill at all, and simply sent that message to Aristomachos to avoid an embarrassing confrontation with an ally. What we need to do...'

There was a small disturbance at the door; one of Aristomachos's slaves came in and whispered to his master. 'Show her in!' Aristomachos ordered out loud. 'Councillors, the Milesian girl is here.'

Dionysia came in a moment later, followed by her ever-present maid. She glanced round the room apprehensively. Then her eyes fell on Isokrates and she cried in alarm, 'Oh, Apollo! What's happened?'

'Bad news from Ephesus,' Aristomachos told her. 'Isokrates had a meeting with your friend Laodike. He wasn't supposed to survive to report on it, but he did – and that seems to have provoked her. At least, that's what we think, but we don't know the people. We were hoping you could advise us.'

Dionysia swallowed several times, staring at Isokrates with so much dismay that he was embarrassed.

'It's just a flesh wound,' he told her. 'And I'm tired and light-headed, is all.'

She flushed and looked away. 'I am most willing to help you if I can, sirs.'

'Good!' said Xenophantes, and proceeded to give her a summary of what had happened in Ephesus.

Dionysia had gone very pale by the time he finished. She pressed her hands to her mouth and shook her head; there were tears in her eyes. Aristomachos, frowning, looked around, then went out and came back with a three-legged stool. She sat down heavily and pulled a fold of cloak over her head.

'Forgive me,' she said thickly. 'Oh, Apollo!'

'It's a shock to you,' acknowledged Xenophantes.

She nodded wordlessly, not uncovering her head. 'I don't ... I never thought ... oh, the stupid *fool*! *Oi moi*, poor Antiochos! I should never have left the court! I've only made things worse!'

'Don't be a fool!' Aristomachos told her sharply. 'Seems to me that Queen Laodike is the one making things worse. I take it you agree it's likely she's poisoned her husband?'

Dionysia swallowed a sob and nodded again. 'Yes. If she thought she was going to be set aside *again*, she'd do it. Antiochos always trusted her too much. She kept telling him that she *loved* him, and he ... he *believed* it! He never could understand that people *flattered* him; he thought that since everybody said how wonderful he was, it must be *true*.'

'Do you know why she was so eager to find you?' Xenophantes asked.

She shook her head. 'I thought before that she wanted to make sure I couldn't tell Ptolemy until the divorce was all settled. But now ... maybe she just wants to punish me.'

'She's taken risks for this,' Agathostratos pointed out. 'When her husband found out about it, it *did* offend him. Is punishing you worth that much to her?'

'I don't know. I wouldn't have thought so. He wasn't *her* husband when he slept with me.'

Isokrates suddenly saw what must have happened. 'The king asked for you!' he exclaimed.

Everyone looked at him, and he struggled to sit up and explain. 'When I told Laodike that you were in Alexandria she said "Well, at least she's not coming back!" I didn't pay attention to it at the time, but she was relieved that you were out of the way! The king had asked for you, and she was afraid you might influence him against her.'

'Makes sense,' said Aristomachos. 'For the king to give up a wife he likes and go back to one he detests is one thing; for him to give her up and console himself with his favourite concubine – that'd be a lot easier. And presumably the queen knew that Lady Dionysia had been trying to persuade him not to divorce Berenike.'

All the others nodded. Xenophantes grimaced unhappily. 'I'd been hoping the explanation would be something *useful*. Ah well.'

He began asking her about the court, about various friends of Antiochos and what they were likely to do now. Isokrates found it impossible to pay attention: his head had started to ache and he felt giddy. Someone caught his arm and tugged: he looked up and saw it was Aristomachos.

'Excuse me,' the trierarch said to his illustrious guests. 'My helmsman needs to go back to bed.' He led Isokrates back along the corridor and deposited him back in the guest room.

Isokrates slept; woke when a doctor came in to see to him; then slept the night through, and woke feeling considerably better. Aristomachos's slaves brought him broth and he drank it, then lay in bed staring out at the garden. It was the middle of the afternoon: he'd lost another

158

day. He tried to work out how long it had been since he was wounded. Six days, he thought. He wondered how long it would be before he was well again.

A boy appeared in the doorway, saw that Isokrates was awake, and hesitated.

'What is it?' Isokrates asked him.

The boy came in. He was nine or ten, with curly black hair and hazel eyes. His tunic was plain and none-too-clean, but his manner wasn't that of a slave. 'You're Isokrates,' he said accusingly. 'You were shot. My father said you're going to stay with us until you're better.'

'That's right. I'm grateful for it. You're Aristomachos's son, then? What's your name?'

'Anaxippos.' Named after his grandfather, like most first-born sons. He regarded Isokrates suspiciously and announced, 'My father said you ran down a hill as tall as the acropolis with an arrow in your back.'

'I don't know how tall the hill was.'

Anaxippos frowned. 'How could you do that? I had to miss the school race once just because I cut my knee.'

Isokrates was amused. 'There were pirates behind me shooting at me. I didn't want to die. That's how.'

The boy stared. 'How many pirates?'

'I didn't count. To tell the truth, I never even saw them. I was too busy running.'

'Then how did you know they were pirates?'

'I'd met one of them just before I started running.'

'Why didn't you fight?'

159

For a moment Isokrates was offended. Then he realized that he would have been similarly puzzled at that age. To be shot in the back while running away was the fate of a coward – but everyone was treating the wound as something honourable.

'When I first met this pirate,' he said, 'he ran away as fast as his ship could row. That doesn't make him a coward. His ship was no match for ours, and if he'd fought, he and all his men would've died. It was the same when I met him again, except that the tables were turned. I was unarmed and on my own; he had friends and weapons. Sometimes running is the only thing you can do, and escaping is the best you can hope for.'

Anaxippos thought about it. 'That was cowardly, attacking an unarmed man with a whole gang!'

Isokrates shook his head impatiently. 'No more cowardly than attacking a fifty-oared pirate ship with a trihemiolia! It wasn't a *fight*. He didn't want to beat me; he wanted to kill me. Going after me on his own wouldn't have been brave, it would have been stupid, because it would've made it easier for me to get away. I did get away. That was a defeat for him, and a victory for me.'

Saying this made him feel better. He became aware that some private corner of his mind agreed with the boy's view. He had run away, leaving his enemy secure, safe in the queen's protection. Andronikos, though, would not be viewing their encounter as a victory.

Anaxippos gave this his considered attention. 'Like when Demetrios the Besieger attacked the city,' he said at last. 'We didn't *beat* him, but when the siege failed, he lost.'

'Exactly!' agreed Isokrates, pleased with the comparison.

'It's like our republic,' said Aristomachos. Isokrates hadn't noticed him, and looked up with a start to find the trierarch smiling at them from the doorway. 'We can't hope to beat a king, but if they don't beat us, we win. Anaxippion mine, have you done your music practice?'

The boy favoured his father with a put-upon scowl, an exaggerated sigh, and a sulky exit.

'I hope he didn't tire you,' said Aristomachos.

'No. Sir...'

'Good! Feeling any better?'

'Yes. Sir, what did the presidents decide to do?'

The trierarch grimaced. 'Not much. We're not sure exactly what's happening in Ephesus, and until we know, we should be cautious: that's the upshot of it.'

'Oh.'

'We're preparing to send an embassy, though. Agathostratos volunteered to head it. The Syrians are bound to treat *him* with respect: if it wasn't for him, Ephesus would still belong to Ptolemy. He'll take one line if Antiochos is still alive, and a different one if he's dead – but he's not going to denounce the queen. At most he'll complain about one of the queen's mercenaries.'

Isokrates frowned unhappily, and the trierarch nodded and sighed. 'Nobody liked it much, but everybody who knows the Syrian court agreed that if Antiochos *is* dead, it's very likely that the next king will be Seleukos, his eldest son by Laodike. Apparently the boy is nineteen, has been at court for the past couple of years, and hasn't offended anybody crucial. If he's king, and owes it to his dear old mother – well, he wouldn't be too happy to have Rhodes denouncing her as a murderess, would he? It would hurt us worse than it hurt her.'

'But if she poisoned his father...'

'Then he's profited by his father's murder, hasn't he? He can't admit it. The *real* point is, the alternative to Seleukos is Queen Berenike's son, who's only three. Everybody at our conference agreed: Antiochos's men won't swallow Berenike as Queen Regent, because they're afraid she'd pay more attention to her brother Ptolemy than to them. According to your girl-friend, they aren't keen on bitch-faced Laodike, but they're even less keen on being governed from Alexandria. Seleukos is descended from his namesake the Conqueror on both sides, and is old enough to be his own man.'

'Ptolemy will go to war,' said Isokrates.

''Course he will. Here, you've got a letter from your girlfriend.' Aristomachos held out a sealed roll of papyrus and laughed at Isokrates' astonishment. 'Didn't you notice it yesterday? She was all in tears over her brave sailor lying there wounded on her behalf. Well, you did look like something washed up on a beach. Something skeletal, I mean, not bloated.'

'But I wasn't wounded on *her* behalf! I...'

'She was in bugger-arsed Ephesus when the queen sent for you, and you told the queen she was in Alexandria. She's not stupid: she knows that if you'd piped up with, "The girl you want is just over the hill!" you'd've been rewarded with gold instead of an arrow in the back. Besides, women love to think that men are making sacrifices for them. I suppose it makes them feel important. Like Helen watching from the walls of Troy as the heroes fought.' He fluttered his eyelashes coquettishly and clasped his hands to his bosom.

Isokrates took the papyrus and broke the seal.

Dionysia daughter of Kleisthenes greets Isokrates of Kameiros. Shame compels me to write you: I have brought you ill fortune. The queen summoned you only to ask about me, and you protected me, though it nearly cost you your life. I am most deeply grateful, and I pray the gods grant you a swift recovery! Farewell.

'You should write back,' said Aristomachos, leering.

Isokrates looked up quickly. 'I thought...' He stopped.

'What?' Aristomachos arched his eyebrows. 'What, you thought *I* was interested? Oh, no. You heard the woman yourself: she's a respectable musician, not a courtesan. I don't go after respectable women: I much prefer the disreputable sort. More fun and fewer complications.'

Isokrates cursed the wave of relief this news

brought. I *can't* go after respectable women, he thought – but he said nothing, looking at the black strokes of ink on the letter in his hand. *I am most deeply grateful.*

How grateful? Enough to give him that shy true smile, and touch his face with those long fingers, and kiss him? Enough to give him what the pirate had taken by force and the king by decree?

Probably not – but even if she was, should he ask it? She'd said, in tears, that she wanted to be a musician, not a courtesan. She wouldn't succeed in that ambition if she started off by sleeping with a naval helmsman as a reward for his help. A rich music-lover like Hagemon might accept a refusal from her if she was chaste; he was unlikely to do so if she was sleeping with a low-born rival.

Offering her marriage would be even crueller. To become, instead of a famous singer, the wife of a poor man – to struggle with dirt and hunger in a rented hovel; to bear children her husband could not afford to rear – that was a bitter sentence. No decent man would ask it of her.

'You write to her,' Aristomachos urged. 'I'll tell the slaves to bring you pen and ink.'

Eight

'What sort of bugger-arsed letter is this?' demanded Aristomachos indignantly, coming into the room that evening flourishing the missive.

Isokrates sat up and glared at him. 'You *read* it?'

'You're in my house. I have a right to read letters sent from my own house! Oh, come *on*, my friend, what do you mean writing the woman such a prissy cold letter? *"What I did I did to serve the Rhodians, not for you. I hope to return to duty soon"*. How far do you think *that's* going to get you?'

'I don't think it's going to get me anywhere.'

'By Aphrodite, it won't, either! What's *wrong* with you? You *like* the woman; that's plain from the way you look at her!'

A slave came in, glanced nervously from face to angry face, then said to his master, 'Sir, there's a man at the door who claims to be this gentleman's father.'

Isokrates stared at the slave in horror.

'Let him in, then!' ordered Aristomachos.

The words, 'No! Keep him out!' struggled to Isokrates' lips – but he swallowed them. A son could not refuse to see his own father.

'Must've heard you'd been wounded,' said the

trierarch, with some satisfaction. 'Come to patch things up with you, I expect.'

'No,' said Isokrates. 'News takes longer than that to get to him. He must've come to Rhodes-town for something else.'

The slave returned, escorting Isokrates' father. It had been eight years since they met, and the hair which had been mostly black was now mostly grey, with the beard entirely grizzled. The old man had lost weight, and his bones stood out starkly; his eyes were bloodshot and uncertain. His tunic was old and patched. When he saw Isokrates he stopped short in the doorway of the room, his big hands clenching and unclenching at his sides.

'Good health!' said Aristomachos cheerfully. 'You must be ... what was the name?'

'Kritagoras, sir,' the old man said, with a nervous glance at the trierarch.

'I am Aristomachos, Isokrates' commanding officer. He is staying with me until he's recovered from his wound. He's an exceptional officer, and I value him highly.'

Kritagoras ducked his head and returned his attention to Isokrates, who gazed stonily back at him.

'They said at the shipyard you'd been wounded,' the old man said at last. 'It's not ... not too bad?'

'No,' Isokrates replied shortly. 'What brings you to Rhodes-town?'

'Came to see you.' Kritagoras cleared his throat uncomfortably and went on hurriedly, 'I wrote you about Theophrastos's daughter. Well,

166

her father won't give her to *me,* but he'd be more than happy to give her to *you.* She's a pretty girl and a hard worker. If...'

'No.'

'You wouldn't have to stay on the farm all year,' coaxed his father. 'Ships don't go out in the winters anyway.'

'No,' Isokrates repeated levelly.

'I wouldn't...'

'The answer is *no,*' Isokrates interrupted. 'And you are mistaken: Theophrastos would not be happy to give her to me. He wants to give her to a man with land, and I have none.'

Kritagoras's face creased in pain. 'Please!'

'I swore an oath by the Sun!' Isokrates told him vehemently. 'That land is cursed. Find yourself some other heir.'

Kritagoras didn't start shouting, the way he always had before. Instead, he began to cry, snuffling and pressing his calloused hands to his face. It was much, much worse, but Isokrates stifled the impulse to pity.

'What is this about?' Aristomachos asked, quietly horrified.

'A stupid girl!' shouted Kritagoras, wiping the tears away. 'That's what it's about, a stupid girl, my second wife, who hanged herself! It wasn't my fault!'

Isokrates shook his head angrily. 'Fourteen years now you've been repeating that. You can repeat it til your deathbed, but it still won't be true.'

'She kept having daughters,' Kritagoras explained, turning to Aristomachos. 'The property's only a small one, sir: how was I supposed to provide dowries for a load of daughters? I wanted to keep it intact, free of debt – for *him*, for my son!'

'A *load* of daughters!' Isokrates exclaimed contemptuously. 'You wouldn't let her keep even *one*! And hitting her, because she cried for them – was that done for me, too?'

'A man comes in from the vineyard, tired,' said Kritagoras, 'and finds the house a mess, no supper, and his wife snivelling in a corner, well, of course he loses his temper! It wasn't ... I was never ... there's plenty of men who...' He trailed off under Isokrates' bleak stare. '*She* always admitted she was at fault in it!'

'*She* always forgave you. *She* was gentle and kind, always willing to blame herself and never anybody else. But I'm *your* son, not hers, and no more merciful than you were. I swore an oath by the Sun, and I'll keep it.'

'You were twelve years old!'

'It was an oath, and I'll keep it. Find someone else to take your land, old man: I won't touch it.'

Kritagoras began to cry again. Isokrates turned to Aristomachos, who stood there appalled. 'I'm sorry, sir, that you had to witness this disgraceful scene.'

'Oh, Zeus!' muttered Aristomachos, shaken. 'Here, old man, you'd better leave it for now. Here, come on, sit down in the dining room and have a cup of wine.'

He came back a little later. Isokrates was lying down by then, pressing his face against his forearm, remembering Agido's body being cut down

168

from the roof beam.

'I gave him some wine,' Aristomachos said uncertainly.

'Thank you, sir.'

There was a silence.

'I was eight when my father married Agido,' Isokrates said abruptly, without looking up. 'She was fourteen. She was never like a mother, but no, if you're thinking of Phaidra, you're wrong. There was nothing unholy about the way I loved her: we were like brother and sister. We played guessing games and told stories; she teased me and taught me how to play the pipes. The farm's up in the mountains, you see, between Karyon and Attavyros: beautiful country, and the grapes make good wine, but there weren't a lot of other people nearby. My mother died when I was small, I didn't have any brothers or sisters, and I had to walk for half an hour to reach the next farm with a boy my age. Until Agido came, it was just me and my father in the house most nights, and it was lonely. The first year after she came was the happiest I've ever been.'

'A lot of men won't raise daughters,' said Aristomachos. 'Dowries are a great expense. I supplied one for my own daughter last year. I was happy to, but I'm wealthy, and I would have struggled to find the money if I'd had more than the one girl.'

'Most men will allow their wives *one* girl, though, especially if the wife has no other child to console her, especially if she's ... she's *wounded* by the loss! Not my father. Agido bore three daughters in a row. The first one my father put out on the hillside; I went to look for her next day, but the birds and the foxes had had her. The next two I carried into Kameiros, in the hope that somebody else might take them up – and now I don't dare sleep with any whore under twenty, in case she's my sister. I watched Agido turn from a sweet, cheerful girl into a shivering, weeping thing that hid in corners. When she was pregnant for the fourth time, I begged my father to promise her that she could keep the child, whatever it was. He would not.'

'Well,' said Aristomachos, after a silence. 'He was wrong, there's no doubt. But...'

'He said he did it to keep the property whole, so I swore he can take it whole to Hades.'

'An oath sworn by a child isn't binding. He was right on that one. Look, he's an old man! He's *crying*. He's your *father*!'

'I want nothing to do with the man. But I'm sorry you had to witness this.'

'Father Zeus! I was told that *he'd* cut *you* off. I suppose nobody believed that a son would disinherit *himself*!'

'I want none of that land. Let it go to ruin. My father can die on it, alone.'

'Gods avert the omen! You'd regret it if he did.'

'Then let him find somebody else to be his heir! You haven't understood, no more than he will. Agido died so that nobody else could share that land, and because of that, I can never work it. It is cursed for me, and I never want to see it again. Tell my father to leave me alone.'

Aristomachos swore and went out.

170

Part of Isokrates wanted to follow, to go speak to his father while the man was still in the house. Those tears scalded his memory: he had never seen his father cry. He stayed where he was, nursing his anger and disgust to keep away the pity.

'You'll come running home again, soon as the winter comes!' Kritagoras had shouted, the summer Isokrates left him. But Isokrates hadn't run home. He'd endured the summers at the oar, the winters in the yard; endured the barracks, the homesickness, the assaults. He'd learned how to fight and how to handle a ship, and now at last he was a success in his chosen career. Kritagoras had come and found that the son he'd sworn would fail was a helmsman, respected by a rich and distinguished trierarch – and he was crying now because he finally understood that he'd lost. Isokrates should be glad of the victory. He'd made sacrifices enough to win it.

In the morning one of the slaves offered to trim his hair and beard; when the man had finished snipping he handed Isokrates a mirror so that he could admire the result. The face reflected was painfully gaunt and disturbingly like his father's. Isokrates searched it for a resemblance to his almost-forgotten mother – the eyebrows, perhaps? the ears? – but he kept seeing his father's face and remembering his father's tears.

He pulled on a tunic, realizing as he did that the garment wasn't his, and that he had no idea what had happened to his own things – apart from the fine new Alexandrian cloak, which he still regretted. He went to find Aristomachos.

The trierarch was in his office, writing letters; when Isokrates appeared he set the pen down with a smile. 'Good to see you up! How're you feeling?'

'Much better, thank you, sir. I should go home today.'

'*Bugger* that! —By "home" I take it you mean that hovel full of screaming brats in the harbour district? No, you'll stay here until you're better.'

Isokrates wondered who'd told him about the screaming brats. 'Sir, I...'

'This is because you're embarrassed about quarrelling with your father in front of me, isn't it? Well, you'll simply have to swallow your pride. That's a considerable task, I grant you, given the size of it, but do your best.'

'Sir, I am grateful for your kindness, but I am a free-born citizen and...'

'If you think I think I own you, you are sadly mistaken.'

'I don't even know where my own *clothes* are!'

'Your officer's tunic must've been torn up for rags.'

'What!'

'What do you expect, after it's been soaked wringing wet with blood and had a filthy great hole torn in it? You ruined it in the line of duty: you can have a new one free. I imagine the rest of your clothes are back at the hovel, and if you're that bothered about them, I'll send someone to fetch them. But you're not going back there until you're better.'

'You say you *don't* think you own me?'

'No,' said the trierarch quietly, meeting his eyes. 'I think I'm your friend. Now, if you want to tell me I'm wrong and walk out the door, go ahead. I won't stop you. I'll feel what any man feels when his friendship is rejected, but I'll see to it that you don't suffer for it.'

There was a silence. Isokrates felt as though he were a string which had been keyed tight with pride and suspicion, going suddenly slack.

'Sit down!' ordered Aristomachos, getting up from the room's only chair. 'You've gone green. Zeus, I wasn't proposing buggery! Frankly, you're about as attractive as a fucking post fence!'

Isokrates sat, then bent over to put his head between his knees. 'Sorry,' he muttered. 'Didn't think you were. I'm not ... not as recovered as I thought.'

'I told you so, didn't I?'

This word *friend,* Isokrates warned himself, was not all it seemed. Kings had friends, to whom they entrusted various tasks, but those friends were not their equals. Aristomachos probably envisaged something similar ... though if he were asked what he meant he would probably say, 'What sort of bugger-arsed question is that?'

Isokrates smiled at the thought and looked up at the trierarch. He still did not want to be a servant, but if it came to a choice between *friendship*, however defined, and an open break with a man he'd come to like a great deal – then he knew what his choice was. 'I would be honoured to call myself your friend.'

'Good! Then go back to bed and work on getting better. I want to take *Atalanta* out for another cruise in eight days' time, and I'd prefer it if you were on board.'

To his surprise, Isokrates enjoyed the next eight days. He pottered about the house, then, as he began to recover his strength, went for walks into the marketplace. He played board games with Aristomachos's son and talked about ships with him; they read one of the trierarch's books. He also found himself starting to learn something about merchant ships and investment.

He hadn't thought about the money he'd invested in the Alexandrian grain shipment until Aristomachos asked where he wanted to put it now – a question which, he discovered, meant not 'where do you want to deposit it?' but 'in what cargoes do you want to invest?' The amount at his disposal, he discovered to his amazement, was four hundred and twenty drachmai.

'Well, your investment was three hundred, yes?' Aristomachos said breezily. 'A hundred from your share of the pirate money, and two hundred from the salvage. We've got the salvage money, by the way; picked it up in Ephesus, and *yes,* I did give the crew their share! They think I'm a splendid fellow, and they're spending it hand over fist. Anyway, the grain made forty per cent profit. That's exceptional, but you can pretty much count on fifteen per cent, and sometimes do much better – though normally you have to pay carriage costs and harbour dues, which cuts it down again. You want to spread the risk, though. A ship gets taken by pirates, or caught in a storm, and you lose everything you put in her – so you don't put everything you've got in her, right? But it's not worth investing less than a hundred-fifty. Syndicates aren't interested in piddling little amounts.'

Isokrates had never thought of a hundred drachmai as a 'piddling little amount'; his father's farm earned little more in a year, once the bills had been paid. Aristomachos's talk of 'per cent profit' and 'bottomry loans' made his head spin. He knew enough of merchant shipping, though, to find an insight into the mechanics of its finance fascinating. He ended up investing a hundred and fifty drachmai in each of two ships and keeping a hundred and twenty, for expenses and to buy some new clothes.

The embassy to the Seleucid court set out and returned during those same eight days. The news from Ephesus was as bad as feared: King Antiochos the God was dead. Queen Laodike had produced witnesses who swore that on his deathbed the king named her son Seleukos as his heir. The court in Ephesus had accepted this and given the young man the royal diadem. There had been no direct news from the rival court in Antioch, but it was widely predicted that Queen Berenike would summon help from her brother in Egypt, and that the war would have begun by midsummer.

The only real question, endlessly debated in

the taverns and marketplaces of the city, was what the *third* monarchy would do. Antigonos, King of Macedon, had long been a friend of Syria and an enemy of Egypt – but would he support the new king Seleukos? Antiochos had been his nephew; he might well be unwilling to back his nephew's murderers.

All of this, however, was public, announced to the Rhodian People at an emergency meeting of the Assembly, and debated by the Rhodian People wherever they happened to meet: there were no more private meetings in Aristomachos's house. It seemed as though the centre of the whirlpool had moved on, leaving *Atalanta* and her crew to continue on their ordinary course.

Atalanta set out again late in May on a regular cruise looking for pirates: southwest to Crete, then north along the western coast of the Peloponnese and on as far as Epirus. These were prime pirate waters, and they employed all the usual tricks to try to locate their enemy. They bought drinks for seamen in taverns, and trawled for rumours; they offered to escort likely merchant ships, and crept quietly behind them, hoping a hemiolia would dart out to attack; they lurked behind headlands and hid in inlets. They saw only one ship that might have been of interest – and it quickly dodged into the harbour at Dreros, where the authorities refused to allow entrance to the Rhodians.

'Well, as least the bastards are too busy hiding from us to attack our shipping!' commented Aristomachos, but he was frustrated and disappointed. Pirates always multiplied during a war, and he had six merchant ships to worry about.

It was June now, and hot; the galley's enclosed oardeck was stifling, for all the awnings carefully arranged to direct air through it; the men's sweat hung in the dank enclosure, so that the taste was forever in the mouth. However much water one drank, it never seemed to be enough. Isokrates, still weak from his wound, struggled to cope. He could not row – the movement pulled the new scar unbearably – and the constant struggle to remember safe landing places and where they could get water seemed to batter his mind numb by the end of the day. The four days they spent on short rations on an isolated beach, trapped by a storm, he actually welcomed as a respite. He thought that his strength must actually be coming back – he never felt any better, but then, if his strength *wasn't* returning, he'd be feeling worse, wouldn't he? He kept himself working by a combination of habit and sheer willpower.

They returned to Rhodes at the end of June to rest and refit. Isokrates was exhausted. Aristomachos, too, was aching and weary: he had conscientiously stayed with his ship every night, and eaten the same rough fare as the men. It had finally won him the respect of the oarcrew, but made him very eager to get home to his own house. When *Atalanta* docked he issued a half-hearted invitation to Isokrates to come to dinner, but was relieved when it was declined: everyone on the ship was sick of the company of everyone else.

Isokrates saw to the needs of the ship, then walked back to his lodgings at Atta's. He had seen his landlady only briefly since he was wounded, and arriving back at the house he found to his dismay that the place seemed even smaller and smellier than he remembered it. It was quiet, for once, though: Atta and her children were eating, a serious business for all of them.

'Oh!' exclaimed Atta, when he appeared at the door. 'I didn't cook for you.'

Isokrates hadn't expected her to, and had brought a handful of barley cakes with him, leftover from the ship's stores; he held them up silently. At once Atta's two children began whining that they wanted some barley cake too: their meal must have been even scantier than usual. Atta told them to be quiet.

'But Isokrates *always* gives me some barley cake!' cried little Leuke.

''Cause you're a greedy little beggar!' Atta snarled, and clouted the girl, which made her wail.

Isokrates thought of walking out again. Instead, he handed two of the cakes to Atta – he had more than enough, and he was heartily sick of them anyway.

'May the gods bless you!' Atta cried, breaking one cake and giving each child a half, keeping the other one for herself. The whole family fell silent again, the children greedily stuffing the coarse bread into their mouths, the mother savouring each crumb.

Isokrates sat down wearily. 'What's the news, Atta?' he asked, and took a slow mouthful of his own cake.

Atta swallowed and exclaimed, 'Oh, all the talk is of that poor Syrian queen!'

'Laodike? Poor?'

'No, no! *She* seems as heartless and cruel as a she-wolf! I mean the other one – Berenike, Ptolemy's daughter. She's dead, she and her little son and all her servants!'

Isokrates nearly dropped his barley cake. 'What?'

'The wicked queen sent men to kill her, just as soon as her husband was dead – and they say that she had something to do with *that* as well, though nobody can prove it! Queen Berenike was at Antioch, you see, only not right in the city, but in her summer house in this garden village outside the city, where there's a shrine to our holy Lord Apollo. Daphne, the place is called: everyone's talking about what happened in Daphne. Laodike sent some ships full of her own soldiers, wicked mercenaries and pirates, and they beached their ships and marched inland and surprised the village. Queen Berenike's people fought – they say the queen herself fought, at the end, with a sword she took from her bodyguards! – but they killed her, and her little boy with her.'

'Herakles!' Isokrates had no particular feelings about Queen Berenike – but still, it was a brutal act. Laodike might have ensured that her rival's child would never inherit the diadem, but at a terrible cost. There would be no half measures now, no pauses for negotiations. Ptolemy would press the war to the hilt – and Seleukos would have few allies.

'It was a most unholy murder!' Atta said, with relish. 'The gods will avenge it. She was murdered, poor queen, before the very eyes of Apollo!'

'I think Berenike's brother will be the one to avenge it,' said Isokrates.

'Yes, but the gods will *help* him,' Atta replied. 'Because Apollo is the patron of the house of Seleukos, isn't he? But he won't favour them now, after that insult to his holy shrine.'

'Nobody much will favour them now,' said Isokrates. He swallowed his barley cake and suppressed the urge to run over to Aristomachos's house to ask the trierarch what he thought of the news. From Rhodes' point of view, Berenike dead made very little difference from Berenike fled: Berenike's brother would still go to war. He doubted very much that Rhodes would join him, though. Condolences and sympathy would be enough to keep Ptolemy friendly, so why should Rhodes give him blood and ships as well? – particularly when the end result would be an increase of Egyptian power in the Aegean. No, neutrality was a much better strategy. He did wonder, though, about the 'mercenaries and pirates' who'd committed the murder. It took no leap of the imagination to include Andronikos in their number. What would the pirate do now?

Not, he suspected, go cheerfully back to Ephesus to see if his employer had another little job for him. It would be as clear to Andronikos as it was to Isokrates that the new king Seleukos was likely to disown the murder in order to pacify popular opinion: *It was my mother's doing, not mine. Women! Passionate and irrational creatures, what can a man do?* The men who'd obeyed the queen's orders would be lucky if the king did no more than banish them.

On the other hand, why would Andronikos want to go back to Ephesus? Laodike had provided him with a ship, weapons, and men. He could take up his old trade again.

Isokrates was disconcerted by the thrill that this possibility gave him. Andronikos the mercenary of the queen could not be touched; Andronikos the pirate was fair game – and the thought of hunting him down made all Isokrates's weariness vanish. How was it that hatred for a man he'd met only twice had such power to inspire him?

Because the man had raped Dionysia, of course. She'd been glad to think he'd harm no more innocents, but he was still free, and still shedding blood.

Isokrates dusted barley off his fingers. 'I'm going to get some sleep,' he told Atta.

'You want me to take those things of yours to be laundered?' she asked hopefully. 'I mended that other tunic, by the way. It's in your room.'

'Which other tunic?'

'Why, your old officer's tunic. Your shipmate Polydoros brought it round while you were ill. Oh, that must have been a foul wound, it's no wonder you were so ill! I had to soak and bleach it *three times* before the stain faded! It had a nasty rip in the back, too, but I stitched it up.'

Isokrates stared in surprised pleasure. Of course, *Aristomachos* thought it had been thrown out; *he* would throw damaged clothes out – but other, less wealthy, shipmates had a better appreciation of the value of fine linen. Now Isokrates would have *two* officer's tunics, one for everyday, and one for formal occasions! Even after he'd paid Atta for her efforts, it would be like getting half a month's wages as a bonus. He felt a rare stab of gratitude toward his landlady.

'Thank you!' he said warmly.

In the marketplace next morning he found that a special meeting of the Assembly had been called. It seemed that ambassadors from Ptolemy and from Seleukos had arrived while *Atalanta* was cruising. Both were seeking Rhodian support.

Pleased that he'd arrived just in time, Isokrates made his way to the theatre on the slope of the acropolis. For an Assembly to be valid, at least five thousand citizens had to be present – but even before he entered the theatre, Isokrates could tell that there would be no problem reaching the quorum. He stepped through the entry arch to find that more than twice that number were already in place: every seat was taken, even those at the top of the rickety bleachers. In the hot sun the massed citizens – all men aged eighteen and above – sweated, gulped down water from the busy water-sellers, and fanned themselves with hats. Farmers and goatherds, in from the country for the day, hoiked off the right sides of their best tunics with calloused thumbs, so as to let in some cooler air; barefoot sailors and dockworkers simply stripped off, and the richer citizens in their fine linen gazed at them enviously. The mood, however, was sober. Usually Assemblies were high-spirited affairs, with plenty of factional joking and jeering – but today the Rhodian people had gathered solemnly to listen to calls to war.

Isokrates, still tired, was not confident of his ability to stand for a couple of hours in the hot sun, and looked for a place in the shade. He was not the only one doing so, however, and all the places were taken. He was ready to give up when an acquaintance from a previous ship noticed him and beckoned from the shadow of an entry arch.

'Heard you'd been wounded,' said the acquaintance. He moved aside, giving Isokrates his own place.

Isokrates moved gratefully out of the sunlight and leaned a shoulder against the wall. 'Thanks.'

'What happened?'

Isokrates grimaced. 'Shot in the back while running away, if you want the truth. A friend's son is horrified by my cowardice. But I was ambushed by a gang of pirates, and didn't have much choice.'

The other man met his eyes. 'I heard you were shot on the orders of Queen Laodike.'

Isokrates looked away, then forced himself to look back into the curious gaze. He had conscientiously repeated the official line that the

183

queen wasn't responsible: the argument that an accusation would hurt Rhodes was convincing. The lie was easier to stomach now that he had hopes of Andronikos. 'Not on her orders,' he said firmly. 'By a pirate she'd hired as a mercenary, while I was on my way back from her house. He had a grudge: I'd sunk his ship.'

The acquaintance and his friends snorted appreciatively. They were ready to ask more, but the city's herald sounded the trumpet to signal that the assembly was about to begin. The ambassadors processed on to the stage, each carrying his herald's staff and escorted by a Rhodian president.

Both ambassadors were tall, well-dressed men with good loud voices; both made much of the friendly feelings their respective masters had towards Rhodes, and the various favours the kings had conferred upon the island. Ptolemy's man had the easier job: all he had to do to gain sympathy was describe the murder of Queen Berenike and her little son. He did so forcefully, with tears and the gestures of a tragic actor, and was rewarded with groans of pity and indignation. He finished with a denunciation of Queen Laodike and an appeal to the Rhodians to 'honour your old alliance and help your steadfast friend King Ptolemy to put an end to her murderous reign!'

Seleukos's ambassador wisely declined to compete for Rhodian sympathy. He briefly justified the murder as a mother's attempt to protect her children from the plots of a usurper – then appealed directly to fear. Egypt already controlled Lycia and Pamphylia, he pointed out; already Ptolemy dominated the Island League. How long, he asked, would Rhodian independence last, if the king of Egypt had no rival in the Aegean?

Some wit up in the bleachers yelled, 'When did Antigonos die?', which brought a chorus of appreciative jeers and left the ambassador flustered. The king of Macedon was also interested in control of the Aegean, and had long been a more serious rival to Ptolemy's ambitions there than the Syrians.

Apart from that one interruption, the audience listened to the speech in silence. Ptolemy's ambassador had received a round of sympathetic applause when he finished speaking; Seleukos's got a bare spattering.

The speeches lasted until nearly noon. When the ambassadors finished, the Rhodian presidents announced that the vote on how to respond would take place the following day, after the Council had met to draw up concrete proposals for the People's consideration. The People applauded.

Isokrates made his way down from the theatre with his acquaintance, then – reluctant to talk about his wound – stopped with the excuse of wanting a drink of water from the fountain in the plaza outside. There was a long queue, and his companions left him. He was waiting there patiently when his name was called. He looked round to see Aristomachos waving at him.

He went over. The trierarch was accompanied by Nikagoras and by Nikagoras's father, a

Council member named Nikolaos. 'What did you make of that, then?' asked Aristomachos.

Isokrates shrugged. 'I didn't hear anything worth fighting for.'

Aristomachos snorted. 'Me neither. But watch out! Apparently Stratokles wants to talk to you: he hopes you'll testify about your reception by Queen Laodike. He thinks it might help his cause.'

Isokrates frowned, trying to remember who Stratokles was ... oh, yes, a councillor, from Lindos in the south of the island. 'He in Ptolemy's pay?'

Aristomachos laughed and exchanged a look with Nikolaos.

'If I answered that, I would have to speak ill of a fellow-councillor,' Nikolaos said, smiling.

'I would've thought you'd be happy to testify against the queen,' said Nikagoras, with a touch of sullenness. 'She tried to have you killed! Are you just going to, to *slavishly* accept that?'

Isokrates regarded him a moment. 'A private quarrel is no grounds for war. If I thought that, I'd be as bad as Antiochos! Whatever I may have suffered last month, it's a scratch compared to the mauling we'd get from King Seleukos even if we won. If we can go after Andronikos of Phalassarna now, I'll be content.'

'So you think we should just roll over and let the kings do what they want?'

'No!' Isokrates said in exasperation. 'I'm saying we shouldn't fight unless it's *worth it*. We don't have anything at stake here: King Seleukos isn't threatening our trade or our freedom, and

Ptolemy won't turn into an enemy if we stay neutral. Berenike was Ptolemy's sister: let him avenge her.'

'Well said!' exclaimed Nikolaos. Nikagoras glowered, and his father slapped him on the shoulder. 'We don't live in the age of heroes, my boy, and you can't have a glorious single combat when you need a hundred and twenty oarsmen to move your blessed ship!' He turned back to Isokrates. 'Come with us!' he said cheerfully. 'We're having a quick meal before the Council meeting; it's at the Council House, and I'll introduce you to Stratokles. You can tell him what you just told us: that'll shut him up!'

Nine

Isokrates was not eager to go along to the Council House and meet Stratokles, but went anyway, so as not to offend. The pro-Ptolemy councillor, however, turned out to be nothing to worry about: when he understood that Isokrates wouldn't help him, he did no more than hurry off to canvass support from somebody else.

The 'quick meal' Nikolaos had promised consisted of bread and freshly grilled lamb, which the councillors ate standing in the portico adjoining the Council House, politicking furiously all the while. Isokrates listened intently, relishing the sense of being in the thick of things. He enjoyed the food, too: he seldom had the chance to eat so much meat. He was still eating and listening to the arguments when Aristomachos clapped him on the shoulder. 'Come along!' ordered the trierarch. 'There's a concert to keep the ambassadors amused during the afternoon, and the Milesian girl is performing.'

Isokrates swallowed hastily. 'I thought she was going to give a free concert during a festival?'

'Apparently she did that while we were away. The city will be *paying* her for this one.'

Isokrates grinned with pleasure: Dionysia's free concert must have been a success! He accompanied Aristomachos eagerly.

His enthusiasm was only slightly dented when Nikagoras joined them. It was natural that the young man should join his uncle, particularly since his father was attending the Council meeting. Nikagoras, however, seemed far less tolerant of Isokrates' presence: all the way to the concert hall he tried to kill with glares.

Most of the benches were occupied when they arrived, but Aristomachos had reserved seats in the third row, and one of his slaves was sitting guard on an array of cushions.

Shortly after they'd taken their seats, the two embassies came in – not just the ambassadors this time, but the whole of the two diplomatic entourages, each accompanied by its Rhodian hosts. The Ptolemaic group were escorted to the front two rows on the centre right, the Seleucids to the corresponding seats on the centre left, with the Rhodian hosts acting as a buffer in the middle.

The Seleucid embassy happened to be in front of the seats Aristomachos had reserved, and as they took their places Isokrates recognized the plump 'royal kinsman' Hyperides, who'd escorted him to the queen's house in Ephesus. Hyperides, however, was too busy talking to his neighbour to notice anyone behind him, and Isokrates scrunched backward into his seat, clenching his teeth. He glanced at Nikagoras, who was seated almost directly behind the fop, but the young bow-officer apparently hadn't recognized the man. They'd met only briefly, after all.

There was a drumroll, and a chorus filed into the sunken orchestra just in front of the stage; musicians appeared, playing the kithara and the aulos, and the first number began, a lively song and dance welcoming unspecified guests to 'the flowered isle, the bride of the Sun above us, lovely Rhodes!'

Dionysia performed next. She came on to the stage, smiling and beautiful in a long chiton of patterned linen under a cloak of sheer silk, carrying a kithara; she struck a chord, then began to sing a hymn to the Sun. Isokrates had heard her sing before, so the voice – pure, supple and strong – was no surprise; what stunned was the skill of her playing. The strings rippled and rang under her long fingers, now supporting her song, now dancing about it, now bold and rhythmic, now sweet and plaintive. Her face was turned outward toward the audience, but her attention was entirely fixed upon the music. Isokrates held his breath listening. He had believed that she was gifted, but his belief had been based on little more than faith: now his faith was justified.

At the end of the song the audience applauded loudly. Hyperides, however, did not applaud; instead, he turned to his neighbour and said in a loud whisper, 'That's King Antiochos's old whore Dionysia! What's she doing here? She's supposed to be in Alexandria!'

At this Nikagoras sat up straight and glared indignantly. 'She's no whore!' he declared loudly.

The fop looked round and sneered. 'Is that what you think here on Rhodes?'

The ambassador, in the front row, glanced back with an anxious frown and made a hushing gesture. On stage Dionysia had begun to play again.

The concert continued with a variety of different pieces, presumably assembled in the embassies' honour out of anything appropriate which the performers already knew. There was a choral hymn to Apollo (patron of the house of Seleukos) and a dance in honour of Dionysos (patron of the house of Ptolemy). There was a lively instrumental trio of aulos, kithara and drums, and an aria from a tragedy. Dionysia's singing, however, stood out above the other acts like mountain peaks above a forest. The songs she had chosen were bits of empty flattery – a song praising the first Antiochos for his defeat of the Galatians; another in praise of the Nile – but her skill gave them dignity and made them wonderful. When the concert finished the audience called for her, improperly by name – 'Dionysia! Dionysia of Miletos, Dionysia the kitharist!' – and when she yielded and came back on stage, flushed and smiling, the applause was thunderous.

Hyperides, however, sat back with his arms crossed. Nikagoras gave him a filthy look and leaned forward so that his clapping hands brushed the other's long hair. The Syrian clapped a hand protectively to his scalp and looked round angrily; Nikagoras raised his eyebrows in open challenge.

'You think that's worth cheering for?' snarled Hyperides, as the noise died down. 'A Milesian slut with a kithara? She was big news in Antioch *years* ago. Doesn't Rhodes have anything *fresh*?'

'Lady Dionysia is no slut!' said Nikagoras hotly.

'She's the old king's whore; he got tired of her and she went off looking for lovers new. I'd heard she went to Alexan—'

'He *never* got tired of her!' replied Nikagoras. 'She ran off to Alexandria to warn King Ptolemy against your Queen Laodike!'

Hyperides looked more sharply at Nikagoras, then glanced along the row and saw Isokrates. He froze.

Isokrates gave him a sour smile. On stage Dionysia launched into her encore:

'For the Sun bears toil in every day...'

The second line was swallowed up by Rhodian cheers, and the rest of the song was accompanied by rhythmic stamps as the audience mimicked the beat of oars.

When the encore finished, Hyperides shot to his feet and edged along to whisper to the ambassador under cover of the applause. Both men looked round at Isokrates, the fop scowling and the ambassador curious. Isokrates groaned.

'What's going on?' whispered Aristomachos.

'That's the man who fetched me to the queen's house.'

'Ah!' The trierarch contemplated the fop with satisfaction. 'Good.'

Isokrates looked at his commander more closely. 'You planned this?'

Aristomachos shrugged. 'Planned what? Yes, all right, I hoped if we sat near the Syrians we could strike up a conversation and maybe learn something. But that's a hope, eh? not a plan.'

As the applause at last died down and people began to leave the hall, the Seleucid ambassador stood, looked at Isokrates, and beckoned hopefully. Isokrates got reluctantly to his feet and came over; Aristomachos came as well, with Nikagoras trailing after him.

'Good health,' said the ambassador, eyeing their party uncertainly. 'Hyperides tells me that you are the Rhodian officer who was so unfortunately injured by a mercenary in the employ of the Queen Mother Laodike.'

Hyperides looked surprised at this description of what he'd said. Isokrates merely nodded. Aristomachos, however, gave the ambassador a broad smile and said, 'Indeed, and I'm his trierarch. Aristomachos, son of Anaxippos. We've been wondering, Ambassador, if you could tell us what's become of that murderous pirate?'

The ambassador blinked, but forged ahead with what was evidently a prepared speech. 'We hope you understand that the queen never countenanced any such attack. Now that she appreciates what sort of man she'd hired, she has dismissed him from her service.'

Nikagoras began to protest; his uncle shot him a quelling look and said, 'Well, Ambassador, that's good to hear.'

'King Seleukos was dismayed when he discovered that one of his mother's hired men had attacked a Rhodian naval officer,' the ambassador continued. 'As I told your Assembly this morning, he values the friendship of the

Rhodians. He instructed me to find the injured officer and offer him compensation. I would have done so before now, but nobody had made a note of the name.'

'You should have asked at the naval board,' said Aristomachos helpfully. 'Everyone there knew about it. So, Isokrates! The king's offering you compensation!'

Isokrates, stiff with outrage, couldn't think what to say. He had refrained from accusing the queen because he'd believed it was best for Rhodes – and now everyone who heard about the matter would believe he'd been bought off!

'King Seleukos greatly regrets...' began the ambassador.

'I don't take bribes,' Isokrates said savagely. 'I swear by the Sun, I want none of the king's money!'

At this Hyperides stared in outrage, and the ambassador winced.

'You've offended him,' Aristomachos tactfully explained to the ambassador. 'You're offering him money for what he was doing out of honest goodwill. We Rhodians value the king's friendship as much as he values ours. May that friendship never be damaged by rash accusations! We're well aware that the pirate had a private grudge, and we've said as much to everyone who asked about it.'

The ambassador smiled in relief.

'I tell you what we would like, though,' Aristomachos continued, 'and that's news of what became of the pirate. Where he is, what sort of ship he has, how many men and so on. We don't like to leave notorious Cretan pirates floating loose about the shipping lanes, creating a hazard to trade. I'm sure you feel the same.'

'Ah.' The ambassador looked embarrassed. 'I fear I don't know what happened to the pirate. I take your point, however, and I will make inquiries at once.'

'Thank you.' Aristomachos gave him another broad smile. 'His name's Andronikos of Phalassarna; when last heard of, he had command of an akatos called the *Nea*. He'd recovered thirty-one of his own crew – the queen apparently gave him a talent of silver to ransom them.'

Embarrassment was joined on the ambassador's face by annoyance.

'She'd given him a crew for the *Nea* as well,' Aristomachos continued cheerfully. 'I don't know whether he's still got them, or whether they went back to the queen.'

'I'll make inquiries,' said the ambassador again, and glanced briefly but tellingly at Hyperides.

'Good, good! If you hear anything, you can send a note to my house. It's near the marketplace; anyone can point it out. You want to make a note of our names this time? Aristomachos son of Anaxippos, and Isokrates son of Kritagoras, of the trihemiolia *Atalanta*.'

'Lady!' interrupted Nikagoras in delight. Isokrates glanced round and saw that Dionysia had descended from the stage and come over. She was still carrying her kithara, cradling the instrument against one silk-draped hip: she might have posed for the lyric Muse, except for the anxious

195

expression on her face.

'Lady, good health!' exclaimed Aristomachos.

'Good health!' she replied nervously. Her eyes quickly skimmed the company and stopped on Isokrates. 'I'm very glad to see that you've recovered, helmsman.'

Isokrates inclined his head, tongue-tied. After the cold letter he'd sent her, he'd expected her to dislike him, but instead she simply seemed nervous.

'You were the best thing in the concert,' Nikagoras told her eagerly.

The ambassador was frowning. 'Dionysia, daughter of Kleisthenes. We were surprised to see you here in Rhodes. We'd heard you went to Alexandria.'

'I did,' Dionysia replied simply, meeting his eyes. 'I came back to Rhodes afterward. Sir, please excuse me. I didn't intend to intrude; I just wanted to assure myself that the helmsman had recovered from his injuries. As you've no doubt heard, his ship rescued me from pirates.'

The ambassador's lip curled. 'Back from Alexandria so soon? What, Ptolemy didn't reward you for your treachery?'

'He'd heard my news already,' she answered evenly. 'Sir, please believe I never meant any harm to King Antiochos. I'd hoped that Ptolemy could persuade him where I'd failed – and I was afraid of Laodike, who'd...'

'Treacherous slut!' broke in Hyperides.

'How dare *you* talk about treachery!' exclaimed Nikagoras at once. 'You and your treacherous bitch-faced mistress have...'

'That's enough!' snapped Aristomachos, grabbing his nephew's shoulder and shaking it hard. He turned toward the ambassador with a false smile. 'Excuse my nephew, sir. Young men, pretty girls...'

'He is excused.' The ambassador was frowning at Dionysia. 'Ptolemy already *knew*?'

'I was delayed, sir, as you must have heard. Someone else reached Alexandria before I did. I don't know who.'

The ambassador thought about that a moment, then grimaced. 'It could have been anyone! The business was notorious within days.' He was silent another moment, gazing coldly at Dionysia. 'The king missed you, you know. He wanted to know where you'd gone. When he was told you'd taken ship for Egypt he refused to believe it. He said that others might be faithless, but not you.'

Dionysia flinched.

'When he was dying – ill and in pain – he kept asking for you to come and sing to him.'

She turned her face away. 'I didn't mean him any harm!'

'Then I'd hate to see how much harm you caused when you meant to!' The ambassador glowered at her a moment longer, then looked away. 'Well. Trierarch, helmsman: I wish you joy! and I will send to you if I learn anything about the pirate.'

He gathered his entourage about him and departed, one of the last of the concert-goers. Hyperides sneered over his shoulder a couple of times as he walked off; Nikagoras looked daggers back.

Dionysia pulled a fold of her cloak over her head and began to walk back toward the stage. Something about the way she held herself reminded Isokrates of Agido. He ran after her and caught her arm, and she turned to him with eyes full of tears.

'Don't listen!' he told her vehemently. 'That man is a hypocrite and a bully!'

She stared in confusion.

'He just tried to bribe me, and he was reproaching you for something that was in no way your fault! He heard you when you started to say Laodike had threatened you, you know, and he ignored it. He knew perfectly well she had; he knew that if you'd stayed at court, you'd be dead by now – but he wasn't going to admit it, particularly with one of the queen's creatures at his elbow. Do you think *he* would have stayed with the king, if it was *his* life that was threatened?'

She was silent a moment. 'No. But it's different.'

'Why? The ambassador was one of Antiochos's friends, wasn't he? He owed the king as much loyalty as you did – but he's now telling lies to protect his lord's murderess.'

'No! To protect his *new* king...'

'Perhaps so, but it still gives him no right to accuse you! And you did *not* harm the king. If Antiochos had listened to you he would never have gone to Ephesus and he'd be alive now: that's true, and you know it.'

Dionysia drew a deep breath, meeting his eyes:

the contact felt so intimate that Isokrates dropped her arm and took a step back. He didn't drop his insistence, though. 'You ran away because you couldn't trust King Antiochos even to protect your *life*. How is that your fault, and not his?'

Nikagoras had thrust forward, scowling furiously. 'You're very bold now!' he sneered angrily. 'No one would guess that you've *also* been telling lies to protect the queen!'

'Nephew, don't be stupid!' snapped Aristomachos. 'He's been telling lies to protect *Rhodes*, and if you don't believe me, talk to your father about it.'

Dionysia looked sharply at the trierarch. 'This bribe – it was to keep quiet about how the queen tried to have him murdered?'

'Well, attempted murder of an allied officer is a bit of an embarrassment when you're visiting the allies looking for support,' said Aristomachos sourly. 'And, to tell the truth, hiring a pirate is nearly as bad. Everybody knows we Rhodians hate pirates. Naturally the ambassador had instructions to try to hush things up.' He snorted in amusement. 'It was so embarrassing, in fact, that as soon as he realized it wasn't current gossip he didn't even want to ask about it, in case that drew attention to the matter! He must be thanking the gods that we're so reasonable. But you should've let him bribe you, Isokrates! Why not collect a couple of thousand for doing what you were doing anyway?'

'I'm not for sale,' Isokrates replied proudly.

Aristomachos grinned. 'I hope your pride gives

you some satisfaction. It costs you enough.'

Dionysia was frowning. 'Does Hyperides *know* you're going to keep quiet anyway?'

'What, you think he'd try murder if he thought bribery had failed?' asked Aristomachos. 'Zeus! What a fine upstanding young man. Never fear: he knows we're eager to keep the new king sweet.'

'I wouldn't be scared of that Hyperides anyway,' said Nikagoras, with contempt. 'He's soft and fat.'

Dionysia shook her head. 'He wouldn't kill a man *himself*. He'd hire people. You wouldn't know who they were, or how to guard yourself.'

'Who is he, anyway?' asked Aristomachos.

'A kinsman of Laodike,' Dionysia replied. 'Son of a niece, I think. I don't know him well. I never met any of her people until we went to Ephesus. The thing I do know, though, is that he's part of her circle, and that all his hopes depend on her. If he thought you were going to embarrass her, he *would* try to silence you.'

Isokrates stared in disbelief. 'Why would he bother? I can see why the *ambassador* cares, but Laodike's people? If she's not embarrassed about murdering a queen, why should she care about killing a helmsman?'

Dionysia shook her head again. 'You don't know courts, do you? A true courtier is more interested in his position *inside* the court than in anything that happens *outside* it. Killing you would be a way for Hyperides to demonstrate his devotion to the queen.'

Isokrates frowned, trying to fathom that, then

shrugged it off. 'Well, he knows I'm no threat, so don't worry.'

There was a moment of silence. Dionysia shifted her kithara. 'Well. They're waiting for me backstage. I ... I simply wanted to assure myself that you'd recovered.'

'I'm fine. I ... I enjoyed the concert.'

That brought the rare shy smile. 'Did you?'

His heart suddenly began beating very hard. She liked him. It wasn't just gratitude and duty: she *liked* him. It didn't change the fact that he could only make her miserable – but, oh, it was sweet!

'You were wonderful!' Nikagoras broke in.

Dionysia gave him a glance of unmistakable irritation, but thanked him dutifully. 'I have another concert in three days' time,' she told them, 'at the feast of Athena of the City.'

'I'll be there!' Nikagoras promised at once.

'If we're still in Rhodes then,' his uncle said severely. 'We might not be.'

Isokrates answered Dionysia's questioning look. 'Pirate-hunting. Wish us luck.' Moved by a sudden impulse he added, 'We hope that now we can go after Andronikos again, and finish him once and for all!' Then he cringed inwardly: the boast was worthy of Nikagoras.

'Ah. Good luck!' Then she smiled. 'Well, if you're still in Rhodes for Athena's festival, I'll get you tickets.'

'If we're here, I'll be happy to pay for my ticket,' Isokrates replied. 'I know I'll enjoy it. You must have managed to get membership of that Guild, the Dionysiac Artists, if you're handing out tickets for concerts.'

She smiled again, her eyes shining. 'Yes. It's what my father always dreamed of, and now I've done it.' She looked down. 'Of course, he always thought *he* would be my guardian – I have to have a male guardian, of course. Hagemon has kindly agreed to stand for me – but the name on the register is mine, and I paid the membership dues myself.'

The thought of Hagemon as her guardian gave him a stab of jealousy, but he dutifully said, 'I'm very glad.'

'I owe it to you,' she said vehemently. 'That is, I owe it to Rhodes, and the kindness I've met here – but you're the one who persuaded me to come here.'

'You owe it to the Muses,' Isokrates replied. 'They're the ones who gave you the gift of music.'

Dionysia's sour-faced maid hurried over from somewhere backstage and whispered to her mistress. Dionysia sighed. 'They're waiting for me,' she said. 'I must go. I'm very glad you're recovered, helmsman – and I wish you joy and good luck, all of you.' She retreated; the maid shot Isokrates a look of deep misgiving as they went through the stage door.

Aristomachos, Isokrates and Nikagoras made their own way out of the now-empty concert hall. Nikagoras kept shooting puzzled looks at Isokrates, and when they started along the street outside he asked abruptly, 'Are you in love with her or not?'

'Are you?'

Nikagoras sighed deeply. 'Oh, yes!' Another glance of puzzled resentment. '*I* certainly would not tell her how "very glad" I am that she's got another man as her guardian!'

'You can't marry her,' Aristomachos told his nephew instantly. 'Your father betrothed you to Neophron's daughter Hipparchia.'

Nikagoras gave his uncle an irritated look. 'So?'

'The Milesian made it very clear that she wants to be *respectable*. Respectable means *marriage*, boy, and you can't offer it. And even if she'd accept concubinage, you're in no position to keep her, not without any money except your allowance and a bow-officer's pay. What do you think you look like to a woman who was the kept mistress of the King of All Asia? You're being *stupid*!'

'If she *liked* me...'

'I'll tell you something you've already spotted: the one she likes is Isokrates – and he isn't pushing it.'

Isokrates set his teeth. 'If I did push it, I'd ruin her. You think she'd keep Hagemon's patronage if she took up with me?'

Nikagoras was taken aback. 'No, but...'

Isokrates met his eyes. 'You know I don't even have a house: you've thrown it in my face. I can't offer her marriage. Probably Dionysia's too intelligent to choose me *or* you, but I'm not praying to Aphrodite for her to be stupid. Membership of the Dionysiac Artists means that she's beginning to succeed in what she wants to do – and she's got the talent; you know she has!

Should I treat her like an enemy ship? Ram her and sink her? May the gods destroy me if I do that to anyone who claims me as a friend!'

Aristomachos sucked his teeth. 'You do too have a house. Your father would cut his throat if that meant you'd take it.'

'I have no inheritance – and even if I did, it wouldn't be enough to compensate her for what I'd take from her.'

Nikagoras had gone a dull red and walked several paces staring at his feet. 'You don't really love her,' he declared, suddenly looking up again. 'If you did, you wouldn't be so *logical* about it.'

'So it's only real love if you don't care what happens to your loved one?' Aristomachos asked in amusement. 'Boy, the difference between you and Isokrates is that he's older and has a lot more experience of what things cost. You sail along believing that things are somehow all going to turn out for the best: he knows that often they get buggered up completely.' He turned his shrewd gaze back to Isokrates. 'I suppose you're right. A pity, but you're right.'

'I know I'm right,' Isokrates said soberly.

Ten

Isokrates was at home next morning when Atta knocked on the door, then opened it, looking anxious. 'There's a foreigner here to see you,' she informed him.

He'd been mending his bed. The rope cradle that supported the mattress had become so frayed that it was on the point of breaking altogether, and he'd tipped the frame up against the wall to restring it. The rope was old and fragile, and the job was taking a long time. He'd been sitting on the dusty bit of floor which had been under the bed, and he was filthy and covered with bits of straw from the mattress; his tunic was the old officer's tunic, which had turned out to be so stained that he'd reluctantly decided it was no use for anything except messy jobs. He was in no state to receive visitors. He swore, tried to brush some of the muck off, then gave up and went to see who it was and what they wanted.

It was Hyperides. The Syrian was standing outside Atta's front door, draped in a short cloak of gorgeous crimson silk, hand resting on a gold sword-hilt; he was looking around at the grubby neighbourhood in disgust. Atta's children stood in the doorway, gaping at him in wonder.

'Herakles!' exclaimed Hyperides, when Isokrates appeared. 'You *do* live in this dung-heap!'

Isokrates had been hot with embarrassment, but at these words his feelings changed to cold anger. 'What do you want?' he asked sharply.

Hyperides looked down his nose. 'To talk to you, Rhodian. I was going to suggest that we go into the house so we could do so privately, but I've thought better of it. Is there anywhere *clean* available?'

Isokrates was strongly tempted to tell him to take himself to Hades – but there was a chance that the Syrian had come to deliver information. 'We can walk,' he said shortly. He set out without even pausing to put on his sandals.

He led the Syrian down the narrow alley to the harbourside: the buildings there were warehouses, and the stones along the breakwater were unoccupied. It was a bright summer day, already hot, and the water before them sparkled in the sun. To their right the head of the Colossus could be seen above the protecting seawall; to their left frowned the high wall of the naval shipyards, which foreigners like Hyperides were forbidden to enter. A quadrireme was floating idly in the centre of the harbour, her oars shipped and mast unstepped. A small boat was rowing around her, presumably looking for the source of some problem in her handling.

Hyperides sneered at the scene. 'What sort of ship is that, then?'

'Quadrireme.'

'Oh, of course! One of your famous Rhodian quadriremes. It has what, half as many men as a *real* warship? Why do you people use them, anyway? Nobody else does.'

'We use them because they're faster and more manoeuvrable than quinqueremes, but require only two thirds of the crew,' Isokrates replied evenly.

'Ah, I see! You use them because you don't have the manpower for real ships. Well, this *is* only a *little* island, isn't it?'

Rhodes was in fact a *large* island, with territories elsewhere. That might not seem much to a Syrian, but Isokrates had no doubt that Hyperides was at least aware of it. Certainly he knew the reputation of the Rhodian navy. He gazed at the fop in silence until the sneer wavered, then asked quietly, 'Did you come here to say something, or only to provoke me?'

Hyperides snorted, adjusted his crimson cloak with a jerk, and rested one plump hand on the hilt of his expensive sword. 'Your trierarch implied yesterday that you had refrained from slandering Queen Laodike. I wanted to check that that was true.'

'I have refrained from telling the truth about my visit to her, yes.'

'Why? Is somebody else paying you?'

'I don't sell my loyalty or my silence! I've kept quiet because a quarrel with King Seleukos wouldn't serve Rhodes. Is that really all you came for?'

The Syrian looked him up and down – then grimaced. 'I don't believe you. How would a peasant who lives in a dung-heap get to be so proud?'

Isokrates spat deliberately on to the breast of that crimson cloak, turned on his heel and began to walk off. Hyperides swore and sprang after him; Isokrates whirled and kicked. Barefoot as he was, the blow wasn't what it might have been, but it had the force of anger behind it, and it landed squarely on the other man's knee. Hyperides shrieked and fell to the ground. The drawn sword in his hand rang out against the stone.

Isokrates moved without thinking: a leap forward and a quick hard stamp on the Syrian's hand, provoking another shriek, then a swift grab to scoop up the sword. Hyperides yelled again, snatching his hand away and gazing up in terror. Isokrates hefted the sword, the weight and balance of it unfamiliar in his hand. It was a *kopis,* the curved, single-edged cutlass favoured by infantry. He'd trained with a spear, but not this awkward thing.

He looked down at the Syrian nobleman, sprawled there in his crimson silk. 'You pathetic blustering idiot,' he said in contempt – and walked off.

He was back at Atta's house before he started to think. Whatever Hyperides had wanted before, what he would want now was revenge – and it would be very easy for him to get it. He was part of a diplomatic mission, and Isokrates had knocked him down and taken his sword. It would be only his word against Isokrates' that the sword had been drawn.

For a moment he was tempted to go to Aristomachos – but what could the trierarch do? A better option suggested itself. He tucked the sword into his belt and started off along the street at a run, aiming for the marketplace. Somebody there was sure to know where the Seleucid ambassador was staying.

The ambassador was lodged in the house of Admiral Agathostratos, who was one of his guest-friends. The prospect of appearing before the great commander barefoot in a filthy old tunic was excruciating, but, increasingly worried about what Hyperides might say, Isokrates forced himself to go to the house and knock upon the door.

The doorkeeper didn't want to let him in, but he insisted: he *must* see the ambassador; it was most urgent – in fact, an emergency. He presented the doorkeeper with Hyperides' sword, and asked the man to deliver it to the ambassador at once.

It did the trick: the doorkeeper returned swiftly, looking worried, and escorted him into the house.

The ambassador was sitting under a vine trellis in the courtyard, with his distinguished host beside him. The sword lay on a small table between them. As soon as Isokrates appeared, however, the ambassador leapt to his feet and demanded, 'What have you done to Hyperides son of Lysimachos?'

'Knocked him down,' Isokrates replied. 'He drew that on me.' He turned away from the Syrian, saluted the admiral and went on, 'Sir, I'm sorry to appear before you in this state, but this fellow Hyperides came to my house while I was busy with a messy repair, and I've had no chance to change.'

Admiral Agathostratos regarded him with a frown. 'You're saying he attacked you?'

'Not immediately, sir. When he arrived at the house he said he wanted to speak to me in private. When I agreed, though, he seemed determined to start a quarrel. He insulted me and Rhodes. Eventually I tried to walk off, and he drew the sword and came at me. I've come here, sir, because I'm afraid that he'll lie about what happened to get me into trouble.'

The admiral's frown grew. 'You claim to be a peaceable man, but that stain on your tunic wasn't made by wine.'

The admiral *would* recognize blood, even faded. Isokrates ducked his head. 'Yes, sir. This is the tunic I was wearing when I was shot. I ... I keep it for messy jobs now. I apologize.'

Agathostratos's face suddenly cleared. 'I remember you now! You're the officer who was almost killed by Queen Laodike's pirate.'

'Yes, sir. That was what Hyperides said he wanted to talk about.'

'Oh Zeus!' groaned the ambassador. 'Is he hurt?'

Isokrates gave him a cool look. 'No.'

'Is that all you can say?' the admiral asked his guest angrily. *'Is he hurt?* A member of your staff just drew a sword on an unarmed Rhodian officer!'

'We don't know that,' replied the ambassador testily. 'We've only heard one side of the story.'

Agathostratos slapped the table, making the sword jump. 'Diodoros, are you stupid – or do you just think I am?'

The ambassador stared at his host, taken aback.

'That young man has been looking for trouble ever since he set foot in my house; if he hadn't been a guest I would have shipped him home in a barrel! If *he* were ambassador, his speech to the Rhodians would have been "submit to the new king's will, or feel the new king's wrath!" – and the Assembly would vote to supply ships to Ptolemy, sure as the sun rises. What is he *doing* here?'

'I'm sorry,' mumbled the ambassador, 'I...'

There was a commotion at the entranceway, and then Hyperides came in. There was dirt all over his fine cloak, blood on one knee, and he was cradling his right hand. When he saw Isokrates he stopped short, his jaw dropping. Isokrates knew that he'd been right to go straight to the ambassador.

Hyperides recollected himself, flung out his uninjured arm in a dramatic gesture, and exclaimed, 'This man attacked me!'

'Other way round, by what he's just told us,' said Agathostratos briskly. 'Where is this confrontation supposed to have occurred? If you have witnesses, we'll ask them about it – but if you don't, I want to know what you were doing calling on the man in private.'

Hyperides was thrown completely off balance. He struggled a moment, then declared, 'I went to ask him about his meeting with the Queen. He...'

'So you agree that you sought him out?' asked the admiral. 'At his house?'

'Well – yes. He...'

'And you asked to speak in private?'

'Yes. He ... I was afraid he'd been repeating a slanderous story about Queen Laodike. I spoke to him, and he used insulting terms about her. When I remonstrated with him, he attacked...'

'Oh, be quiet!' broke in the ambassador suddenly. 'Do you have no sense at all? He'd already agreed to keep his mouth shut. You went after him and picked a quarrel – blatantly you did! – and you're lucky you came out of it alive. The man came here with *your sword* – and given that he had it and you didn't, he might as easily have come with your head!'

Hyperides gave him a look of astonished indignation. 'I am a royal kinsman! Is this how...'

'Yes, you're a royal kinsman!' the ambassador interrupted. 'And when I talk to the queen about this affair – as I'll have to, no doubt – I'll beg her not to let you risk your precious neck again. I'll also tell her that you went into the city to pick a fight with the Rhodian who offended her, and that the Rhodian – having previously kept quiet when he might have spoken – graciously spared your life when he might have taken it. You blithering idiot, if you *had* succeeded in killing the man, do you think I could've hushed it up?'

'I wasn't going to kill him,' Hyperides said sullenly. 'I was just going to give him a thrashing for his insolence.'

At this Agathostratos laughed harshly. 'But he

thrashed *you* instead!' He turned a broad smile on Isokrates. 'Well done!'

'This is outrageous!' exclaimed Hyperides angrily.

'Indeed!' replied the ambassador. 'We are on Rhodes, in case you hadn't noticed, trying to persuade the Rhodians to alliance – or, failing that, to neutrality – and a member of my entourage thinks he can thrash a Rhodian officer for insolence! By all the gods and heroes! Get out of my sight!'

Hyperides went crimson and stood where he was, quivering. His eyes went to the sword on the table.

Isokrates stepped over and picked it up, then decided that the precaution was unnecessary: Hyperides would never attack him in front of two witnesses. He extended the hilt to the Syrian. 'Take it back,' he said. 'I don't want it. The weapon I know best is the ram.'

There was an odd, almost dislocated moment as their eyes met: it was as though Hyperides saw him for the first time, and, for the first time, understood that he was dealing with someone who destroyed ships and drowned men for a living. He went pale, snatched the sword, and ran out of the courtyard.

'I apologize,' said the ambassador curtly. 'He is young and foolish. He was born inland, too, at Seleucia-on-the-Tigris: he is accustomed to dealing with barbarians, not free Greeks.' He inclined his head to the admiral. 'You know me better, I hope, than to believe I share any of his opinions.'

'The queen wished him on you?' asked Agathostratos.

'Yes – though I believe he volunteered for the mission,' replied the ambassador. He gave Isokrates a wary look and added, 'He said he wanted to see for himself whether Rhodes had any real grounds for its pride. He should have seen that it does, but he's been very reluctant to admit it.'

The admiral grunted. 'You said something about the helmsman agreeing to keep silent.'

The ambassador winced, but nodded. 'The king had authorized me to offer compensation to the Rhodian injured by the queen's mercenary. Hyperides pointed out the helmsman here to me yesterday, at a concert, and I offered him the money, but he called it a bribe and refused it. I must say, his refusal didn't offend *me*, since it was accompanied by expressions of goodwill toward King Seleukos, but Hyperides was very ready to be offended.' He turned a sober face to Isokrates and continued, 'Again, I am sorry – and I thank you, truly, for sparing the stupid boy. If he'd been injured, the queen would ... would have made my life very difficult.'

Isokrates inclined his head shortly, not trusting himself to say anything. He had no doubt that the ambassador would've preferred to believe Hyperides' version of events: it was Agathostratos who'd forced him to inquire more deeply. While the ambassador's exasperation with his subordinate was undoubtedly genuine, he'd only arrived at it because he'd been pushed.

He turned to the admiral. 'I won't take up any

more of your time, sir. Thank you for your help.'

Agathostratos smiled broadly. 'It was a pleasure, helmsman. I wish you joy!'

Isokrates saluted and went out.

At the meeting of the Assembly that afternoon, two proposals were put to the Rhodian people. The first, sponsored by Stratokles of Lindos, was to provide a force of twenty ships to assist King Ptolemy; the second, sponsored by Agathostratos, was to remain neutral and seek to maintain friendly relations with both kings. A third motion – to supply a force to King Seleukos – had apparently failed to win enough support to be carried forward from the Council to the Assembly. Isokrates voted for the second motion, and was relieved when it passed by a margin of two to one.

The following morning brought an invitation to lunch from Aristomachos. Isokrates arrived at the house in good time and was escorted into the dining room. The master of the house was still busy somewhere, but the boy Anaxippos came in looking bright and eager. 'Good health!' he said politely.

'Good health!' Isokrates replied. Anaxippos regarded him in expectant silence until he added, 'Is something the matter?'

'Papa says that one of the Syrians attacked you with a sword,' the boy said at once, 'but you took it away from him, even though you were unarmed!'

'Well, yes,' Isokrates said, embarrassed. He wondered who'd told Aristomachos about it. 'He

215

didn't really know how to fight.'

'How did you do it?' asked the boy eagerly.

'Kicked him on the knee.'

Anaxippos glanced round, then snatched a scroll off the sideboard and held it clutched like a dagger. 'Show me how?' he suggested hopefully.

Isokrates obligingly turned his back, then spun round, miming a kick to the boy's knee. Anaxippos gave a yell of delight and pretended to collapse on the dining room floor; Isokrates snatched the scroll.

'My turn now!' exclaimed Anaxippos, leaping to his feet again.

Isokrates' rush was feigned, but Anaxippos spun about with ferocious enthusiasm and delivered a real kick. Isokrates yelped and clapped both hands to his shin, dropping the scroll. The boy's face crumpled in dismay.

Aristomachos hurried in. 'Anaxippion! What are you doing?'

'He was showing me how he disarmed that Syrian,' explained Anaxippos.

The trierarch's face brightened. 'Yes? I was wondering that myself. Are you hurt?'

'Mortally wounded,' agreed Isokrates, rubbing the bruise. 'I kicked the Syrian's *knee*, Anaxippos!'

'It's because you're so tall,' replied Anaxippos shamefacedly. 'Your knee's too high up.'

Aristomachos laughed. 'You'll have to grow a bit before you try tackling any murderous Syrian swordsmen, son. Isokrates, some wine?'

They sat down with a cup of white wine, well-watered, since the day was hot. Anaxippos hovered, hoping for something interesting. Isokrates sipped his wine – then, surprised and puzzled, sipped it again. The dry fragrance filled his mouth, bringing memories of hot afternoons picking grapes, and the sour winter smell of fermentation. He set his cup down, staring at the trierarch suspiciously.

'What's the matter?' asked Aristomachos. 'Oh, the wine! Zeus, that was quick. Yes, I bought it from your father. We talked wine a bit, the night he was here, and I ordered an amphora, out of curiosity. I'll buy more, next year: it's nice stuff.' He swirled the wine in his cup and took an appreciative swallow. 'Now, to what I asked you over about – Ambassador Diodoros sent me a letter. It's on the sideboard ... oh. What happened to the bugger-arsed thing?'

Anaxippos darted forward and collected the scroll from under the couch. 'Is this it, Papa?'

'What was it doing there?'

'I was pretending it was a sword.'

Aristomachos snorted. 'That disarming trick seems to work, then. Give it here. Don't you have any lessons?'

'Not *now*,' replied his son, rolling his eyes. 'It's *lunch-time*! Papa, I want to hear about *Atalanta*. I'm going to be a trierarch one day, so I need to know about ships, don't I?'

'A point, a point!' agreed Aristomachos, with a lordly wave of the hand. 'Don't get in the way.' He took the scrolled letter, opened it, glanced over it, and put it aside. 'The gist is, our friend Andronikos didn't keep that akatos. Instead, I'm afraid, he got another fucking hemiolia – the *Kratousa*, built at Patara.'

'Decked?' asked Isokrates.

'The ambassador didn't include that detail.'

'Does it make a big difference?' asked Anaxippos.

'Undecked ships are a lot easier to take,' replied his father. 'Particularly if you want to take them intact. You injure even a few oarsmen, it puts all the others off their stroke. Andronikos apparently managed to collect enough mercenaries from among the queen's forces to crew his ship, and they're well armed. As we suspected, he was involved in that business at Daphne. In the forefront of it, in fact. He came away from Berenike's summer palace with a shipload of loot, and hasn't been seen since.

'Now, I won't deny that I was hoping we could go after him, but I think we may have to give up. My guess is that he's gone home to Phalassarna. It's what most pirates dream of, isn't it? Strike it rich, and go home to buy an estate. I don't think we'll see him again for years. He may get bored with farming eventually, but it'll take more than one season for that.'

Isokrates locked his fingers together, frowning, remembering his two brief meetings with the pirate, thinking through all he knew of the man. 'I don't think so,' he said slowly. 'He's a bold, ambitious man, and there's a war just starting, with all that means in opportunities to pillage. He's got a new ship: why should he sell her before he's had any real use of her? He's flush with loot, too, and his people are all

218

praising him. I agree he's likely to have gone home, but I don't see him just settling down to prune vines.'

Aristomachos pondered that and grimaced. 'You sure this isn't just wishful thinking? You want to go after the man: that's been plain enough every time his name comes up.'

'You do, too,' Isokrates pointed out, though with an uncomfortable awareness that the trierarch had a point. 'You were the one who thought of fishing for information from the Syrians.'

Aristomachos waved that aside. 'Well, yes. I don't like the example he set, escaping from a well-deserved ruin by royal patronage, and I don't like him attempting to murder a Rhodian, *my own helmsman,* and getting away with it. If we take him out, everybody will applaud the deed – and my trierarchy would end in a blaze of glory. That would do no harm at all, would it? But I don't feel as strongly as you do. *I* wasn't forced to run away from him with an arrow in my back.'

You didn't have to listen to Dionysia, either, saying how glad she was that the man who abused her wouldn't harm any more innocents, Isokrates thought unhappily. 'I don't think it is just wishful thinking,' he insisted honestly. 'There's his new crew to think of as well. His original men were all from Phalassarna, but we know nothing about these mercenaries who've joined him. It's very unlikely that they're all from his home city, so they won't want to disband there. What's more, if he does go home with a shipload of treasure, he'll have a lot of young Phalassarnans wanting to join him for the war. I think he's going to set out again – and that he'll have more than one ship when he does.'

'What a cheerful fellow you are!' said Aristomachos. 'Anything more? Where he's likely to turn up, for example?'

Isokrates frowned and shrugged irritably.

'So all we can do is another bugger-arsed cruise past Crete, hoping?'

'No!' Isokrates scowled, trying to think it through. 'He won't do what everybody else is doing. That raid on Lycia, where we met him – that was unexpected. So was running to the queen. He'll head for somewhere that's supposed to be safe. I think the northern Aegean's the best bet. He's made himself very obnoxious to Ptolemy; he'll want to stay out of Egyptian territory. I think we should do a cruise through the Cyclades, try to see if we can pick up any rumours. Then we can find a merchant ship and trail her through potential trouble spots.'

Aristomachos looked sceptical.

'Yes, I know it's long odds!' Isokrates exclaimed irritably. 'But even if we don't catch Andronikos, it might net us somebody else. Ptolemy will be moving his fleet north, and the scavengers will be just beyond what he controls. Besides, most of our ships are cruising around Crete and Epirus, and pirates are looking out for them. We'll never make another kill this season if we stick to familiar waters.'

Aristomachos snorted appreciatively. 'And that's very true! Right, the Cyclades it is.'

'Won't it be dangerous if the pirates have lots

of ships?' asked Anaxippos, frowning.

'I don't think it'll be "lots of ships",' Isokrates replied. 'It'll be this hemiolia and one or two smaller craft. It'd only be dangerous if the pirates got a chance to board.'

'Most pirates have small craft,' Aristomachos explained to his son. 'They pack in all the men they can carry, but they don't have rams. They go for unarmed merchants, or raid unprotected villages near the coast. They can't face warships and don't want to meet any.'

'But what if they *do* board you?' demanded the boy. 'With lots of these "well-armed mercenaries", in lots of little ships?'

'Then we're in trouble,' said his father bluntly. 'But don't worry: they're no match for *Atalanta*. She's fast, and she's nimble: she can ram those bastards before they throw a grappling hook.' He pursed his lips. 'One of my ships is due in Delos with a load of grain before long. We could meet her there, and ask her captain what the rumours are. Delos is a good place for rumours, and merchant captains hear things naval officers don't.'

'That would be good,' Isokrates said. 'But we'll want to trail a different ship coming away again. Pirates don't usually go for grain ships.'

Aristomachos nodded. 'So – we have a plan! My Delos-bound ship is the *Melpomene*; she should be on her way from Alexandria now. How soon can you get *Atalanta* ready?'

'She should be ready now,' Isokrates informed him. 'She didn't need any repairs, and I've already arranged for provisioning. It's just a question of rounding up the men.'

Aristomachos glowered at him. 'Some of us, Isokrates, like to see our families and sleep in our own beds occasionally! We'll leave the day after tomorrow.'

Isokrates ducked his head. The thought that now he could go to Dionysia's concert leapt unbidden to his mind. He was determined not to pursue her – but it would be all right to go and just listen, one man among a thousand, wouldn't it? And to see her again, to hear her voice – he ached for it.

The trierarch drew in a breath and let it out again. 'Now, there's another matter,' he said, cheerful again. 'The ambassador wrote to me about it, because he'd seen the sort of answer he was likely to get from you. It seems that the king actually handed him a purse of coin to buy your silence – 'scuse me, to compensate you for your injury. When you turned him down, he was a bit unhappy about it. He's got to account for the money to the royal treasury, and to hand it back looks like failure. After you spared the life of that prick of a royal kinsman, he decided to give it to you as a reward, instead.'

Isokrates stared, sceptical and affronted. 'I don't...'

'I know you don't, and so does the ambassador. I, however, *do* – which is one reason I'm rich and you aren't. I accepted the money on your behalf, and swore by the Sun that I'd see you took it. Where do you want me to put it?'

Isokrates continued to stare. The trierarch grinned. 'Don't look at *me*! *You're* the one who spared that prick's life after he drew on you. If...'

'I was never going to kill him! It would be like ... like killing a lapdog!'

Aristomachos laughed. 'I'm glad the bugger didn't hear that! It would make him hate you even more than he does already – and that man is more of a viper than a lapdog, my friend. If the ambassador hadn't carted him off home this morning, I'd be worried about you meeting some nasty accident. No, why shouldn't you accept a reward for sparing him? Think how he'll feel when the ambassador informs the treasury what he did with that money!'

Rather against his will, Isokrates smiled.

'That's better!' said Aristomachos kindly. 'Let's have some lunch, and I'll tell you about some ships you might want to invest in.'

'Boring!' groaned Anaxippos, and left his elders to it.

Eleven

The king's bribe was two thousand drachmai. Isokrates had never conceived of owning such a sum, and when he'd invested it in another three of the trierarch's ships, he found it difficult to believe that the money really existed at all.

He nonetheless felt agreeably wealthy as he walked back from the trierarch's house, and for the first time in years found himself contemplating the possibility of a life beyond the navy. Two thousand drachmai – or whatever it came to by the end of the year – was enough to buy a house, and perhaps put down some rent on a little vineyard...

He wondered if it was the taste of his father's wine which made him think of a vineyard. He tried to change the daydream to an olive grove or a fishing boat, but the memory of tending the vines crept back at him – the scent of them, and the way the leaves moved, and the joy of the harvest.

Vineyard or olive grove or simply more investment in ships, it was still a future. For the first time since Agido's death, he could hope for the sort of life he'd once seen as natural and inevitable: home, wife, children...

A little house and a rented vineyard wouldn't

be enough for Dionysia, though. He once again saw her standing on the stage, fingers flying over the kithara, her face intent and inward as her voice filled the hall. No, he could not offer a goddess the life of a tenant farmwife.

He stopped short in the street, his heart suddenly beating hard with grief and anger, *wanting*, fiercely and painfully, something he knew he couldn't have. He swallowed several times, reasoning with himself. His situation was better and more hopeful than it had been since Agido died. He'd *won* the contest with his father, made an independent life for himself; he had the rank of helmsman, and every prospect of more ships in future; he had this new wealth, which with the help of Aristomachos might grow into house and land of his own. Why, then, this desperate sense that everything he'd worked for was a handful of ash? It was stupid!

He shook himself angrily and walked on to the shipyard, where he put up a notice requiring all of *Atalanta*'s crew to report to the ship in two days' time. Then he checked the trihemiolia over and inquired about her provisioning.

It was evening by the time he finished, and he took care to stop at a cookshop on his way home, as certain of Atta's 'But I didn't cook for you!' as if he stood at the door.

When he knocked on Atta's door, however, there was no answer. He stood on the doorstep a moment, nonplussed. It was beginning to grow dark: Atta and her family should have finished their supper by now, and be preparing for bed. Had something happened in the neighbourhood to inspire an outing – a funeral, a new baby? He knocked again, uncertainly this time.

A sound came from inside the house: a moan.

Isokrates froze, shocked. He had spoken to Atta when he left the house that morning: she'd been in good health then. What could have happened to her in only twelve hours? He stifled the impulse to run away, and instead tried the door. It wouldn't open: the bar was down. He squatted, got his fingers under the sill, and lifted the door off its hinges.

The room stank of vomit. It was dark, too: the faint light of dusk behind him revealed only a black huddle in the corner, where Atta and her children slept at night. Isokrates groped for the lamp on the shelf beside the door, but when he found it, couldn't strike a light. The fire on the hearth was cold, and he couldn't find the fire-lighter. He went over to the bed, treading in something slimy, and gingerly reached out to touch what he hoped was a shoulder. 'Atta?'

There was another moan.

Trembling a little, he ran out of the house and banged on the door of the next neighbour. This was a dockworker called Bion, whom he normally despised: a drunkard and a wife-beater. When the man came to the door, however, irate at being disturbed after supper, Isokrates greeted him with relief. 'Something's happened to Atta!' he cried. 'Can I borrow a lamp?'

Bion's pale, downtrodden wife appeared behind him, her hand over her mouth, her eyes huge. Bion glanced round at her disapprovingly, but made no objection when she darted back into the house, to return with a lamp, lit from the embers on the hearth.

The unsteady lamplight revealed Atta curled up in bed with her arms wrapped around her children. Vomit, streaked here and there with red, had overflowed the chamber-pot and made a foul wetness in the clay of the floor. Bion's wife gave a wail of dismay and ran over; Atta moaned again as the other woman touched her, but the children in her arms didn't stir.

'Get away from her!' ordered Bion abruptly. 'You'll catch it!'

'She's not ill!' protested Isokrates indignantly. 'She was perfectly fine this morning!' – and only then began to suspect.

'They must've eaten something bad,' said Bion's wife, wringing her hands. 'Oi moi moi, the poor things! I told her, don't you eat the stuff the fishmongers throw out! But they were always hungry, poor things, poor things!'

Eaten something bad. There was a basket on the table, a small basket made of woven rushes, with a lid. Isokrates picked it up and opened it: it contained honeyed sesame balls. They did not quite form a layer over the bottom of the basket: there was space for two or three more. A scrap of papyrus lay on the sweets: 'Dionysia daughter of Kleisthenes to Isokrates son of Kritagoras, in token of my joy at your recovery.'

'Oh, Zeus!' Isokrates said quietly. He looked from the basket in his hands to the woman and her children on the bed, and felt a wrench of anguish, a physical pain, as though the poison was biting his own guts.

227

Little Leuke had been born a couple of months after he arrived in the house: he had known her all her short life. He remembered the child embracing his knees and looking up at him hopefully. What had he brought to her now? He went over and touched her soft hair: her head lolled, the eyes half-open with only the white showing, her chin covered with a slime of blood and vomit. He could not tell if she were still alive.

He left Bion's wife with Atta and ran to fetch a doctor: it was the only thing he could do. By the time he returned to the house with the man, though, the women of the neighbourhood had already begun to wail in mourning. Atta continued to breathe for another hour, but the children had been dead for some time.

He had very little recollection of the rest of that night. He remembered agreeing to pay for the funerals, but then nothing until dawn, when he knocked on the door of Aristomachos's house, carrying the basket of sesame sweets.

The trierarch wasn't up, but the slaves admitted Isokrates to the dining room, and presently Aristomachos came in, rumpled and yawning.

'You'd better have a good reason for this,' he said. 'Herakles, man, what's the matter?'

'Atta's dead. My landlady. Both her children, too. I think they ate some of these.' Isokrates set the basket down on the table.

Aristomachos stopped yawning mid-gape. He stared a moment, then gingerly opened the basket. He read the note, and looked up incredulously 'You think the Milesian pois—'

'No!' Isokrates exclaimed angrily. *'Hyper-ides.'*

'Ah.' Aristomachos stared into the basket a moment. 'Did he know – yes, of course he did; he was there at the concert.' He shook his head unhappily. 'Oh, by Apollo! You say your land-lady is *dead*?'

The image of Leuke, dead in the arms of her dying mother, forced itself back into Isokrates' mind. He pressed his hands against his eyes, trying to block it out.

'Easy!' exclaimed Aristomachos, and came over to pat his shoulder.

'He meant it for me,' Isokrates said thickly. 'But they ate some; of course they ate some! They were always hungry: leave a basket of sweets on the table all day, untouched? The little girl was only five!'

'Are you certain of this?' asked Aristomachos seriously. 'That house is in an unhealthy quarter. The sweets may really be from the Milesian girl, and perfectly wholesome.'

Yes, the quarter was unhealthy, and, yes, as Bion's wife had exclaimed, Atta often made soup from old fish. She'd always had a fine judgement of what could and could not be eaten, though, grumbling angrily about traders who didn't drop their prices until the food had to be thrown out.

'I'm sure of it.' He picked up the note from the basket. 'I still have Dionysia's other letter, and this isn't the same hand. Besides, it's addressed to me as "son of Kritagoras". That's how you gave my name to the ambassador, but I always say, "of Kameiros", and that's how she addressed the other one. If you have any doubt, though, we can feed one of these to a rat and see what happens.'

Aristomachos winced. 'I certainly wouldn't want to eat it myself. What do you want me to do?'

Isokrates drew a deep breath. What *did* he want Aristomachos to do? Why had he come *here,* rather than ... who *should* he turn to?

'I should go to Agathostratos,' he said aloud. 'He was hosting the Syrians.'

'Very well. I'll send a note to Agathostratos.'

Isokrates stared at the trierarch. 'I didn't mean...'

'Well, you came here for support, didn't you?'

Isokrates replied with what he suddenly understood was the truth. 'I came because you're a friend I trust. I need your good sense. The man is a royal kinsman. I don't know ... I don't know if...' He set his teeth, suddenly trembling with impotent rage. He didn't know if there was anything he could do against Hyperides; worse, he didn't even know if he should *try*. If accusing Laodike might injure Rhodes, did he dare to accuse her favourite? He wanted, with a violent hot yearning, to punish the man who had put poisoned sweets in the way of an innocent child – but there were many other children on Rhodes, and how would it serve Leuke to bring war down upon them?

'We'll talk to Agathostratos,' said Aristomachos. 'He'll know.'

* * *

The admiral evidently rose early, because his response to Aristomachos's note arrived by return of messenger. It was an invitation to come and discuss the matter at once.

The two of them walked across the market, which was just waking up. Baker's stalls were piled high with fresh-baked bread; fruit-sellers sold cherries, peaches and strawberries; country-women squatted by the roadside with bundles of herbs and wild asparagus. To Isokrates it seemed incredible that another day had begun, and Leuke wouldn't see it.

At Agathostratos's house the slaves were washing the entrance hall, tossing buckets of water on to the stone and sweeping the slurry out into the street. Aristomachos and Isokrates removed their sandals and edged through, their muddy footprints swept away behind them.

Agathostratos was in his garden, eating a breakfast of bread and olives. He nodded to Aristomachos, who bowed his head respectfully before sitting down on the garden bench. Isokrates perched beside him.

'Thank you for agreeing to see us,' Aristomachos began. 'My helmsman...'

'Has had some trouble from that Syrian viper Hyperides?' the admiral finished for him.

'Yes,' said Isokrates. 'At least, sir, I think so.' He held out the basket of sesame balls. 'This was left at the house where I lodge sometime yesterday. My landlady and her two children are dead.'

Agathostratos drew in his breath with a hiss. He took the basket and looked into it warily.

'My helmsman says that the note is *not* from

the Milesian kitharist Dionysia,' supplied Aristomachos. 'It's a different hand. Besides, she knows him as "Isokrates of Kameiros", not by his father's name. Hyperides knew that she was a likely source for a gift: he was present when she came up after a concert to thank Isokrates for his help. But we can send for the woman and ask, if you like.'

The admiral nodded unhappily and closed the basket. 'I was ... no, to say I *expected* this is too strong. I was uneasy. That young man Hyperides felt himself very ill-used, both by the royal ambassador and particularly by your helmsman here – and Diodoros, for all that he was head of the embassy, was clearly worried about him. My comfort was that they all left yesterday morning. That he sent you a parting gift – no, I'm not surprised. I'll send for the woman, but I don't doubt she'll confirm these did not come from her.'

He summoned one of his slaves and gave him a message for Dionysia. Then he regarded Isokrates a moment. 'As I understand it, Diodoros offered to buy your silence. You refused the money, but have been silent anyway.'

'Yes, sir. My trierarch advised me that to accuse Queen Laodike would not serve Rhodes, and I was persuaded by his reasoning.'

'So you should be: it's well-founded.' Agathostratos grimaced. 'The fact that Diodoros was so worried about the opinion of a spiteful young fool shows that the queen has great power in the new court – and I suppose it's natural that she should, since her son owes his title to her ruthlessness. The critical question now is how much support Hyperides can expect from his patroness.'

Aristomachos stirred. 'The new king needs friends. Surely...'

'The new king likely *has* friends,' the admiral said sourly. 'Antigonos of Macedon may not have declared himself yet, but he's been a friend of Syria and an enemy of Egypt all his life. Even if he rejects Seleukos, though, does anyone seriously believe he'll stand aside and let Ptolemy take control of the Aegean? And if he has Antigonos behind him, Seleukos isn't going to worry too much about conciliating Rhodes. We've voted to stay neutral.'

'Your motion!' Aristomachos said sharply.

'Yes, by Apollo! And I don't think it was a mistake. But still, the new king knows that neutrality is all the favour he's going to get from us, so he's not going to go out of his way to be helpful if we come to him complaining about one of his mother's favourites. It might be dangerous even to try.'

'A woman is dead,' said Isokrates. 'A woman and two children, Rhodian and freeborn. They're owed justice!'

Agathostratos sighed. 'I don't dispute it. But Justice, that star-born goddess, left the earth with the Golden Age. Whether or not our complaint has any hope of success depends on how much support Hyperides can muster in the court of Syria. I say again, it might be very dangerous to pursue this – not to Rhodes, son of Kritagoras: to *you*. Hyperides seems to have been your enemy even before he arrived in Rhodes – I suppose he resented it that you survived your interview at the queen's house and made trouble for her. When you took away his sword and embarrassed him in front of the ambassador, he hated you even more. If we complain and our complaint fails, he'll find a way to kill you – and I, at least, would regret that. Rhodes can't easily afford to lose men of your quality.'

'He's already trying to kill me!'

'While he was here in Rhodes! I doubt he's moved enough to pursue the matter once he's back home again – unless, as I said, he knows we complained about him to the king. I tell you this plainly: it would be safer to let the matter drop.'

Aristomachos stirred, but said nothing, only looked at Isokrates doubtfully. Isokrates thought again of Leuke's dead face. He shook his head angrily. 'People are *dead*. I swear by the Sun, I will not let the matter drop without even making a complaint!'

The admiral sighed. 'Very well. Can I at least persuade you to leave this in my hands, and not talk about it to anyone else?'

Isokrates gazed at him a moment warily. He'd been happy to turn to the admiral, but now he remembered that Agathostratos was pro-Syrian, with many friends in the Seleucid court.

'What I would do is this,' the admiral said evenly. 'I would send secretly to my guest-friend Diodoros, who's already familiar with the situation, and tell him what's happened. Evidence of attempted murder might be something he could use to make the queen withdraw her favour from

Hyperides – in which case, we would be free to prosecute. If, on the other hand, he reckons that Queen Laodike would actually be *pleased* by what her favourite did, Diodoros can keep this a secret from her, and instead inform the king privately. He'd have strong motive to make the king distrust Hyperides, and I could insist that he consider your safety in his report.'

'That sounds good to me,' said Aristomachos quickly. His eyes darted to Isokrates. 'It would not make the complaint any less likely to succeed,' he coaxed.

Isokrates pondered it unhappily: this creeping, secretive approach seemed a betrayal of poor little Leuke ... but Aristomachos was right that a headlong approach was unlikely to be any more successful, and might well achieve even less. It was true that Ambassador Diodoros had every reason to blacken Hyperides' name with the king, if only to justify himself. It was probably the best that could be achieved. Reluctantly, he nodded.

A door opened, and then Dionysia came into the garden, escorted by her maid and by one of the admiral's slaves. She was dressed very soberly in a voluminous cloak – woollen, despite the heat – and her face was anxious. The anxiety gave way to surprise and unmistakeable pleasure when she saw Isokrates.

'Daughter of Kleisthenes,' said the admiral, inclining his head. 'Thank you for coming so promptly. May I ask if you know anything about this?' He picked up the basket and held it out to her.

She regarded it a moment in surprise, glanced uncertainly at Isokrates, then reached out hesitantly to take it. She flipped open the lid, picked up the note and stared at it blankly. 'No,' she said in confusion. 'I didn't write it. It's not from me.' She looked up at Isokrates, and something in his face gave him away: her eyes widened and she set the basket down abruptly. 'What is it? It's not ... you didn't...'

'I think my landlady and her two children ate from it,' Isokrates told her. 'They're dead.'

'Oh, Apollo!' Dionysia clapped her hands to her mouth, staring at Isokrates in horror. 'I didn't send it; please believe I didn't send it! It ... Hyperides! He was there when I spoke to you, he...'

'That's what we thought, too,' said Aristomachos, with satisfaction.

'I would never do anything to hurt you,' Dionysia told Isokrates breathlessly, her face flushed. 'You've done more to help me than anyone alive – rescued me from the pirates, and brought me here, and introduced me to friends and patrons, and never asked anything at all in return. I would never...'

'Please!' Isokrates protested, embarrassed. 'We just had to check. We'd feel very stupid if we complained to King Seleukos, and then it turned out that you'd sent those, and Atta and her children died of eating bad shellfish.'

Dionysia stared. 'You're going to appeal to King Seleukos? Oh, no! Don't, please don't! Hyperides will kill you!'

'I will see to it that the business is managed

discreetly,' Agathostratos said sharply. 'The helmsman should be in no danger – provided the matter is managed discreetly here in Rhodes as well.'

'But...' she began.

'Thank you for your assistance,' Agathostratos said forbiddingly. 'We will also thank you for your silence.'

She looked unhappily from him to Isokrates.

Isokrates bowed his head to the admiral. 'I'll leave it in your hands, then, sir. Thank you.' He turned to Dionysia. 'I can escort you back to your lodgings, Lady, if you like.'

'Please,' she said faintly.

Dionysia said nothing as he accompanied her back through the house, but when they reached the street she said in a low voice, 'I'm sorry. I've brought you nothing but grief.'

'No,' he said forcefully. 'Your enemies have brought me grief. Don't for a moment blame yourself for their crimes.'

She looked up at him with sad eyes and repeated, 'I'm sorry.'

'Which way is it to your lodgings?'

She gestured to the right. 'I'm in the Guild's house for now. Near the theatre.' They started along the street, the maid trailing silently behind them.

'My landlady had two children,' Isokrates said abruptly. 'The little girl was five. I used to give her scraps, though her mother didn't like it.'

Dionysia winced. 'I'm so sorry!'

'It's not ... I just want you to understand why I can't take your advice.'

'Where will you go now?'

He hadn't thought of that. He had no idea who would inherit Atta's house, but he did know that he couldn't spend another night there. The place now seemed to him cursed – just as the house where he'd been born had become accursed, the moment Agido's body was cut from the roof-beam. Suddenly sick and giddy, he stopped short in the road. He felt as though a plague had struck every place he'd called home, and that everything he looked back on was tainted.

Dionysia reached up tentatively to touch his shoulder. 'Isokrates?'

He shivered and caught her hand. Her slim musician's fingers curled around his own, and her beautiful face, looking up into his own, seemed the only safe haven in a world of horror.

'I ... I would like to help,' she said earnestly, 'if there's any way I can. If you need money for a new place to stay, I could...'

'No!' he said, stung with shame: was he an object of charity, to *her*? He flung off her hand. 'When autumn comes, I'll *buy* a house. Until then I'll find a room in barracks, or stay with Aristomachos.'

There was a silence, and then she said hesitantly, 'I was told that you were disinherited by your father after a quarrel.'

He shook his head and began walking again, careful not to look at her. 'I quarrelled with my father, certainly. But I do have some money now, from salvage and from a reward the Syrian ambassador gave me for sparing Hyperides' life...'

'What?'

238

He told her about the sword.

'Oh, Apollo!' she exclaimed in horror. 'The whole court will be laughing at him about that! No wonder he tried to poison you!'

Isokrates glanced round anxiously, but the street was empty, and no one had overhead. 'Don't talk about it!' he ordered.

'Please!' she said, with a catch in her voice. He paused, surprised, and found her standing several paces behind, her hands pressed together.

'Don't hate me!' she pleaded. 'I want to be your friend, if you'll allow it!'

He stared in consternation. 'I don't hate you, I ... I *am* your friend, of course I am!'

'But...' She stopped, biting her lip. 'I need to talk to you. Is there somewhere...'

The maid Dyseris made a noise of contempt, and Dionysia looked at her angrily.

'He's ashamed because he's too poor for you,' Dyseris said bluntly. 'And when you offered him money you rubbed it in. There: I've sorted it for you.'

They both gave her identical shocked stares.

'If you need to talk, do it in public,' Dyseris continued. 'Lord Hagemon won't be at all pleased if word gets back to him that a penniless navy man was seen leaving your room in the morning.'

'Dyseris!' exclaimed Dionysia angrily.

'It's true, and you know it,' the maid replied.

Dionysia glared at her, then turned back to Isokrates. 'There's a public garden by the temple of nymphs, just a block from here. We can talk there.'

The garden was a tiny sunken one beside the small marble shrine; it was visible from the street, but, at this hour, empty. Roses, jasmine and Rhodian hibiscus grew along its stone walls; the pond in its centre held lilies. Dionysia seated herself on the stone bench and arranged her cloak carefully; Isokrates crouched uncomfortably on the edge of the pond.

'Hagemon's not my lover,' Dionysia declared, her eyes hot. 'If that's what you think, you're wrong. I told him I'm not a courtesan, and he accepted it.'

In spite of everything, Isokrates' heart rose at that declaration. All he said, though, was, 'If you refused him, he won't want you accepting anybody else.'

Dyseris snorted. 'Smart man! Listen to him!'

Her mistress gave her another angry glance, then said, 'Is it true what she said – that you ... that you've kept away from me because you're poor?'

It was a relief to have it out in the open. 'The Muses favoured you, and their gifts will make you rich and famous. I don't even have a house of my own. I can't offer you anything.'

Her eyes sought his and held. 'You want to?'

He closed his eyes. 'Yes. Of course.'

'I wasn't sure,' she said softly. 'I thought ... but your letter was so *cold*! I was ashamed that I'd written to you at all ... but then when I saw you at the concert you were so very kind. I couldn't work it out.'

'If you were fool enough to love me, it would cost you your patron and all your hopes. I don't injure my friends – and I hope I am your friend.'

'A very true and dear friend!' Dionysia exclaimed in a choked whisper, twisting the edge of her cloak in her hands.

Isokrates locked his hands together between his knees. Some corner of his mind wanted Dionysia to protest that he *could* make her happy – that she would be happy in his love. She hadn't done that: love without music would make her miserable, and she knew it. He felt suddenly much calmer, and with the calm, deeply weary.

Dyseris gave a snort of contempt. 'Men and women can never be friends.'

'That's not true,' Isokrates told her quietly. 'Agido was my friend. My stepmother; she's dead now, but we were like brother and sister.'

'She was the reason you quarrelled with your father,' Dionysia said quietly.

It wasn't a question. He nodded, then suddenly found himself telling her about Agido, and about the farm up in the mountains, beautiful and cursed. Dionysia listened in silence.

'Oh!' she whispered, when he stumbled to a stop. 'Oh, I ... I understand now.' She drew a deep breath.

'It wasn't a big place anyway,' he told her. 'Not like your manor in Miletos.'

'No, but ... but I understand now. You have been my friend.' She drew another breath, then said urgently, 'Now let me be yours! Please. I ... I could at least lend you some money.'

He shook his head. 'I ... thank you, but no. I'll be well, once I've rested. As for money, I'm better off than I've been for years. I may not

241

have enough for ... enough to support a proper household, but I have plenty for my own needs. I will buy a house in the autumn. Until then ... well, I doubt I'll be in Rhodes for more than ten days, anyway, until the end of the sailing season. We're leaving on another cruise the day after tom– no, *tomorrow*.' The realization that *Atalanta* would set out the following morning shook him.

She regarded him anxiously. 'Are you well enough to go?'

'I'm not *ill*.' He was silent a moment, then said, 'Your concert was today, wasn't it?'

'Yes. Don't worry; I have plenty of time to prepare for it.'

'I was going to come. But the funerals will be this afternoon.'

She hesitated, then said, 'I pray the earth is light on them. Look, you should go back to your friend the trierarch until then. I'm *sure* he'll want you to stay in his house; he obviously cares about you, and if he isn't already expecting you to stay, he will be as soon as he thinks about it. I can find my own way home!'

He smiled weakly: she was probably right about Aristomachos. He nodded and rose heavily to his feet.

'Let me ... let me know how you are,' Dionysia said earnestly. 'Send a note before you leave, and when you get back. I'm going to be away later this month, but you can always leave a note for me with the Guild.'

'Very well. But you're going away? Where?'

'To Athens.' She smiled shyly. 'I've been

242

invited to compete in the Panathenaia, in the "singing to the kithara" class!'

'Oh!' This was news. The 'Great Panathenaia', held every fourth year in Athens, included musical competitions as well as athletics, and attracted performers from all over the Greek world. To be invited to compete was no small honour: the only music festival which carried more glory was the Pythian Games. 'I wish you every good fortune, then!'

'And you,' she said, looking up at him intently. 'I wish you joy, my friend.'

Twelve

Isokrates had never liked Delos. On this occasion, with his heart still raw from the death of Atta and her children, he detested the place.

True, the island was very holy. Stony hub of the Aegean, surrounded by the great wheel of the Cyclades, it belonged to the gods. Under the sacred palm tree in its centre Leto had given birth to Apollo and Artemis, brightest of all divinities. Delos-town was splendid with a multitude of temples, all lavishly adorned with gold and ivory, rich hangings, and beautiful statues in marble and bronze; the marketplace, with its long colonnades, was nearly as magnificent and bustling as that of Alexandria.

The island's sacredness, however, meant that birth and death, those two messy and unclean extremes, had both been excluded – and with them, all real life. Healthy adults came to Delos to worship the gods or to trade in the famous market; others sailed over from neighbouring islands to cater for them. No one actually lived on Delos for more than a few months: the land was untilled, and no children grew up there. Travellers who fell ill were whisked away to neighbouring islands before they could pollute the sacred soil with death. It had always struck

Isokrates as a false place, like the painted back-drop of a theatre.

The thing he really disliked about it, though, was the whiff of piracy. The island's sacred status meant that anyone could trade there without fear of reprisals for crimes committed elsewhere, and, as a result, it was home to the biggest slave market in the Aegean. The slave trade had always been the ally and support of piracy, and he hated it. Aristomachos was right, though, that Delos was a great place for rumours.

'Not as many as usual,' remarked Timon, the captain of Aristomachos's part-owned ship *Melpomene*. 'Not about pirates, that is. All the talk is about the war.'

He was sitting with Aristomachos and Isokrates in one of the overpriced Delian taverns with a jug of indifferent wine. *Atalanta* had arrived at the island that evening after a slow, rumour-hunting voyage, and found *Melpomene* docked, her cargo already offloaded. Timon had been happy to join them for a drink, but was not proving as helpful as Aristomachos had hoped.

'The place is heaving!' objected Aristomachos, looking out from the shady terrace to the market-place. It was dusk, but the great plaza was still crowded.

'Oh, it's busy, yes!' agreed Timon. 'Sold the grain soon's we touched the quay; made twenty-six per cent on it. But that's because people are trying to get a cargo home before the war starts. There's less gossip than usual, and what there is, is about the war.' He shook his head. 'People from the Asian coast aren't even sure whether their cities will have the same constitution when they get home as when they set out. And there's Macedon, too: nobody knows whether it's going to jump in or stay out of the water, and that affects everything. There's less about pirates than there normally is.'

'Bugger that!' said Aristomachos impatiently. 'You trying to tell me that merchant skippers aren't interested in where they might meet a pirate?'

Timon, a slight, wispy man of middle age, awarded the sarcasm a weak smile. 'Nnoo-oo ... but they're spending less time on it than usual. Besides, everybody *knows* where you're *likely* to meet a pirate. It's when they appear where you don't expect that everybody talks about it.'

'And that hasn't happened?' asked Isokrates.

The captain shrugged. 'Not that I've heard of. The only rumour I've heard is that Euboia is a good place to stay away from just now.'

'Ah!' exclaimed Aristomachos eagerly. 'Who told you that?'

Timon shrugged again. 'Captain of the *Dioskouroi*, also out of Rhodes. I don't know where he got it from, though, or why Euboia is supposed to be dangerous. It's just one of those rumours that gets passed around.'

The trierarch grunted in recognition.

'Might be something to do with King Antigonos, for all I know,' Timon continued. 'He holds that shore. The Macedonians always get itchy when Ptolemy ventures north, and they say the whole Egyptian fleet has sailed to Pydnai. I heard our Assembly voted to stay neutral?'

'Two to one – with sympathy and good wishes to Ptolemy,' replied Aristomachos.

Timon nodded. 'Good. Good. Not our war.' He took a sip of wine and added, 'Though I've no doubt, trierarch, that we'll still suffer because of it. If Ptolemy's fleet is at Pydnai, it won't be patrolling Cyprus and Cyrenaica. If the dog's in the vineyard, the fox can raid the henhouse.'

Aristomachos made a rude noise. 'Ptolemy's fleet wasn't much of a guard dog anyway, was it? Too many bugger-arsed quinqueremes, no use at all against small craft. *We'll* guard the henhouse, as we always do.'

Timon smiled at that and raised his cup. 'And may all the gods favour you while you do it!'

They all tipped a little wine out on to the stained floor as an offering to the gods for their favour. 'So,' concluded Aristomachos, drinking off what was left in his cup, 'you're saying the only rumour you've heard was this one about Euboia?'

Timon nodded, and Aristomachos thanked him. He tossed the wine-dregs into the basin in the corner and jerked his head for Isokrates to follow him from the tavern.

They started back toward the north harbour, where *Atalanta* was beached. Their route took them through the great market by the Sacred Harbour. It was night, and the stalls were closed, but the place was still crowded with travellers who might have come to Delos to worship Apollo and Artemis, but were celebrating Dionysus and Aphrodite in the taverns and brothels. It was a hot July night, and the air was still, the stars huge and shimmering in the clear sky. The air smelled of wine, honey and spices, and the sound of flute and kithara drifted across the marketplace.

On the northern side of the harbour, though, they met a different scent: stale urine and shit. The slave-pens stood there, and the next day's merchandise waited, shackled, for the coming of the morning. As he passed the dark sheds, Isokrates wondered, as he always did, how many of the people in them were the victims of pirates.

'They ought to shut this market down!' he said angrily.

'People need slaves!' protested Aristomachos. 'I couldn't live without mine, I know.'

Isokrates gestured impatiently. 'You didn't buy them *here* though, did you? If they closed this place, the pirates would find it harder to make a living.'

'No,' said Aristomachos, 'They'd just go somewhere else. They do anyway. Shut this place down, and all that would happen would be somewhere else would get rich.'

Isokrates grimaced, unconvinced: there were other slave markets, it was true – but none was as central and convenient as Delos. He didn't want to argue, though, so he just grunted.

They trudged past the slave-pens and across the rocky spur of land that separated the Sacred Harbour from the sandy crescent of the North Harbour. 'So,' said Aristomachos, after a silence. 'With luck we might meet these pirates within the next few days.'

'May the gods grant it!' Isokrates replied vehemently.

'Yes,' said the trierarch, sounding uncharacteristically unsure of himself. 'Um. There's something I've been meaning to talk to you about.'

'Sir?'

'Yes.' Aristomachos swallowed, then came out with it. 'I got to thinking about what we're trying to do – that the men we're going after outnumber our deck-soldiers, and maybe all our crew. If they manage to board us, it'll be sticky. Even my son could see that.'

'*Atalanta*'s a good ship, sir,' Isokrates replied at once, 'and the crew know their business. We can outmanoeuvre them.'

Aristomachos brushed the words away impatiently. 'Yes, but things can go wrong! Anyway, what I meant to say was, I drew up a new will, before we left Rhodes.'

Isokrates wasn't sure what he was supposed to say to that, so he merely made an inquisitive noise.

'I named you as executor and as guardian of my son.'

Isokrates stopped short, staring, trying to make out the other man's face through the darkness. 'Sir,' he said, shocked, 'that's ... you honour me, but your kinsmen...'

'Would cream off money,' Aristomachos said resignedly. 'The best of them wouldn't take much, but if they were a bit short, they'd raid my funds to cover themselves, instead of hitting their own or borrowing. Bugger it, that's what *I'd* do, if I were in charge of somebody else's estate! Maybe they'd pay it back and maybe they wouldn't, but even if they did pay it back, Anaxippos would lose the interest. If nothing else, they'd neglect his business in favour of their own. You, though – you'd look after my son's inheritance to the very best of your ability, and you'd hand the whole lot over as soon as he came of age. The boy likes you, too – admires you, if you want the truth. He'd listen to you, and you'd look after him.'

'He's a good boy,' Isokrates said, feeling helpless. Manage an estate? Six ships, a grand house, lands, capital enough to pay for a trierarchy?

A trierarchy! He, Isokrates, could become a trierarch!

Even as he thought it, he recoiled. He could conceive of wanting that high title – but not at the cost of Aristomachos's *life*. 'Sir,' he said, ashamed, 'I'm not ... I don't have the experience to...'

'You can always get experience: all you have to do is keep at it. Honesty, that's what I need in a guardian for my boy, and it's a rare commodity. Anyway, I put your name down, and if anything happens to me, you'll have my house to go home to.'

'I'm ... I'm honoured. But...' He stood a moment, peering down at the other man, still trying to come to grips with what he'd been offered – and, more, how much he was trusted. He understood, quite suddenly, that he respected his trierarch profoundly, and that he wanted Aristomachos to live long and rise high. The thought of *his* trierarch as a president, directing the republic shrewdly and sensibly, gave him a stab of pride. 'I'd die myself, sir, sooner than let anything happen to you!' he exclaimed.

Aristomachos let out his breath in a huff. 'Well, thank you! But I hope nobody dies. 'Cept pirates, of course.'

'We ought to be in a position to ensure that, sir.'

'I hope so.' The trierarch sighed again, then said, finally, 'The fact is, Isokrates, I've never been in any bugger-arsed battles. I don't ... I haven't ... you have any tips?'

Isokrates stared, finally understanding what the conversation was about.

'I did my naval service, yes!' Aristomachos exclaimed, brushing aside the unvoiced objection. 'But we didn't *meet* any pirates, did we? And now ... well...'

'You'll be *fine!*' Isokrates said hastily.

'You think so?' asked the trierarch uncertainly. 'I keep having these visions of breaking down and trying to run, of *failing,* in front of everyone.'

'Sir, I'm sure you won't,' said Isokrates, with perfect sincerity. 'In Ephesus you got the ship out safely – and then took her back. Demanding to see the king, that was no coward's work!'

'Yes, but that's *talking.*'

'Sir, you kept your head in time of danger and you made good decisions. There are a lot of things I'm worried about now, but you failing us – that's not one of them.'

Aristomachos let out breath in a short *huh.* 'Thank you.' After another silence, though, he said, 'When we meet the enemy, though, I want you to give the orders. I *don't* have any experience of battle. I might get something wrong.'

'No, sir,' Isokrates said firmly. 'You're the trierarch, and the men expect the orders to come from you. But if you like I'll remind you of things, and let you know what I think is the right timing. That's the hard bit, when it comes to manoeuvres, getting the timing right.'

The trierarch nodded, smiling now. 'I can believe that.' He trudged on a few more steps. 'Well, now that we've settled the thing, we just have to find the buggers, don't we?'

'Maybe they're in Euboia,' Isokrates said hopefully. 'Maybe we'll find them soon.'

They continued companionably along the beach. *Atalanta* was drawn up about a third of the way along the North Harbour, next to a Ptolemaic courier ship: she had again made a tent of her mast and mainsail, but in this hot season the awning was stretched high, a shelter against sun, not rain. Isokrates' practised eye scanned the huddled shapes visible beneath it and shook his head. 'Half the men must be off drinking!'

Aristomachos grinned, a flash of teeth in the darkness. 'Well, why not? We'll hardly leave crack of dawn: we need to find ourselves a merchant ship bound for Euboia first. That's assuming we're still going to trail one, and I didn't hear any reason we shouldn't.' He sighed and rubbed his neck. 'I swear by all the immortals, when I get home I'm going to buy myself a new slave. She's going to be young and pretty, and her job will be to give me backrubs until I'm rid of all the aches from this bugger-arsed voyage!'

Next morning they had no difficulty finding a ship to trail. The *Tyche* was a *keles,* a small, fast vessel bound back to her home port of Chalkis in Euboia; her captain had heard the rumour, too, and was delighted to have a Rhodian warship to protect him. His cargo was slaves freshly purchased in the Delian market.

Aristomachos found it funny; Isokrates did not. Apart from his moral outrage, though, he had to admit that *Tyche* was perfect: pirates preferred small, fast ships, and slaves were one of the most profitable, and most tempting, cargoes.

They rowed ahead of *Tyche* during the first day of the voyage, and spent the night on a tiny beach on the southern shore of the island of Andros. Their consort caught up with them during the night, but waited off the tip of the island until *Atalanta* appeared and signalled.

From the western tip of Andros the Euboian shore was already clearly visible. *Tyche* sailed southwest into the Euboian Sea, her half-furled sail showing white from a good distance. *Atalanta* crept after her with her mast stepped, hiding below the horizon.

It was about noon, and the sea was beginning to narrow between Euboia and Attika, when *Tyche* hoisted a red shield to the top of her mast – the agreed signal for danger. It seemed that Timon's rumour had some foundation.

There was a rush as the crew hurried to their

253

stations. Isokrates had to warn Damophon the bo'sun not to speed up the stroke: he did not want the oarcrew exhausted when they met with the pirates. It was enough that every oar was manned: *Atalanta* raced toward her consort with the water foaming against her prow. Nikagoras climbed up on to the forefoot and gazed eagerly at the ship ahead.

'There's a longship bearing down on her!' he yelled. 'A big one; it's rowing out from the shore of Attika! It's *red*!'

'What!?' asked Isokrates, much taken aback. Pirates favoured blues, to fade into the sea: he'd never heard of one painted red.

'It's, it's undecked,' called Nikagoras. 'It's ... it's ... it's a *trireme*!'

Aristomachos and Isokrates exchanged a look – and then Isokrates said aloud what they'd both realized. 'Naval vessel.' Royal navies favoured triremes as couriers and guardships; pirates never used them.

Aristomachos nodded, went to the hatch, and shouted. 'Easy oars!'

'The *Tyche*'s brailed up her sail and is heaving to!' called Nikagoras. 'The trireme is coming up ... she's got a big standard, purple and gold...'

'Bugger it!' muttered Aristomachos. 'Stay away from bugger-arsed Euboia: Antigonos fucking king of Macedon is assembling his fucking fleet there!' He started forward.

'We could turn around,' Isokrates called after him, but the trierarch shook his head glumly. Isokrates supposed he was right. Run, and the trireme would conclude that they were enemy

254

spies, and if they ended up in a fight with a Macedonian naval vessel they'd cause a major diplomatic incident. Surrendering was the better option.

He felt guilty, though: this had been his plan, and now at best there would be a long delay while they tried to convince the Macedonians that they were neutrals, not spies; at worst, the Macedonians would arrest some of *Atalanta*'s crew. There was a handful of Athenians among the professional oarsmen: they'd fled their home city after the disastrous Chremonidean War, and were all rabidly anti-Macedonian. It was very likely that the Macedonian-installed government of Athens had sentenced them to death.

The trireme veered off from *Tyche* as soon as she saw *Atalanta*, and raced over with all oars beating. She was faster than *Atalanta* – the only class of vessel which could claim that honour. Though the two craft were the same length, the trireme, broader at stem and stern, carried fifty more oars and, being undecked, was lighter.

Isokrates dropped through the central hatch to the oardeck, and gave the order to ship oars. 'We didn't find pirates,' he told the men. 'We found the Macedonian fleet.'

There was a cry of alarm from a couple of the thranite oarsmen – Athenians, of course.

'What we'll tell them is that we're *all* Rhodians,' he announced, glaring up and down the deck. 'Neutrals, and on friendly terms with Macedon. The Macedonians have no cause to detain any of us – and if any of you are tempted to inform on a shipmate, you'd better be prepared to go into exile, because you'll never be able to live among Rhodians again. Understood?'

Somebody cheered: *'Atalanta!'* – and then they all yelled it, *'Euge! Atalanta!'* Isokrates nodded curtly and went back on deck. He'd done what he could, and it should be enough to keep the Athenians safe for a few days at least. If the Macedonians were suspicious, though, if they detained *Atalanta* for a long time, and the trihemiolia ran out of food and money ... well, he would worry about that if it happened.

The trireme was close now, and slowing. Her standard was now clearly identifiable as the eagle-and-oak-wreath of Macedon: the third great kingdom, the one whose stance had been the great question of the marketplace.

'What ship?' yelled her bow-officer; and Isokrates called back, *'Atalanta,* of Rhodes!'

'You'll accompany us back to base!' shouted the Macedonian, as Isokrates had feared.

The Macedonian fleet was assembled on the famous beach of Marathon, and it was immense: the prows of the king's warships were lined up along the shore like brazen towers in a city wall. The ships themselves were painted in bright reds, greens and purples, their figureheads and stern ornaments touched with gilding. Most were quinqueremes – three-banked galleys with five files of oarsmen to a side, the oars in the upper tiers manned by two men apiece. There were bigger ships as well, though, with six, eight, nine files to a side: huge ships, crewed by up to a thousand men; ships which relied, not on ramming, but on catapults mounted in towers on their decks, and on large forces of marines to board their enemies; ships which, to the Rhodians, seemed scarcely ships at all, but floating forts.

Atalanta was directed to an empty patch of beach in the middle of the fleet, and the trireme backed in beside her. The trireme commander came over as soon as the anchor stones were in place. He was a weedy man in a splendid silk tunic, an Athenian of the Macedonian-approved stamp, very full of himself. What were they doing in the Euboian Sea? he wanted to know. Where had they sailed from? When? How many in the crew?

Aristomachos answered him patiently and allowed him to inspect *Atalanta*.

'And your crew are all Rhodian?' asked the trireme commander, looking down his nose at the oarsmen.

'All from Rhodes and Rhodian territories,' Aristomachos agreed. 'Military service.'

The trireme commander appeared to accept this, though he had his clerk make a list of names; he snorted at some of the names, but apparently it was only the pronounciation that offended him, because he mimicked a Dorian accent to his clerk. Aristomachos bore it politely. Only at the end did his patience crack a little. 'And when can we leave?' he asked.

The trireme commander replied, with a supercilious look, 'At the king's pleasure,' and departed.

'Well, that'll be a long time!' muttered Aristomachos. 'Fucking Antigonos Knock-knees has not enjoyed *anything* for years!'

'I'm sorry,' said Isokrates unhappily.

Aristomachos looked at him, then sighed. 'No, your reasoning was sound enough. I agreed with it, didn't I? Just ... this fucking war is buggering everything up!'

A couple of hours later a royal official turned up at the ship. The crew had rigged the mainsail as an awning by this time, and most of them were sitting in its shade, while a few were cooling off in the sea by the ship's prow. Some of the trireme's crew had joined them in the water, though others, including several archers, were standing guard to ensure that none of the Rhodians tried to slip away into the camp.

The official was a man of middle age with a magnificent beard, plainly dressed apart from a gold-and-ivory wand of office. He approached them along the beach, and Aristomachos descended the ladder to greet him as soon as he glimpsed the gold wand; Isokrates scrambled down when it became clear that the official was indeed making for *Atalanta*.

'Good health to you, Rhodians!' said the official. 'I am Apollonios, a friend of King Antigonos.'

'Good health!' said the trierarch, with an ingratiating smile. 'I hope you've come to tell us we can go?'

Apollonios shook his head. 'You are Aristomachos son of Anaxippos, trierarch of this vessel?'

Aristomachos agreed that he was.

'King Antigonos sends me to ask if it was a man from your ship who was involved in an encounter with Queen Laodike's mercenaries last month.'

'Ah.' Aristomachos glanced uneasily at Isokrates.

Apollonios caught the glance, and nodded as though the trierarch had answered. 'In that case, the king invites you to dine with him, you and the officer who was injured.'

'My ship...' began Aristomachos.

The official raised a hand to stop him. 'I will see to it that your men are supplied with food and drink. King Antigonos has no quarrel with the Rhodians.'

King Antigonos was staying inland from his fleet, in a camp beside the stream which filled the marshes at the northern end of the beach. The walk there took over an hour, and they arrived at the king's pavilion hot, sweaty and dishevelled. The pavilion was about the size of Aristomachos's house in Rhodes; it was of plain bleached canvas, but surmounted by a golden eagle trailing a banner of purple silk. Men in the severely handsome armour of the Macedonian royal guard flanked it on all sides.

Apollonios escorted them to an awning stretched between three olive trees adjacent to the king's tent, and left them. A guard brought them watered wine, and another provided a basin so they could wash their hands and feet; after that they were left to their own devices. There were no seats under the awning, but the bare ground had been strewn with reeds from the marsh. Aristomachos sat down heavily on them, then shifted uncomfortably. After a few minutes he got up again, and went over to the nearest guard to ask how long they would need to wait. The guard didn't know, and Aristomachos returned to the shade of the awning, plucked a couple of the unripe olives, then sat down and irritably shredded them.

Isokrates sat hunched, hugging his knees, tense with doubt and fear. It was obvious that the king had heard something about what had happened in Ephesus. He was not sure how much he should say. If he told the truth and the Syrians found out, they would not be pleased.

On the other hand, would the Macedonian king believe the official version of events? He clearly already knew enough to have doubts, and if he was suspicious he was likely to detain *Atalanta* until he was satisfied. That would be hard on all the men, and for the Athenians could be fatal. He thought of restless, greedy Simmias, his second: there was a man who'd inform if he thought he could get away with it. He wished he could consult Aristomachos, but didn't dare, not while they were surrounded by the king's men.

As the shadows lengthened toward evening, their guide Apollonios at last reappeared and invited them to enter the king's tent.

The pavilion was partitioned into rooms by linen walls, but several of these hangings had been drawn back to create a banqueting hall. The gold-banded post of the royal standard stood at one end, and couches had been arranged about it; the floor was covered with sumptuous rugs. A number of men were clustered about the wine-bowl at the far end of the room: they were all magnificently dressed in scarlet and silk, gilded armour and jewelled brooches. Among them, however, was a tired-looking old man with a scraggly white beard, and he wore the richest ornament of all: a ribbon of purple silk tied about his thin hair with the ends trailing – the royal diadem. Isokrates stopped short, struck against his will by a kind of awe. Antigonos might bear the nickname 'Knock-knees', but he was the son of Demetrios the Besieger, and in his youth had contended with Ptolemy the Thunderbolt and Seleukos the Conqueror. All his old opponents were nothing but ash, but still he lived on to trouble their successors. It was like meeting Agamemnon, or some other hero from the age of legend.

Antigonos seemed to feel his gaze: he glanced round, stared a moment – then smiled and approached. 'The Rhodians!' he said genially. 'Be welcome!'

Aristomachos and Isokrates both bowed deeply.

'I'm told that you came to the Sea of Euboia chasing pirates,' said the king, smiling.

'Yes, o King,' agreed Aristomachos. 'We misinterpreted a rumour to avoid the area.'

'Well, it is my good fortune!' replied the king. 'I've wanted news from Rhodes. Come, have some wine!'

Slaves poured wine into silver cups and escorted the reluctant guests to a couch upholstered in crimson, close to another with gold fittings up-holstered in purple. Antigonos took his own place, and his friends arranged themselves about the room. Slaves brought in loaves of fine wheat bread flavoured with cardamon and saffron, and meat in a sauce so rich and spicy Isokrates had no idea what it was.

The king asked about Rhodes' stance on the war. He seemed to have heard all about the vote for neutrality, but was curious about the arguments of the Council. Aristomachos disavowed knowledge of anything beyond what had been said in the Assembly, though he gave a full account of that: the company was most amused by the heckler's question about when Antigonos had died. One of their fellow guests at the king's table inquired whether Rhodes would build ships for Ptolemy; Aristomachos said politely that the question had not been raised before *Atalanta* left Rhodes. Isokrates, keenly aware that he was the poorest and least-educated man in the room except for the slaves, kept his mouth shut. Nobody said anything about what had happened in Ephesus, however, and after a while he began to relax just a little.

'Why did you think there might be pirates in the Sea of Euboia?' one of the guests asked Aristomachos, with an arch look.

Aristomachos explained again about the rumour, adding the information that they were hunting a pirate known to be particularly daring and unconventional. The king's friend looked sceptical, but didn't make an open accusation of spying. Isokrates began to hope that *Atalanta*

262

really would be allowed to leave next morning.

The second course appeared – grilled sea bass with a piquant sauce – and the talk became more general: the weather, the prospects for the harvest; a play several of the king's friends had seen in Athens a few days before; the Panathenaic festival, now about to begin. The Rhodians had nothing to add to this, and ate in silence.

The meal at last began to draw to a close; by ones and twos the guests took their leave, prostrating themselves to the king before heading out into the night. Aristomachos started to get up at one point, then subsided at a slight shake of the royal head.

At last no one was left in the room except the king, Apollonios, the Rhodians, and the king's slaves. Antigonos gestured for the slaves to refill everyone's cup, then dismissed them. He smiled broadly at the Rhodians.

'Now we can speak freely,' he said, settling himself more comfortably on his couch. 'No one here will gossip. I gather, gentlemen, that you were both in Ephesus immediately before the death of my nephew Antiochos. I would be grateful for any light you could shed on the matter.'

Isokrates was slightly taken aback by that reference to *my nephew*: the family relationship had hardly seemed relevant to monarchs who had never even met face to face. He looked uncomfortably at his trierarch, still unsure what he should say.

'My gratitude is worth having,' said the old king, after a moment of silence. 'On the other

263

hand, if you are unable to give an account of yourselves, I will have to conclude you had no honest purpose coming here – in which case your ship will be subject to seizure and yourselves and your men to imprisonment for the duration of the war.'

Aristomachos cleared his throat. 'We are both strangers to royal courts, o King. Why should you think we know the truth about a king's death?'

Antigonos merely smiled. His friend Apollonios said evenly, 'You were in Ephesus. Your helmsman there was invited to the queen's house, for what reason, nobody seems to know. He returned a couple of hours later, running, and collapsed in front of the gates with an arrow in his back. You took your ship out in a great hurry, then returned the following day demanding to speak to King Antiochos. The king agreed to see you, then fell ill; when news of this was brought to you, you departed again in haste.'

'Come, come!' said the old king genially. 'What harm is there in telling me what happened?'

'One of the queen's mercenaries used to be a pirate,' Isokrates said uncomfortably. 'He had a grudge against me for sinking his ship. He laid an ambush for me on the way back from the queen's house.'

The king gave him a look world-weary and indescribably knowing. 'That is the official version, yes. The Syrians should be satisfied by now that you're repeating it. All my courtiers heard me asking you about the stance of Rhodes, and if any of them are reporting to Seleukos, they'll tell him that that's what I asked about. I've told you that nobody now in this room will gossip: you can speak freely.' He leaned forward, meeting Isokrates' eyes. 'I'm in this war anyway: I don't dare give Egypt the freedom of the Aegean. Antiochos *was* my nephew, though, my dear sister's son, and his house and mine have long been friends. I'm still pondering whether I should go beyond opposing Ptolemy's fleet to supplying active help to my grand-nephew Seleukos – and in that, yes, it *does* matter to me whether Seleukos got the diadem by murder. A man who'll connive at the murder of his own father is hardly going to scruple at betraying a great-uncle. What did Queen Laodike want with you, Rhodian?'

Isokrates gave Aristomachos a hopeless look – then told the king the truth about his visit to the queen's house. When he'd finished, Aristomachos described his attempt to report the matter to the king, what had come of it, and what conclusions the Rhodians had drawn.

Antigonos listened in silence, a silence that lasted after Aristomachos ended his account.

'We don't really know that he was poisoned,' Aristomachos said at last. 'And even if he was, there's nothing to say that Seleukos knew about it.'

The king sighed. 'He was poisoned. Seleukos may not have approved it beforehand, but if he doesn't know it now, he's exceptionally stupid, and won't last out the summer. I don't believe he's stupid – and if he disapproved of what his mother did, he would retire her to some remote country estate. Instead she's been accorded full royal honours and has unparalleled influence in the Syrian court. She always was a nasty piece of work. I still have the report one of my spies drew up at the time of her marriage. Apparently when she was still a child, she had another girl killed, because the poor thing had beaten her in a game.' He snorted. 'And her parents hushed it up, instead of punishing her for it, so it's no wonder she now believes she has a right to get rid of inconveniences by any means she pleases.'

He sloshed his wine about the cup, then tossed it into the basin undrunk. 'Well, well; I'm obliged to you. I had rumours; now I have an eyewitness account. What can I do to show my gratitude?'

'If you're grateful for our bad news, o King,' said Aristomachos politely, 'well then, we're glad that Rhodes has been a friend to you.'

'How diplomatic,' replied Antigonos drily. 'In other words, you don't want money, because then the Syrians might suspect that you told me the truth.'

'My helmsman has already survived an attempt to poison him, o King.'

The king raised his eyebrows. 'This I hadn't heard. Tell me.'

'It was a man named Hyperides, son of Lysimachos,' Isokrates said, embarrassed. 'A kinsman of Queen Laodike. He ... well, I suppose he was angry that I got away and made trouble for the queen. He got himself attached to an embassy to Rhodes, apparently so that he could thrash me.'

'On an *embassy*?' asked Apollonios, shocked.

'He misjudged his man,' said Aristomachos with satisfaction. 'Isokrates knocked him down, took away his sword, and brought it to the ambassador with a complaint. That infuriated the young viper so much that he sent a basket of poisoned sweets, purportedly from a friend, as a parting gift.'

'My landlady and her two children are dead,' Isokrates said bitterly. 'We're trying to complain to King Seleukos about him, sir, but discreetly, because we don't know how much influence he has.'

Antigonos snorted thoughtfully. 'That, actually, is useful information – a straw in the wind, as you naval men put it, that shows which way the wind's blowing. This man was *able* to get himself appointed to a sensitive embassy, was he? Who was the ambassador, may I ask?'

'Diodoros, a guest-friend of our admiral Agathostratos.'

'I know the man: a good man, able and loyal. My nephew used to send him here occasionally as well. What did he make of this Hyperides?'

'I don't think he liked him,' Isokrates said slowly, 'but he would have preferred to believe that he wasn't at fault. When he was convinced that he was, he was angry and exasperated, but he was also worried about what to say to the queen. Agathostratos remarked on that – that it was a bad omen that Diodoros was worried.'

The king let out a breath. 'A bad omen indeed.

Thank you a second time.' He tapped the arm of his couch, then gave them another thin smile. 'I say again, I am obliged to you. I still wait to hear how I should express my gratitude.'

'We're happy that you still consider Rhodes your friend,' said Aristomachos, 'and that *friendly* ships are allowed to come and go from Macedonian ports.'

Antigonos waved a hand. 'Of course your ship will be allowed to leave in the morning! Tell me, were you really hoping to find a pirate? In the *Euboian Sea*?'

'Yes, o King, we were. An unconventional pirate by the name of Andronikos of Phalassarna. He has reason to stay away from Egyptian waters and a tendency to appear where he isn't expected, so we were chasing rumours. I know pirates are small fry to you, o King, but chasing them is what our ship was built for – and even you, I think, would be glad to see the end of a man like Andronikos. He was involved in the attack on Daphne, and was last seen sailing away from that atrocity in a hemiolia called the *Kratousa*, loaded down with loot.'

The king looked mildly interested. 'One of Berenike's murderers, and a pirate on top of it? A common enemy of mankind, it seems. Apollonios...'

The official, who'd listened in frowning silence, nodded. 'I can look into it, my lord. I can't promise anything, and I'll need at least three days.'

'Look into it,' ordered the king. He surveyed Aristomachos a moment, then said, 'You are free to take your ship and go whenever you choose. I suggest that you might want to stop in Athens for a couple of days, though, to enjoy the Pana-thenaia and trawl for rumours among the crowds. If Apollonios meets you there ... why, you might want to share a drink with him.'

Aristomachos sat very still a moment, then got up and bowed deeply. 'Thank you, o King. We are in your debt.'

Thirteen

Athens during the Panathenaia was a nightmare: high prices, a shortage of water, scarce food, and everywhere crowds, crowds, crowds. The port of Piraeus was crammed with merchant ships; the road between the port and the city was jammed with carts; in Athens itself there were people everywhere. It was noisy, dirty, and swelteringly hot.

Walking into the city had been Aristomachos's idea. There was no real need to leave the Piraeus. Apollonios would undoubtedly contact them on the ship: there was nowhere else he could be sure of *finding* them. He had said, though, that he needed three days; getting to Athens had taken only one – and Aristomachos wanted to see something of the festival.

Isokrates was nervous about leaving *Atalanta*. They had obviously not been able to tell the crew that they'd come to meet Antigonos's spy-master, as a reward for information received: that would have betrayed them to any Syrian spy who troubled to investigate. The men, though, were understandably dubious about the excuse that they were trawling for more rumours: festival-goers would know less about piracy than the traders on Delos, and *that* hadn't turned out too well. The Athenians in the crew were particularly apprehensive – though most of them were plainly intending to sneak into the city to see their families, a prospect which made Isokrates very uneasy, though he didn't forbid it. He had to leave Simmias in charge, as well, and he didn't trust the second. He joined Aristomachos anyway, though, because he hoped to hear Dionysia sing.

By the time they reached the Athenian marketplace he was wishing he'd stayed on *Atalanta*. Aristomachos had invited his nephew as well, and the two of them were pointing out the sights to one another and exclaiming. Neither had visited Athens before, but they'd read any number of Athenian orators, philosophers and playwrights; they seemed to know the sights of Athens nearly as well as those of Rhodes. Isokrates couldn't help a gloomy suspicion that Dionysia would be similarly knowledgeable, but to him the city seemed a rundown place full of mean mud-brick houses and unfriendly people – though the public buildings were very fine.

Aristomachos gazed up at the Parthenon on its hill above them. '"Shimmering, renowned and with violets crowned,"' he recited enthusiastically, '"Athens the glory of Greece!"'

Isokrates stirred irritably. 'That must've been when it was a democracy.'

'Of *course* that was when it was a democracy!' said Nikagoras with contempt. 'That's *Pindar*! *Everybody* knows that one.'

'I didn't,' Isokrates said morosely.

'Choose your venue and I'm sure you can hear

it set to music,' said Aristomachos cheerfully. 'Probably in any one of three settings. The Athenians are very fond of that poem. I wonder if our Dionysia will sing it? We need to find the Guild of Dionysiac Artists: they'll have a schedule.'

It was the second day of the festival. The first day had been devoted to the religious rituals; now the musical and athletic events were in full swing – but finding out what was on where was difficult. Aristomachos asked a shopkeeper for directions: the man professed ignorance – with a sniggering imitation of the trierarch's accent. A passerby turned out to be from Syracuse, and had no more idea of the city's layout than the Rhodians. Isokrates wished they'd enlisted one of the Athenian oarsmen.

They eventually found a waterseller who directed them to the theatre, on the other side of the acropolis from the marketplace. The Guild of Dionysiac Artists had a house there, which, in the usual way, had been made available to visiting members of the guild. The Rhodians arrived to find pandemonium, with actors and musicians charging about in various states of undress clutching masks and instruments. The inquiry about the competition for singing to the kithara did, however, eventually produce a harried secretary with a ledger.

'Dionysia daughter of Kleisthenes of Miletos?' he asked, running a finger down the ledger. 'No, nobody by that name is entered.'

'She told me that she'd been invited to compete,' said Isokrates. 'Perhaps you have her

272

down under the name of her guardian, Hagemon?'

Dionysia was not listed under Hagemon's name either, nor had she been misplaced in the categories of 'singers' or 'kitharists'. The secretary refused to check any further, and raced off to deal with a complaint about a missing kettledrum.

'You must've misheard or misunderstood,' Aristomachos told Isokrates. 'Ah well, never mind! Let's go watch the horse races!' The hippodrome wasn't too far from the theatre, and to find it all they had to do was follow the sound of cheering.

Isokrates watched a couple of races without registering the winners. He was sure he had not misheard or misunderstood: Dionysia had told him she was to sing at the Panathenaia. Somebody had clearly made a mistake, and it seemed much more likely to have been the Guild secretary than Dionysia.

He excused himself after the third race and went back to the Guild house. An inquiry about the competition eventually found another competitor, a foppish long-haired tenor from Corinth. The competition would take place the following day, the tenor informed him – but no, he'd heard nothing of Dionysia. 'Daughter of Kleisthenes of Miletos?' he said, with interest. 'I didn't know he had a daughter! I've heard him play, of course – the most *divine* touch on the strings! That man's skill came straight from Apollo; I kiss his hands for it! His voice, though ... well, he wisely let somebody else do the singing. What does his daughter sound like?'

'Like a goddess,' said Isokrates.

The Corinthian looked uneasy. *'Re*-ally?' Then he brightened. 'She can't have come. If she was here, I would've heard something. *Very* well known, her father: if his daughter was about to compete, everyone would be talking about it. You must be mistaken.'

'Perhaps she was delayed in Rhodes,' Isokrates said, but he was worried.

He looked for the Guild secretary again, and eventually found him in a courtyard arguing with a drum-and-flute duo.

'No, it was *not*!' the secretary was saying angrily. 'I don't know what you two did to it...'

'We didn't do anything!' protested the flautist.

The secretary gave a snort of contempt, glanced up, and spotted Isokrates. 'Oh, there you are! I was hoping you'd come back. The woman you were asking about, the daughter of Kleisthenes – the name was familiar, so I checked, and you're right, she *was* supposed to compete in the singing-to-the-kithara contest. She hadn't turned up by the start of the festival, though, so she was struck off the list.'

'It just broke!' argued the drummer. 'We didn't do anything!'

'You two drunks fucking *broke* it!' exclaimed the secretary. 'You can fucking *pay*!'

Isokrates thanked him and got out.

He had no more appetite for the festival, and he started back to the ship. Piraeus was an hour's walk from Athens, time enough for worry to settle into fear. Dionysia's absence could not be

274

explained by anything trivial: the invitation had been important to her career. She had no family ties to bind her, and there had been no storms to delay her. Was she ill? Had she met with some disaster, in Rhodes or on the sea?

Perhaps she simply had a sore throat, and couldn't sing, or had hurt her hand, and couldn't play ... though wouldn't she have sent a letter in that case? Perhaps she had, but she'd sent it to whoever it was that had invited her, and the secretary hadnseen it. Isokrates almost turned around and went back to ask who'd invited her, but it seemed unlikely that the secretary would even know. Besides, by the time he thought of it, he was almost at the port.

Piraeus was a town in its own right, and Isokrates found it a deeply unsettling one. The naval base spread out over its three harbours had once had space for nearly three hundred warships, and the Athenian triremes which docked there had ruled the Aegean. A bare fifth of the shipsheds were still in use, and even those now stood empty, the ships they'd contained off serving King Antigonos. Athens had once been stronger, prouder and more glorious than Rhodes; now it was a Macedonian possession and a destination for tourists. Rhodes would suffer the same fate, if the republic's wisdom ever failed it.

The Athenian navy might have shrunk, but the merchant harbour was busy enough: *Atalanta* had been forced to run up well away from the central quays, much to the disgust of her crew.

Isokrates trudged along the edge of the Kantharos Harbour, past one merchant ship after another, and finally reached his trihemiolia, beached among the light craft and fishing boats and looking like a ferret among rabbits.

The ship was quiet: most of the crew had gone to see the festival. Isokrates scrambled up the boarding ladder, and found Simmias playing dice on the stern deck with Damophon the bo'sun and one of the deckfighters. They had a large jug.

Simmias looked up in bleary alarm. 'What are you doing back early?'

'What are you doing drinking on duty?' Isokrates replied, scooping up the jug. 'You're relieved, and confined to the ship until we leave port!'

Simmias glowered and stamped off. Isokrates sat down heavily in the command chair and gazed bleakly out at the harbour.

Damophon came over, embarrassed and apologetic. 'Sorry, sir.'

'*You* weren't in charge.'

'Well, no, but we all put money in the kitty for the wine.'

Isokrates snorted and handed him the jug, which was almost empty.

Damophon ducked his head in thanks. 'Don't be too hard on Simmias, sir. He's not a bad fellow, even if he is a bit too eager to get hold of money. He's unsettled; we all are. We don't know what we're doing here. We'd like it better if we just cruised pirate waters, the way everybody does.'

Isokrates shook his head. 'We wouldn't *catch* anything if we did that. There's going to be blood in the Aegean soon: that'll fetch the sharks.' He met the bo'sun's wary eyes and went on, 'You think I'm being a fool?'

Damophon pursed his lips. 'That's not your reputation, sir. I think maybe you're a little too eager for revenge on this Andronikos, though, and you're chasing whispers. What you said about sharks, though – that's true.' He grimaced. 'That was a great, great fleet up at Marathon.'

'Yes.' Isokrates imagined the vast ships setting out into the Euboian Sea, slicing the waves with their towering beaks while all those thousands laboured at the oars. Ptolemy's equally huge fleet would be setting out from Pydnai in Lycia to meet them. Blood in the water, and men drowned by the hundred. Why? he wondered. He could understand being willing to die for city and friends. He would be willing to die for Rhodes himself – but why would any man die for a king?

'A fleet like that,' said Damophon, 'they'll be shipping in supplies from all over to keep everyone fed. And kings always grant amnesties to pirates who attack their enemy's shipping. Oh, you're right about the sharks! But it seems to me that by the time there's a rumour about where they are, they'll be somewhere else.'

'Worth a try, though.'

'I suppose,' Damophon said doubtfully. He saluted with the wine-jug and went to join the deckfighter dicer in the shade of the mainsail awning.

Aristomachos and Nikagoras had not returned to the ship by dark; Isokrates was becoming seriously worried when a boy arrived with a note from the trierarch, saying that they would be staying in the city that night.

'He gave this to you himself?' Isokrates asked the boy anxiously. 'He was well?'

The child sniggered. 'He was rollin'. Him and his nephew, they're banqueting at *Aspasia's Vineyard*, eating grilled mullet and drinking honeyed wine, with the most beautiful girls in the city singing and dancing for 'em. He said you shoulda stayed with 'em.'

It wasn't until noon the following day that Aristomachos climbed up the boarding ladder, sweaty and dishevelled and smelling of spilt wine. 'Zeus, it's hot!' he exclaimed, collapsing into his chair. 'Apollonios show up?'

Isokrates grimaced and made a hushing gesture, though in fact the stern deck was empty. 'No, sir.'

'Well, may he rot! There's a performance of Euripides' *Iphigenia in Tauris* today, in the very theatre where it was first put on, but I left my nephew to watch it on his own and plodded back here in this filthy heat so I wouldn't miss the bugger!'

'Have some water,' Isokrates said tactfully, offering him a jug.

'They have chariot racing today, too,' said the trierarch regretfully, taking a swig of water and wiping his mouth.

'It's a pity. Sir, I checked back at the Guild yesterday, and Dionysia *should* have been there.

Her name was taken off the list of competitors because she hadn't showed up by the beginning of the festival.'

Aristomachos gave him an anxious frown, then shook his head. 'Maybe she's ill. You can ask her what happened when we get back to Rhodes.'

Apollonios did not show up that day; in fact, he did not show up at all. That evening, however, a port official appeared at the ship, gingerly carrying a sealed letter-case.

'It's addressed to Aristomachos son of Anaxippos, of the Rhodian trihemiolia *Atalanta,*' said the port official.

'That's me,' agreed Aristomachos, taking the letter-case. The official gave him an apprehensive look and departed hurriedly.

'Bugger it!' muttered Aristomachos, studying the seal. 'That fellow obviously recognized this, even if I don't! Probably thinks we're spies.'

Nikagoras and a couple of deck-soldiers had come over to see what was going on, and the trierarch glared at them. 'This must be some sort of follow-up to our encounter with the king, all right? Bugger off, and let me read it in private – not *you,* Isokrates!'

It was growing dark, and they had to go to a nearby tavern and borrow a lamp before they could read the letter. Aristomachos then took it out the tavern's door and read it in an undertone while Isokrates held the lamp for him.

Apollonios son of Phylarchos wishes health

to the trierarch Aristomachos. First, I regret that the pressure of my duties forbids that I meet with you – *yes, so you drew attention to us by sending a letter with a Master Spy seal on it, you bastard!* – I have made inquiries respecting the pirate Andronikos, and have discovered the following:

Firstly, the man was in the employ of Queen Laodike, as you said, and was provided by her with a ship, the *Kratousa*, which he crewed with mercenaries recruited from among the forces in Asia – *That's right, you stupid bugger: we told you about it!* –

Secondly, he was indeed among the foremost of those at Daphne, and has been included by King Ptolemy on the lists of wanted criminals – *we know that, too!* –

Thirdly, – *now we're coming to it* – Thirdly, after departing from Daphne, Andronikos returned to his home city of Phalassarna, where he boasted of his deeds and spent silver to the value of three or four talents. He discharged some crew, but recruited many others, and set out from Phalassarna again about eight days ago, as I learned from one recently come from that city. In addition to the hemiolia *Kratousa*, he is reported as commanding two lighter craft, one of twenty oars, the other of thirty, both carrying men armed for raiding. Among his boasts was that of receiving information and help from Syria if he raids Egyptian shipping, and he is thought to have made for Lycia, an area with which he is familiar.

'Lycia!' exclaimed Isokrates, seeing again the blue seas around the Olympos headland, and the hemiolia going down. Lycia belonged to Egypt: he'd been sure that Andronikos would avoid it. He'd known that the man was bold, though: he shouldn't have ruled it out.

'Lycia,' repeated Aristomachos in disgust. 'Coast like a fig leaf, all ins and outs and islands. Could sail right past him and miss him completely.'

'No, I might know where to go. Given where I met him before.'

Aristomachos raised his eyebrows, frowning. 'If his base has been found before, he won't use it again.'

'But I didn't find his base! I just know that coast well enough to work out where it was. See, I met him mid-morning. Dionysia said that they'd spent the previous night in a small inlet. There's only one or two places it could be.'

'Oh, well done!' Aristomachos said warmly. 'If it wasn't ever found, he'll be confident about it – particularly since he doesn't know *we're* on to him.'

Isokrates shook his head unhappily. 'If he set out eight days ago, he'll be in Lycia *now*. That's if he was really bound there at all: he may have been spreading false rumours about his destination. Even if he is there, it's a long way. He may be gone again before we arrive.'

'Don't be so gloomy!' said Aristomachos. 'He'll be thinking he can afford to be picky, and take time to collect only the best plunder to take home. Ptolemy's garrisons will've been stripped of men for the campaign, and if ships disappear everyone will put it down to war, not piracy: Andronikos won't be expecting anybody to come after him. There's a very good chance he'll still be around, if we hurry. There's more to the letter:

> While my lord the king would not be grieved to see Ptolemy's ships harmed, he judges that this wicked pirate is a common enemy of mankind. Accordingly, if you are in need of assistance, you may show this letter to any of the king's people, and they will be required to give you whatever you may require for the pursuit of the criminal Andronikos.

'It has the royal seal!' Aristomachos exclaimed, holding the letter up to the light. 'At least, I *think* it's the royal seal. Eagle and oak-wreath. It's not the same as the one on the case, anyway. Well. Probably won't need it, but it's a useful thing to have.'

Isokrates did not smile. A worrying possibility, still vague, was beginning to take shape in his mind. Andronikos had set out from Phalassarna eight days before; Dionysia had set out from Rhodes ... when? Five or six days before, to arrive in time for the start of the festival? Would their courses have intersected?

It seemed far-fetched, but ... she should have been at the Panathenaia, and she wasn't. And perhaps the coincidence of timing wasn't accidental. If Andronikos still had contacts in

Laodike's court, and if Laodike still hated Dionysia – no, there was no 'if' in it. The queen *would* hate Dionysia now, much more than before. Laodike's attempt to get rid of Dionysia was what had caused her final confrontation with her husband: she would certainly find it outrageous that after causing her so much trouble, Dionysia should be alive and thriving in Rhodes. That invitation to the Panathenaia, where had it come from?

With a sudden icy sickness, Isokrates realized that wherever the invitation had come from, it must have arrived while Hyperides was in Rhodes.

'So!' exclaimed Aristomachos, slapping his shoulder. 'Lycia it is! We set out first thing tomorrow!'

Atalanta set out at dawn, though Isokrates was obliged to scour the taverns of Piraeus to manage it, and left two men behind. That long hot day and the next he drove the men hard, rowing in shifts from dawn to dark. They did not complain: they understood perfectly well that the mysterious letter had contained news, and they were eager to take another ship. That worried Isokrates, in a remote fashion: if the Syrians ever set someone to inquire into the matter, it would be obvious to them that he and Aristomachos had done a deal with Antigonos. Most of his mind, however, was absorbed in the overwhelming need for *speed*. The crew believed that he was eager to take revenge on Andronikos. The real fear – that Dionysia had fallen back into the hands of her abuser – that was something he couldn't bring himself to mention even to Aristomachos. The image of her as he'd first seen her, battered and despairing, burned his mind, making it impossible to rest. Sleepless at night on some isolated beach, he thought of her twisting her cloak in her hands and calling him her true and dear friend.

He had failed her. He had not killed Andronikos at their first encounter; he had fled from him at the second. Now he struggled to drag a ship across the infinite blue of the Aegean, knowing even as he did so that perhaps he was heading to the wrong destination, or would arrive too late.

She may just have a sore throat! he told himself repeatedly. *She may have hurt her hand!* But he felt as though he were in some nightmare, tangled in a snare or wading through mud to save her, too slow, always too slow.

They crossed the Cyclades, turned south, and arrived back in Rhodes at night, three days after leaving Athens. Isokrates wouldn't have stopped at the island at all, but they had run out of supplies. He refused the men leave to go into the city and sent them to sleep in the shipyard barracks instead, so that he could be sure of getting away early. He himself slept aboard *Atalanta* and rose before dawn to chivvy the shipyard for supplies of food and water.

Then he had to wait for the trierarch: Aristomachos had gone home to sleep in his own bed. He finally turned up at *Atalanta* at the fourth hour of the morning. By that time the ship had been sitting in the water for an hour, all oars manned.

Aristomachos scrambled aboard, looking worried. 'Sorry,' he told Isokrates. 'I had some business.'

Isokrates nodded curtly, too furious to speak, and gave the order to cast off. Aristomachos caught his arm and drew him over to the command chair. 'Agathostratos came round,' he said in a low voice. 'Last night I sent a report on our meeting with King Antigonos to him and to Xenophantes. I thought somebody ought to know.'

'Oh.' Isokrates hadn't thought of that. Aristomachos was right, of course.

'Yes. Anyway, Agathostratos came to tell me he'd heard from his friend Diodoros, the ambassador. Apparently he'd sent him that basket of poisoned sweets, with an account of what happened.

'Diodoros had already had a meeting with the queen, which apparently didn't go too well: the queen was angry about his "disrespectful" treatment of her kinsman, and thought he should've insisted on your being thrashed for quarrelling with a diplomat. The ambassador was so apprehensive that he didn't try to meet with her again. Instead he took the sweets to King Seleukos. The king summoned Hyperides and told him what Diodoros had said. Hyperides denied any wrongdoing – so the king asked him to eat one of the sweets.'

Aristomachos paused, waiting for some response. Isokrates said nothing: he was finding it difficult to concentrate on his friend's words. Only the steady beat of the oars seemed real,

285

carrying them on toward Lycia.

'Well, Hyperides refused, of course,' Aristomachos continued at last. 'And this is the bad bit: the king did nothing more than *dismiss* him. Oh, apparently he made it clear that *he* wouldn't tolerate diplomats who took advantage of their status to poison personal enemies – but he didn't try to get his mother to send the viper away. He just summoned Diodoros and asked whether we're likely to change our mind about neutrality over this. Diodoros told him we won't.' Aristomachos grimaced. 'Which is true, I'm afraid. Even if we made a big noise about the poisoning, the Assembly wouldn't overturn the vote, not now. Nobody wants to join this war. And look, my friend: *don't* make a noise about it. Please. If you do, it won't get justice for your landlady, but it will get you killed. At the moment the only comfort is that the Syrians won't try to kill you again any time soon, because they think you're dead. Agathostratos had the good sense to let Diodoros think *you'd* eaten the bugger-arsed poison, and that it was *your* death we were complaining about.'

Isokrates stared numbly, again remembering Leuke's face. Aristomachos touched his shoulder. 'I'm sorry.'

'They'll find out I'm not dead,' Isokrates said at last. 'Particularly if they ... if they discover that we met Antigonos.'

Aristomachos shrugged. 'Well, yes – *if* they ever look into that, we're both in trouble. But right now the Syrians have more urgent things to worry about. By the time the war's over – well, even if Hyperides and Laodike are still alive, we'll be stale news. They'll have fresh grievances and new enemies to occupy them, I don't doubt *that* for a moment. If you don't stir them up again, they'll forget you.'

Isokrates stared out over the trierarch's shoulder at the blue Aegean. He had never been able to help Leuke: not against her brother's bullying or her mother's neglect; not in her hard life and not in her cruel death. He had been both witness and cause of her end – exactly as he had for Agido.

'I'm sorry,' said Aristomachos again. 'And there's more bad news, too. I made some enquiries about our friend the Milesian. It seems she *did* set out for Athens, shortly after we left for Delos. I'm sorry.'

Isokrates hadn't wanted to ask – hadn't wanted to waste the time, and more, had been afraid to know. 'I thought that might be the case,' he said at last, heavily.

Aristomachos let his breath out slowly. 'So that's what's been goading you, is it?'

Isokrates gave him a sick look. 'I don't know how invitations to the Panathenaia work. She was expected there, but I don't know whether somebody could've arranged for her to be nominated. She must have received the invitation while Hyperides was in Rhodes – and the letter said that Andronikos still has contacts in Syria.'

'Oh, that's a foul thought!' Aristomachos exclaimed, startled. 'I hope you're wrong – and I hope we *find* the filthy bastard.'

* * *

The men rowed hard all day, and the island of Megiste came into sight early in the evening. Isokrates wanted to continue on; Aristomachos gave the order to put in.

'The men are tired,' he said firmly, in reply to Isokrates' look of angry reproach. 'They need a good night's sleep – particularly if you want this ship to take on a horde of pirates in the next couple of days. We need to sit down and plan our tactics very carefully, too.'

Isokrates scowled; the trierarch sighed and expanded. 'The bastard is going to have, what, seventy or eighty on the hemiolia, and at least as many on the smaller craft? Their numbers may be about the same as ours, but you know as well as I do that their people are better armed than ours and a lot tougher. If we just row up and attack their fucking base they'll slaughter us. If they manage to *board* us, they'll slaughter us, too. Even my son could see that!'

Isokrates stood still a moment, looking down at his friend. What the trierarch said was un-doubtedly true; that he hadn't seen it himself was probably because he hadn't wanted to. He hadn't had a clear idea what he would do if he found Andronikos, but there had been a hazy expectation that he would cut down the pirate and rescue Dionysia. It wasn't going to happen like that. *Atalanta* couldn't match the pirates by land, and by sea could do so only by employing her superior speed and agility in order to ram. That would kill or disable the pirates, but it was likely to do the same to any prisoners they had aboard. A naked seaman might have some chance of swimming to safety after his ship was swamped, but a captive would drown.

If they wanted to be sure of rescuing the pirates' captives, they needed a force which could attack the pirates' base on land – and they had none. Rhodes did have a small army, but the process of applying to the navy board for assistance, and then getting the men round to the pirate base, would take too long, even if the republic was willing to commit forces to his tenuous hope – which wasn't likely.

'There's no hope of getting any help from Ptolemy's forces, is there?' he asked the trierarch pleadingly. 'We can't send to the garrison at Pydnai or Phaselis and ask for land troops to back us up?'

Aristomachos shook his head. 'Not a chance. I don't think the king's garrisons were eager to do any marching even before, judging by that sack-arse in Phaselis, but now, with a war on, the forts will be stripped and everybody who can hold a spear will be attacking Syria.' He frowned at Isokrates, then patted his arm. 'Don't despair, man! If Andronikos *is* still in Lycia, it'll be because he's being picky and only grabbing the choicest bits of plunder. That means he'll be keeping his booty shut up back at his base until he's ready to go home to Crete. If we tackle his ships on the sea *first*, his captives will be safe until we come to rescue them.'

Isokrates let out his breath slowly and nodded. That was indeed the most likely scenario, if Andronikos was still in Lycia.

If Andronikos was still in Lycia. If he'd even

gone to Lycia to begin with. If, if, if.

Dionysia had left Rhodes nine days before, and not reached her destination: there was no 'if' in that. Where was she now? Was she helpless on the pirate's ship, already bound back to Crete for a life of slavery – frightened, hurt, humiliated and alone?

He remembered how before she had preferred death, throwing herself into the sea rather than letting Andronikos use her as coin. This time even that choice might have been denied her.

Oh gods! he prayed, in anguish, Apollo and the Muses, you love her and gave her gifts: keep her safe! And you who see all, Sun above us, let me find her!

Fourteen

At Megiste they had what felt like the first piece of good luck for a year.

'If you're going east, could you do some escort duty?' asked the commander of the island's naval base. 'There's a merchantman bound for Antioch who's been sitting in port since yesterday, hoping for protection.'

Aristomachos looked hopeful. 'What sort of merchantman?'

'She's the *Colchidis,* four hundred tons, bound for Antioch with a load of timber from the Euxine. Her captain owns the ship himself. Kylon son of Polemon, of Rhodes town. He's afraid that the Egyptians will impound his cargo if he sails on unescorted. Ptolemy's ships have been up and down this coast since the start of the month, and the timber's suitable for ship-building.'

'We'll escort him,' said Aristomachos. 'I'll send him a note to tell him we want to leave early.'

'I know Kylon and the *Colchidis,*' he told Isokrates a little later. 'Nice, roomy ship, and fast, too. She's rigged in the Euxine fashion, with doubled stays, and her figurehead is Medea of Colchis, holding up the fucking *golden fleece*!

291

Any pirate who sees her will say to himself, "Luck of Hermes! A ship from the Euxine! Maybe it's carrying *gold*!" and rush out to have a closer look. All we have to do is sneak along after her.'

'We should do our sneaking inshore,' Isokrates said eagerly. 'That way, not only will the land mask us, but if the pirates do rush out, we'll be able to cut them off from their base.'

Aristomachos summoned Nikagoras, Simmias and Polydoros and announced that he hoped to meet with a substantial force of pirates within the next two days; Nikagoras seemed to be the only one this news took by surprise. The five of them discussed tactics over a light supper. Glancing round the others' faces in the lamp-light, Isokrates was comforted: for all the differences he'd had with his bow-officer and his second, now they all seemed of one mind. Tomorrow the ship must work like a single living creature – and the omens that it could do so were good.

Atalanta and her consort set out from Megiste in the grey pre-dawn. There was an inshore breeze and the *Colchidis* struggled to get out of the harbour; in the end *Atalanta* impatiently gave the merchant a tow.

Once they left the bay, though, the tables were turned. The sea was choppy, making the galley buck and the oarsmen struggle, while the roundship shouldered the waves aside, her folded sails taking her close to the northeasterly wind, bearing her eastward. *Atalanta* hurried to the calmer water closer to shore. The rising sun

292

showed the Lycian coast rising steeply to their left, its headlands and islands a hazy tourmaline against the dark blue of the sea. A pod of dolphins surrounded the galley, leaping and frolicking in the foam about her prow: the men pointed them out to one another and grinned, taking it as a sign of the gods' favour. Despite the rough water they were in high spirits.

The men rowed steadily in shifts, clinging to the coast, which, besides concealing them, provided some shelter from the wind. The *Colchidis,* however, swung well out to sea, making the most of the contrary wind: most of the time she was visible only as a patch of white sails. Noon came and went. They reached Phoinikos beach at about the eighth hour, and saw the Olympos headland rising steeply before them, shadowed with pines. *Atalanta* rowed parallel to the long line of surf, her oars beating in time to a melancholy tune on the pipes. The men were too tired to sing.

At the end of the beach, they could see the white sails of *Colchidis,* far out on the blue water, narrowing as the roundship adjusted her trim to round the headland. Then *Atalanta*'s look-out shouted wordlessly, and a moment later Nikagoras's voice rose, shrill with excitement: 'Longship, there! Rowing out toward the *Colchidis*!'

Isokrates and Aristomachos both hurried forward through the crowd of off-shift oarsmen and climbed up on to the ship's forefoot. Nikagoras grinned madly and pointed: there was indeed a galley moving out from some cove in the headland before them – a slim blue needle, almost lost against the sea. It was small, though, and undecked: not a hemiolia. Isokrates, straining his eyes, thought it might be a *myoparon,* the smallest class of warship, possessing only twenty oars. The light prow showed that, whatever it was, the vessel wasn't armed with a ram.

'Easy oars!' shouted Aristomachos, and the trihemiolia coasted forward in a sudden silence.

A second blue needle slipped out from behind the headland, this one much larger. Its thicker outline showed that it was decked: a hemiolia, undoubtedly.

Aristomachos gave a whoop of glee and slapped Isokrates' shoulder. 'All oars!' he yelled. 'We found the bugger!'

'Hard a port!' Isokrates yelled, suddenly terrified. If they could see the pirates, the pirates could see them – and there was still time for those ships to return to the safety of their base. *Atalanta* needed to get out of sight.

Kleitos the tiller-holder obeyed, and the trihemiolia's beak turned toward the land. The decking sounded as the off-duty men poured below to join their comrades at the oars, and the trihemiolia's speed began to pick up. Isokrates walked back to the stern: Kleitos glanced at his face, then handed over the tiller. Isokrates nodded to him. The tug of the bar in his palm seemed to draw away all his fear, and, after so many anxious hours, he felt curiously calm. There was no place now for emotion: what was done next had to be done perfectly, or it would fail.

The *Colchidis* and her attackers disappeared behind the rise of the land, but he steered the ship still closer inshore until the steep cliffs towered over them. There was a strong current running toward the cliff, and he had to work to hold the ship steady.

Aristomachos came back to join him, his face pale with excitement. 'Sir,' Isokrates said quietly, 'the men should be rowing in short shifts.'

Aristomachos winced. 'What about *Colchidis*?'

'Let the pirates take her. Her crew know we're here, so they won't fight, and if they don't fight, they won't be harmed. They'll be needed to sail *Colchidis* back to Crete, and at the journey's end they'd fetch at least two hundred apiece.'

The trierarch grimaced, but gave the order: he knew as well as Isokrates that it was necessary. *Atalanta*'s oarcrew had been rowing all day on rough water, but the pirate crews would be fresh. The trihemiolia had to conserve her men's strength until the crisis was over.

Half of the beating oars rose and stilled smoothly. The ship had become a single being whose hundred and twenty limbs moved purposefully as one: the ragged performance of the previous April belonged to another age. Isokrates knew that below-deck half the oarsmen were leaning on the hafts, catching their breaths. Damophon would let the others carry on for sixty strokes, then switch over.

Aristomachos went forward to the central hatch, called down, 'Pass the water round!' then continued as far as the forefoot. He spoke briefly to Nikagoras, then came back, sat down in the command chair, and fidgeted. After a minute he stood up again. 'Gods rot it!' he muttered, glaring at the cliffs to their left. 'If the buggers saw us, they could be back at their base by now!'

Isokrates said nothing. What Aristomachos had said would be true even if they'd continued with all oars. They just had to hope that the pirates had been concentrating on *Colchidis* during the brief interval when *Atalanta* was visible.

They rowed on, clinging to the shelter of the cliff. The oar shifts changed, then changed again. The beat of the drum amidships was a constant heart, even and untroubled: *bang,* two, three, *bang*, two, three, the oars digging into the turquoise inshore water and propelling the longship swiftly athwart the current.

At last they rounded a curve of the land and caught sight of *Colchidis* again. The roundship was hove to, her prow toward the wind and her sails limp, apparently alone ... no! Not alone: the myoparon was snugged up against her. Where was the hemiolia? Where, for that matter, was the third ship Andronikos was supposed to possess?

The cliff on their left fell away and they rowed out into a deep blue bay: there was no more possibility of concealment. 'All oars?' whispered Aristomachos longingly.

Isokrates shook his head. 'Sir, we don't *need* all oars. They're caught.' *Colchidis* and her attackers were still so far away that he could scarcely make out the shapes of the men aboard – but they were to *starboard,* seawards of *Atalanta.* The pirates could not get back to shore without passing the trihemiolia.

Atalanta swept majestically onward toward the centre of the bay, her bronze beak biting the water, her standard gleaming, her drum maintaining the same steady beat. It seemed an eternity before the galley tucked up against *Colchidis* began to stir. Then men began scrambling off the merchant, into the pirate ship: they'd seen the Rhodians, and knew they had to fight or flee.

The hemiolia reappeared suddenly, shooting out from *behind* the roundship. There was a stir on her forefoot, then a flash of light: a sailor had scrambled up and was signalling with a polished shield. The pirate ship turned her prow toward *Atalanta* and bore down swiftly, all her oars beating. Her smaller consort moved in parallel, close to her flank. Isokrates understood the intention perfectly: whichever ship *Atalanta* attacked first, the other would close and try to board.

The hemiolia was much the more dangerous of the pair: not merely larger, but protected by decking and armed with a ram. Kill the hemiolia, and the myoparon would be easy.

'All oars,' he said, under his breath, and Aristomachos bellowed, 'All oars! Deckfighters, to your stations, both sides!' Then he added, under his breath, 'Right between the pair of 'em, yes? Disable one, ram the other?'

Isokrates glanced up at the bright sun on the

standard, nodded, and adjusted the tiller.

'Right down the middle!' the trierarch confirmed, shouting it for the whole crew to hear. 'If we can't outmanoeuvre a pair of bugger-arsed Cretans, men, we're not worthy of Rhodes!'

The men cheered, though the cheer from the oarcrew was ragged: the men were pulling hard, and didn't have much breath to spend on cheering.

Suddenly the pirates were close – close enough to see the the men crowded on deck, their shields held high, the spears in their hands gleaming, with the archers and slingers crouched in their shadow. Two of *Atalanta*'s deck-soldiers had taken up station in the stern, and they raised their own shields to protect themselves and their officers against the oncoming menace. 'Rush speed,' whispered Isokrates, and Aristomachos shouted it: 'Rush speed!'

The drumbeat picked up at last: *bang* two, *bang* two, the heartbeat suddenly racing as in anger or in fear. *Atalanta* leapt forward joyfully; 'Port a point!' shouted Nikagoras shrilly from the bow, and Isokrates tilted the tiller. He could see both ships now, the hemiolia to port and the myoparon to starboard, with the pirates crowding the sides. There was a sudden explosive *cracking* against the decking: slingstones from the enemy. Aristomachos gave a yell of pure excitement, smacking a fist against his palm. Isokrates drew a deep breath: wait, wait...

The air filled with arrows, and men were screaming the warcry; the sound of spears beaten against shields almost drowned the drum.

298

'Ship the oars!' he whispered

'Ship oars!' yelled Aristomachos, and Isokrates shifted the tiller again.

The hemiolia had swerved at the last moment, trying to brush against *Atalanta*'s portside oars and disable them – but the oars were flat against the vessel's side, and *Atalanta* had swerved as well: from the corner of his eye Isokrates glimpsed the enemy prow gliding past, its painted eye wide in surprise. A spear splintered the trihemiolia's high stern post; the deckfighter to his right swore horribly and dropped to his knees. Isokrates paid no attention, only pulled the tiller sharply. There was a jolt and a splintering crash. Aristomachos howled in glee, and slapped his shoulder so hard that he made the tiller wobble. Then there were only the blue waters of the bay before him.

'Port, full about!' yelled Aristomachos, needing no prompting. *Atalanta*'s starboard oars stayed high; her port oars dug into the water at rush speed; Isokrates leaned against the tiller. The trihemiolia spun about, almost in place: as she turned he spared a glance for the myoparon, and saw that she was drifting helplessly: *Atalanta* had brushed against her stern, tearing a steering oar out of its socket and shattering the tiller. A pirate was hanging over the side screaming curses.

The hemiolia had veered to port and was also starting to turn. She was slow, though, much too slow: most of her crew were fighters, not sailors, and the very number of men aboard burdened her.

'All oars, rush speed!' shouted Aristomachos; and, in an undertone, 'The next call is yours.'

Isokrates nodded. The tiller in his hand seemed a part of him, and he felt as though he *was* the ship, that it was his head which now turned toward the enemy, his own brazen tusk that lunged hungrily at the pirate's slowly turning side.

It was a tricky angle, broadside on to the hemiolia: at anything more than walking pace, the ram would lodge in the pirate's side – and then that crowd of armed men would struggle over the prow and on to *Atalanta*. The trihemiolia hadn't time to build up much speed, but still he gave the order, 'Back oars!', and *Atalanta*'s greedy rush paused. 'Ship oars!' he bellowed, hand closed on the tiller – then the ram bit.

The impact heaved the hemiolia up on to her side, and her planking cracked and splintered. Her oarcrew howled; somebody forward was bellowing a warcry and somebody else was screaming. 'Back oars!' yelled Isokrates, 'Back oars!' The tiller was twisting in his hand, and he fought to hold it straight.

There was a rain of missiles, and from somewhere forward a slither of metal striking metal, the noise sharp against the deep groaning of wood. *Atalanta* began to move backwards, slowly at first, then more rapidly. The screaming continued, and terrified curses joined it. Breathing hard, Isokrates looked around for the myoparon.

The smaller vessel was rowing toward *Atalanta*, raggedly, steering with the rearmost oars on each side. The pirates on deck were in a frenzy, beating their shields and screaming in rage as they watched the hemiolia founder. They would have been wiser to flee.

'All oars!' Isokrates roared, shoving the tiller hard over. *Atalanta*'s oars moved obediently as one, even before the drum beat began again. The trihemiolia turned away from her victim. Several of the pirates had hurled themselves off the hemiolia's deck, dropping their spears and shields, trying to swim over to grapple with their antagonist, but already *Atalanta* was moving too fast for them to catch her. She swept about in a graceful curve to starboard, with the myoparon struggling after her.

Aristomachos glanced up at Isokrates, face alight, and there was an instant of perfect understanding between them. 'Rush speed!' yelled the trierarch.

The drumbeat picked up again: *bang,* two, *bang,* two. *Atalanta* raced ahead of her adversary, curling to starboard gradually at first, then more and more sharply. The crippled myoparon could not match that sharp curve, and was slow to understand what it meant. By the time she realized, it was too late. *Atalanta* went about and bore down to ram on the perfect oblique angle from behind.

Some of the pirate oarsmen jumped up from the benches and leapt into the sea; some of the fighters dropped their weapons and copied them. The rest wavered helplessly, screaming in terror or in rage, covering their faces or waving their fists.

'Ship oars!' ordered Isokrates: on this occa-

301

sion, he judged they could ram at full speed.

The ram struck. The myoparon was so lightly built that she simply disintegrated under that blow, and *Atalanta* rode right over her with a terrible crashing and shrieking. She dragged to a halt on top of the wreckage, on water full of timbers and struggling bodies. One of the pirates grabbed a Rhodian oar.

'All oars!' shouted Aristomachos in alarm, and the other oars stirred, one striking the pirate, who screamed, but did not let go. One of *Atalanta*'s archers went to the side, took careful aim, and shot the man in the neck. He screamed – the sound bubbled horribly – and fell backwards into the water.

They rowed clear of the wreck, then coasted to a halt. Forwards somebody was crying. Around them the blue waters of the bay sparkled in the late afternoon sun, as though nothing had happened.

Aristomachos was flushed and sweating heavily. 'Oh, Father Zeus!' he exclaimed, wiping his face. 'Oh, gods!' He glanced round dazedly. Off to starboard the hemiolia was a swamped hulk, and behind them the timbers of the myoparon bobbed on the waves. *Colchidis* was busily sailing away.

'Nikagoras?' the trierarch called uncertainly, and made his way forward.

Isokrates released the tiller. His hand was numb, and his fingers had gone white. He stretched them cautiously, then looked round. The deckfighter who'd collapsed when they passed between the two ships was sitting by the command chair, cradling his right arm and rocking back and forth. Isokrates went over to him, saw that it was Kleophon, who'd hauled Dionysia out of the sea that spring. His shoulder was at a peculiar angle.

'Fucking slingstone,' muttered Kleophon, as Isokrates examined it.

'Looks like a broken collarbone.'

'I'll live,' Kleophon said, in tones which were probably intended as stoical, but emerged as relieved. Isokrates nodded. He called Kleitos over to take the tiller, then went forward to see who else was injured.

One of the deckfighters was dead, killed by arrows; another four, including Polydoros, were wounded. The deckfighter captain had an arrow through his foot, and sat on the tabernacle cursing. In the prow, Nikagoras sat in a pool of blood, clutching his thigh and sobbing in pain. His uncle crouched beside him, holding his hand and trying to calm him. The wound looked like one made by a spear – a deep gash, still bleeding heavily – though the weapon that caused it was nowhere to be seen; tossed overboard, perhaps.

Isokrates went below and told Damophon the bo'sun, who had more experience with injuries than anyone else on the ship, to go up and see to the wounded. Damophon nodded and went on deck. Isokrates turned to the oarcrew, who were all resting on their oars, watching him expectantly. He opened his mouth, then found himself unable to speak.

'Well done!' he managed at last. 'They had two ships, and we sank both.'

303

Somebody cheered.

'Our deckfighters bore the brunt of it,' he continued. 'The pirates outnumbered them, and if we'd been boarded it would've been very nasty, but they fought them off. Onomarchos is dead, and there are five wounded, including Polydoros and our bow-officer. We owe these men a debt.'

That was received in sober silence.

'Now...' he continued, and stopped, swallowing. It was hard to think what to do now.

'They got any plunder?' called one of the Athenians hopefully.

'We think they might, at their base,' Isokrates replied, finding his stride again. 'First, though, we've got to find our consort and check that she's all right. Then we'll see if we can find their base. It's on an inlet in this bay, I'm sure of it.'

Colchidis was unharmed, and had stopped her flight from the bay as soon as she was confident that the pirates had been sunk. Kylon, her captain, was worried that Aristomachos was going to try to claim salvage – in fact, his sullen expression showed that he suspected the trierarch of having delayed his attack precisely so that he could claim salvage, since it made a difference whether the roundship had been in pirate hands. Aristomachos assured him that such a brief interval didn't count, and that he had no intention of cheating a fellow Rhodian. At this the captain, relieved, thanked them warmly for saving his ship.

'Perhaps you could help us, as well,' Aristomachos said. 'We have wounded. Can you put in tonight when we do, take them on board, and carry them back to Megiste?'

The merchant captain frowned. 'I'll carry your wounded, but I'm bound for Antioch, and already late. If it's a doctor you want at Megiste, there are several in Phaselis.'

Aristomachos scowled: like Isokrates, he would prefer the wounded to get treatment from the naval surgeon at the base on Megiste. Kylon, however, refused to turn back, and in the end Aristomachos was forced to agree to the trip to Phaselis. 'There's another thing, then,' he said, when he'd yielded. 'We want to round up any of the bugger-arsed pirates who didn't drown: could you carry them for us? We'd be sure to get a good price for 'em in Antioch: the king will want slave labour for his war.'

'I'll do it if you accompany us,' said the merchant. 'I don't want to carry pirates unless we have some back-up.'

Aristomachos was muttering as he descended the boarding ladder: 'The bastard! We save his bugger-arsed ship and he can't even be bothered to sail back to Megiste! A *Rhodian,* and he's happy to leave his countrymen to the butchers in Phaselis! Fucking bastard!'

Atalanta cruised over to the hulk of the hemiolia, but there were only three men perched on the tabernacle. All the survivors who could swim were undoubtedly heading for shore. The bay was small enough, and the enclosed waters calm enough, that they had a good chance of making it – though what they'd do, naked at the foot of a cliff without even a pair of sandals, was another matter. Aristomachos cursed, and ordered the galley to do a sweep toward the closest shore, looking for swimmers.

The second man they pulled out of the water was greeted with a chorus of Rhodian jeers: 'What, you again?' and 'Remember us?'

Isokrates forced his way through the crowd, and the young pirate who'd been dangled from the forefoot looked up at him fearfully.

'You were with Andronikos before,' he said. 'Was he on your ship?'

The pirate shook his head wretchedly.

'What ship were you on? The myoparon?'

'The *Kratousa,*' whispered the pirate. 'The hemiolia.'

'And Andronikos wasn't?'

The Cretan shook his head again. One of the other captives started to tell him to be quiet, and was himself clouted to silence by a decksoldier.

'You're going to be sold,' Isokrates said in a low voice, 'but slavery can be heavy or light. Answer me truthfully, or I swear by the Sun, I'll see to it that you go to the mines, where you'll be buggered by every guard who takes a fancy to you, and then worked to death.'

The youth looked up at him in terror. 'He wasn't on the *Kratousa* today, I swear it! The *Lykaina*'s being overhauled; she sprung a leak and she won't be fit for sea until tomorrow. Andronikos stayed ashore so's her crew'd be happy we weren't goin' to cheat them. When we saw that cursed Euxine merchant, see, we thought it might be carrying gold, and *Lykaina*'s people were afraid we'd cut them out, even though we'd all sworn to split all the takings. The only way Andronikos could convince 'em they'd still get their fair share was to stay with them. Her deckfighters went with us, though, so he's just got her oarcrew with him. That's only thirty men, and they aren't armed much better than your lot.' The pirate began to cry. 'You can kill him and good luck! This is his fault! We didn't *need* to go out raiding again; we were rich men, after Daphne! I wanted to stop home and get married, but he told me I was a coward if I didn't join him just once more!'

'Where's your base?'

'Little inlet,' said the youth, wiping his eyes, 'round the northwest end of the bay.'

'And you say Andronikos is there with about thirty lightly armed men? Is the camp fortified?'

'Fortified?' asked the Cretan. 'No, of course not! If any *soldiers*'d showed up, we would've put to sea straight away.'

Isokrates glanced round his men. 'Tie him up,' he ordered, and went to find Aristomachos.

The trierarch was sitting beside his nephew again, holding his hand. Damophon had come and gone, and Nikagoras's thigh was now bound up in sailcloth. He was lying flat on the foredeck, with the other wounded; the sail crew were rigging an awning. The young man was very pale and limp, but his breathing was steady and the bleeding appeared to have stopped.

'Sir,' said Isokrates, and Aristomachos looked up with a frown.

Isokrates told him what the pirate had just said.

'Oh Zeus!' said the trierarch wearily, and wiped his face. 'What is it you want to do?'

'Sir, we should take their base. At the very least we're bound to seize or destroy the remaining ship. If we don't they'll just seize another merchant and head home with their loot.'

Aristomachos looked up at him wearily. Then he patted Nikagoras on the shoulder and stood up.

'Uncle?' said Nikagoras, opening his eyes.

'It's all right,' Aristomachos said gently. 'Just going to talk to Isokrates. I'll be close by if you need me.'

They walked aft a few paces. 'I don't know what I'm going to say to my sister,' Aristomachos said unhappily. 'I promised her I'd look after the boy. You want us to storm a base on *land*? Half our deck-soldiers are wounded, and we don't have more than twenty spears on the ship!'

'What's the alternative?' Isokrates demanded. 'Let that pirate escape again? Sir, I believe that boy told me the truth – that there really are only thirty or so oarcrew in the camp with Andronikos. It fits: the other two ships were overcrowded. We ought to move at once. Otherwise, anyone who swam clear of the wrecks will have a chance to join Andronikos, and the odds will get worse. Most of our men have some training, and we can share out the arms among the best fighters.'

Aristomachos groaned. 'Sun above us, what a

day! Very well; you're right. We'll have to get the wounded below: I'm not leaving them on deck if we're going back into action.'

Fifteen

The pirate base lay on an inlet where a little stream had cut through the cliffs and deposited a crescent of gravel where a few ships could run up safely. This beach could not be seen from the water from most angles, and it was hard to reach by land, a combination which made it ideal for pirates. When *Atalanta* crawled cautiously toward it, the sun was going down, and the inlet was in shadow. It was still apparent, though, that there were two ships there: a galley, hauled up on the beach for repairs, and a large merchant ship, beached at the stern and anchored at the prow. There were some makeshift huts of driftwood and canvas at the foot of the cliff – but no people in evidence.

Atalanta turned and backed on to the beach, then rested her oars. Still nothing moved.

'They've run,' said Aristomachos in disgust. He had borrowed a shield and spear from a downed deckfighter, and he hefted the heavy things with a grimace. 'They saw what happened to their friends and took to their heels.'

Isokrates shook his head in denial: the possibility that Andronikos had escaped *again* was too painful to accept. 'Maybe they're hiding in those huts,' he suggested, and went to the boarding ladder.

Aristomachos caught his arm and shook his head, then gestured for one of the remaining deck-soldiers to descend first: Isokrates had no shield, and was armed only with a sling and a hatchet from ship's stores. The proper weapons had gone to the men most skilled in their use, which Isokrates was not.

The deckfighter grinned at the trierarch, saluted, then, disdaining the ladder, jumped down from the side of the ship, holding his shield up high. The precaution was unnecessary: no arrows flew.

The rest of the spearmen began to disembark. The first decksoldier crunched up to the nearest hut, jabbed it with his spear, then ran to the next. It quickly became obvious that all the huts were empty.

Colchidis was following *Atalanta* at a safe distance. When it became clear that the base was deserted, she moved in and anchored beside the other roundship. *Atalanta*'s crew began moving the wounded off the galley.

The light was fading fast now. Isokrates walked into the middle of the abandoned camp, angry and despairing. Andronikos had run; he was alive and free. One day he would show up again, undoubtedly with more blood on his hands. Was Dionysia with him? Or was her body already rotting in some shallow pit nearby?

The embers in the camp's central firepit were still hot, and there were a couple of torches laid ready; he lit one and made a quick tour. The pirates had obviously abandoned the place in moderate haste. The huts were stuffed with bulky items of plunder: expensive carpets and hangings, finely painted cups and bowls, flasks of Attic oil and Chian wine. There should have been lighter items as well, though – coins and jewellery, certainly, and possibly metalwork and spices or perfume as well – but none of these things were in the huts. The loot had been sorted, and the pirates had taken only light, portable items which wouldn't impede their escape. An unwilling captive would be even more of an impediment than a rug, and it seemed highly unlikely that Andronikos had taken her.

Dead, dead. The words beat his mind like a drum at rush speed, making it hard to think. He tried to tell himself that there was no evidence she'd ever been here; that it was entirely possible that her ship to Athens had sprung a leak, and that she'd already returned to Rhodes, safe and well – but his heart was unconvinced. He ached to find her body and cradle it, to give her the ritual of burial – but he wanted even more to find her murderer.

The only real route off the beach was the gully of the stream: the cliffs were so steep as to be almost impassable. Isokrates picked his way over to the gully, his torch held high. In this late summer season the stream was almost dry, but the bed was half-choked by thorny scrub and full of tumbled stones and boulders. It would be very hard going even in daylight, and dangerous, too: besides the hazards of falls there would be snakes and scorpions. *Atalanta*'s crew were mostly barefoot. He could not take them up this rough path blind in the dark – but if they used torches the pirates would be able to see them coming. The confrontation was likely to be bloody enough without giving the enemy a chance to spring an ambush.

That was assuming the pirates were still around, of course. They'd had a couple of hours of daylight to make their escape: probably they would already have reached the head of this gully. How could he track them then? The dry stony ground did not take marks easily, and whatever trail Andronikos had left would be impossible to find in the darkness. If he waited until daylight, though, the pirates would be far away.

The light from the torch he held wavered madly: his hand was shaking. He dropped it and stood still, breathing hard. He wanted to howl and beat his hands against the stones – but what good would that do? All it would achieve would be to make the crew doubt their helmsman – and he couldn't permit that. He might, still, think of *some* way to go after his enemy.

There was a shout, and Kleitos the tiller-holder ran up, out of breath. 'The merchant ship!' he exclaimed, dismay clearly audible in his voice.

Of course: the most secure lock-up the pirates had had available was the hold of their captured merchantman. That was where they'd kept their captives; that was where the bodies were. Isokrates snatched up the torch and ran back toward the sea.

Aristomachos was waiting on the sterndeck of the pirates' roundship, holding a lantern. When Isokrates ran up he said, 'I'm sorry.'

'Dionysia?' Isokrates choked.

The trierarch hesitated. 'I didn't see. It's too dark. I sent Glykon to fetch a lantern; he's only just come back with it.'

Isokrates extinguished his torch: the habit of never taking an open flame on board a ship was so ingrained it survived even his current anguish. He scrambled up the ladder, and he and Aristomachos descended the stern hatch.

The hold had been barred on the outside, but now stood open: the scent that came from the blackness inside was unmistakeably the blood-and-shit stink of violent death. They picked their way down the ladder, Aristomachos holding the lantern.

The bodies were at the far end of the hold, against the stempost, as though they'd run as far as they could. They were all girls and women, dressed only in torn chitons. The eldest might have been twenty-five; the youngest couldn't have been more than fourteen. Their eyes still gleamed in the dim light of the lantern, and the expressions of terror on their faces made them seem almost alive. The deck underfoot was sticky and wet with their half-congealed blood.

Isokrates stepped closer, shuddering at the feel of the blood, but driven by the need to find one particular face.

It wasn't there. The sight of the dead girls was so horrifying and so pitiable that it took him a moment to realize that there was another absence.

'There are only a dozen of them,' he said, his voice sounding unnatural in the thick air. He looked round and met Aristomachos's eyes: the trierarch was standing well back, clear of the blood, an expression of grief and revulsion creasing his face. 'They must've had more than a dozen captives: their camp has the pickings from lots of different ships! Where are all the others?'

'Maybe they took the rest with them,' Aristomachos said uncertainly.

Isokrates shook his head. 'Not up that gully. Not in the hurry they were in.' He turned and began to make his way back out of the hold; he could feel the blood on his feet sticking to the decking, and choked on bile.

'Well, what then?' asked Aristomachos, following him. 'Maybe they let the rest of their captives go! They didn't *need* to kill any of the poor creatures!'

Isokrates paused, wanting desperately to believe it. 'I don't know. But – they killed those women to spite us, because we'd sunk their ships and they were angry. Does it seem likely to you that they were suddenly filled with *pity*?'

'It's *possible*,' replied Aristomachos, warming to his idea. 'Killing lovely young girls like that – even a heart of bronze must find it hard! The rest of the captives may be hiding somewhere nearby – they *would* hide when they saw us coming. For all they know, we could be another lot of pirates!'

'Oh, gods grant it!' Isokrates cried passionately. A grimmer possibility occurred to him: that the pirates had *tried* to take their captives along. The women in the hold had refused to

315

come, and been killed outright; the rest would be found on the way up the gully, struck down wherever they failed to climb a rockfall, or tried to escape.

Dionysia, he was quite sure, would try to escape. He told himself furiously that he didn't even *know* that she'd been captured, but his imagination persisted with a vision of her tearing away from Andronikos and collapsing with a spear in her back.

They emerged on the roundship's deck. On the beach, the men were making camp, spreading out the fine rugs from the huts and dismantling the huts themselves to build up the fire – in this season, there was no need for shelter at night, and *Atalanta* planned to leave again before the sun was high. The wounded had been moved near the fire. They wouldn't be put on board the *Colchidis* until morning: a bed on land was more comfortable.

'Assemble the men and tell them we're going up the gully,' Aristomachos ordered. 'That is, we'll leave a force here in camp, to guard it, but all the men with proper weapons are to come with me.'

'They won't be enough,' Isokrates told him. 'There must be at least thirty pirates, and they'll have the advantage of high ground.'

The trierarch made an impatient gesture. 'All the men with proper weapons *and* some of the light-armed men, then! But we need to be quick about it. We'll see if we can find the rest of the captives – but at the very least, we have to make sure that those murdering bastards aren't waiting

316

for us to go to sleep so they can come back and kill us.' He looked at Isokrates and drew a deep breath. 'I assume you're coming too, but you'll stay toward the rear. That hatchet will be no use at all against a spear.'

Isokrates was as quick as he could be, but it still took a little while to prepare the expedition. They had to arrange sentries for the camp; they had to assemble as many torches and lanterns as they could scramble together; they had to collect suitable rocks to use as slingstones; at Isokrates' insistence the men without sandals had to bind their feet in sailcloth. At last, though, they had a small force ready to climb the gully: a dozen men equipped with shields, spears and helmets; another ten with only spears; and finally, at the rear, another dozen armed with slings and either knives or hatchets. All the men were nervous, but all were willing. They all knew now what had been found in the hold of the pirate ship – and they were not eager to sleep without being sure that the enemy were far away.

The path up the gully was as difficult as Isokrates had expected, a painful scramble over boulders and through thorns; the only mercy was that they didn't encounter any snakes. They had been going only about half an hour, however, when Aristomachos halted the party. The men at the back crowded forward when the men at the front stopped, and were irritably ordered to be still. There was silence for several breaths – a silence broken only by the crackle of the torches. Then Isokrates heard it: a chink and rattle, the sound of something ahead moving over loose stone. He felt in his purse for a stone and dropped it into his sling, praying desperately that it wouldn't be needed.

'Who's there?' shouted Aristomachos into the darkness. 'We are Rhodians, here to fight pirates!'

For a long time there was no reply. Two of the deckfighters began to advance, their spears raised and their shields high.

'Don't!' came a frightened voice from the darkness – a man's voice, speaking with a Cretan accent. 'We surrender!'

There was another silence, this one startled. Then the trierarch said angrily. 'Then throw away your weapons and come forward with your hands behind your head.'

After a moment the man shuffled forward into the torchlight: a dirty, unshaven oarsman in a short tunic, his bare feet bound up in sail cloth. He tossed a knife on the ground in front of himself, then linked his hands behind his head.

'Kneel!' ordered Aristomachos. 'Keep your hands together behind your head!'

The pirate obeyed at once, kneeling on the stones. At this another man, apparently reassured now that he wouldn't be killed outright, also came forward into the light. He threw down a cutlass, and knelt beside his comrade. Then another two came together: one bleeding from a head injury, his arm about a friend's shoulder; then another pair, one limping, his foot covered in blood, the other supporting him...

There were fourteen of the men in all, and half of them were injured.

'Where are the rest of you?' asked Aristomachos in confusion. 'And, by Apollo! what happened?'

'It was those mad bitches!' exclaimed the first pirate, suddenly talkative with outrage. 'They *threw rocks at us!* From high up, and it was just starting to get dark. We couldn't hardly even see 'em to fight back! They got the chief. He fell down, and they kept throwing rocks at him, with him screaming and cursing, and there wasn't anything we could do. Any man that tried to help him, he got the same treatment!' He was suddenly crying. 'We couldn't fucking get through! *Women!* Fucking whores!'

Isokrates forced himself through to the front. 'The women *escaped*?'

The pirate stared at him, the tears on his face shiny in the torchlight. 'Fucking bitches got off the bugger-arsed ship while we were watching ... while we were watching *you* sink our ships, oh Father Zeus! They ran off up the gully, and the chief said, "Well, we'll just round them up when we reach 'em," but they'd got up the sides of the gully, and they *threw rocks at us*!'

Aristomachos let out a whoop of admiration. 'Brave girls!' He slapped Isokrates on the shoulder. 'Here we were thinking we had to *rescue* them! Fit to mother heroes, every one of 'em!' He turned back to the pirate. 'What's the situation now? Are the women still there? What happened to the rest of your people?'

The man shook his head, still crying. 'I don't know. We came back because we couldn't get through. If there's any of our people left up there, he's dead.'

Isokrates felt numb and short of breath; his heart was beating at rush speed again, only now it said *alive, alive!* 'Sir,' he said. 'Let me take a few men up the gully to see if I can find the women.'

Aristomachos grinned. 'Very well. But be careful, eh? Make sure they know who you are before you step under any rocks!'

In the end, however, Isokrates took more than a 'few' men. Aristomachos and one half of the men took charge of the prisoners, while Isokrates led the other half of the Rhodian force up the rocky streambed. The small band struggled over the boulders and through the scrub, listening intently and occasionally calling out, 'Friends!' After a little while, though, Isokrates began to wonder whether the women – if they were still up on the cliffs somewhere – would *believe* that any armed men marching up the gully were indeed their friends. He wondered what he could do to convince them he wasn't a pirate – and found a ready answer.

'For the Sun bears toil in every day,' he sang, his voice strained and thin in the darkness. Dionysia, certainly, would recognize that song, and he was sure now that she was with the women hidden up ahead.

The men joined in the familiar hymn:

>   ...without ceasing in any way
>   his horses run when rosy Dawn
>   rises from Ocean to heaven each morn...

They walked on, singing; when they reached the end of the hymn they started it over again. They'd reached the middle of the second repetition when their torches showed the first body ahead. It was half-buried under a pile of stone, but it seemed to have been a man. The song faltered and stopped.

There was a silence. Isokrates stepped forward and knelt to inspect the corpse: definitely a pirate, and, while the stones might have knocked him down, somebody had made sure of him by cutting his throat.

'Ladies?' he called at the night ahead. 'Ladies, we're *friends*!'

From somewhere up ahead a woman's voice called uncertainly, 'Rhodians?'

He knew that voice: everything inside him seemed to leap at the sound of it. 'Dionysia!' he cried, standing straight and holding his torch up. 'Dionysia, it's me!'

'Isokrates?' she called back, and her voice was shaking this time. There was a movement in the darkness behind the torchlight, a flutter of white – and suddenly she was there, slim and frail in a blood-spattered chiton, her hair loose and tangled, a knife in her reddened hands. She tossed the knife aside and stumbled over to him, bursting into tears, and he had just time to set the torch down before she threw herself into his arms.

It took a couple of hours to get all the escaped captives back down the gully. There were about

321

fifty of them – mostly women, though there were a few boys as well. They were all exhausted and battered; one girl had been stung by a scorpion, two had been badly injured by slingstones thrown by the pirates, and most had older injuries from days of abuse. They were all very quiet, and even the worst injured ones refused assistance from the Rhodians. Their friends had to take turns helping them.

'They don't want to be touched by men,' Dionysia told Isokrates. She didn't seem to feel the same: she was holding his hand tightly. The two of them were leading the rest of the party back down the streambed, Isokrates holding the torch up to throw as much light as possible. They'd extinguished half of their torches and lanterns, to preserve the fuel.

'I'm so sorry,' he said. He could imagine what Dionysia and her fellow captives had been suffering, for days – and his admiration at their escape was mixed with guilt, because *he* hadn't rescued them.

'Why should *you* be sorry?' she demanded. 'You *came after me.* You came after me and you sank their ships! How did you do that? How did you *know*?'

'You weren't at the Panathenaia. And we were given some information, and ... but we were so *slow*! I should have killed the bastard the first time I met him: I'm sorry.'

'He's dead now.'

There was a flatness in her tone. Isokrates had checked over the bodies before they started back, and had found that of Andronikos. The

322

stones had battered him badly, but that fierce black-bearded face was still recognizable. His throat, too, had been cut, though he'd probably already been dead when it happened. Isokrates remembered the bloody knife in Dionysia's hands, and he stopped and turned to face her, meeting her haunted eyes. 'You were very brave,' he told her fiercely. 'You and your friends. You succeeded where I failed. You can be *proud* of what you did.'

'It was horrible!' she replied, her voice shaking. 'He screamed and...'

'Of course it was horrible! But he was an evil man, your enemy. He hurt you and was glad of it. If you hadn't killed him, he would've killed you. There is no shame in what you did.'

She sighed heavily, then leaned against him. He put his arm around her shoulders. The shape of her body as it pressed against his was sweeter than any music. He turned his mind from the future, and devoured the sensation of having what he loved safe at his side. Tomorrow he could be formal again: tonight was his own. They started forward again.

'What happened to the others?' she asked, after a silence. 'The girls who wouldn't come with us, I mean, who stayed on the ship?'

He hesitated.

'They're dead?'

'Yes. I'm sorry.'

She shook her head. 'I told them that the men would kill them. I begged them to come – but they were frightened. They said, "If we run away, we'll be punished!" They thought they'd be safer where they were.' She was silent a moment, then said quietly, 'Maybe they would gave been, if the rest of us hadn't run – but I don't think so. Oh! You don't know, you don't know! That merchant ship they took, the *Eleutheria,* it had a crew. At first they were going to keep the crew alive to sail the ship back to Crete, but some of them tried to escape, and then the pirates got tired of having to guard the rest, so they ... they buried them all up to their waists in a pit on the beach, and took turns throwing stones at them. They made a *game* of it, so many points for an eye, so many for a hit on the mouth ... those poor men, they were blind and bloody and sobbing, and those foul monsters kept throwing rocks, and *laughed*!'

'How did you get away?'

She brushed a tangle of hair out of her eyes. 'The lookouts saw a Euxine merchant, and the ships went out to take her, taking all the men apart from Andronikos and the *Lykaina*'s oarcrew. Most of them went over to the western end of the beach, trying to see. Then we heard them shouting that there was a *galley* in the bay. And I *knew*,' she glanced up at him, face intent, 'I *knew* it was you, and I *knew* you were going to sink them – and I knew that then Andronikos would kill us, because he couldn't drag us along with them and he wouldn't let us go free. So I told the others, and we agreed we had to try to escape, right away, while the men were all down the western end of the beach. We pretended to have a fight, and Myrtis banged on the hold and begged the guards to come in and stop it. There

324

were only two of them on duty, but they still weren't afraid to come in. Men used to come in every evening, by ones and twos, to pick out a girl, and they expected everyone to cower and cry. They never expected us to attack them. We didn't kill them, though – we were hoping that if we spared them, they might spare the girls who were too afraid to come along. We just tied them up, and then we crept out of the ship and ran along the beach and up the gully.'

'And when they followed you,' Isokrates said, still stunned by it, 'you fought them and beat them.'

She walked a few more paces, then said abruptly, 'You make us sound braver than we were. We didn't *want* to fight at all. All we were trying to do was get away. But – but the way up this gully was so *hard*, and we didn't have any sandals, and most of us were hurt. We couldn't go fast enough, and I knew the men would be coming after us. So when the gully opened up a bit, I had everyone climb up, as high as they could. I told them to collect heavy stones, and to throw them down at the men if we were spotted – but really I was hoping it would be dark and they'd walk past without noticing us. I didn't really think we *could* hurt them.'

'So you were the general, then?' He found that he wasn't surprised.

She shrugged. 'I suppose so.' She glanced up at him again, uncertainly.

Did she suppose he *disapproved* of her courage? He tried to imagine her, imprisoned with the others in the hold of that ship, whispering to her fellow captives, planning the escape.

He imagined the men coming in every evening to 'pick out a girl' for the night. Had she suffered that, or had Andronikos reserved her to himself?

He would not ask. He would not compound her shame by making her relive it. She was alive and whole, and her body was pressed against his own, shivering with relief. That was what mattered.

'You were very brave,' he said again. 'You suffered, but you fought on, and in the end, you won.'

She smiled, but her eyes were suddenly shining with fresh tears. 'Oh, I hoped so much you would say that! When I was locked up with the other women in the hold we talked a lot about men. The others said that men never see women as anything but slaves, that when we're young and pretty they use us, and when we're old they jeer at us and work us to death. And I said, no, I knew men who weren't like that – but when they asked me who, the only man I could think of was you.' She slipped her arm about his waist. 'I *knew* it was you, in that galley. Andronikos told me that you were dead, but I knew you weren't. He...'

'You talked about *me*?' he asked in surprise.

'Oh, yes! He had that cloak you bought in Alexandria, and I told him that he'd stolen it from a better man. It made him angry, and he tried to tell me that he'd beaten you, that *he* was the better man. And I told him, no, the first time you met Isokrates, he sank your ship, and the second time he escaped your ambush and drove your patroness to desperation. If you ever meet again, I told him, it will be your death.'

'But *you're* the one who defeated him, Dionysia – you and your friends!'

She sighed deeply, her arm holding him close. 'You sank their ships. You came for me. Oh, you are my sun, and I never want to lose the light again!'

Sixteen

Isokrates woke in full sunlight with a muzzy head and a strong sense that he was being watched. He opened his eyes, and found himself staring up into Dionysia's face. She smiled at him and brushed a lock of hair out of his eyes.

He moved without thinking, reaching up to put a hand behind her head and pull her down so he could kiss her. She returned the kiss, and when their lips parted continued to smile at him. For a moment he smiled stupidly back at her. Then reality washed over him: it was broad daylight and they were lying on a rug on an open beach surrounded by nearly two hundred men and fifty or so women. It had seemed natural to lie down side by side the previous night, but the light of day revealed the act as wildly improper, for all that they'd done nothing but sleep.

That he loved her was something he had been painfully aware of for a long time; he knew now that she loved him, too. Love, though, wouldn't pay the rent. She'd agreed that he was too poor for her, and nothing important had changed.

He drew away and sat up; Dionysia leaned back on her heels, frowning a little. 'What's the matter?'

'I have to...' He waved vaguely at the ships. He

noticed Damophon the bo'sun nearby, sitting with a couple of the oarcrew. They were all grinning at him: he scowled back. 'Lady, forgive me. I have work to do.' A trihemiolia to get ready for sea, prisoners to check, and a salvaged merchantman to be cleared of bodies and loaded with recovered loot.

Her frown deepened. 'What's this? I'm *Lady* again? Last night you were calling me by name!'

He drew a deep breath, unable to answer. He knew what he *ought* to say, but could not bring himself to say it.

Her frown turned into a look of deep hurt. 'Last night you told me I'd suffered in a war – and that I'd won. Am I just a pirate's dirty cast-off this morning?'

'No!' he said appalled. 'I don't ... Dionysia, I'm no richer now than I was when I spoke to you before!'

'I don't *care* any more!' she cried passionately.

'You should. Do you know what it's like to be poor? To have to worry over how to buy each meal – and go to bed hungry, when you don't have enough for food as well as rent? It's bad enough for a man, but for a woman – it's trying to raise children that's the worst of it. My landlady, who died – she must have been young and happy once, but all the time *I* knew her she was savage and sour. To have your children cry for food, and be unable to give it to them – that would turn most people sour, I think. And *you*!' He reached out and caught her hands. 'So gifted, so beautiful! How could I live with myself, if I turned *you* into another Atta?'

329

The frown was back. 'You said you had enough money to buy a house.'

'I do. Just this summer. But ... not a big house.'

'Well, if you have enough for a house – I *was* earning enough to live on this summer, even though I was having to pay rent to the Guild. If I didn't have to pay rent, I'd be *better* off, not worse! And if I lose Hagemon's patronage, y*ou* could be my guardian.'

He stared at her. It actually sounded *possible*, and he struggled to think it through. Going out to work would be a disgrace for most wives, but music was different: if anything, a married female musician would be *more* respectable than an unmarried one.

He hated the idea of living on a wife's money – but he hated the idea of losing Dionysia even more. If he added her earnings to his own, and if his investments paid well ... he would have to buy slaves, though: he couldn't ask Dionysia to scrub floors and grind grain, not with those kitharist's hands. That meant money to feed and clothe the slaves, and a bigger house to provide room for them. The two thousand drachmai, which had seemed such a huge sum a month before, dwindled to inadequacy – but perhaps if they *both* scrimped and made do...

Could he ask that of her?

'We should wait until we're back in Rhodes,' he said at last. 'You should think about what you're saying.'

She shook her head emphatically. 'I won't change my mind.'

He swallowed, afraid to believe it. 'Even so,' he managed, 'we should wait until we're back in Rhodes. Then, if you haven't changed your mind, we can talk about ... about how we might manage.'

Her hands, still cradled in his own, suddenly clutched hard, and her face lit in that wonderful shy smile.

'Isokrates!' someone called, and they both looked round to see Aristomachos bearing down across the beach.

'Good, you're up!' said the trierarch. 'Good health, Lady. Isokrates, you know this coast. What's the nearest town?'

'Melanippion,' Isokrates replied, taken a little aback. 'It's on the headland east of here, just outside the bay. It's only a small place, though.'

'Would there be a doctor there? And a market-place?'

'Both, I should think.'

'Good,' said Aristomachos, with satisfaction. 'What I was thinking was this: we take the ship over there, fetch a doctor for the wounded, buy some supplies, and spend the next day or so here. The wounded would do better here than a ship, and it would give the rest of us a chance to rest – and I don't know about you, but I could use a day or two on dry land. We could finish the repairs on that pirate ship and load up the merchantman we've salvaged. Then we could head back to Megiste.'

'What about *Colchidis*?' Isokrates asked doubtfully.

Aristomachos spat. *'Colchidis* can rot. If

Kylon won't turn back to Megiste for Rhodian wounded, he can go on to Antioch alone! And we don't need *Colchidis* now we've got a merchant ship of our own – a *nice* ship, too. I had a look at her. Syracusan, built of Italian fir with a beautiful deep keel of Epirot oak. She'll fetch a talent of silver at auction – and I can say that for sure, because I'm planning to bid myself.'

'Sir,' said Dionysia hesitantly, 'my luggage is aboard that ship.'

'You'll have it back intact,' promised Aristomachos at once. 'What happened to your maid?'

Dionysia's smile vanished instantly. 'They left her on the *Lindia* – on the ship they took me from.'

'So she needs passage from Athens?'

'No. They sank the *Lindia,* after they'd picked out what they wanted from her. Dyseris...' Dionysia stopped abruptly and pressed her hands against her eyes.

Isokrates and Aristomachos both stared. This was extraordinarily brutal, even by the standards of Cretan pirates.

'I'm sorry,' Dionysia said, after a moment. 'She ... she was my nurse when I was small, and my honest advisor when I was grown. But I shouldn't burden you with my tears. I've wept for her already, and I'll weep more when I have leisure. Right now you want information about the pirates. They sank all the ships they took, except for that one, the *Eleutheria.* They were trying to keep their presence here a secret, and didn't want anyone to report back. Sir, I can tell

332

you one thing which might be of value. Andronikos had a letter from Hyperides. It told him
when the *Lindia* meant to sail, and that I would
be aboard: it said that Queen Laodike would be
pleased if I came to grief, and that they could
rely on her to protect men who'd helped her. And
it said, too, that Isokrates had eaten poison.
Andronikos showed me the letter. I think it's still
in his cabin – that is, in the captain's cabin on the
Eleutheria.'

Aristomachos let out his breath in a hiss.
'We'd guessed most of this, but an incriminating
letter – now, *that* could be very useful indeed.'

Isokrates frowned. 'If Seleukos won't force his
mother to get rid of Hyperides for poisoning,
why would he do it for corresponding with a
pirate?'

'I wasn't thinking of giving the letter to *Seleukos*,' said Aristomachos, smiling beatifically. He
glanced from Isokrates' puzzled face to Dionysia's equally puzzled one and said, 'Pydnai's
right on our way home. We can hand it to King
Ptolemy's people, along with the letter from
Apollonios.'

'What?' protested Isokrates. 'Won't handing
Ptolemy a letter from King Antigonos's *spy-
master* simply make him disbelieve us?'

'Oh, no, no!' replied the trierarch, eyes gleaming. He flung out a hand in a dramatic gesture.
'King Ptolemy's greatest rival is willing to help
him against such a notorious pirate – a pirate
who doesn't just *raid* shipping, but goes on and
sinks it! Queen Laodike's favourite, though –
King Seleukos's own kinsman – corresponds

with him and tells him where to find his victims! You think King Ptolemy won't find a use for a story like that? Ha! Lady, can you and your friends put together a list of what ships that monster took, and when? We can give that to King Ptolemy as well! *Lindia* was Rhodian, and that lovely *Eleutheria* is Syracusan. Hyperides encouraged attacks on *neutral* shipping!' He grinned savagely. 'Seleukos will have to get rid of the viper after that – exile him, at the very least. And there's a war just started, remember: if Hyperides is ever captured by the Egyptians, those letters will cost him his head.' He beamed at them, like a host who'd produced a particularly magnificent dish at a dinner party.

'I'll be very glad to make a list of the ships,' Dionysia said eagerly.

'Good, good!' Aristomachos clapped his hands. 'So! I'll take *Atalanta* on round to Melanippion with half the men; Isokrates, you get the other half to work on that pirate galley; and you, Lady, compile this list of ships – and if you and your friends can help with our wounded, as well, we'd be very grateful.'

They remained on the beach for two days. *Atalanta* visited Melanippion and came back with a doctor and medicines, as well as a good supply of food and firewood – and a few more pirates, survivors of the rammings, who'd swum ashore and been caught in Melanippion when they tried to steal a fishing boat. The pirates were locked in the hold of the Syracusan ship *Eleutheria;* the bodies of the women they'd murdered were removed, given the funeral rites,

334

and burned on a pyre constructed on the beach. The bodies of the dead pirates, in contrast, were left to rot in the gully – though the Rhodians did send a working party up to collect all the portable plunder.

Aristomachos insisted that they collect Andronikos's head as well. When the men returned with the grisly object, he sealed it carefully in a jar of oil. 'I'll send this to King Ptolemy as well,' he told Isokrates. 'A gift from Rhodes: the head of the pirate who murdered the king's sister. That'll please him.'

'We don't know that he personally...' began Isokrates.

'It doesn't *matter* whether he personally killed her or not!' Aristomachos replied. 'He was certainly part of that attack, and Ptolemy has named him as wanted.' He snorted. 'There may even be a reward in it. That letter from Apollonios will show the king that we were working hard to find the man. But even if Ptolemy doesn't reward *us*, it'll make him say to himself, "Ah, yes, the Rhodians are fine people! They can have the run of the Aegean, as far as I'm concerned."' He grinned at Isokrates and added, 'It won't do my own reputation any harm, either, will it? with the king *or* with our own dear democracy! Zeus, I'll be a statesman yet!'

'I'll vote for you,' Isokrates said, smiling back.

When the Rhodians at last set out again, the men were in high spirits. The hold of the *Eleutheria* was full of a fortune in recovered plunder and a total of twenty-four pirates to sell as slaves – and there was, as well, the pirate ship, *Lykaina*, a thirty-oared lembos well-suited to becoming a naval courier. One of *Atalanta*'s wounded had died, but the other four – including Nikagoras – were making a good recovery. *Atalanta*'s prow was now decorated with four *akrostolia*, and the men had anointed the figurehead with scented oil and searched out a wild laurel to make a garland for her. *Atalanta* was unquestionably a lucky ship, a bringer of victory and wealth to all who served on her.

At Megiste they stopped the night. A dozen of the women who'd crowded the decks of the three ships disembarked there, hoping to make their ways home either from the island or from the town of Antiphellos on the mainland opposite. Aristomachos gave each of them some coin from the plunder, to help them on their way.

At Megiste there was news of the war.

'Ptolemy has taken Antioch!' the base commander told them excitedly, when he greeted them on their arrival. 'He took his fleet along the coast from Pydnai, as many ships as he thought the harbour at Seleucia could handle. When he put into Seleucia all the leading citizens came out to welcome him, wearing crowns and carrying garlands!'

'Zeus!' exclaimed Aristomachos in amazement. Seleucia, the port of Antioch, had been founded by King Seleukos's great-grandfather the Conqueror. For it to turn out to welcome a Ptolemy was extraordinary.

The commander of Megiste nodded. 'And when he took his army up to Antioch itself, it was the same thing!'

'Queen Berenike must've been popular.'

'Her murder certainly wasn't! At any rate, King Ptolemy is sitting in Seleukos's own palace, listening to petitions and handing out judgements!'

'Where was Seleukos while all this was going on?' asked Aristomachos. 'Still in Ephesus?'

The base commander didn't know: he'd had no news about the Seleucids. 'It just goes to show, though,' he declared piously, 'not even a king can offend the gods. Apollo himself turned against Laodike when she sent murderers to defile his shrine at Daphne.'

'Apollo has a lot of company in finding that offensive,' replied Aristomachos. 'You could say that even a king has to worry about what people think.'

They left Megiste next morning and rowed northwest along the coast. It was afternoon when they reached the Ptolemaic naval base at Pydnai, on the western end of Patara beach. This was almost empty – Ptolemy's fleet was still at the port of Seleucia – but the men who remained there were on high alert. They were polite to the Rhodians, however, especially after Aristomachos told them that he had valuable information for the king, and a gift which would please him.

'A gift?' asked the commander of Pydnai, frowning at the sealed jar dubiously.

'The head of the pirate who murdered Queen Berenike!' Aristomachos announced triumphantly.

The commander of the base stared. He touched

the jar gingerly, then looked up at Aristomachos with a broad smile. 'That is indeed a *noble* gift!' he exclaimed. He took charge of the package of letters and the sealed jar, promising to send them on to Antioch with the next courier.

At last, on the third day after leaving the pirates' beach, they came back to Rhodes, arriving in sight of the Colossus early in the afternoon.

Aristomachos had transferred on to the *Eleutheria* for the last leg of the voyage: the round-ship would dock in the merchant harbour, not the naval shipyard, and the trierarch wanted to make the arrangements for her himself. He'd left a supply of coin on *Atalanta*, however, to be distributed to the men as an advance on the salvage money. When Isokrates handed out the money, the crew cheered and went off in high good spirits to spend it and to boast of their ship's achievements.

Isokrates spent the rest of the day in the shipyard, looking after *Atalanta* and the captured pirate galley, the *Lykaina*. He tried not to think about Dionysia. She had travelled on the *Eleutheria*. During the voyage she had been very busy looking after her fellow captives, who all regarded her as their leader. He imagined her trying now to find accommodation for them and asking after ships to take them home. She would once more be beautifully dressed and impeccably groomed – she'd recovered her luggage, and one of the captives had taken up the position of her maid. She would deal with officialdom with perfect composure.

He wondered if she had changed her mind, now that the joy of the rescue had worn off. Part of him hoped that she had: he feared that if she married him, she would come to regret it. A larger part of himself, though, was praying to Aphrodite to bring her to his bed.

He arranged some maintenance work for *Atalanta*, found a place for *Lykaina*, and placed an order for some supplies of canvas and leather. At last he went to the navy's headquarters to see if there was any word about the two men he'd been obliged to abandon in Athens.

They had both managed to get themselves home, and had put their names back on the ship's list a few days before; they would be available when *Atalanta* set out again. Satisfied, Isokrates left a message for them to speak to him. He was about to leave the headquarters again when the clerk said, 'Isokrates of Kameiros? There's a letter for you.'

It was from his father. He accepted it with misgiving, and took it outside to read in the evening light.

Kritagoras to his son Isokrates, greetings. I am not well, and I fear never will be again. I beg you, come home and bid me farewell.

He read the letter over twice, then sat down on the steps, staring at it numbly. He remembered his father's tears – remembered Agido weeping in a corner – then, suddenly, remembered being very tiny, sitting on his father's shoulders during the Sun Festival and watching the ships process

339

into the harbour.

He read the letter again, remembering how he'd answered Aristomachos: *'I want none of that land. Let it go to ruin. My father can die on it, alone.'* And the trierarch's reply, *'Gods avert the omen! You'd regret it if he did.'*

He went back into headquarters. 'This letter,' he said to the clerk. 'When did it come?'

It had arrived five days before. Isokrates thanked the clerk and started back toward the shipshed, where he'd left his luggage, already planning the journey. From Rhodes-town to the city of Ialysos was an easy walk, a few hours along the level coastal road; if he set out now he could get there before midnight. Then he could rest a few hours, and at dawn continue on; he could reach Kameiros by evening, and if he kept going he'd arrive at the farm by midnight...

He was leaving the shipyard, a small sack of luggage over his shoulder, when somebody called his name. He glanced round and, to his surprise, saw Aristomachos hurrying toward him.

'I'm lucky I caught you,' panted the trierarch. 'Come back to my house; we'll talk.'

Isokrates hefted his luggage. 'Sir, I'm sorry, but I've had some bad news and I have to...'

'Your father's already buried,' said Aristomachos bluntly. 'It would be a wasted journey.'

Isokrates stared at him, stunned. Aristomachos caught his arm. 'Come on,' he said gently. 'Come back to the house and have some wine.'

Isokrates had followed him numbly as far as the house before he thought to ask, 'How do *you* know that my father's dead?'

'Sit down and have the wine, first,' replied the trierarch. 'Then I'll tell you.'

In Aristomachos's house there was a scent of cooking and a murmur of voices from the kitchen. A slave washed their feet, then brought them wine in the dining room. Anaxippos appeared, eager to hear about pirates.

'In a little while, Anaxippion,' Aristomachos said absently. 'Isokrates has just had some very bad news about his family.'

'Oh,' said the boy, disappointed and embarrassed. 'I'm sorry.' He went out.

'How do I know about your father?' asked Aristomachos, and took a swallow of wine. 'I arranged to buy his land, that's how. He had title until his death, at which point the land passed to me. The *price* of the land – which is eleven thousand drachmai – also becomes due upon his death, and is payable to his heir – you.' He took another swallow of wine. 'He insisted on a clause that if you chose to farm the land, the deal was void – but I think he did know that you wouldn't.'

Isokrates stared down at his hands – like his father's hands, big and bony, but where his father's hands had callouses from the pruning shears and the plough, his own were marked by the shipyards and the oar. 'Whose idea was this?' he asked, after a long silence.

Aristomachos hesitated. 'To be honest, I'm not entirely sure. It was settled when he came here about the wine. We started talking about you, and somehow we ended up with this deal.

'He asked me about you and your career, you see. He was very pleased, very proud, when he heard about your success and your reputation for honesty and courage. He asked me whether you'd be able to marry, if you had enough to buy a house of your own. Then he said he'd sell his land, since you refused it – only then he'd have nothing to live on.'

Isokrates covered his face. 'Did he die alone?' he choked.

Another hesitation. 'I don't know. There was a neighbour, Theophrastos, who'd been checking in on him during his illness; he'd given the man instructions to contact me when it was over.'

'What ... what was wrong with him?'

'Fever. Dysentery. That's all I know.'

'A broken heart?'

Aristomachos sighed. 'Fever and dysentery, Theophrastos said. Theophrastos saw to the funeral rites.'

'And you – *you* own the land now?'

'I don't expect to lose out by it,' the trierarch said. 'Prime vineyards.'

'Eleven thousand is more than the land's worth. The place is remote. Everything has to be carried up and down that road.'

'I still don't expect to lose out. I can get more for the wine than your father did. Believe me, my friend, any curse on that land was personal to you: I'll make money on this deal. Don't refuse his bequest, my friend. He did an evil thing, certainly, but he loved you. Let his death end the curse.'

Isokrates drew a deep breath, then another. He

342

was starting to cry, and he wiped impatiently at the tears. His father was dead – alone. 'You were right,' he said thickly. 'I do regret it.'

Aristomachos got up and came over to put a hand on his shoulder. 'Drink up your wine, have some supper, and go to bed. Death is a bitter cup, but it's one we all drink sooner or later.'

Isokrates slept badly, falling asleep in the grey hour before dawn, only to be woken a couple of hours later by one of the slaves tapping him on the shoulder and telling him that there was a lady at the door asking for him.

It was Dionysia, of course. The place of Dyseris a few steps behind her had been taken by Myrtis, one of the girls from the ship. She started to smile when she saw him, but the smile quickly became a look of concern. 'Oh, Apollo! Has something happened?'

He clung to the doorframe, trying to shove his mind into motion. 'I had bad news last night,' he managed. 'My father's dead.'

'Oh!' She gave him an uncertain look.

'I didn't think it would hurt,' he told her. 'I haven't forgiven him. But I wish I'd been there to say farewell.'

'I'm so sorry.'

'Let's walk,' he said abruptly.

They started down the street toward the marketplace; the stares they received from the passersby made him aware that they were a very mismatched pair – Dionysia beautiful and elegant in a rose-coloured cloak over a cream chiton; himself scruffy and unshaven in his ship-going tunic, which was badly in need of a wash.

'I came to tell you that I haven't changed my mind,' Dionysia said quietly. 'Perhaps you don't want to talk about this now, but I'll say just that, so that you know. I haven't changed my mind, and I'm not going to.'

He swallowed painfully. 'My father ... he sold the farm. To Aristomachos, so that I would have the price of it. Eleven thousand drachmai.'

'Oh!' exclaimed Dionysia, stopping short in the street. 'Oh, that's enough for a *big* house, isn't it?'

'Yes.' He swallowed again. 'It's enough for a big house, with a garden – and what's more, it would mean that I could keep ... that I could keep investing the rest of the money I got this summer. If I'm ever to become wealthy, that's the way I'll manage it.'

'That's wonderful!' Dionysia exclaimed excitedly.

Her new attendant hurried to her and caught her hand. 'Does that mean I can stay?' she asked eagerly. She turned anxious eyes to Isokrates. 'I'd be no trouble, sir! I can cook and garden and weave and sew, and I'll work very hard if you let me stay!'

Isokrates stared in confusion. Dionysia patted the girl's shoulder gently and explained. 'Myrtis and Thaumarete have asked if they can stay with me. Their husbands won't want them back, now that the pirates have had them. I said I didn't know if there'd be enough space for them, but...'

'Stay with you?'

'As paid attendants.'

'I was thinking I had to buy slaves!'

'No, no! I'd much rather help my friends than have slaves. I could pay their wages, if there was enough space in the house.' She stopped suddenly, studying his face. 'You will *accept* the money?'

Let death end the curse. 'Yes,' he said, choking on the exquisite blend of joy and anguish. 'Yes.'

Author's Note

This book is set during the summer of 246 BC, during the outbreak of the 'Laodicean' or 'Third Syrian' War. It was the height of what's called the 'Hellenistic' period – an epoch so thoroughly ignored in popular history that I probably need to explain to many readers what it actually *was*. When Alexander the Great died his generals tore his empire to bits and made themselves kings of the pieces: the Ptolemies ended up with Egypt (but also governed Cyrene, Cyprus, and bits of Anatolia); the Seleucids originally had the whole Middle East from the Mediterranean to Afghanistan; the Antigonids eventually settled for Macedonia and Greece. All these monarchs were Macedonian Greeks, despite the use of the term 'Egyptian' or 'Syrian' for some of them, and their realms are littered with Greek inscriptions. The period traditionally extends until 30 BC, when Egypt, the last Hellenistic monarchy, was swallowed up by Rome – but in fact, that was just the burial of something that had been dying for over a century.

Rhodes was, as I have tried to represent, a maritime republic which punched above its weight due to its importance to trade. Its influence actually extends to the present day: the

'Rhodian Law' is the basis of all codes of maritime law ever since.

The poems quoted are, on page 40, first a scolia (drinking song) taken from Athenaeus, included, with notes in Campbell's *Greek Lyric Poetry* (no. 904); next (repeated) Mimnermus frag. 10. The quote on p. 101 is Euripides, *Electra,* 1163–4. The translations are my own.

Those who have had the good fortune to have taken a holiday on the 'Turquoise Coast' of Turkey may wonder why my pirates are Cretans, rather than Lycians or Cilicians, since the guidebooks say, quite truthfully, that piracy was a problem on that coast in antiquity. That, however, was *later,* after Rome kicked out the Ptolemies and Seleucids and crippled the Rhodians; in the third century, the worst pirates were Cretans. (As for those who have never visited the region – do! It's fantastic. So is Rhodes – and yes, of course it's a tourist trap, but it has withal to catch tourists, in spades. Beautiful, beautiful island!)

Any depiction of life in antiquity is a reconstruction. Sources for the third century BC are comparatively scarce, which means I've had to reconstruct this edifice not from walls and roof-beams, but from post-holes and the odd brick. I'm tolerably well informed and I've done my best to be accurate, but where there's a lot of guesswork there will be errors; what's more, storytelling requires a simplified background. If you're really interested in Hellenistic history, don't rely on me. Go try Peter Green's *Alexander to Actium* and M.M. Austin's fascinating sourcebook, *The Hellenistic World.*

To avoid overburdening the narrative with Greek terms and titles, I've used English ones except where there's no good translation: thus *helmsman, bo'sun* and *tiller-holder* rather than *kybernetes, keleustes* and *pedaliouchos,* but *trierarch* instead of *captain.* I am not confident about the rendering of King Antigonos's title *Gonatas* as *Knock-knees.* Kings did often have disrespectful nicknames as well as official cult titles, so it's possible that that's what it meant – but nobody's sure.

I am not the best person to write sea-stories – I get seasick on trains! – but, really, the standard of writing about ancient warships is so abominable that anything's an improvement, and at least I did my homework. I am particularly obliged to two authors: Lionel Casson, *Ships and Seamanship in the Ancient World,* and John Morrison, *Greek and Roman Oared Warships.* The design of galleys with more than one bank of oars is still controversial, though the contention that three superimposed banks were *quite impossible* did rather get blown out of the water by the reconstruction of a three-banked Athenian trireme, the beautiful *Olympias.* Check out the website of the Trireme Trust for photos and details of her performance in sea trials.

This brings me to the issue of galley slaves. Some readers may think I had my galleys rowed by free citizens because I was reluctant to accept the brutalities of history. Please, go read Casson and Morrison: there you will see the evidence for the use of galley slaves – or rather, you won't, because there isn't any. There is, how-ever, a *lot* of evidence for free oarsmen. Medie-val and early modern galleys may have used slave labour; ancient galleys did not.

The Hellenistic heyday was short, and in many ways the Laodicean War was the beginning of the end. Ptolemy's fleet was defeated by that of Antigonos at the Battle of Andros, but against Seleukos his campaign was overwhelmingly victorious – his army got as far east as Babylon. Before he could cement his victory, however, he was called back to Egypt by a native revolt, and his brief triumph marks the high tide line of Ptolemaic power. As for the Seleucids, the eastern provinces took advantage of the troubles to secede, and were never recovered. To make matters worse, Queen Laodike persuaded her son Seleukos to make his little brother Antiochos 'the Hawk' his colleague in kingship: Antiochos promptly revolted, and the Laodicean War was followed by 'the War of the Brothers', during which more provinces seceded. Seleucid power declined even more than that of the Ptolemies.

Into this weak and divided east stepped the rising power of the Mediterranean, Rome – invited, as it happens, by the Rhodians and the Pergamenes, who were feeling threatened by an Antigonid–Seleucid pact. Rome swallowed all, friend and enemy alike: her treatment of Rhodes is particularly depressing to contemplate. The 'Colossus' of Rhodes, completed in 280 BC, col-lapsed in an earthquake in 226, and was never rebuilt.